Nyifie Brothers Publishing

THE BEAM

Season One

JOHNNY B. TRUANT

SEAN PLATT

Copyright © 2024 by Sterling & Stone
This edition published by Johnny B. Truant and Nyfie Brothers Publishing.
All rights reserved.

No part of this book may be reproduced in any form or by any electronic or
mechanical means, including information storage and retrieval systems,
without written permission from the author, except for the use of brief
quotations in a book review.

Thank you for supporting my work.

THE BEAM

| Episode 1 |

Chapter 1

Of all the truths and lies perpetrated about Natasha Ryan in The Beam news feeds and so-called independent media, the only story that truly bothered Natasha was the one claiming her voice was enhanced by an add-on called an Audibox.

Rumor said that once, when Natasha had gone in for a resurfacing of the skin on her long neck and aristocratic chin (a job nanobots were notoriously bad at, given that it involved so many dying surface cells), she'd discreetly called a high-end enhancement dealer and ordered an implant that would subtly tune the reverberations of her larynx and make her perfect pitch that much more perfect. Beam reporters didn't have details on exactly how the Audibox worked (seeing as its existence was a damnable lie), but they claimed it worked via biofeedback and that Natasha had needed to train herself to use it — to hold discreet notes in her mind so the Audibox could help her produce them. But that was utter and total bullshit. If she'd have to train herself to use a device, why wouldn't she use that same time to train herself to sing properly instead?

None of the other lies bothered Natasha nearly as much. The gossip sheets claimed she'd cheated on Isaac with his

3

brother. They claimed she'd been *so* early to try nanobot injections (nearly predating The Beam's 1.5 iteration, back when it was known as the Crossbrace project) that she'd been over forty when her first album had dropped — a fact that would make her almost a hundred today. Both were bullshit. She'd cheated, but never any of the times the press had accused her of it and never with Micah. And when she'd released *Via Persephone* in '36, she'd been twenty, as claimed. And as to the rest? Well, Natasha denied most of what came up about her on sheets inside The Beam, but the truth was that most of those stories were true. It was hard to argue too much without losing the ability to look yourself in the eye, so Natasha usually allowed her winning smile to speak for her, neither denying nor accepting.

As she stood in the spotlight on the Aphora Theater's stage, the footlights nearly blinded her to the crowd. Still, she could see them well enough to know what her unenhanced voice (still raw and naked, as had been her signature since her debut) was doing to them. A girl with Natasha's credits and social circle couldn't be blamed for having a filter lens installed while she was getting a surgical eye lift, or for directing her circulating nanobots to spend extra time on her rod cells so as to see better in the dark. Because oh…*what* she could see! The dress circle in the front, decked in the very best finery, hung from her every note, their eyes wet and dreamy. The main floor (decked in still-decent finery) leaned forward, their lips slightly parted, occasionally holding hands. Even the lottery and contest winners at the back (in mismatched suits that shone at the elbows; God bless their hearts for trying) were rapt with attention.

Natasha didn't need any goddamned Audibox in her throat to sound amazing. She was *Natasha Fucking Ryan.* Some singers could shatter glass with their voices, but *Natasha Fucking Ryan* could shatter hearts. She hadn't *risen* to fame. She'd taken fame by the balls and demanded her due. Back then, in 2036, she'd been a fat girl with a dream, standing onstage as nature had made her. Today, she was thin, supple, beautiful, and would live longer — and yes, she had had some help, but her *voice* hadn't changed. Her pitch hadn't been enhanced, nor the power of her songs altered. No one wrote Natasha's lyrics other than herself, and while the source of the soul-tearing torment beneath her songs had changed, the torment itself remained. The people watching her performance would never know the elite nature of her daily hardships, but they all knew what it was like to be human. And in the end, human was human.

Natasha held up her arms, raising her voice an octave, increasing her volume precisely without artificial help. She held it, cascaded down, and ended in an elasticized note that trembled to a whisper. The crowd followed her movements, their eyes and chins lowering subconsciously. She could almost see pieces of their souls wisp from their chests and float away. Right now, Natasha could make them do anything. Right now, every person watching — live or via the Beam feed — was totally in love with her, as they always had been.

Natasha brought her hands down as her voice shimmered away. She lowered her head, looking toward the foot of the stage. Her posture caved, curling her shoulders down and forward, defeated. The note collapsed, then died. The lighting director dimmed the lights on cue. The last thing the crowd saw in the faltering light were Natasha's eyes — her deep-green irises, soulful enough to penetrate all the way to the cheap seats — as they wet, as they fell, as the crowd hushed.

The spotlight winked out. The stage fell dark. For a moment, there was nothing, not even a whisper. The world had vanished.

Then, all at once, the hall erupted in applause. The house lights came up, and Natasha watched as the crowd stood, beating their hands together, most of their faces plastered with tears. In the back, where inhibitions were lower, the questionably dressed attendees jumped and clapped overhead, cheering, whistling, crying out. The stage lights went bright. Natasha bowed. A rose landed at her feet, followed by another. A full bouquet.

Natasha bowed again, her heart full.

The few people who hadn't already stood came to their feet. Their faces didn't look reluctant or goaded; they looked overwhelmed. It had taken them a while to rise because they hadn't felt emotionally capable of standing. These last applauded slowly and quietly, because it was all they could muster. Yes, Natasha had done her job well.

She bowed again and again, letting her face portray more exultation and astonishment overwhelm than she actually felt. The room's emotional swell was impressive, but adoration had long ago stopped giving Natasha a high. These days, it merely saved her from depression, and got her back to normal.

She could hear a few people in the crowd calling her name.

Natasha, we love you!

Natasha, you're beautiful!

Get off the stage, bitch!

Her head jerked up. Something else landed on the stage amidst the roses. It was a tomato. An honest-to-God *tomato*.

Natasha wasn't the only person who'd heard the anonymous heckler. All across the crowd, heads searched the room, looking to see who dared to ruin the mood and the moment. The voice had seemed to have come from Natasha's right. But then from the other side, a chorus of boos burst out, becoming a taunting chant.

Natasha was turning to find the source of the discord when some sort of heavy rubber ball struck the stage at her side and skittered away, making her jump. Boos bounced through the crowd from every direction. Natasha spied a few of the people making the boos, hands clapped to mouths and faces angry. The offenders were among the most shabbily dressed, their appearances unenhanced, the grit of below-the-line living embedded in their skin. There were only a few of them, but they were so loud…and they looked so *angry*. It was a species of anger Natasha vaguely remembered but had mostly forgotten: the anger she'd once had for those who had plenty when she'd had so little. It was the anger of a young girl whose family had barely gotten by — who'd seen the way the rich got richer during the disaster years, while the rest of the world crumbled.

Now, that same anger was booing *her*. Hating *her*. Throwing things at *her*.

A shoe struck the stage. Who would throw a shoe? How would they ever get home? The shoe was heavy — someone's idea of a dress shoe simply because it was black. The shoe nearly hit Natasha's foot. She jumped back, shocked.

The man who'd thrown it yelled, "Thieving cunt!"

And Natasha thought, *This is Directorate.*

Natasha stepped back, away from the tomato, the shoe, and the rolling rubber ball as if they were bombs. This wasn't how things were supposed to go. She'd poured her heart out. They were supposed to love her. She wasn't supposed to be booed. She wasn't supposed to be the whipping girl for the world's social woes. She'd gotten her fame and fortune through hard work, clawing her way through the same system that was in front of everyone. The difference was *she* had taken a chance. *She* had gambled. *They* — the bastards who were booing her — had just accepted their government dole and complained. Who were they to boo her? But that was what the venue got for selling cheap seats, for giving away tickets as promotions. Elegant affairs were supposed to be accessible only to elegant people — *especially* this close to Shift, when things always went to crap and when mixing classes was always a recipe for disaster.

The boos grew louder. It was so unfair. Natasha's well-deserved applause had been shocked into silence, and a handful of loudmouths were getting all the attention. And this was going out on the Beam feed, too, so everyone was watching her moment crumble thanks to a handful of assholes. Soon, boos were the only sounds in the seats, oddly harmonizing with the thunking of objects landing onstage.

A well-dressed man, his eyes offended on Natasha's behalf, jumped onto one of the jeering miscreants. The booing man fought back, throwing them both over a chair. Those around them stepped away. One of the malcontents closer to the stage turned to stare at Natasha as if she'd caused the fight and threw something at her. Natasha flinched away. Whatever the man had thrown struck and shattered a light, and with the explosion of glass and sparks, the paralysis remaining in the seats started to crumble. A few of the rabble in back began changing sides, apparently swayed by well-reasoned arguments from the troublemakers — sage truisms such as "Get the diamonds out of your ass! And Fuck you!"

"Natasha!" hissed a voice. She turned to see Jane, her tour manager, beckoning her.

Natasha looked out at the brawl unfolding in the theater — the same theater that, moments earlier, had harbored a sea of adoring fans. What had gone wrong? She looked back at Jane. In the second it took to look away, Jane had easily grown twice as impatient. She had doubled the size of her gestures, and the number of arms used to make them. Her eyes looked angry, baffled by Natasha's stupidity.

"Natasha!" Jane repeated. "Get the hell over here, will you?"

"They threw a tomato," was all Natasha could say.

Jane rushed forward and grabbed her star by the wrist then began to pull on Natasha's arm nearly hard enough to yank the limb from its socket. Natasha's high heels threatened to spill her, but she'd had years and years of practice at remaining stylish and beautiful even under duress, and managed to keep her footing. She shambled along behind Jane like a dog on a leash. They stepped through a black curtain as something broke onstage. It sounded like glass or porcelain.

"Your hover," said Jane. "Go with James. *Now.* Get the fuck out of here."

"But I'm supposed to sign autographs," Natasha said, dazed.

Jane jabbed at the curtain with a pointed finger. The gesture made the black drape swing, and Natasha saw through it that security and police had come to the front of the stage. The crowd was trying to climb up. Were they trying to escape the melee, or had they *all* turned on her?

"You want to sign for this crew?" said Jane. "You'll need a riot mask. They're falling apart out there!"

"Why?"

James's hand was already replacing Jane's on her wrist, and a moment later, the bodyguard's strong arm was around her shoulder as well. Jane was supposed to manage tour dates; James was supposed to protect her. Only Jane would yank her along. James, on the other hand, knew better ways to move her.

"Come on, Ms. Ryan," he said. James shaved his head but wore a brown porkpie hat like a hipster. It was a strange look to counterpoint his broad, muscular body.

"I need Kiki."

"I have your dog, Ms. Ryan. Come with me. It's not safe here."

"But they love me. They're supposed to love me," she said. Beyond the curtain, there was a yell, the scampering of feet, and the thump of a police slumbergun, followed by the sound of a body hitting the polished wood floor.

"Come with me. Come on. Let's get you home."

Natasha allowed herself to be led toward her hovercar. She was so catatonic that James had to buckle her in before taking his spot up front behind the steering fork. There was a small pink bag beside her on the seat. As the hover climbed, she reached inside it, pulled out the small white dog, and set him on her lap. She proceeded to tell Kiki that it was all fine, that Shift always caused a little unrest, and that other than the actions of a few rabble-rousers, the performance had gone quite well. They loved her. They really did.

As James steered the craft into the thin traffic above District Zero and banked it toward Natasha's penthouse, the star looked down and saw a dozen or more police cars arrive at the foot of the Aphora, their presence incongruous amongst the limousines and high-end hovers. She watched police swarm from their vehicles like ants rushing the theater, face shields donned and slumbers held across their chests.

"It's fine, Kiki," said Natasha, petting her dog in short, quick strokes.

Kiki accepted his owner's reassurances without protest or disagreement.

Chapter 2

"Isaac."

After touching his flashing countertop to take the incoming call as voice-only with track-and-follow (necessary because he always paced while talking), Nicolai Costa said his one-word greeting then listened as Isaac blabbed on for three full minutes to unburden himself. Yes, Nicolai was Isaac's speechwriter. Yes, he was Isaac's right-hand man, and yes, he was his chief adviser. But really, the core of Nicolai's value to Isaac was as a buffer. Nicolai wasn't responsible for *giving* Isaac information so much as he was responsible for *intercepting* information that would only worry or confuse him. And on the other side of the buffer, it wasn't Nicolai's job to act on Isaac's fears and worries so much as to listen to them, then assure Isaac that it would all be okay. Nicolai didn't precisely *do* most of what Isaac wanted done. It was Nicolai's job to determine what actually needed to be done versus what was just Isaac being Isaac, then to handle things in whatever way he saw fit.

"They threw shit at her, Nicolai. Tomatoes. Fucking *tomatoes*, like Vaudeville. It took fifty police to stop what almost became a full-scale riot. She's terrified. Well, of course, this is

Natasha, so she's not outwardly terrified, but she is just the same. I can see it. But she's also…hang on, Nicolai."

Nicolai had seen this move before and knew what was coming. Isaac was going to run out to his patio to say something he didn't want Natasha to hear. Despite taking the call as voice-only, Nicolai could almost see Isaac scamper outside in his mind. Couldn't Natasha see right through it? His departure had to say more than his words ever could.

Nicolai paced, waiting. He crossed the bank of windows looking out onto the city night below. As he passed his grand piano, his fingers feathered the keys. He kept promising himself he'd learn to play it one of these days, but a man only had so much time. Right now, he had his work writing for Isaac plus his private creative writing projects. The piano would have to wait.

"You still there?" said Isaac's voice. It seemed to be right in front of Nicolai.

"Where would I be?"

"I'd know if you'd use video like a normal person."

"Not everyone wants to be on video all the time, Isaac. What if I'm naked?"

Isaac made an impatient noise and continued. "Anyway, I was going to say that Natasha is *hurt*. Not, like, injured, but like…well, you know how she is."

Nicolai knew. Natasha had practically grown up in the spotlight, and appreciation was, for her, like blood to a vampire.

"I understand."

"The rioters were from our own party, from the Directorate. I don't like it. It makes us look like a mob."

"Of course it was our people," said Nicolai. "Enterprise don't riot." And it was true. There were plenty of Enterprise members in the rabble (there were more Enterprise than Directorate below the line, actually, seeing as Directorate received support from their party whether they worked or not), but those poor Enterprise were starving artists, not disgruntled workmen. Artists didn't rise up. When artists took a gamble and failed their way into ghettos, they sat in dark corners, slit their wrists, and listened to Morrissey drawl on from a century in the past.

"What does that mean?"

"Nothing, Isaac. Is she okay?"

"She's fine. But I have a speech tomorrow. A speech to these…these *fuckers*."

Nicolai couldn't help but chuckle, keeping the sound low in his throat. He paced his apartment as Isaac's voice followed.

"I'll rewrite your speech," Nicolai said. "This could be good. Don't worry. I can spin anything."

Isaac blurted, "How could it be good?"

"Unrest over inequity should actually work in our *favor*, not against us. Sure, Natasha is your wife, and you're Mr. Directorate, but where's most of the wealth outside of Directorate leaders? Is it in the Directorate?"

"Well…no…"

"Of course not. So do you see what I'm saying?"

Isaac was probably nodding. It was an affect some people had when they took most of their calls via video.

"So get some rest," said Nicolai. "Tell Natasha I said it'll all be fine. I'll get you a new draft of the speech, and you'll see. This is good. We *want* the Directorate upset. If they aren't upset, they might decide to go Enterprise when Shift comes. But if they *are* angry and make noise, then not only will it solidify them against a common opponent and make them want to stay where they are, but their bitching will also raise the antenna of some of the complacent Enterprise — folks who are living below the line and might move to us just so they don't starve. You'll see."

Isaac mumbled, mollified.

Nicolai said his goodbye and then swiped the air, ending the call. A beep said he was alone again, so he made another circuit of his apartment, looking out over District Zero.

As he paced, Nicolai looked at his piano — an astonishing black-and-white trophy appropriate to a man of his station. The thing was worth thousands upon thousands of credits — and was, as Nicolai saw it, a giant status symbol begging in vain to be used for the creation of art. Nicolai didn't have room for any more art in his life, though. He told himself for the millionth time that his scattered bursts of creative writing were enough. They would have to be. Eventually, he'd find time for music, just as he'd find time to birth a painting on the decorative easel that now supported a plant.

He plopped onto his couch, swiped a square in the air with his fingers, and watched as the overhead Beam projector gave him a screen. Then he reached over and grabbed a keyboard from the end table beside him. A canvas as expensive as Nicolai's could project him an airboard, but Nicolai had never understood how people could use those things. It was neat to wave your fingers in the air as if hitting keys, but without tactile feedback, the experience was clunky at best. Such failures of common-sense understanding were almost standard in a lot of modern (elite) technology. Sure, it was *neat* and *cool* and *fun*. But was it *practical?* In Nicolai's opinion, airboards were for people who wanted to pretend they were writing but never actually did.

His fingers clacked on keys. Words lit the screen. This went on for a while until Nicolai realized he was just rehashing Directorate propaganda and rewriting an old speech — one of the few standard speeches from the party's archives that had been given by Directorate leaders over and over and over again. He had told Isaac that unrest was good, but the problem was that Nicolai didn't know if he actually believed it. You couldn't quell unrest; you could only redirect it. Those people had come after Natasha because she was at the top of the credit/income ladder, not because of her party affiliation.

Nicolai couldn't make that class-based anger vanish, so his best bet was to refocus it in a useful way. The rioters' problems — and all of the problems plaguing the Directorate — were the result of the Enterprise. *They control the wealth. They are keeping you down.*

With a strange punched-in-the-gut feeling, Nicolai realized that it wasn't the first time such deflection had been used. Back when there had been mass immigration into America (in the days before it joined the North American Union), economic woes had been usually blamed on foreigners coming in and taking jobs. Before that, the default enemy had been the Jews.

Nicolai swiped the window closed then set the keyboard back on the end table. He stood, walked to his window wall, and once again took in the streets of District Zero below. The city was alive with light, but the sky above it was a smooth nothingness. Nicolai missed being able to see the stars and the moon through the Shell miles above as he had in his youth, but night objects weren't bright enough to blast through the three-layered defensive barrier like the sun did. The nights seemed so dark, even in the city. It was the price you paid for protection.

From all the way up high, the city seemed peaceful. But that was the thing about distance: From far enough away, everything became an average. There were rich, and there were poor. There were Enterprise and Directorate. There was the NAU and the Wild East, out past the ant farm wall that covered the continent. But if you kept pulling back, eventually everything averaged out to people. And when the Mars project was finished — and if the elite then moved a planet away — the only thing needed to restore a sense of equity would be to zoom out another level or two.

Nicolai sighed. He had to clear his head. He needed someone to talk to and to be with. Someone who wouldn't care about socioeconomic woes. Someone who could make the world vanish for a few hours at an exorbitant price — or sometimes longer than a few hours, if she was feeling generous.

"Canvas," Nicolai said to his empty apartment.

A single chirp answered him.

"Get me Kai Dreyfus."

Chapter 3

THE TRICK to being a good escort, Kai knew, was to make the man she was with feel like he was the only person in the world she'd ever care about. That meant she couldn't discuss other clients, leave remnants or mementos of other clients around, halfass her affection, or talk business. For the time she was booked, Kai *became* her client's girlfriend, wife, confidant — whatever he wanted. She kept extensive records of each client's background in a characteristics file in her canvas. Subtle cameras in her apartment and embedded in her retinas recorded every second of their every interaction, and a sophisticated AI algorithm stripped the footage for relevant details.

Client A had three kids. His oldest knew about his dalliances, but didn't care.

Client B had a cluster of moles on his arm that Kai had once said looked like the constellation Orion, and he'd thought that was delightfully clever.

Client C had insecurities surrounding his manner of dress; she'd once innocently commented on his shoes and incited a mopey incident that it had taken her hours to rescue him from.

Client D liked to fuck her from behind every single time,

because he wanted to pretend that she was his wife, whom he was desperately attracted to but who'd turned icy after their only child.

When a night with Kai ended, it was like she and the client pressed a giant pause button on their relationship. When the client booked her again, their relationship resumed. They always picked up exactly where they'd left off. An intuitive program in Kai's canvas even told a bot, through her Beam connection, to arrange the apartment exactly as it had been when the client had last left. A man could leave a half-eaten pizza in Kai's fridge, then wander back a month later and pull a piece from the fridge as if it were the same pizza. If he'd left crusts in the box, the same number of crusts would still be there, just as his memory told him they would be.

Being a great escort was only half about the sex. Men didn't just need sex from her. If all they wanted was physical release, they could beat off. Kai knew her clients didn't come simply to insert tab A into slot B. They came to feel wanted, to feel desired, to feel understood and comfortable. So yes, she had to move as they wanted and do the things that pleased them. But she also had to stock her racks with the towels they liked, have their preferred sheets on the bed (in both thread count and color), and set her walls to project the art most pleasing to *their* eye. Each client wasn't just a man. He was a project.

So when Nicolai's call came through, his identity rang into a small cochlear implant in Kai's ear, too quiet for her current client — a new man who liked it a little rough — to hear. And because she was busy smacking her new client around, she couldn't take Nicolai's call even though she very much wanted to. Nicolai was her favorite…but right now, *this* man was her boyfriend. And because Kai was her new client's girlfriend at the moment, she wouldn't get calls from other men because she was his and his alone. So as Kai's petite frame sat atop her man's back in red lingerie with her black hair swinging in her face, she sighed internally as she subtly cocked her head to decline the call.

My current boyfriend, she thought as she slapped him across the back with a small black crop, *is an asshole. And playing coy.*

First of all, his name clearly wasn't Ralph McGuinness, as he'd told her it was. Kai's AI software had already filtered that name through the Beam servers and found nobody close to his description. Second, the AI had already analyzed the timbre of his voice and determined (quite redundantly, in Kai's opinion) that he was probably lying. None of this was really unusual. All of Kai's clients were wealthy and hence were more often than not people of significant standing. Many of them were high-ranking officials within either Enterprise or Directorate. Those kinds of men didn't want people to know they visited an escort, but it usually didn't matter because Kai always found them out no matter what bullshit story they fed her. It was her business to know. The more she knew about a client, the better she could satisfy him. If she knew, for instance, that a man who claimed to own a textile company was, in fact, up for a Senate seat, she'd know those days he was in most need of relief and which topics she should and should not broach. Knowing a man's true identity helped her know which opinions and leanings she should pretend to have, and guess at how empowered or subservient to be.

And of course, if Kai knew a man's true identity, she could attach video of the acts, infidelities, and atrocities they committed together to those identities in her database. A bit of information like "A man calling himself 'Ron Barber' likes to dress in young girls' panties" was of limited use, but "The Commissioner of Such and Such likes to dress in young girls' panties" was quite valuable indeed. Kai had never, ever, ever revealed any of the millions of secrets she'd collected over the years...but a girl had to have a Plan B (or a nest egg) saved for the inevitable rainy day.

She looked down at her client's back then rose up enough

to turn him over onto his back. He had a handsome face with a square jaw, with a five o'clock shadow spread across it. He had hazel eyes and sandy-blond hair. His chest and arms were well muscled. In most ways, he was an ideal client for Kai, if for no other reason than that she would probably have been attracted to him anyway. He'd come at her with such flair and bravado that she'd decided on impulse to quote him twice her normal rate. He hadn't blinked. So he was rich, and probably connected.

"Have you had enough?" said Kai.

"Not even close," he said.

She slapped him across the face. "Speak when spoken to, Ralph," she said.

He smiled — not at her command, but at the name. He knew she knew, and found it hilarious.

She hit him again, harder.

The smile widened.

He'd hired her for the entire evening and night. Seventeen hours. "Ralph" had picked her up at five, and she was his until ten in the morning. They'd gone to a ridiculously expensive dinner, and he'd become moderately lubricated with a multi-hundred-credit bottle of champagne. Then they'd headed to the Aphora, where they'd watched what Kai felt was perhaps the most raw, heartbreaking performance from Natasha Ryan she'd seen in all the years Kai had spent following her. Then those assholes had started booing, and things had quickly fallen apart. Kai had been totally shocked by the incident, but throughout it all "Ralph" had seemed totally nonplussed. That in itself was a clue to something. Kai wondered what her canvas's AI would make of it, if anything.

As she straddled her client with her hand cocked back, Kai looked down at the mystery man. She probably didn't truly *need* to know who he was. She might never see him again, and he might simply be a horny man with a ton of credits to blow. But Kai didn't like a puzzle she couldn't crack, and so far, she hadn't been able to crack this one. She had a tiny nano-enhancement in the index finger of her right hand that allowed her to read Beam IDs without a scanner, but the man either didn't have one (unthinkable; he was too conservative-looking to be an Organa) or had had it encrypted. So she'd used another enhancement to sample DNA from a piece of his hair, but again, she came up empty. It made no sense that he'd be off the grid. He *had* to be hiding something. But how? And why?

"Take off that bra," he said, reaching up to paw at Kai's small breasts through the lace.

"I give the orders here," she said, then slipped her bra off and tied it around her client's head at the mouth, halfway gagging him.

Kai hid it well, but she was pissed. Or rather, she was *indignant*. After her years in this business (more years than she'd care to admit, though she looked twenty-five at most), she'd come to see information as an entitlement. "Ralph" wasn't doing anything overt to keep her out, but the mere fact that he represented an impenetrable wall irked her something fierce. Kai wanted to hit him again to vent her frustration, but he'd like it too much.

Even if she didn't need to know who he was, she absolutely did.

Kai climbed off her client. He twitched to the side, reaching for her ass. She dodged the hand then slapped it away. Oh yes, he was quite the character. He couldn't decide if he was the sub or the dom. Or perhaps he was the bad boy who was an asshole…and hence needed to be taught a lesson.

"Where are you going?" he slurred around the bra in his mouth.

"What fucking business is it of yours?" She gave him the smallest of sexy smiles, to make sure he understood that this was all still just part of the play.

"Come back here," he said.

Kai turned, fast, and grabbed her client by the chin. "You're bad," she said. "You ask too many questions."

"I'm bad," he mumbled between his compressed cheeks. Farther down, his biology indicated that the way she was treating him wasn't a problem.

"I'm going to have to punish you."

"Oh no," he said, falling back onto the bed.

Kai reached into the end table and removed a pair of handcuffs. Before closing the drawer, she also palmed a small vial with a tiny sponge on its top.

"I'll have to restrain you," she said, securing the first handcuff to the headboard.

"Mercy," said the man, now smiling openly.

Kai straddled him to reach the second cuff, and he responded beneath her. As she raised his arm to secure the second cuff, she discreetly swabbed her neck with the sponge on the vial. Then, as she lowered her face toward his, she tucked the vial under the mattress.

The man inhaled, drawing her scent. As he did, his eyelids fluttered.

"Hey, Ralph," said Kai.

"Hey," he said. "I've been bad."

"*Very* bad. Kiss my neck."

She pushed her neck against his mouth, moaning. It would take at least a half hour for the engineered pheromone to soften his brainwaves, but it didn't matter. She was a girl of her word, and the man had paid for a service. So she removed the rest of their clothing and delivered.

Afterward, with "Ralph" satisfied and flagging, Kai resumed kissing his neck, giving him more of the pheromone. After a while, his movements grew sluggish. His eyelids started to flutter again as he drifted into something between sleep and wakefulness.

"Hey, Ralph," she said.

"Mmm," he said.

"Relaxed?"

"Mmm," he repeated.

Kai reached behind him, untied the bra gag, and tossed it aside. She ran a red-painted nail down his chest, idly. "What's your name, beautiful?"

"Ralph."

Kai laughed girlishly. "No, silly. What is it really?"

Ralph started to snore lightly. She shook him.

"What's your name, baby?"

"Ralph," he slurred.

Then he fell asleep. But it was okay. His brainwaves should have loosened even if his tongue hadn't, and he'd be imperturbably asleep for hours now. She could get what she wanted directly from the source.

"Let's get you online, 'Ralph,'" she said, picking up her diagnostic tablet and setting it beside him on the bed. Something inside her was sizzling. It shouldn't bother her so much that she couldn't get "Ralph's" identity, but the only people she'd run into before with a level of identity encryption she hadn't been able to hack like a cheap lock were a few unlucky subjects during her dalliances as an amateur assassin. Usually, when someone was locked up this tight, someone else, somewhere, wanted him dead. What were this man's secrets? And if she didn't discover them, might those same secrets come back to haunt her, as a girl who'd once given him a good time?

Kai unfolded her sleeping client's hand, laid it on the tablet screen, and scanned it. No identity came up. No surprise there, but it wasn't what she was after. Usually, a person could access their personal array of upgrade diagnostics via their Beam ID, voice recognition, retinal scan, or fingerprint/palmprint, and usually those first-degree cross-pollinations were vulnerable to one such as Kai. "Ralph's" Beam ID might have been hidden, sure…but unless whoever had done his encryption was especially thorough, his handprint and Beam ID should still both be connected — not to his identity, but to each other — in the lesser-protected protocols within his upgrades.

Kai swiped the surface of the wall behind the bed. A screen appeared. She watched the tablet scan his hand then began poking around in the diagnostic tools. He'd had a few upgrades (there were several types of nanos in his system, and he seemed to have an extra memory buffer, for instance), but she couldn't access stats on any of them. Kai tried to use his palmprint to identify him to the system but found she'd need a password.

And...*FUCK.* There was a firewall between her canvas, the tablet, and the lowest identification protocols. So much for finding his Beam ID through a back door.

Kai looked down at the naked man on her bed, lying on his stomach with one strong arm up. She wondered if any of his muscularity was natural, or if it was all the work of nanos. Even as a woman who'd cheated her way to a flat stomach and gravity-defying breasts, she found herself strangely judgmental of Ralph's muscles. It was probably because she was feeling so resentful about his secrets, but she suddenly thought that if he hadn't grown those arms himself, he was a fucking pussy.

Yes, she was letting it get to her. But Kai Dreyfus was a girl who always got what she wanted, and she didn't like this one bit. The idea that someone had put up such a thorough firewall around this man's true identity made her wary. Who was this man on her bed? What was he up to? Was he just here for a good time, or did he know something about Kai? Did he know the secrets she'd taken over the years — and if so, what might he be planning to do to retrieve them?

She slapped his sleeping face lightly, playfully.

"What are you hiding, buttercup?" she asked him.

Regardless, it would be prudent to wipe his memory. It would be impossible to do a decent job with all the protections in place, but she might be able to force a soft reset with a few nanos that could go in and manually induce some light damage to his hippocampus. She'd have to be careful. Too many nanos, and he'd end up burned. She didn't want him burned, just mildly forgetful. Then she wanted to get him the fuck out of her apartment.

Kai pulled up the diagnostic screen, checked for perimeter protection at his ears, and found none. Then she pulled a small lancet from a sterile pouch, slid it into a doser attached to a nano pack, and gave instructions to six scavengers. She pushed the lancet into the skin behind his ear, tossed it into the garbage, and started to clean. She could have the doorman take him away. She'd owe the doorman a quickie for the favor, but it was okay. The doorman was kind of hot.

Just as Kai was about to retrieve her tablet, something on the screen caught her eye. It looked like a software tag left by the developer who'd put her mystery man's protections in place. She chuckled. Watch it be Doc. But of course, that was stupid. Doc didn't deal in upgrades this sophisticated.

But when she looked closer, she saw that it wasn't an identifier tag at all. It was a prime sequence — a piece of code that was meant to form an interface with another piece from an external source. It meant he was prepped for an upgrade that could be taken on and off of his body, like enhanced glasses. But as much as she tapped her tablet and searched her mind, Kai couldn't place the prime sequence. It certainly wasn't for enhanced glasses.

Mystified, she entered the code into her canvas and sent it to her network on The Beam.

The response returned three words that, to Kai, meant nothing but smelled like poison: *Stark Centurion Program.*

Chapter 4

It was only 8 a.m., and already the streets were filled with assholes.

Thomas "Doc" Stahl sat in a cab, looking down at his wrist. As he straightened his arm and rolled it back, the tattoo faded away. It was an unpopular upgrade, and people who didn't know Doc sometimes commented that looking at his wrist to see the time was something that made him look stupid, not retro. The local time was on every canvas, every surface in any public building, in the corner of every heads-up display (retinal, projected, or even the poorest VR glasses in the ghetto) and available for the asking at just about any place in the NAU. Most people in the better parts of the city had cochlear implants for audio calls, and even some of the bums had ancient phones. The time was on every digital billboard, every screen.

But Doc hadn't gotten the watch upgrade because he wanted to see the time on his wrist. He'd gotten it because he liked the affect of looking down. The gesture conveyed class when he wanted it to, and it conversely conveyed "Fuck you, hurry up" about a thousand times better than anything else a man could do. People hadn't worn functioning watches for over fifty years, but tapping one's wrist still meant "Let's hurry up" in the same way people still referred to "getting something on tape" when they meant making a recording. And looking down at a cocked wrist was still singularly insulting in a way that checking a display could never be. It told the person he was talking to that he gave less than a shit about whatever they were telling him, and that they were just wasting his precious time.

"Run them down," Doc told the driver.

"Hey, they've got a right to protest," the balding man in the driver's seat said without turning back.

Doc drew a deep breath then exhaled, watching the line of protesters through the cab's window. He touched the glass, brought up a tint panel, and dragged a screen across the glass to block his view. The cabbie would, of course, be sympathetic. Here he was, carting some uppity Enterprise man around in his cab while a bunch of his fellow low-end Directorate protested the same uppity Enterprise bastards. Doc wanted to argue — to point out to the cabbie that every single one of those protesters could have chosen to make their own way in the Enterprise instead of accepting a fixed government dole that was barely adequate — but his words would fall on deaf ears and possibly result in an "accidentally" higher cab fare. Directorate members didn't want to hear that they'd made the wrong choice. *And you know what?* Doc thought. *They wouldn't move over to Enterprise when Shift came, either.* It was easier to bitch about how the system was unfair and suggest taxing the wealthy members of the Enterprise so that Directorate stipends could be increased. All while half of the fucking Directorate sat on their asses and didn't work at all because so much could be automated.

"Look, fella," said Doc. "I'm not trying to be uppity. But I've got an 8:30 sixteen blocks down, and that parade ain't getting any thinner. Can we go around?"

The cabbie looked at the meter, and they both watched the fare click up. "Not really."

"Can I ask you a question?" said Doc.

"Hell, *you* can do anything," said the cabbie.

"You don't have to work. This cab could drive itself. So why do it?" Doc wasn't trying to be rude. He wanted to know. Besides, Doc — always an entrepreneur and a fierce determiner of his own future — believed there was a little Enterprise logic in everyone.

The cabbie opened the window and stuck out his arm. "Scintillating conversation," he said.

"But it could have an AI driver, and you could sit in your house and…"

"Sometimes the dole ain't enough," said the cabbie. He hooked his arm over the headrest and looked Doc over from top to bottom. Doc was wearing jeans, boots, and a simple suit coat, but it was all expensive. Doc's shoulder-length blond hair had a sheen that could only be maintained by nanos. "Not that you'd know that."

Doc wanted to debate, but it was pointless. The cabbie had already judged him, just like Directorate protesters always leapt to judge the well-off Enterprise every six years, in the weeks preceding Shift. He wanted to argue that he'd scraped his way up from the bottom, but he stopped when he remembered that he was talking to a man who'd taken a job that existed solely so that he could take it. If the cabbie died, AI would drive the cab the next day, and the city would save money. It was a loop that existed only within itself.

Doc fished a twenty-credit note from his pocket and pushed it toward the driver. The fare stood at $8.70. Doc told him to keep the change and announced his plans to walk the rest of the way. As he exited the cab, the driver gave him an angry look. Doc had meant the tip as a make-peace gesture, but of course the driver had taken it as condescension.

Doc skirted the protesters, stuffing his annoyance low,

figuring they were doing him a favor. Yes, the streets would be thick with assholes for a while, but Doc felt that there was no objective "good" or "bad" about anything. A self-made person understood that it wasn't what happened to you in life that mattered, but what you did with those happenings. So yes, this all meant opportunity. The protestors wanted an end to decadence and inequality between the rich (who could afford the best upgrades) and the poor (who had no upgrades and accessed The Beam via old consoles and handhelds). Doc didn't usually sell upgrades to the truly rich or truly poor; he sold mainly to the upper-middle, middle, and lower classes. This hullabaloo meant he had an opportunity to show the poorer of his customers that they could, indeed, afford upgrades on his easy payment plans. And for the upper tier of customers? Well, they'd buy fancier upgrades than ever if they thought their rights were being threatened. They'd consume out of fear. They'd consume to justify their previous consumption. And they'd consume to raise their middle fingers — to show the protestors that they intended to do whatever the fuck they wanted.

Doc cocked his arm and the nanobot-generated tattoo reappeared on his wrist, seconds ticking off near where his forearm began to thicken. He had fifteen minutes. And there wasn't a cab — hover, wheeled, or pedi; human- or AI-driven — to be seen. The rails would take him too far out of his way. He'd have to run, and he was going to be late.

Doc hoofed it toward Xenia Labs, referring to his wrist every few minutes like a compulsion. Twelve blocks left. Eight blocks. By the time he had five blocks remaining, his time was up, and he was sweaty as hell. He sold an upgrade that short-circuited perspiration and cooled the user via a rather toxic coolant circulated and (hopefully) contained by nanos, but Doc didn't have it. Now, approaching Xenia, he wished he did, despite the occasional disastrous side effect. He was going to look and smell disgusting. Then, because he decided he might as well embarrass himself fully, Doc tapped his ear and rattled off the voice message to Nicolai that he kept forgetting to send. Nicolai had been bugging him for days. Doc let him know that his new upgrade was in and that he could stop harassing Doc about it and come pick it up. With Doc running, Nicolai would get the message and hear his dealer panting. Not exactly the professional image Doc hoped to convey, but what the hell.

He kept running, his boots smacking pavement. He arrived at Xenia ten minutes late, rushed into a bathroom, and splashed cold water on his hot face. The bathroom didn't have a groomer, so he ran his fingers through his blond mane. His suit coat was dark. Hopefully it would hide his sweat-stained pits. He took a final look in the mirror, trying to feather his hair away from the sides of his face where he refused to stop sweating. He failed. Doc's hair stayed plastered to his skin like a dark-blond halo.

That done, he crossed the hall to Xenia's suite and trotted up to the receptionist. The girl behind the desk had three different clips on her ears. Doc wondered if she ever hit the wrong one and ended up rattling off her hilarious drunken stories to her boss instead of her girlfriend by mistake.

"Hey, sweetheart," said Doc. "My name is Thomas — although people call me Doc — and I'm here to see…"

"Oh, yes!" the girl said brightly. "You're the salesman. You're early. Mr. Killian is in with a distributor. I apologize that he's a little behind. He's been tied up with a bunch of loose ends. The other day, some protestors beat in the door of our warehouse and disturbed a swarm of nanos that had been developed for police use. It was almost a disaster. You wouldn't believe the mess, but luckily nobody was hurt, and now…"

Doc held up a hand. "Hang on a second, darlin'. I'm here to see Mr. Nero." Every other Friday, Doc stopped by to see Nero for more stock and to see what was new, if anything. Nero was a prick of immeasurable proportions and despised even the slightest delay, but he also cut Doc a tremendous wholesale deal since Doc moved so many upgrades. When Nero wasn't being pricky (which was rare), he sometimes told Doc that none of the other independent salesmen could sell to the wide spectrum that Doc did. Most of the reps who sold Beam-enabled personal upgrades catered to the low or high end of the market, but Doc could sell to both and everyone in between. Doc sold rudimentary tablets and handhelds to people below the line, but also sold memory and creativity enhancers to those near the top of the food chain. He didn't discriminate where profit was concerned.

The usual desk jockey — an uppity little cocksucker named Templeton — knew Doc and would have rebuked him for his lateness. But Templeton wasn't here, and his replacement had no clue.

"Oh, Mr. Nero isn't here," said the girl. "He's dealing with the police. The swarm, like I said. You'll be meeting with Mr. Killian. Have a seat over there." She pointed to a chair in the waiting area, near a plant.

Doc's heartbeat was still coming down from his run, so he forced himself to breathe slowly and sit. While he waited, he tried to fan his armpits and cool off. He wasn't late after all. This Mr. Killian wasn't even ready for him. Doc wondered if Nero had told Killian to give him his usual discount. He'd be pissed if he had to pay full price and would grill Nero about it in two weeks if he did. Nero had a big bark, but ultimately spoke credits. If Doc threatened to move and start buying from Yeardley, he'd immediately cough up a rebate to cover the discount.

Ten minutes later, a tall man in a white lab coat with dark-black hair appeared at the end of a hallway and greeted Doc. Doc rose and shook the man's bony, clammy hand.

"I'm sorry we're so chaotic today," said Killian. "We had a bit of an incident with the protestors, see, and…"

"I heard," said Doc. He thought of adding something

about how obnoxious the protestors were to grease the conversational skids, but he'd yet to gauge the man's political temperature.

"Well, it's led to a bit of a kerfuffle. Anyway, I apologize. Don't let your first impression get to you! We're ordinarily very composed and professional around here, and if you're going to…"

Doc laughed good-naturedly. "It's hardly my first time here."

Killian stopped and looked at Doc, confused. "Really? I understood I was introducing you to our product line."

Doc shrugged. "Have you gotten new products in lately?"

"Oh yes." Killian's confused look vanished; something delighted replaced it. "We get new shipments constantly. The pace at which we're cracking the neural nut, so to speak, is staggering. Once the Series Six nano software patch was developed and we learned that we could up-or-down-regulate CNS neurons, the cortex became our playground. What Einstein said about how we only use 10 percent of our brains? Well, that leaves a lot to uncover. I can't discuss it all yet because it's preliminary, but let's just say that what's becoming possible by the week has us all quite excited." Killian's eyes had grown wide. He seemed positively giddy with discovery.

"I haven't seen the Series Six nanos," said Doc.

"Really? How long have you been in this game?"

Doc gave his disarming smile. "Long enough."

"Well, they're hardly new," said Killian. "But of course, you wouldn't call them Series Six, would you?" Doc had a moment in which he thought Killian was going to slap his own forehead. "You'd call them Paradigm."

"Oh, of course," said Doc. But he'd never heard of Paradigm nanos either.

"Anyway, I don't mean to imply that it's all about nanos. The neural mapping field is also very promising, of course," Killian added, making for a doorway at the end of the hall that Doc had never been through before. He'd thought it was a utility room.

"Of course," said Doc.

They reached the door. Killian bared his arm and allowed a concealed scanner to read his Beam ID, then used his fingers to draw a complicated pattern on a swipe screen near the door. Doc was looking directly at Killian's hands, but he'd never be able to replicate the pattern. It seemed almost random.

The door beeped and hissed open. "Well, come on in," said Killian, leading the way.

Once inside the room, Doc's breath evaporated. The lab was stark white, and every surface chattered with Beam activity. Even the floor under Doc's boots hummed in response. The room was filled with devices Doc had never seen before, arranged on what almost looked like display racks. There were long work benches circling the room's perimeter. Some of these seemed to be staffed by electronics workers who were peering at tiny devices through magnifiers, but other areas looked like biological wet benches. Doc saw vials of reagents, manual and auto pipettes, and what looked like jars filled with gel.

"Most of the actual production is automated," said Killian, "but for research — at the macro and not nano level, of course — it's all done by human hands unless it's too precise or dangerous. Our technicians all have the latest ocular implants. You've seen these?" Killian snatched something from a rolling cart and then extended his hand. Two eyeballs stared up at Doc.

At first, he was repulsed, but Doc couldn't resist reaching out and taking one of the things between his fingers. It was soft and squishy and slimy, exactly like it looked.

"Interior is carbon nanotubes," said Killian, dropping the remaining eye to the floor and then stomping on it with his shoe. He reached down and retrieved the eye, which was completely unharmed. "Just let Moe try to poke you in the eyes with these suckers," he said, miming a *Three Stooges* eye-jab. Hardware is all NextGen biologic, grown with synthetic neurons and innately dependent on resident Series Six nanos."

He tossed the other eyeball to Doc, who caught it. Doc looked down, shocked. The best ocular upgrades Nero had shown him were either small sensors implanted at the back of the cornea or full robotic orbs made of glass.

"The software is uploaded via BioFi, of course, same as your skills downloads."

"Skills downloads?" He ignored "BioFi," which seemed to be the less important of the two totally foreign things Killian had said.

Killian waved his hand. "Like learning ballet or whatever."

"Oh," said Doc, mystified.

"And that's the other thing. This is BioFi version 7.6, which enables zettabytes of data to be transmitted in minutes. We *could* operate at much lower speeds and fidelities for skills transfers, of course," Killian continued, "but we do still get better fidelity with a hard connection. And I don't have to tell you what the arrival of 7.6 means for the transfer of meta-neural data."

"You can say that again," said Doc, feigning a laugh.

"It's just all so exciting to us," said Killian, still giddy. "And for you too, if you're to educate your customers. You know about the dislocation paradigm?"

"Well…"

Killian was so excited, Doc didn't even have to pull a response from his ass. The scientist rushed to explain: "With an upload, I mean. Where people worry about emergent properties like consciousness, identity, and all of that, because who wants to become just bits in an archive, without being who they were before?"

"Not me," said Doc.

"Exactly. But what we've done, thanks to the arrival of 7.6 and the speeds it allows — especially when tethered; you don't have to go wireless — is to create a buffer during the transfer process, allowing neural data to exist not just within the body and not just within The Beam, but effectively in *both*, with sixteen separate redundancies to ensure that..."

A bell-like noise cut Killian off. He and Doc turned to look at a rectangular screen that had appeared on the wall to Doc's right. The screen showed the girl Doc had met at the front desk, still seated. Something had changed in her manner. Before, she had been bubbly and exuberant, but now she seemed somehow bothered.

"Um...Mr. Killian?" she said.

Killian smiled. "Yes, Vanessa!"

"Um...there's someone here to see you."

"Well, I'm in with a client now," he said then swiped the screen closed. A moment later, it opened again.

"Mr. Killian?"

"*Yeeeees...*"

"You really should talk to him."

"Well then, Vanessa," said Killian, annoyed, gesturing toward Doc. "Maybe you'd like to explain to Mr. Greenley why..."

But of course, Doc wasn't Mr. Greenley. He suddenly understood why Killian thought it was his first time here, why the girl thought he'd arrived early rather than late, and why none of what Killian was taking for granted made a molecule of sense to him.

"That's the issue," said Vanessa, looking side to side nervously. "*The person out here to see you* is Mr. Greenley."

Behind Doc, a magnetic door lock clicked into place, and an armored guard began walking toward him.

Nicolai sat to the side of the lectern, looking on as a cluster of glass eyes watched Isaac Ryan deliver the speech Nicolai had written for him. The speech was thick with rhetoric, because rhetoric worked. People didn't want to hear new information. They wanted to hear the same old things over and over, until they began to sound true.

Nicolai listened to his words pouring from Isaac's mouth, annoyed. Annoyed with himself for writing them, and annoyed with the people watching Isaac's persuasive dark eyes on their tablets, walls, and countertops for believing them. There was nothing in the speech that was literally untrue, of course, but there was nothing in it that was really true, either. The whole thing was bullshit…shades of meaning cobbled together in such a way that, when taken together, appeared to say something.

Isaac's speech explained how the Enterprise — his own party's opposition — was only concerned with itself. It was and always had been the party of the selfish. Enterprise's organizers had said, "We will not take care of you," and people had flocked to their ranks. Those people couldn't be blamed, said Nicolai's words on Isaac's lips. The party attracted gamblers who were happy to trade the security of aid (all expenses paid and credits supplied for living expenses, like in the Directorate) for a shot at greatness. But how many people among the Enterprise ever became great? How many amazing creative talents ever earned more than a handful of credits' worth of income? But on the other end, how many among the Enterprise starved because their party wouldn't provide for them when they failed? How many were downtrodden because those in the Enterprise's upper echelon wouldn't reach down and help their brothers and sisters to stand?

Nicolai listened as Isaac attempted to soothe the Directorate unrest that had culminated in the riot at Natasha Ryan's concert. Nicolai was particularly proud/ashamed of that bit of spin doctoring. "We forgive and understand those people who were responsible for causing the riot and seek only to help them rise up," Isaac told the lenses in front of him. It was so perfect/hideous. Forgiving the rabble-rousers showed the Directorate's compassionate heart. *You can harm us, and we will still forgive you*, Isaac's quote said, *because we are family*.

What a bunch of bullshit, thought Nicolai.

But that was true of politics in general, was it not? If Nicolai were an Enterprise speechwriter, he'd be doing the same things as he did for the Directorate: just doling out bullshit of a different flavor. He'd be writing words for Isaac's brother, Micah, instead, telling the NAU that the *Directorate* were the greedy ones. *They* were the Robin Hoods who wanted to tax the profits that Enterprise members had worked hard to earn from the sweat of their own brows and wills. Why should the Directorate (many of whom chose to sit around all day without working) benefit from the Enterprise's intellect and guts?

"There is no perfect system," Isaac said from the lectern. "There will always be problems, but we cannot draw flame from a match of unsteady premise. We cannot abandon those who are unable to succeed on their own, as the Enterprise does. The Directorate is committed to providing for our members — *for every single one.* You will never starve as a member of the Directorate. As more and more tasks become automated by AI and service robots, you will not truly need to work. We have the best of both worlds. We receive what we need without having to break our backs to get it. When turbulence approaches, always remember who we are and what we have. We cannot riot. Riots make us look like a mob. We are no such thing! We believe in our family, and our family is proud!"

None of it was untrue. Directorate members were not required to work. But it was also not really true, because a Directorate living was meager. You got a place to live, you got your services and healthcare taken care of, and you got a stipend for living expenses. But the technology that handled base tasks and made it possible not to work was a double-edged sword because it gave members things to want. Too many Directorate Party members spent their credits on gadgets then found themselves short on food. So what did they do? They took some of those jobs back in order to earn extra credits. All of their work was based on a fixed income, with few legitimate chances for advancement. Nicolai couldn't live like that. He was Directorate, but only in the way Isaac was. Both of their fixed credit allowances, based on their positions, were so high that it felt unlimited. Isaac had even found a slippery way to reclassify Natasha as Directorate. She was a self-made performer who'd come up Enterprise, but now received an exorbitant salary. The irony was that while her scrappiness had gotten Natasha to where she was, her flat pay rate meant that no matter whether her next album and holoconcerts thrived or flopped, she'd generate exactly the same number of credits.

There was something unappealing to Nicolai about guarantees. Risk — the Enterprise's bread and butter, which the

Directorate thought of as gambling — was more exciting. Risk felt like standing on the top of a cliff, feeling your heart beat out of your chest. You might die if you jumped from that cliff, and it was smarter to head over to the wading pool where things were safe. But Nicolai, who'd grown up wealthy, had fled Rome as it burned, trekking through the Wild East with only a pack and a crossbow. He knew the rewards that came from risk. But that had all ended when he'd arrived at the NAU border and met Isaac, and the other bookend had snapped into place.

Still, Nicolai had that seed of adventure and self-determination deep inside him. He wore his black hair too shaggy for a man who could afford follicle-pausing treatments and wore small, round glasses that had stopped being necessary a hundred years earlier with the advent of Lasik eye surgery. Nicolai could afford eyes that could see through walls, but he wore glasses and instead used his credits for creativity add-ons that were experimental at best and reckless at worst. He had a wetchip in his cortex that scanned his mind when he worked on his books, tried to draw or paint, or touched the keys of his piano. The chip watched the firing patterns that came with creativity then fired those neurons while tuning down centers that seemed most responsible for internal criticism. Seemed was the operative word. Creativity was one of the least understood emergent properties, and tinkering with it was considered pseudoscience at best. Even his dealer, Doc, warned him to proceed slowly lest he do damage that couldn't be undone, but Nicolai swore that every time he used his creativity chip, he found inspiration more easily. Each time, he got a little bit more out of his own way. Every day, he was inching closer to writing more stories and books…and maybe one day, fewer bullshit political speeches.

"The NAU, even today, still has the world's only stable government," said Isaac, looking earnestly at the glass eyes in front of him. "Our two parties were formed at a time of unrest, as our borders closed, as our enemies tried to storm our gates. And in the midst of that unrest, the Enterprise decided it was more important to fight over the resources we had and let the strongest survive. It was shortsighted then, and it's shortsighted now. One citizen should not be rewarded if another must suffer. In the Directorate, we are *all* equal."

Nicolai felt his gut tighten. *That* was the only outright lie in the speech. But it was okay; that particular lie had been told often enough that nobody knew it was a lie. Repetition had turned it true. The spirit of Directorate "equality" said that everyone was taken care of and had a chance to advance. In reality, equality meant a ton of low-level managers, number crunchers, data shufflers, and representatives from industries that could easily be automated all juxtaposed with the highly paid Directorate elite. Nicolai himself was paid well, but there seemed to be a secret club above his pay grade, in the realm of the Isaacs and the Natashas. He'd heard Isaac and Natasha use the term "Beau Monde." Although Nicolai probably wasn't supposed to so much as know the phrase (he being merely in the 95th or so percentile), he suspected it referred to the truly elite — the 1 percent of the population that possessed 99 percent of the wealth.

But as Nicolai had written and Isaac had said, no system was perfect. There *were* a lot of starving artists and failed entrepreneurs in the Enterprise. Maybe the Directorate system was the best that could be done. Nicolai couldn't make up his mind. In an ideal world, he'd knock down the iron rule that said you chose one party or the other and would plunk himself squarely in the middle.

Nicolai looked out across the live audience — a group of several hundred Directorate who'd come to the Orpheum to watch Isaac Ryan speak in person. Their faces were pleased and optimistic, their mouths set in determination. A few nodded along. Part of their fervor was probably due to the add-on Isaac had in his throat — a little gadget that caused his voice to reverberate at the most psychologically persuasive frequencies — but mostly it was Nicolai's words, coming from Isaac's mouth. One day, Nicolai would finish his novel. One day, he'd be known for something other than speeches…if, in fact, he got any credit for the speeches at all.

Nicolai's fingers twitched — an unconscious gesture he made when he wanted time to hurry.

He'd written the speech; he knew it was almost over. When it was, the crowd would applaud (of course; he could see them dying to shower Isaac with praise right now), and for another night, the Directorate's image in the minds of its members would be secure. They would sleep, having decided to remain in the Directorate when Shift came. Their earlier dissatisfaction would seem less vital, less insistent. Groups who had previously felt inequity would feel kinship instead.

In the glow of post-speech adoration, Nicolai would shake a few hands as Isaac liked him to then run off on a very important errand. Listening to the speech hadn't moved *him* toward pacification. Listening to his own hypocrisy coming from Isaac's lips made him want to do something very, very Enterprise. He wanted nothing more right now than to run over to Doc's and pick up his newest purchase — a 2.0 version of his current wetchip. He'd paid a fortune for it and was dying to try it out, to explode into an impulsive, reckless, unstable tsunami of creativity. The new chip was supposed to be safer, deeper, and much, much more effective.

He'd had a frustrating few days. First, the riot at Natasha's concert, then the panicked call from Isaac. He hadn't been able to reach Kai Dreyfus, who not only calmed him but also helped him to think. Kai knew all about Nicolai's implant. She'd always encouraged him to write his books and make his art. And sure, she was a whore, and a whore would tell her clients whatever they wanted to hear. But Nicolai, always a good judge of character, suspected that Kai might just be the only honest person in his life.

But everything would be fine once he got out there and got his new implant. It wouldn't matter that he'd done plenty of his own whoring here tonight.

Onstage, Isaac closed his speech.

Applause.

Heads nodded in the live audience, just as they would be nodding in Directorate households all across the NAU.

Nicolai smiled a plastic smile, shook hands, and muscled through too many minutes of mingling. Then he slipped out, hailed a hovercab, and soared through the city toward Doc's apartment.

Chapter 6

Doc sat in an overstuffed chair in his apartment on the forty-seventh floor of Tuco Towers, a conjoined pair of skyscrapers connected to one another by bridges. The bridges were a novelty and branding angle for Tuco and nothing more. Even if there was any point in going from one building filled with apartments of people you didn't know to another, the people at the top of the towers were rich enough to afford hoverskippers. Even Doc could afford a hoverskipper. He didn't have one because hoverskippers were (like the city's ancient, horse-drawn hansom cabs) for tourists. He had his car, though, and while it would be clunky to climb into it through the magnetic port at the end of his hallway and cross to the other tower, he could do it. He'd do that before walking across those stupid bridges, which were mainly used by the Towers' teenagers to hook up and fuck.

Right now, Doc was supposed to be watching a holo to unwind from a long day of scrambling, as a hustler like himself always did.

Instead, he was *trying* to watch the holo but couldn't move his mind from what he'd seen in the lab.

The upgrades he'd seen were troubling enough. Revolutionary new nanobots? Eyes that looked real but could do… well, whatever they could do. BioFi? What did it all mean? And how had that lab been there the whole time he'd been visiting Xenia…and yet they'd kept it from him? He was one of their best salesmen. Doc hadn't just been plunked into Tuco Towers, where the rents were exorbitant because the security was top-notch. He'd *earned* his way into wealth. Xenia couldn't possibly think he wouldn't be able to sell those upgrades.

And that led to the most troublesome thing about Doc's afternoon — a crawling certainty that the only reason Doc wasn't supposed to see the upgrades in that lab was because his customers would never be allowed to buy them.

When Greenley (the salesman Doc had been mistaken for — a man whose elite clients *were* allowed to buy those elite upgrades) had made his unfortunately timed appearance, Doc had realized the depth of the shit he'd landed in. He had learned, quite accidentally, just how far the field of human advancement had come. If what Killian had told him was even half-true, people who used those upgrades would be almost like superheroes. How much of a person's mind could be backed up on The Beam these days? How far had virtual meetings advanced? If the level of immersion that *seemed* possible was, indeed, possible, users of the new technology would be able to sit in a chair beside a canvas and feel themselves fully somewhere else. With a snicker, Doc's mind immediately drifted to the applications in immersive porn. Just imagine the filthy knots into which fetishists could twist themselves when those new tricks came onboard.

And that was just the stuff he'd seen. His new, unauthorized knowledge didn't include the other devices Doc had seen around the lab — items Killian hadn't had time to tell him about before they'd been interrupted. Some of those things had looked like weapons. Others had looked like spare body parts. The human arm hanging on the wall…what could it do? Could it shoot deadly rays like in old movies about the future? Could it punch a hole in Plasteel? Could it disrupt the life energy of anyone it touched, thus making it a hand of death? There was no way to know.

In the lab, Killian's eyes had been panicked when he'd realized his mistake. The guard had advanced. A few minutes later, another two guards had entered, and Doc had found himself surrounded. He hadn't been able to help himself. He'd raised his hands. Killian, regaining his composure, had then laughed and told Doc that there had been a mistake, but that he wasn't in Nazi Germany. Killian had smiled wide and waved the guards away, chastising them for giving their guest the wrong impression. But Killian, Doc noticed, still hadn't unlocked the door, or told the armed men to leave.

"I'm so sorry, Mr. Stahl," Killian had told him. "We seem to have made an unfortunate mistake."

"Hmm," Doc replied, noncommittal.

"Fortunately, our gaffe is reversible."

Doc had looked at the guards, his eyes wary. He was usually cool and in control, always smooth and often sarcastic — a sometimes-cocky asshole. But as he'd eyed the guards and their weapons (a sort he hadn't seen before), Doc felt his usual persona melt away. He stood in the middle of the room, unable to move.

"Oh, please," said Killian, laughing. "What is this, a standoff?"

"I don't know," said Doc. "Is it?"

"Of course not," said Killian. "You're one of our best salesmen." But he was merely mouthing the words. Killian hadn't even known who he was, and still didn't.

"Hmm," Doc repeated. His arms were raised slightly from his sides when the guards had approached, even after he'd lowered them from over his head. He looked like a man about to sprint, once he determined the correct direction in which to run.

"But I hope you understand," said Killian, "these upgrades are for a client who demands high levels of discretion." But that, too, was bullshit. Doc, who was well steeped in the art of bullshit, knew bullshit when he heard it. What he was seeing wasn't a custom order. It was a product line. This wasn't all for one company or person; it was for a whole *class* of people — a class that Doc, while well off, wasn't elite enough to represent. What he was seeing represented a widening of the gap. Doc thought, *The rich get richer.*

"Uh-huh," he said.

"So…and this is awkward, I know…we can't allow you to remember these items. For the client's privacy, you understand."

"I see," said Doc. And now, he did see. They were going to wipe his memory. They wouldn't have a Gauss Chamber because this was a lab, not a hospital. Wholesale erasure wouldn't be necessary anyway. They'd use a hand unit. Doc would lose the last fifteen minutes and would later find himself unsure whether he'd seen any new wares this week or not. He'd probably call Nero on Monday and ask for a new appointment. Nero, duly briefed, would play along.

And so he'd told Killian that he understood, and he'd allowed Killian to wave him clean. Afterward, he'd affected the vacant, vaguely optimistic expression appropriate to a fresh wipe while a tech ran a small sensor above his long blond hair. The tech had declared him current as of approximately the time he'd been in the bathroom washing his face. Then Killian had led him out without hurry, knowing that Doc's ability to form new memories would be impaired for several more minutes. He'd told him that there was nothing new this week and had suggested Doc call Mr. Nero on Monday. Doc had thanked him, gone back down to the street, and had hailed a cab. He'd gotten the same cabbie as before. The cabbie had jerked the cab at every stoplight, nearly causing Doc to plow his face into the divider.

Sitting in his apartment, mulling his troubling (and unforgotten, unwiped) time at Xenia, Doc swiped the air to make the holo he'd been pretending to watch vanish. It was a stupid show anyway. Whiny people with their whiny problems. It wasn't even distracting him. He could still see everything that had happened today, thanks to the wipe firewall he'd had implanted and the accompanying spoof under his hair. As a man who'd had to scrap and connive his way to success as a salesman, it wasn't the first time someone had wanted Doc to forget what he'd seen.

"Canvas," Doc said.

His wall chirped.

"Search biological enhancements."

A large globe of Beam pages appeared in the air in front of him. Doc preferred his results visually clustered in an intuitive web, like a Beam-generated mind-map. Closest to Doc was a window showing a common distributor of artificial limbs, and beside it was Hammacher Schlemmer. Neither were helpful. He wasn't looking for replacement parts, and Hammacher Schlemmer hadn't changed in the fifty years it had been selling upgrades instead of shoe buffers from in-flight magazines. All of HS's add-ons were useless novelties for rich people who had literally nothing else to spend their credits on: bioluminescent toes to show users see where they were walking at night; tongue modifiers that made everything taste like ice cream. He frowned.

Doc held the index finger and thumb of each hand up in front of him then peeled the web open between the limb distributor and Hammacher Schlemmer. Deeper pages rolled forward, and the outer layer curled back like a banana peel. Nothing. He turned the globe, peeled the other way, following the HS path, toward upgrades and away from medical limb replacement. But it wasn't right.

"Search biological upgrades."

This time, the front page was Omnipedia. Of course. But

he didn't want to know the theories behind biological enhancement, particularly the vanilla'd version. He twisted the web, spun it to find its edges, and saw that the scope was still wrong. He was already feeling discouraged. If Xenia had tried to wipe his mind to make him forget what he'd seen, what were the chances that it would be available, publicly, on The Beam?

Doc sighed then looked down at his router, which he kept visible so that he could look at it and make himself less paranoid. The *SECURE* light was still lit. The router had been ridiculously expensive, and used AI/key encryption, a hybrid model ensuring that all but the most advanced systems would never know where his queries originated.

Duly secure, Doc said, "Search Series Six nanobots."

This time, even the front page wasn't close. He found a line of Series Six radial grass cutters and plenty on nanobots, but nothing related to both. He peeled the web and looked inside for the hell of it, but knew there was no point.

"Search BioFi 7.6."

This time, the results were even less relevant. There was nothing at all on BioFi (except for one weblog in which the teen author had written that she'd scored poorly on a test in bio and then had run-on with the next sentence, about a friend named Fi) and a few useless hits that included the number 7.6. Doc exploded the BioFi weblog just to be sure, but the creator was a nondescript kid whose network pages held nothing. Even her parents seemed unremarkable.

"Visit Utopior Enhancements."

Utopior's virtual storefront appeared before him in a window, complete with a ping asking if he'd care for immersion. Doc touched the ping, and his apartment became ghosts of furniture buried in a life-sized holo. Doc stood and wandered the exclusive shop's aisles, paddling at his sides to scroll the store underfoot. He picked up holo objects and tapped a few for detail. Each time, an enhanced holo of the upgrade appeared in his hands, each time disappointing. Utopior was the most borderline-illegal shop he knew, and the kind of place he could get tossed in jail for visiting. *This* was supposed to be what the law was keeping from Doc, but even the fanciest upgrades here were nothing compared to what he'd seen at Xenia.

Doc sighed, swiped to close the store, and visited the other shops he'd hacked into over the years: Gillead, Philharmonic, even Fremd Geshenk, which trafficked with Eurasia and was home to any number of biological perversions. If you wanted an ear that could listen to seventy simultaneous pieces of music, you visited Philharmonic, but if you wanted a double cock or an asshole that could shrink to carry a pin or expand to swallow a bookcase, you went to FG. But in all of the stores, what he found paled in comparison to the equipment at Xenia by a factor of ten.

Doc shook his head, annoyed. Then he swiped the search away, rose, and circled the room, snuffing lights by pinching his fingers at them. A tune rose as his canvas recognized his movements, and after that, Doc let the computers do the rest. The light in his bedroom came on low. The music was mellow, almost hypnotic, filled with subaural reverberations that would tune his CNS neurons while he slept. The bathroom light came on, beckoning him. Doc washed his face, changed, and tapped the mirror to bring up the next day's weather. Much of the weather was artificial inside the NAU's protective lattice, so predictions were usually accurate and conditions fairly good. Doc called up the report and swore. They were letting it rain tomorrow. He'd probably end up hiking through the city and getting soaked on his usual rounds, thanks to the fucking protestors.

Doc shook his head, left the bathroom without swiping the lights off, then watched as they went off anyway. He climbed into his bed, feeling it adjust to his body and warm beneath him. The music and lights dimmed. In ten minutes, they'd both be off, and so would Doc. After the same routine night after night, sleep came easy no matter the preoccupation of his mind.

But after just a few minutes, when the lights and music were only down to half volume, Doc heard a noise in the living room. He stopped and listened, then heard the noise again.

"Canvas," he said.

He heard no answering chirp.

"Canvas."

Nothing.

Doc turned, keyed at the headboard of his bed. When nothing happened, he felt his heart pound. Like almost every non-Organa citizen of the NAU (and, let's be honest, plenty of Organa citizens, too), Doc wasn't comfortable when severed from The Beam. The Beam comprised Doc's extra senses. Since it was always there, he'd gotten used to knowing anything he wanted to know, being able to see wherever he wanted to see, and being able to tell with certainty that it was going to fucking rain tomorrow.

He checked his wrist. His nano tattoo was still working fine, and he saw that it was nearly midnight. But the enhancements in Doc's body that required a Beam connection to function were quiet. He felt like he'd lost a limb, or several.

He jumped out of bed and called for lights, already forgetting his link was down. Then he tapped the wall to turn them on seconds later, forgetting again. He slammed his toe into the doorjamb and winced, suddenly thinking that the glowing toe enhancement maybe wasn't so stupid after all.

His heart pumped harder. Something was wrong.

He heard the sound again, but this time recognized it as the clatter of his doorknob. Someone was trying to break in. That wasn't supposed to be possible. Tuco was tied down tight, inaccessible at the outer door and elevator to anyone without an embedded Beam ID that matched the supposedly unhackable resident roster. There were two guards at the door and a lobby attendant. And how could anyone pick his lock? There was a manual piece to the lock, of course — a plain old ordinary thing that fell on a deadbolt, to provide a tangible feeling of security — but of course, if his link was down, that deadbolt would be the only game in town. The Beam-enabled locks and security wouldn't be functioning. There was supposed to be a triple-redundancy in the system — a box inside the door that wasn't wired into The Beam, plus a fail-safe in the lock itself. The power supply was supposed to be self-contained. But despite all of that, Doc could hear someone picking with regular tools, as if the lock were nothing more than a stick shoved through a hole.

"Who's there?" Doc called out, feeling stupid. It was the kind of thing people used to do in old movies, back before identifiers and Beam tracking. Before locks that you could command to repel a specific person from your door if you wanted…and if your link was up.

Instead of getting an answer, Doc watched as his front door burst open and a silhouette sprinted toward him. He saw lights on in the hallway.

The intruder was halfway toward him, running. Had he been discovered? The guy wasn't fucking around. Was he here to wipe Doc's memory for good? Or was he here to wipe *Doc* — as in "wiped from existence"?

The intruder's thundering feet told Doc that the intruder hadn't come for tea.

Doc turned, grabbed a lamp, and swung. He was swinging mostly blind in the dark apartment, but his swing hit pay dirt. He felt his arms shudder as the lamp found something hard. The attacker grunted, staggered back, and slammed into the wall. A picture (a real one in a frame; his mother had given it to him, and he'd laughed) fell at the attacker's side. Doc heard glass shatter. He tried to see the intruder's face by the wan city light through his windows, but it was too dark.

The attacker leapt up. The blow had only disoriented him.

Before his pursuer could gain his feet, Doc sprinted to the end of the hall at the back of his apartment in his boxers, yanked open the door at its end, and jumped into his car. Then he disengaged the magnetic docking lock, fired the engine, and whirred away, leaving his attacker's silhouette in the door behind him.

Chapter 7

Nicolai touched the glass front of a store as he passed and glanced at the time. It was nearly midnight. It was late, but Doc's message had said he could come by and pick up his new creativity chip whenever. Nicolai, realizing how overly eager it made him look, intended to take Doc up on his offer.

He hadn't been able to come straight over, and the delays had given him upgrade blue balls. Once he'd left the Orpheum, he'd been summoned back by Isaac, who was in a celebratory mood and wanted the speechwriter to have his due. Nicolai said it was quite all right and told Isaac to take the credit, but Isaac was having none of it. Besides, Isaac said, Natasha wanted to thank him. Then Natasha, once she got him alone, told Nicolai that she'd been very flustered during the riot. She said that she wanted to thank him, to tell him that she felt much better now that the speech he'd written for Isaac had soothed a lot of Directorate nerves. That was what her lips said, anyway. But this was Natasha, and her eyes — when she spoke to Nicolai — always said something else.

Hours and hours had dragged by. Nicolai's fingers twitched then twitched again. He didn't want more Directorate bullshit. The event was politics at its worst. Nicolai shook more hands in an hour than he normally did in two weeks, his fingers twitching the entire time. All he wanted was to write. Sometimes, the need seized him, and he wanted to nurse it immediately. This was one of those times. So he screencapped what he was sure had to be a firestorm of neurons using his current implant, but what he really wanted was to get his new implant and see what *that* baby could do.

Midnight.

It would be okay. Upgrade dealers were like drug dealers, and used to the schedule. Just like with drugs, it was possible to become addicted to add-ons. Dealers of both were always available, no matter the time.

Still, he should call. Doc might be in bed.

But if he called, Doc might not answer, or might tell him to come back tomorrow. Nicolai didn't want to come back tomorrow, so he didn't call. Doc had told him to show up whenever, and whenever happened to be midnight. Paying Doc through the nose for upgrades bought Nicolai a lot of leeway. He reassured himself that it was okay to take it.

Nicolai's Beam ID was registered — via Doc's invite and via his status as high-ranking Directorate — on the permanent guest list in Doc's building. He nodded to the guards, stepped into the elevator, and tried to still his breathing. He felt like a piece of art was trying to be born inside him. He *had* to get his fingers on a keyboard, or explode in an orgasm of creativity.

The floors couldn't pass quickly enough.

Nicolai arrived at the forty-seventh floor to find Doc's door ajar. That was strange, but it wasn't as though doors had to be closed at all times. So he stepped inside and found the room dark. That was stranger. The lights should have sensed him and gone bright.

"Canvas," said Nicolai.

Nothing happened.

He stepped farther into the apartment, tentative, already thinking he should back out. It was hard to see, but the hallway light showed him that a lamp had been shattered and that a framed picture had fallen from the wall. What used to be the frame's glass overlay was in shards on the carpet.

"Doc?" he called.

Nicolai said nothing further because at that moment, a strong hand clasped him from behind, and the cold blade of a knife pressed against his throat.

Chapter 8

Micah Ryan stood at the head of a small group in his office at District Zero's Enterprise building. His shoulders were straight, his hands clenched behind his back. He had a sculpted, handsome jaw and steely eyes that were technically brown but that sometimes seemed closer to silver. He had a carefree, unassuming haircut with nary a hair out of place, and wore his trim blue suit and silk band tie as if he'd been poured into them.

The group was as elite as its tiny size suggested. There was nothing especially difficult about its current mission, but this mission above all others required trust and clearance. It was the kind of mission that nobody could know about because it would make the Enterprise seem two-faced and unsettled. And of course, that was exactly the impression they wanted people to have about the Directorate.

"We were stationed around the Aphora's crowd," said a thin black man named Eams. "Bernie started with the boos, like you saw on the Beam feed. The tomatoes — the first ones, anyway — came from Gloria. Her idea, by the way."

"High-five, Gloria," said Micah, showing a few teeth in a

friendly smile. He held out a hand. Gloria was nowhere near him, but she raised her own, and air-clapped toward him.

"I still think we shouldn't throw shit that isn't natural to carry. Why would anyone bring tomatoes to a concert?" said an agent with a surfer's swept-back blond hair. He was dressed immaculately now, but Micah had seen the feed from his sister-in-law's concert and had managed to pick out Craig, with his surfer's hair. He'd worn a shabby 2060s vintage tux and had looked as absurd as the rest of the attending Directorates.

Gloria started to answer, but Micah, pacing, beat her to it. "It doesn't matter. You'd bring tomatoes if you knew in advance that you wanted to throw them, same as you'd bring a bouquet of flowers. Throwing things at Natasha Ryan's feet is an NAU pastime. So if they aren't running a search at the door, we're allowed to bring whatever. It's fine. Upset Directorate would bring tomatoes to throw."

"But why would they attend at all?"

Micah locked his eyes (charming, not threatening) on the agent with the surfer's hair. "To cause unrest, Craig. To unsettle the populace. To riot. What is it you don't understand?"

"It just seems like it'd be a waste for them. Most of the people have to buy their way into places like the Aphora. Do you know how many credits it costs?"

"Yes, of course I do. I authorized the tickets. It would have been nice to win tickets like the rest of the raff in the back, but it seemed a smarter use of our resources to order them rather than trying to win them one at a time."

Several agents snickered. A few looked toward Micah as they did, hungry for their leader's approval, dying for him to know they got his joke and thought it funny.

"Look," said Micah, still pacing, his voice taking on a lecturing tone, "you've seen the feed. The boos start at the edges and then bleed through the room. The things you threw came from everywhere. But the rear and middle were open seating, and the tickets there are priced so that lower-ranking Directorate can still theoretically afford them if they don't mind blowing a ton of credits for a special occasion. But you can win tickets for all of those areas, so nobody would assume that rioters paid through the nose in order to come in and make trouble. Have you seen the reactions from people who don't know we planted you there? It comes off as a genuine riot caused by Directorate malcontents. At an affair like a Ryan concert, party lines are sharply drawn. It's almost all rich Enterprise, then a few high-ranking Directorate who actually allow themselves to enjoy art, then a small group of raff who won their tickets somewhere. So just put yourself in the shoes of a Directorate contest winner: You're barely scraping by, living on a credit dole that hasn't risen in years, despite inflation. Maybe you've picked up an extra job — one that's held off automation specifically so you can do it, like a pity job. Either way, you're edging it, barely feeding your family and never going on vacation. You've had almost six years in your current situation, and it's terrible, but you can't blame the party because you know that deep down, when Shift comes, you'll stay Directorate. You're not equipped for Enterprise. I mean, what would you do if the government didn't pay for your everything? You've developed no skills and have no faith in your ability to make your own living. You know that as much as you're in the raff now, you'd be *trampled* in Enterprise. So what can you do? You can't improve your financial or living situation no matter which party you're in, so the best thing to do is to argue that it's not your fault. So you raise your Directorate flag and start telling the world that the Enterprise is greedy and evil. You bitch, and you riot. Maybe you throw a few tomatoes."

"But why would they riot *there?*" said Craig. "Natasha is Directorate, not Enterprise."

Micah gave a sideways smile. "Really? I had no idea."

The agents snickered again.

Of course Natasha was Directorate. Her husband, Micah's brother, Isaac, was Directorate too. The same question had been raised early on, when Micah had first instructed the agents to go undercover and riot at the concert.

"This isn't really about parties, Craig. Think about it. This is about haves and have-nots. But rioting and protesting rich people is shooting at a moving target. It's hard to define the enemy — the group that's them as opposed to us — if the differentiator is their credit balances. But if we can make this whole thing — this feeling of pre-Shift unrest — about Enterprise and Directorate? Then we give people a *them* that's clear and well defined. Having a clear *them* solidifies people, which is why we're here to begin with. We're trying to create a *them* in the eyes of the Enterprise. We stage riots as if the Directorate were causing them. The Enterprise starts to hate and distrust the Directorate more than ever. *Us* versus *them*. Solidarity. Strength. Generally making the other side look like shit. You see?"

Craig said nothing, either mollified or pretending to be. But what Craig felt or thought was immaterial. Micah, as always, knew what he was doing.

With Shift approaching, the Senate's balance of power was up for grabs. More citizens in Enterprise meant more Enterprise seats in the Senate. Shift seldom resulted in much movement between the parties, seeing as people seldom changed their natures. The choice, for most people, was a crapshoot. Would you rather have a living provided for you and not really need to work but know you'd be stuck with a barely sufficient lifestyle for the next six years? Or would you rather roll the dice at building a bigger future by making your own living…knowing that if you failed, there was no safety net? The lushest spires and the lowliest gutters were disproportionately filled with people who'd chosen Enterprise, whereas the low end of the middle were mostly Directorate. Those Directorate weren't excited about life, but their situations weren't dire enough to motivate change. The way Micah saw it, Shift really was a pick-your-poison scenario for most people, with both options equally toxic. The Directorate was mostly downtrodden but complacent. The best way to shake that complacency — and gain a few new members — was to show that life in the Directorate wasn't a bed of mediocre-smelling roses.

Micah looked around the group of seven agents. He had managed to spot them all in the feed, but he'd had to enter a 3-D projection, augment, and rotate for quite a while to find some of them. That was good. They were supposed to be invisible.

Now, in Micah's office, all of the agents were nodding, ready to do whatever their fearless leader said. All except for Jason Whitlock. Whitlock's bearing bothered Micah. He'd given his report just like all of the others, but he seemed somehow *off*. He wasn't articulating well. He seemed distracted, and kept turning his gaze to the window. He also seemed to be forgetting large parts of the evening. Whitlock had commented earlier that he'd been shocked by how short the concert was. When another agent told him that it had lasted over three hours, he'd seemed surprised. So Micah had quizzed him, and he hadn't remembered a single title out of Natasha's twenty-seven-song performance. He'd made guesses, but it seemed as if he were pulling them from the Beam Top 50 list rather than memory.

"It's late," said Micah. "Go home, everyone. Good job. We'll talk tomorrow, same time."

The gathering began to disperse. Micah approached Whitlock and set hand to shoulder.

"Jason."

Whitlock looked up.

"You seem distracted."

"Just tired, Micah."

Micah rubbed the man's back then gently turned him so they were facing each other. "You're not just tired. There's something wrong. You don't remember the concert."

"I remember it fine, just feeling a bit swimmy. That's all. I'm okay. I guess I've got some stuff on my mind."

"What do you have on your mind?" Micah's voice came out as concern. The second question layered under the first said, *How can I help?*

"It's nothing. I'm fine."

"Family troubles?"

"No, really, I'm fine. Thank you, though."

Micah's hand was still on Whitlock's shoulder. "It's important to me that your head is clear. You know if you need anything, you can let me know, right?"

"Of course."

"Who was the woman with you at the concert?"

Whitlock looked up, disarmed.

"I saw her in the feed. I wanted to understand how everything went down, so I subscribed to a holo immersive. Almost as expensive as attending." Micah flashed a smile. "Walked around a bit. Paused and exploded. Found all of our people. You were the only one with a date. Or perhaps you got lucky and just ended up sitting beside a beautiful woman who was also alone."

Micah knew from the holo that Jason had left with the petite woman with dark-brown, almost black hair. The holo's resolution and camera positioning weren't high enough to see her well, and her face had been mostly extrapolated. He wouldn't be able to pick her out of a lineup, but he'd seen her well enough to know she wasn't Whitlock's wife, who was taller than Jason and blonder than Craig.

Micah watched Jason's eyes, waiting for the agent's denial.

"Look..." said Whitlock.

"It's okay, Jason. I'm not judging. I just need to know who she was."

He blinked twice, looked up and then around the room.

"It's okay, Jason," Micah repeated.

"I know. It's just that…I don't *know* who she was." He looked into Micah's steely gaze then rushed on. "I mean, I know I was there with her, obviously. But she's…it's like there's a fog in my head."

"You've been wiped."

"Maybe."

"You should have reported it. Immediately." Micah tried not to sound angry, but this was beyond idiotic. Whitlock stammered to defend himself.

"It's more than that! I've been wiped before, and this is different. The timespan is longer, like you'd get from a Gauss Chamber. But also not. I mean, I don't know that I've *lost* anything, but I'm *foggy* on the whole fucking night. I guess she was an escort, okay? And I guess I hired her. But I don't remember how or when. I might have met her at the show. I don't remember her name or what she looked like. I didn't even remember her at all until you started asking me for details, which is why I didn't say anything earlier."

"A modified wipe?"

"Maybe."

Micah drew a deep breath, assessing, then clapped Whitlock twice on the shoulder and said, "Okay, Jason. Go get your head checked. It's probably nothing. You probably had too much moondust."

"I don't do that shit," said Whitlock.

"It was a joke. Too much wine then." Micah smiled.

After a beat, Whitlock smiled back. "I did have a lot of wine."

"That's probably all it is."

"Sure! I was drunk." But his face was uncertain. You couldn't drink inside the Aphora, and it would take a lot of consumption beforehand to fog an entire three-hour concert and what had surely come after.

"Get your head checked anyway."

"Sure, Micah."

Whitlock picked up his coat and walked through the door, leaving Micah alone in his empty office to contemplate the small woman with the missing face.

Chapter 9

Dominic Long walked through the District Zero police station to the Quark annex, his footfalls echoing in the same creepy way they always did down here, too light and too sharp.

Walking through the main part of the station was like walking anywhere else — industrial flooring made of rubberized Formica in an ugly green pattern, dark enough to disguise the blood, urine, and dirt that somehow always ended up plastering a police station's floor. Out there, his shiny black shoes sounded muted, not echoing because the sound was absorbed by the detectives and blue-uniformed patrolmen as they came and went. Out there, his footfalls flew out the windows. He heard street noise. And of course, he could feel the air coming in through the windows and from the temperamental vent system that, these days, was used more for distributing pacifying pheromones than temperature-controlled air.

But once he crossed from the old part of the station to the new section Quark had added after the company had started to take over the whole fucking world, all of the noises changed.

When Quark had initiated its partnership with the police

to handle Beam-related crimes, they'd built this tomb-like monstrosity. You had to submit to a Beam ID scan to enter, and once inside, every surface was wired. Dominic watched a digital shadow of himself walk along the wall to his right. Beneath his feet, as he made those odd, clacking footsteps, he watched red footprints appear below his shoes. Walking in the annex, Dominic always felt judged. Because he was.

"Good afternoon, Captain Long," said a deep, soothing voice that seemed to come from everywhere.

"Fuck off," said Dominic, annoyed. This entire wing represented an invasion of his body's privacy, and he resented it.

"I can recommend a masseuse for that pain in your shoulder," said the voice, unperturbed.

"No offense, Noah," said Dominic, "but get your sensors off my body."

"You're carrying a lot of tension," said the voice.

Dominic shook his head. In order to enter the secure Quark wing, you had to walk through this bullshit gauntlet of holier-than-thou. The old police station was on the north side of the building. The Quark wing was on the south side, and you could only enter it through the old station, via this long white hallway. Quark PD's offices and cells were in the wing's center, and the hallway wrapped around it in a 360-degree spiral. If Dominic were nervous or uptight in a way that might suggest aggression, his posture and gait would betray it, and the hallway would stop him. If too many people (or too much weight) tried to leave the wing's core through the hallway, the hallway would stop them. And that was only on the surface. There were a billion other things the hallway gauged, assessed, and calculated. It was watching his eyes, scanning his body for weapons, talking to any nanobots he had in his system regardless of their encryption (Dominic had none) and measuring his breath's temperature. Dominic didn't understand most of it and didn't want to. To him, the hallway was a perfect example of how The Beam had gone too far.

"This job makes me tense," he said.

"I'm sorry," the voice replied, its deep timbre adjusting in a way Dominic knew was intended to soothe him, setting up subaural resonance to shift his brainwaves. You could resist it if you knew what was happening, so Dominic did. "Would you like me to set up an appointment with a counselor?"

Dominic rolled his eyes. "Decades of development in artificial intelligence, and still, stupidity abounds," said Dominic.

"What do you mean, Captain Long?"

"You don't know what stress is," said Dominic.

"I did when I was alive," said the voice.

Dominic reached the hallway's end. Synthetic response surfaces gave way to plain beige floor tiles, and once again Dominic found himself inside what was more or less just a police station — albeit a squeaky clean, technologically enabled, and window-free one. But this station — Quark's station — wasn't the anomaly. The station on the other side of the building was the anomaly. The old station hadn't changed much since the unrest in the '30s, when it was built amidst supposition that the entire country could fall at any time. That was before America had joined the NAU, back when leftover optimism and the unbridled air of discovery from the '20s still hung in the air like the scent of soured wine. The old station still accessed The Beam through terminals and wasn't gesture-enabled. Part of that was sensible (opening the Fi to general access could lead to security problems with all of the nut jobs coming and going), but most of it was due to apathy and shortsightedness. Police funding, even now, still got fucked right up the butt.

Dominic stopped at a flat silver panel in the foyer that looked almost like a full-length mirror. An Asian woman appeared on its surface and seemed to walk toward him, holding a clipboard.

"How are you, Dominic?" she said.

"Fine, Akari," he replied. The woman in the panel was as artificial as Noah, the voice in the hallway, but the programmers had soothed out Akari's idiot edges. There were iterations of Noah on The Beam that were nearly as sharp as the real Noah had once been, but the station's copy was — in Dominic's mind, anyway — beyond obnoxious. Akari was also cute, and Dominic was a sucker for cute girls, no matter his level of annoyance.

"How can I help you?" she said.

"I got a call about the breach at QuarkTechnic."

Akari looked down at her clipboard — an affect the programmers had added to make her seem more real. "Of course. Holding room fifteen."

"Thank you."

Dominic walked through the Quark station, peering around at the officers working their full-gesture canvases. One was rotating a relational web, peeling it back to search through The Beam's pages. Another sat with her eyes closed, probably downloading images into an implant behind her retinas. Dominic wanted to swear. You had to be half cyborg to work here. It was one of the many things Dominic hated about the annex, aside from the sheer presumptuousness of it all. Quark thought it was important enough to impress itself into the fabric of the police themselves. What a load of bullshit.

Dominic arrived at holding room fifteen. Beside the door was another silver panel, this one smaller than the one at the entrance. Akari appeared, visible from the chest up, still holding her clipboard.

"I can read," said Dominic, his testiness returning in a wave. The fucking Beam was always checking on him, as if he was as burned as the nut jobs they picked up on the street. There was a large black *15* printed beside the door. He didn't need Akari to confirm that he was in the right place.

"It's not that, Dominic," she said. "This suspect is classified security beta. I'm going to need a palm scan." She held up her hand. It looked like she was on the other side of a window and had planted her palm against it from the inside.

"You scan-raped me on the walk in. What did I have for breakfast, Akari? What, exactly, is in my colon right now?"

"I apologize, Captain," she said, subtly shifting in formality. "But I still require the scan."

Dominic grunted and set his large, beaten-up policeman's hand against Akari's small, delicate one.

"Thank you," she said. In front of Dominic, the door swung open.

The room was small and white. Inside, two Quark cops were interrogating their subject at a rather clichéd wooden table. One stood. The other sat at the table's edge. Dominic assumed the standing one was supposed to be the bad cop, and the seated one was the friendly good cop.

Across the table was a woman who appeared to be in her twenties (though who could say these days?) who gave Dominic a tiny smile when he entered. Her hair was matted in giant dreadlocks that were dyed a bright, almost luminescent pink. She had a small silver ring through the right side of her lower lip and another in her eyebrow. The ear on her other side had two piercings connected by a short silver chain. Her index fingers were both tattooed with swirls of black ink.

"Sorry I'm late," said Dominic.

The bad cop wasted no pleasantries and handed him a small tablet with a look of resentment. Quark cops didn't like the regular cops any more than the regular cops liked the Quarks. Dominic was only here because he was the captain, and because this was a high-level inquiry.

"Leah," said Dominic, reading from the tablet. "That's it. No last name. No Beam ID."

"It's not a crime to not have a Beam ID," said the young woman. "Nor to not have a last name."

The standing cop gave her a look then addressed

Dominic. "She's been arrested before. We have her code on file. She really does seem to have no last name. Registered simply as Leah, a student at QuarkTechnic. She was flagged trying to access a classified section of The Beam nowhere near her access level."

Dominic handed the tablet back to the Quark cop, looked at the girl, and waited for her response.

"It was an accident," she said. "I was trying to order lunch." She looked at the Quark cops. "Donuts."

The standing cop moved toward her, but Dominic held up a hand.

"She was in Quark's server. Got through the Blanket, which in itself requires a 128-bit encryption key."

"You can't hold that against me," Leah said. "Who still uses 128-bit encryption? I was composing a nursery rhyme and accidentally accessed the server. Luckily, some citizen scouts stopped me before I accidentally went any further. I hear the next level of security was a velvet rope."

Dominic stared at her.

"A thick one," she added then circled her fingers to show the rope's girth.

Dominic shifted his gaze to the seated cop. He was the only one who hadn't spoken, and was thereby Dominic's final hope of learning something useful.

"What's she talking about?"

"All you need to know is that she was where she wasn't supposed to be, getting at stuff she wasn't supposed to get."

"Cake recipes," said Leah. "Quark's are the best."

"One-twenty-eight-bit is old technology, but the Blanket still blunts brute-force hacks enough to give us time to cut off people who try to get in," said the seated cop. "There's data there not suitable for public consumption, but it's fairly innocuous. She burned through it so fast, we couldn't stop her. Naturally. she was traced, and Quark on-site at Technic brought her in. She was transferring terras of data from one lane to another. Not even to a slip drive for the road. She won't tell us why."

"It was an accident," said Leah. Her hands were cuffed in front of her, but she still managed to tip her chair back on its rear legs. She hadn't yet nursed the gall to put her legs up on the table.

"So she didn't remove anything from the server?" asked Dominic.

"No."

"And she didn't breach your inner security?"

"No…"

"So what's the crime?"

"Digital trespassing," said the standing cop.

"You brought her in here for *that?*" said Dominic. "Aren't there jaywalkers you should be hunting?"

Dominic was annoyed. Hacking was a multi-tiered thing, and the lines between modification and true hacking were gray at best. Most kids could break the security on their canvases to access porn, and the ability required to do it, back in the early computing age, would have sent them to jail for life. But in a world where encryption could be enhanced with conscious choices made by Beam-resident AI codemakers, using a brute-force algorithm was a lot more like hopping a fence and entering a neighbor's yard than breaking into a house. Sometimes, people out on The Beam couldn't resist taking shortcuts. It was technically illegal, but only barely.

"Digital trespassing *at Quark,*" said the cop sitting on the desk.

Dominic actually laughed. These pompous assholes.

"We want to hold her and check out her known associates," said the other cop.

"The associates from my file?" said Leah. "Oh sure, call Binky. Tell him I said hi. I haven't seen him since we burned the preschool firewall so our naptimes could coincide."

"Shut it," the cop snapped, turning.

Dominic met the cop's eyes and shook his head.

"You're just going to let her go? This is Organa shit. Just look at her."

"That's not fair," said Leah. "I haven't judged you based on the way you look." Dominic watched the woman's eyes, willing her not to continue. But then her will broke, and she added, "So, which enhancement did you order to make your jagger bigger and longer?"

The cop moved toward her again, but Dominic held up his hands.

"Ms...." Dominic began then remembered that she didn't have a last name. "Leah," he said instead. "What were you trying to do at QuarkTechnic?"

The girl brought her chair down to four legs and leaned forward, elbows to knees. Her green eyes settled on Dominic's with a smile. "Okay, I'll tell you the truth. I was trying to change my grades. Satisfied?"

"You were at Quark," said the standing cop.

"A mistake." She gave the cop a look. "Your encryption looks the same, and you'd know that if you'd look for yourself. And frankly, you share a lot of the same back doors."

"There are no back doors at Quark."

Leah laughed.

The cops turned to Dominic. The standing one said, "Look. I don't want to pull rank because you'll bluster and pretend you outrank me, but we both know that what Quark says goes in the end. If you let her go..."

The Quark cop was right; you didn't step into a state-run institution like the police and build yourself a new wing staffed by superior forces if you didn't have a lot of power. So to counter, Dominic went on the offensive.

"I'm not going to let her go, you idiot," he snapped. "I'm going to interrogate her. Properly. She needs to be in the public police system, not your proprietary one. If the Organas found out that Quark booked someone without going through proper channels and released that information to the world, it'd look like a conspiracy. And believe me, those hippies have the hackers to release whatever they want."

The standing cop looked at Leah and said, "That's what I've heard."

After a small bluster, the cops relented. Dominic used the Quark station's canvas to transfer Leah's records to the DZPD Beam sector and cleared her for access through the outer corridor. During the walk, Noah's deep, soothing voice expressed a concern for Dominic's blood pressure and urged him to see a physician for an injection of diagnostic and scavenger nanos. Then it complimented Leah on her hair color and admonished her to stay out of trouble. He added that her shoes, which were little more than canvas with individual toes, were better for her back than Dominic's synthetic leather clod-hoppers. Dominic swore.

Once they'd exited the Quark hallway, Dominic marched Leah straight-faced through the DZPD station, past the desk clerk, and through the front door. Officers and detectives watched him pass with the pink-haired girl. He said nothing to answer their stares. It was amazing what you could get away with if you acted like you were allowed to do it, and if you were the captain.

They walked outside then skirted the corner and stopped in front of an Amino stand. The stand was unoccupied, the vendor apparently off at the bathroom or stoned somewhere on moondust. The second seemed likely. Dominic walked by the stand every day after parking his hover in the subterranean garage, and the guy who ran it was as Organa-looking as Leah.

Dominic unlocked her cuffs. Leah looked up at him, rubbing her wrists.

"Stupid, Leah," he said.

"I had a man on the inside who I knew could spring me," she answered, giving Dominic a satirical salute.

"Sloppy, too. I thought you were better than that."

"I'm not sloppy. I'm freewheeling." When Dominic continued to stare at her, her serious glare finally broke, and she groaned — a gesture that said, *Fine!*

She held her tattooed fingers in front of Dominic's face.

"You're not seeing the whole picture, Dom. Those cops were both Beam clerics. Did I not tell you about my new enhancements?"

"You've had those since I met you."

"Not the tattoos, shitter."

"What? Did you add some nano reservoirs?"

"Nano *fabricators*," she clarified. "Under my nails. Problem with Quark security is that the encryption can only be bypassed from the inside. Once these — " she wiggled her index fingers again, " — saw what kind of nanos the clerics had filled those meat sack bodies of theirs with, they fabricated cloned soldiers to match. So I spoofed them and left a few dozen on that table. Now my nanos are inside the clerics, and they'll never know."

"Behind the firewall?"

"Right."

"You *wanted* to get caught."

Leah shrugged. "I needed something to handshake with. Not that this makes things any easier. Hax0r encryption has evolved to ridiculous levels. One of the advantages of having computers doing all of the computer development in The Beam."

Dominic closed his eyes and shook his head. "Dangerous. They could find out."

"They won't."

"They'll trace you. And then they'll wonder why you weren't questioned further. They'll look into the records and notice that all trace of your visit today was purged. Then maybe a few people will remember who took you in for that supposed further questioning." He made a fist and planted his thumb in his chest.

Leah extended her hand and slapped Dominic lightly a few times on the cheek. She had to strain to reach him. She was probably five-five, and Dominic was over six feet tall, at least fifty pounds too heavy. Being a captain, he could afford fat scavenger treatment, but he didn't give a big enough shit about his potbelly to put machines in his body.

"I'll see you around, Dom," she said.

"Fuck you, Leah," he said. But of course he didn't mean it.

"I'll say hi to Crumb for you," she said, and was gone.

Chapter 10

Doc Stahl was grinding like hell down the A05, the airborne avenue that roughly followed Broadway from above. All of the autocops stationed by the buoy lines marking the skyroad's sides should have been lighting up and following, but Doc's hover had a jammer — a good one, too, bought from the same crooked son of a bitch who'd sold him his anonymous router. Doc had another anonymous router in the car, but given what had happened back at his apartment, he was afraid to use it. Luckily, he knew where to go without Beam guidance. That was unusual these days. Most people couldn't find their asses without The Beam showing them where to wipe. Doc saw both sides of the tech coin. Selling add-ons — some of questionable legality — had made him rich, but dependence on machines was fucking society six ways from Sunday. The Enterprise, at least, still had a work ethic. But the Directorate? If their Beam connections blitzed out for a day, a handful would be despondent and panicked enough to commit suicide. You could set your nano-tattoo watch by it.

Doc exited at A14, then banked like a maniac down toward the AP41. Noah Fucking West, was the air map complicated. No wonder people couldn't find shit up here.

The AP41 was packed. Autocops were patrolling a stopped line of hovers jammed in tight as if they might catch the dead line of vehicles for speeding. Doc almost rear-ended a Daimler Sport, veered to the side, and crossed the buoy line. The car behind him, which he'd just cut off, laid on the horn. The line inched up, and he jockeyed back into the column of cars. Doc swore. Back when hovers were new, they were few enough that District Zero had let them simply float up and go where they wanted. But after hovers went from novelty to seeming necessity and there were enough midair accidents, the skyroads were built. Now there was barely an advantage to driving above the ground. Gridlock was officially everywhere, even on a Saturday.

Duly halted, Doc looked down at his dashboard's small screen, where his guidance map would normally be. He had to get onto The Beam, if for no other reason than to figure out who might have broken into his apartment. It had to be because of what he'd seen at Xenia. He remembered Vanessa's and Killian's reactions when they'd realized that Doc was where he wasn't supposed to be. He remembered how the guards had moved to block the door. He remembered the implication that he was going to have his mind wiped whether he was willing or not. Doc wondered what people so paranoid might do if they knew about his wipe-blocking implant.

Of course, it now seemed likely that they did know.

He put himself in Killian's shoes, or the shoes of whomever Killian reported to. Would they simply let a man leave after having seen classified wares and chalk it up as a mistake? Would that be enough? Or would they do some research to find out if the man might be a problem? Doc knew he would, and Xenia had deeper access to The Beam than Doc's official level — maybe even deeper than Doc's *actual* level. Xenia could probably find out that Doc sometimes bought wholesale from a man in Little Harajuku named Ryu. They might be able to find the rumors that Ryu dealt in illegal wares…such as autocop jammers, anonymous routers, and implants that could deflect handheld memory wipers.

If they knew that, they'd know that Doc hadn't forgotten the upgrades he'd seen. Doc knew that biological enhancement ability had far, far, *far* surpassed public awareness. What might the people in charge of that dangerous secret do to preserve it? And how good might their own tracking ability be, given their superior technology? Might they be able to trace a connection even through one of Ryu's routers?

Doc looked down at his dark screen and resisted the urge to log on. He took a deep breath, telling himself that he wasn't like the fools who couldn't be disconnected from The Beam for more than a few hours without their worlds crumbling. He was able to walk to the wall and flip his own manual light switch. He could use a match to start a fire in his apartment's fireplace. He knew how to write letters with a pen, on real fucking paper.

And he didn't need to know who'd broken into his apartment. He only needed to know that they hadn't been coming to say hi, that they had the ability to hack (or force) their way into a highly secure building and an even more secure penthouse apartment. And, of course, that they were surely still somewhere behind him.

Doc swore at the line of traffic then made a decision.

He decreased altitude, submerging below the line of hovers. The car behind him honked, as did several others. But Doc was already gone, speeding through the open air off the skyroad like a land car crashing through a barricaded highway median. Several autocop cars broke from the buoys and descended after him. They were behind; he could outrun them. His destination was nearly directly below him, so he dove, nearly nose-down. His back pressed into his seat like an astronaut in a centrifuge. The gap between Doc and the autocops widened as they shied from his reckless dive, taking a more level approach. Official-sounding entreaties to stop where he was blasted around him, but even if Doc stopped now, he'd end up being fined half a year's profits just to retrieve his license — if, that was, he was lucky enough to remain undiscovered by his pursuers.

Doc's hover dove between the buildings below. He banked hard right, nearly striking a large glass office spire. You weren't allowed to fly this low, and Doc caught sight of several shocked faces staring out at him. He slipped down a street he didn't recognize then darted down a smaller one lined with quaint-looking shops and parked with a lot of wheeled vehicles. Pedestrians looked up, and hoverbikes braked hard as drivers rubbernecked at him. He heard at least one accident, and hoped no one was hurt.

Doc sped through a residential neighborhood, eventually flying out near Houston, by the old bomb crater that had been kept as a themed tourist district.

Shops. Spires. People still watched him, aghast. So he slowed down, dipped into a line of traffic, and continued at street level. After a few more blocks, people stopped looking. The autocops were long gone. They'd communicate his car's description along The Beam, and every traffic light would be looking for him, but Doc drove a Ford Magnum, powder blue — the most popular hovercar and color on the market. And thanks to his jammer, they'd only gotten the car's spoofed Auto ID, which he'd already toggled to a new value.

His heart still thumping, Doc pulled the car to the side of the road, engaged the security, and half walked, half jogged the remaining five blocks on foot.

It was noon. Doc knew he'd wake Kai when he rang her buzzer because she worked at night. And he knew she'd be pissed.

But Kai was also the only person in the world Doc could trust to help him.

Chapter 11

ISAAC SWIPED his connection closed by raking his hand in front of his kitchen wall. In its place, his projection of Picasso's *Les Demoiselles d'Avignon* reappeared. This was bullshit. Nicolai earned an incredible living, placing him just below Isaac and Natasha in the Directorate. A few more notches up, and Nicolai would be in the Beau Monde, the top 1 percent of the wealthiest NAU citizens, where life truly got interesting…not that anyone in the lower 99 had any idea about that, of course.

And what was Nicolai paid so well for? Not just for being Isaac's speechwriter, but his right fucking hand. The person Isaac bitched at. The person who, when he was fired up about something, made it all better — just like he'd done when that riot erupted at Natasha's concert. Isaac was supposed to be able to reach Nicolai 24/7, and right now he needed a sounding board: someone to make the bullshit disappear.

He should have left a message.

Isaac sighed, swiped the connection open again, and waited while his canvas tried to locate Nicolai's ID on The Beam. If he was anywhere remotely civilized (and alive, Isaac mentally added), The Beam should know where he was and should light up any Beam-enabled surface around him — the wall of a building, a counter in his apartment, the tabletop in a coffee shop. Failing that, Nicolai wore a communicator in his ear. He seldom answered with video, but wouldn't flat-out ignore the call even if he was with a woman. Isaac had tried to call half a dozen times, so Nicolai was sure to see the missed calls and know it was urgent. But still. Isaac should leave a message, even if only to put it in bold type.

The connection trilled. Then, instead of hearing Nicolai's voice, Isaac watched as a young man with a sober, professional haircut appeared in the connection window.

"My name is Simon. How can I help you, for Nicolai Costa?" said the young man, giving no indication that Isaac had slammed a window in his face thirty seconds ago. Virtual assistants reset if no business was transacted, so the program was oblivious to Isaac's earlier brash manners.

"Where is Nicolai?" Isaac demanded. But this was already stupid. If the assistant had picked up, Nicolai was unreachable. He was only asking out of frustration, as if the man in the window were a real person who would respond to anger.

"Nicolai is unavailable," Simon said. "How may I help you?"

"Tell Nicolai to call me," he grumbled at the composed young man. The assistant was infuriating. He was grinning at Isaac like an idiot.

"Of course, Mr. Ryan," said Simon, reading Isaac's Beam ID.

"Tell him it's urgent."

"I will."

Isaac stared at Simon's perfectly combed virtual hair and wanted to yank it in frustration. But of course, Simon's hair was fake, just like his wide public relations smile.

"Where the fuck is he?" Isaac demanded again.

"Nicolai is unavailable," said Simon.

"He's paid a ton of money to *stay* available! He can't just go off the grid! Not without okaying it with me first!"

"Of course, Mr. Ryan."

"If he doesn't return this call soon, he's going to lose his fucking job!"

"Certainly, Mr. Ryan."

Isaac was moments from slamming the connection closed in Simon's face (Simon would remember it this time because Isaac had left a message), but he couldn't quite let the whole thing go. If Nicolai was gone for a while, then he was gone for a while. But Isaac needed an estimate of how long he'd have to wait, at the very least. The open-ended nature of Nicolai's desertion was intolerable.

"Simon," said Isaac, calming himself — again, as if Simon might respond to emotion, which he wouldn't.

"Yes, sir."

"Could you please tell me where and when you last tracked Nicolai?"

"I'm sorry, Mr. Ryan," he said, "but I cannot reveal private information."

Well, that wasn't a surprise, but it caused ire to bubble into Isaac's throat anyway. He was in a crisis. Who was he supposed to vent to if not Nicolai?

"Simon," said Isaac again.

"Yes, Mr. Ryan?"

"Go fuck yourself!"

Simon started to reply, but Isaac raked the connection shut and once again found himself staring at *Les Demoiselles d'Avignon* and the naked figures that weren't quite naked. They were ideas articulated in broad strokes, like so many manifestations birthed from The Beam.

Isaac paced his apartment. He knotted his hands behind his back and lowered his head, treading heavily as if showing the universe his agitation, hoping to encourage its sympathy. But the world, the universe, and the room remained impassive, and all Isaac heard were his own footfalls echoing off the Plasteel walls. Maybe Natasha knew he was out here pacing, and maybe she didn't. The last time Isaac had seen her, she was slamming the door to her "office." Not that it was an office of any sort. Isaac wasn't sure what she did on The Beam while she was "indisposed" in there, but Natasha allowed no interruption, and the walls were soundproofed. She wouldn't hear him or likely care if she could (Natasha could be a real self-absorbed bitch sometimes, if not most times) yet still Isaac paced, as if to show someone how intolerable this situation was. *Anyone.*

This should be a moment of celebration. His speech had gone beautifully. For the appropriate number of hours, the entire Directorate had praised their Czar of Internal Satisfaction and told him in various sycophantic ways that he'd managed yet again to turn lemons into lemonade. Isaac's peers had promised him great swings in pro-Directorate sentiment. Underlings had kissed Isaac's ass. Natasha had stood beside him, looking beautiful, even with her stupid dog peeking out from the open mouth of her purse. For a few hours, things had looked rosy. He'd seen Nicolai sneak out, and even his right-hand man had seemed pleased.

Then this morning, the bullshit with Micah had started. Typical. Lemonade turned back into lemons, then into piss. The entire Directorate found itself waist deep in their own bullshit, and all of a sudden Isaac's brilliant reframe was crumbling. The riots again started to feel like riots. Unrest among the Directorate citizenry regained its previous feeling of unrest rather than rosy camaraderie. The public anti-Directorate sentiment that had fallen to quiet over the past twelve hours again blistered like a festering sore.

Isaac tried telling himself that he was especially sensitive because he was getting hurled through the storm's middle. He tried telling himself that the average citizen wasn't feeling the swings like he was. He tried telling himself that Micah's posturing only seemed so damaging to him because his brother had owned the ability to get under Isaac's skin since birth, when Isaac had found himself no longer an only child, suddenly having to fight for maternal attention.

He closed his eyes and tried calming himself. Behind drawn lids, Isaac saw Micah's calm and trustworthy face telling the world a version of the story that made so much more sense than Isaac's.

Isaac snapped his eyes open.

"Canvas."

A chirp answered him.

"Get me Dominic Long."

A soothing female voice came from all around Isaac and answered, "Captain Dominic Long is in a meeting."

"At the DZ station?"

"It's a virtual meeting," said the voice.

"With whom?"

"I'm sorry, Mr. Ryan," said the voice Isaac had programmed into his apartment's canvas — a voice Natasha didn't know was mimicked from a synthporn star Isaac had been fascinated with once upon a time. "I don't have that information."

Isaac went to the nearest horizontal surface and tapped a series of commands.

"Now: With whom?" he repeated.

"It's his weekly cooperative meeting with the other district captains," said the woman's sexy voice.

"Interrupt him."

The woman started to protest, but Isaac kept tapping the countertop, and she stopped midsentence. Being a founding member of the Directorate had its privileges. There was a chirp of acknowledgement, and the room fell silent.

A moment later, a trilling of notes announced an incoming holo call. But holo was for douche bags and lower-downs who couldn't afford nerve immersion, so Isaac declined and answered with video. The counter beneath his fingers opened a window to show a three-dimensional rendering of a man in blue who looked much younger and much more attractive than Dominic — who in reality was old and tired, and less interested in the cosmetic augments and add-ons enjoyed by most other citizens of his pay grade. The rendering had the same almost-real-but-not-real look of all avatars. Computer graphics had improved immeasurably since the first days of simulated reality, but for some reason avatars never stopped being creepy. It was like talking to a doll.

"Who the hell do you think you are?" blurted the man in blue on Isaac's countertop.

"Jesus, Dominic. Get that rig off, and look at me proper. You know how I hate those things."

Dominic's Beam-generated avatar ignored him and kept ranting. The avatar's angry expression was overdone, making its eyebrows rise into furious points. Its skin bloomed red like a sunburn. "I don't care what your title says! You can't just break into a meeting like that. You pompous little…"

"Watch it," said Isaac. "Just in case you've forgotten how rude it is to condescend to your elders — no matter how young and impetuous they may look — you might want to keep in mind who controls rank advancement within public service. PD and FD aren't exactly Enterprise jobs, Captain."

The avatar's eyebrows didn't fall, but it stopped huffing and puffing. On Isaac's countertop, he could only see Dominic's electronic visage from the chest up, but it seemed to have its hands on its virtual hips.

"Now slip off your rig, and look at me. Your avatar is creeping me out."

"I have to get back to the meeting. This isn't just about me. There are six other captains in there. This is their time."

"They'll get by without you. I've sent your regrets to the nexus. Now get out of that rig."

The man on Isaac's counter sighed. Then the screen went

blank, and Isaac could imagine the police captain pulling off the clumsy A/V rig that provided what most people thought was fairly good artificial reality — at least as far as two of the five senses were concerned. He pulled a stool from behind him and sat then dragged the black window to a wall behind the counter so that when Dominic returned, he wouldn't be staring up Isaac's nose.

A moment later, Dominic's barely shaven face was staring at Isaac, his hair tousled from the rig he'd been wearing when Isaac had burst in.

"What?" said Dominic. He looked angry, and days without sleep.

"I need to find Nicolai. He's gone off-grid."

"So? People go off-grid."

"Not Nicolai. Not without telling me."

"Maybe he's getting laid," said Dominic.

"He's always reachable. Sometimes, he'll answer with audio only, and every once in a while he'll click me over to an autoreply to buy a few minutes, but this is different. If he were in Manhattan, he'd be within the core network. He'd have to have left to get off-grid — and by left, I mean like *left*, way off into…"

"I get it. So he ran out. Met some girl. Got wasted and went on a bender."

"Not Nicolai."

Dominic shook his head slowly. "What do you want me to do, Isaac?"

"Track him."

"I can't track anyone."

"Via City Surveillance. Just tell me where he was last registered."

"I don't have access to…"

Isaac tapped his countertop. In the communication window, Dominic's eyes popped at something to his right.

"You've been temporarily promoted," said Isaac.

"Is this the entire city?" said Dominic, now reaching off-frame to grab and grasp at something.

"I don't know. I'm not a cop."

"I don't even know what to do with…"

"Look," Isaac snapped, "just find him, okay?"

Dominic nodded, still wide-eyed at whatever data had just become available to Dominic the Commissioner that had been unavailable to Dominic the Captain. He killed the call with a promise to call back once he knew more.

The apartment was again too quiet. Isaac considered turning on some music or a vidstream but knew it would only make his mind rebel and fight even harder than it already was to dampen his decaying spirits. So Isaac turned into the line of fire, opting to face whatever the world had waiting for him head-on.

He walked over and sat on his couch.

"Canvas."

Chirp.

"Visit Beam headlines."

A holographic ball appeared above the coffee table. The page at the cluster's front was The Beam's main news feed. Isaac reached toward the ball and gestured with his fingers to bring the feed closer to enlarge it. Unsurprisingly, Micah's speech had been voted to the top. Eight of the other remaining top ten stories on the front page were all reactions to the speech. The final item was a story about one of Natasha's pretentious singer friends, Gregory Whitman, who'd punched a waiter in a drunken fit a few nights before. In spite of his dour mood, Isaac chuckled then pulled the story from the page and tossed it to the side like a ball of trash. He scanned the reactions to Micah's speech. Four were from Directorate outlets and hence meant nothing. In the public eye, Micah's speech would be an open wound until Brother Isaac replied. Isaac wasn't even really the right person to reply, but the public was obsessed with the Ryan brothers and had been since the beginning. Micah and Isaac would always be yin and yang to the citizenry, no matter their job titles.

But of course, there would be no reply from Isaac without Nicolai.

Isaac grabbed the four Directorate responses and tossed them then scanned the remainders. One was from an Enterprise toady, and the other three were meaningless us-too responses. Isaac didn't bother to toss them. He grabbed the top headline ("Micah Ryan Claims Riots Were Inevitable") and pulled it forward then dragged it open like parting curtains. The page contained some meaningless text and video. Isaac had seen the speech already, when he was still angry and panicky from news that the video existed. He was calmer now. Maybe it wasn't as bad as he remembered.

There was a POV feed where you could slot in your avatar if you wanted to use an A/V immersion rig and pretend you had a front-row seat, but like all lower-end feeds, the only thing it provided over simple viewing was peripheral vision. Isaac touched the video's top-favorited bookmark to set the vidstream playing, driving the knifelike feeling in his stomach deeper into his gut.

The bookmark started the video at three minutes and seven seconds in. Micah's perfectly groomed head smiled from atop his perfectly beautiful suit. His smile collapsed, and he resumed speaking after what, in the full speech, had been a brief pause for effect.

"The recent unrest is the exclusive doings of Directorate raff," said Micah, addressing his Enterprise audience. "Maybe these idle minds would be better served with work, where they might mine more from their days through concrete uses of their time."

Isaac gritted his teeth. He wished Nicolai were here. Nicolai would be able to couch the insult in a way that bleached its sting. The debate over work was hotly contested between the parties, but whenever Nicolai broached it, the fact that a person didn't *have* to work in the Directorate seemed like an obviously, self-evidently good thing. Still, Micah had turned that little Directorate benefit on its head, same as he always did. Micah made work sound noble. But when the Directorate provided everything a person needed, why *not* rest? Why *not* spend your time learning more and exploring rather than slaving away through your life's every minute?

Micah gave a carefree, charming toss of his head and turned his palms up, feigning something between realization and resignation. "Maybe it's the nature of the Directorate to act as a mob," he said, sounding almost defeated. "Maybe the rioters are angry. Maybe they feel that there has been an injustice. That's how an idle mind thinks — it sees only the thing it wants rather than the effort required to achieve it. The rioters are targeting symbols of aspiration: music halls, restaurants, sports stadiums, places where dreams have been forged from the steel of human spirit. So maybe they feel that the people they look up to have been given everything whereas *they've* been given nothing. But it's not true! No member of the Enterprise believes they have been *given* anything. We have built what we have; they are prevented by their party from building what they want. Is it any surprise that they're angry? The Directorate preaches equality. And that much *is* true. The party doles out *mediocrity* in equal measure." Micah leaned into the audience. "When everyone is equal, no one has value. These riots are a clear sign of the Directorate's faltering moral compass and its eventual, inevitable collapse."

Isaac, watching and feeling a mixture of anger and panic — panic because, to his horror, he found himself agreeing with Micah (a persuasive ability that was one of the younger Ryan's many significant talents) — didn't have to have already seen the video to know what was coming. He knew his brother well enough to anticipate his *dénouement*.

"Shift is coming," Micah said. "So to all in the Directorate who are rightfully, justifiably angry about those things you want but cannot have, I ask this: *Stop destroying what you wish could be yours.* Stop blaming others for achieving their dreams. Stop believing that the only way to stand tall is to eradicate the things that make others stand above you. The things that anger you were achieved through hard work…and if *you* work hard, you can make them for yourself. Do you understand? *You can have the things you want!* In twenty-eight days, you will face a choice: you may choose to remain in mediocrity, or you may choose to stop settling for what is given to you, and instead become what you were meant to be."

Isaac stood from the couch and, in a single motion, threw his fist in a giant roundhouse toward his brother's head. His canvas took the punch as a swipe and closed the projection, but Isaac's momentum caused him to tumble onto the floor and bang his head on the coffee table. Then, insultingly, the canvas's sexy voice asked him if he was all right and indicated that he was bleeding. Isaac touched his scalp, felt blood, and snapped that he was fine.

He was getting to his feet to head into the bathroom and treat his wound (Natasha still hadn't emerged from her office despite Isaac's crash) when a trilling noise indicated a new call.

It was Dominic Long, who told Isaac that Nicolai was last traced entering the apartment of one Thomas "Doc" Stahl, but that Doc had also gone missing or off-grid.

Isaac swore and said the police and City Surveillance were beyond incompetent. Dominic said that the riot and then Isaac's speech had set city tempers flaring, and that Micah's speech today had made things ten times worse. Isaac cut Dominic off with an announcement that he was officially a captain again and snapped that he wanted some answers.

Dominic, unintimidated, stared at Isaac and told him that he wasn't the only one, and to get in line.

Chapter 12

THE BULLET TRAIN dropped Leah at the end of its line, in Pillman, a tiny city situated just where the hills started, but well before the mountains. Pillman was well trafficked and circled by an expressway and had excellent Beam coverage, but it was one of the last towns that did. Past Pillman was a series of increasingly rustic burgs that could access The Beam through a fiber line, but the line had been laid thirty years earlier, back before The Beam had the seemingly bottomless capacity it did now. Access was spotty, and few people in the area had fully Beam-enabled houses. Many had only small personal canvases or even just handhelds, living as people had a hundred years earlier, spending large portions of their days totally disconnected. Beyond these lagging areas was a series of even smaller, more rustic towns that were served only with high-bandwidth air signals and satellite, where some people didn't even have Beam coverage beyond voice communication. And beyond *those* areas, The Beam grew truly dark. City dwellers looked on Appalachia with a sort of superstitious dread, unable to imagine a life so disconnected and so ignorant of the world around them.

At Pillman, Leah transferred to a conventional non-mag

train and rode it up through a series of small stops until she reached the end of the line again, where she disembarked and walked up a series of quiet, dangerously vertical streets past ramshackle homes cut into the steep hillside. Chained dogs barked at her. She saw a few people she recognized and waved, calling out hellos.

She came to a large red barn and walked through the open front door. Halfway down on the right side was a brown-and-white paint horse named Missy. Leah reached in to scratch her, and the horse pressed her nose against the bars on the stall's door. Leah, being duly prepared and knowing what the horse expected, pulled a few nugget-like horse treats from her pocket and held them in her hand, palm flat. Missy's big lips flapped the nuggets from Leah's open hand.

She brought Missy out of the stall and tied her, grabbed her saddle, and secured all of her tack. The Milsons hadn't poked their heads into the barn, but Jen and Paulie were fine with Leah coming and going. So she untied the horse and rode through the barn door then turned up a small dirt path leading farther into the mountains. The path was rough, winding, and sometimes steep. Missy, usually a dutiful trail horse, had grown to hate the path quickly. Leah, however, had found a way to surmount Missy's reluctance. From the second time she'd taken this trail, Leah had started to reward the horse with an apple after reaching their destination. Missy never saw apples other than when she arrived at the Organa compound, so the horse learned to love the path, and now traveled it with enthusiasm.

After a half hour of riding, they emerged into a wide plateau in the heart of the Appalachian Mountains. There was a split-rail fence circling two pastures where several horses grazed. Between the pastures was a path leading into the Organa village. At the gate, as usual, was Crumb.

"Afternoon, Crumb," said Leah.

Crumb looked about seventy-five and had a long, bushy

gray beard. The beard was large enough to require grooming, but Crumb had never groomed it once, so far as Leah knew. It was always packed with crumbs from whatever the old man had eaten last. His lips were dark and cracked, and he was always filthy. He wore dark-green pants with pockets lining the length of both legs. Most of the pockets were ripped and hanging in flaps. Crumb did appear to change his pants because there was a pattern to how different pockets were ripped on different days, but all of the pants were the same style. Crumb always smelled sour and had dirt smeared on his face — not because he tussled in the dirt, but almost as an affect, because any town's "crazy old fucker" had to have dirt on his face. Crumb's black boots were never tied, and he was always stepping on his laces. His shirts were all plain, singular colors, but the hues of each were highly questionable because all were stained, and all were disgusting.

Crumb had been at the village for as long as Leah had been alive. He'd become a fixture…a kind of mascot for the Organas. Nobody ever knew what Crumb was saying, but it didn't matter. He seemed to enjoy talking, and the little village loved him like a pet. Crumb sometimes stalked the Organa settlement. But usually he was out front, standing guard where no guard was required.

"Leah. Leah. Noah Fucking West, Leah. How are ya. How are ya." The last were questions, but Crumb said them like a nervous tic, watching her with darting eyes.

Leah reined her horse, looking down on the gray-bearded man. Today's crumbs looked like breakfast cereal. Leah could make out whole, unchewed nuggets, as if Crumb had simply thrown the cereal at his mouth in the hope that some would make it into his maw.

"How's the border, Crumb?" Leah asked, looking around at the pastoral mountain setting and the grazing horses.

"Threatened," Crumb mumbled. "End times. End times, Leah. Noah Fucking West, end times. You know what I saw today? Saw a squirrel. Three of them. The big one said, 'You ain't foolin' nobody' and then ran off up a tree where he had nuts. I tried to follow, but I'm not wearing shoes."

"That's really something," said Leah, looking down at Crumb's ancient boots.

"You don't know what it was like before The Beam. We made the first. Me and the squirrels. They ran off. I couldn't follow. You don't understand. Neither does Leo. But there was a day. I remember it. We talked in our brains. You lived, and you died. Then I got old, back when I was young. But then I was not who I am. And neither were you. None of us were. You call this a village? But it was all like this. Back when I was young. Back before The Beam. Noah Fucking West!"

Leah looked at Crumb, saying nothing and waiting for him to finish.

"Oh, they're gone now, those fuckers!" said Crumb. "The squirrels, I mean. Leo knows. Did you know that I knew him, back in the day? Noah Fucking West!"

Leah nodded along. This was simply how Crumb was. When Crumb came up and started babbling (sometimes he talked about the stars; he kept saying that Betelgeuse was overdue to supernova and had many theories about it), a lot of people simply walked away. Crumb didn't see this as rude because he didn't seem truly capable of thinking anything beyond the basics of keeping himself fed, clothed, and alive. But Leah still felt that he was human and deserved respect. Once upon a time, Dominic Long had been ordered to send Crumb to Respero and had decided the man was worth saving. Walking away without listening to Crumb for a few minutes felt to Leah like spitting in the face not only of the filthy man himself, but also into the eye of Dominic's mercy.

Leah smiled, said that she totally agreed, then nudged Missy forward with a "See you later." Crumb saw that Leah was leaving and turned to wave, like an overly enthusiastic child.

"Noah Fucking West, Leah!" Crumb yelled.

She turned and saw cereal snowing from his beard. He trotted forward a few feet. Three crows swooped to the ground behind him and pecked at the cereal. Leah was reminded of a dog she'd had growing up who knew to lie beneath her chair at dinnertime because she'd always dropped food as she ate.

"Noah Fucking West and end times!" He seemed to think then lowered his voice to a mere holler. "Well, not end times. But I saw that squirrel, and he told me. Brains aren't what they used to be, I'll tell you. The squirrel, he said it was The Beam. Holy shit! Think like The Beam!" He laughed maniacally. *"Noah Fucking West on The Beam, Leah!"*

Leah waved once more at Crumb and continued riding between the split-rail fences that defined the pastures. Beneath her were two shallow wheel ruts in the dirt with a strip of grass growing between them. Missy was walking fast, just shy of a trot. She always did this at the ride's end. With the long trail behind her, the horse was eager for her apple. The faster she got to the village's barn, the sooner she'd be sinking her giant teeth into it.

They reached the barn. Leah led Missy into her stall and gave her an apple, scratching the mare behind her ears. Then she left the barn and crossed the village.

The air was cool and crisp in the mountains. Leah took off her pack, slipped out a rainbow sarong, and tied it over her shorts. The sarong was loose and billowy, but kept the chill from her legs. Then she slung the pack over her back again, tugged her dreadlocks out from between it and her shoulders, and crossed an open square with a gazebo in the middle. Around the gazebo were purple and red flowers. Leah paused to bend and sniff them. Then she stopped, down on one knee, and drew in the surrounding activity.

The Organa settlement was a bizarre mix of old and new. There were no motorized cars or bikes in the village, but most of the villagers carried handhelds because Organa or not, they felt they needed to know the weather forecast, had to check train schedules from Pillman, or might need to send mail. There were villagers who lived here permanently, but most were transient, coming and going with hybrid lives. Their main houses typically had at least one point of neutered Beam access via a simple terminal canvas. For most Organas, this was what "unplugged" meant. There were purists who lived without any access at all, but even the electrical grid these days was controlled by The Beam. To live totally unconnected meant not just unplugging from The Beam's omniscient data stream, but also from electricity, phone, mail (except hand-couriered OldMail written on paper), vidstreams, most music, and even the simplest conveniences like central cleaning, mechanized washing and mending, banks, and so on. Finding power tools without a Beam chip was nearly impossible except in specialty antique stores at exorbitant prices, so the purists had to build with handsaws and hammers. Orthodox Organas lived much like the pioneers who had settled the NAU, back even before it was called America. Most Organas weren't that dedicated, which was why so few were truly orthodox.

Leah, kneeling amongst the flowers, thought it was bullshit.

In a few minutes, Leo would be chewing her out about getting arrested in the city and about her new nanobot fabricators, which Dominic would likely have told him about. But again: *bullshit*. Didn't Leo have his own add-ons, even if they weren't in his body? Didn't everyone? Sure, most of the Organas didn't have nanos in their blood. Sure, they didn't have chips in their heads. Sure, many of them didn't even have Beam IDs, thanks to Leah. Sure, they had to access Beam terminals like vagrants, without any of the cookies that caused systems to remember who they were. But did they not ride mag trains? Did they not communicate via mail when they were on the grid? Did they not use rolling sidewalks and stairs? Did they not have bank accounts and pay their electric bills in the only way The Beam allowed — by fingerprint?

Despite their fashions and their posturing and their horses and their ritualistic use of moondust, the people in the village were still all connected. They *could* unplug, but they never would. Organa was fashionable as an ideal, but like most ideals, it fell apart the minute someone realized they'd need to light a candle if they wanted to piss in the middle of the night. Leah, at least, was honest about who she was.

She found Leo in the meeting hall, reading a book. A *paper* book, which was its own kind of irony. Organa life was supposed to be spartan and full of self-denial, but Leo's books were a symbol of wealth among the poor. Old pulp paper-backs were everywhere in the poorer neighborhoods, but good, sturdy hardbacks like Leo's were impossible to find. Each would bring a fortune at auction.

Leo looked up, closed the book, and set it on the table beside him. He was sitting alone in a circle of chairs that were often used for moondust parties. His legs were crossed, and his old, wrinkled face looked at Leah from under a head of gray hair. Two braids with feathers hung at the sides of his head, and a blue headband with a sun stitched on it wrapped his forehead.

"Well," he said.

"Hey, Leo."

"You got caught."

She'd known this was coming. Leo had told her to lie low, no exceptions. He wanted her to hack the Quark server, scout for holes in the inner security layers, and transfer everything out that she could possibly get safely onto a slip drive. But Leo was a data hoarder. Brick by brick, he was recreating the most innocuous, most useless parts of Quark's dataset. It was pointless. Everything Leah brought back was obsolete by the time she returned, and Quark was always gathering new data faster than she could bring it back for Leo to stick somewhere and never get around to cataloguing.

"Check."

"You did it on purpose. So you could try out some new hole in your head."

That was how Leo thought of enhancements and add-ons — as "holes in the head." To an old guy like Leo, biological enhancement was about drilling holes and shoving chips into brains. No wonder he didn't get it.

"I wanted to see what was on the other side," said Leah.

Leo looked at her for a long moment, narrowing his steel-gray eyes. He reached toward a dish beside his book where he'd set a carved wooden pipe. The concoction he smoked was laced with moondust, and Leah could smell the drug blended in with the burning tobacco. It had an acrid, almost chemical scent. To Leah, it was the smell of space.

Leo puffed the pipe, looked at Leah again, then set the pipe aside.

"Sit down," he said.

"I'd rather stand."

"Sit down, Leah."

She watched the old man with the braids and headband, trying to decide if this was an argument worth having. She decided it wasn't. Yet. So Leah sat in the chair farthest from Leo, opposite him in the circle, and crossed her arms across her chest.

"You think we move too slow," said Leo.

"Yes."

"You think that we're fighting a losing battle."

Leah tried to decide how she wanted to answer. It was a trick question. She believed in Organa, but she argued for it on shaky ground — she with her new nano-fabricating implants.

"I think that we need to keep up," she said. "Quark is

taking chances, and they get smarter every time. I got caught because I wanted to, because…"

Leo shook his head side to side. Leah watched him and trailed off. Then, reservedly, he picked up the pipe and puffed it again.

"I know why you got caught. I know about your new implants. I seem to recall telling you not to get them."

"We need a presence on the inside. And now thanks to me, we have one. We have…"

"We have a traceable path right back to our front doors!" Leo snapped, his voice rising. "We have a girl who thinks she's so goddamn smart that she doesn't need to listen! We have someone who forgets that she's not the only Organa in this game!"

"Dominic will erase my record," she said.

Leo laughed a humorless laugh. "Oh, I see. And you were talking to the average person on the street, right? Beat cops who will just forget about you. The Beam doesn't forget, Leah. They have you coming and going. They know every feature on your face, and they have a voice record of everything you said. You're blind if you think that data stayed in the station, or that Dominic has access to a tenth of it. Who really controls the cops? Who polices the police? Do you really think The Beam will forget you? You were where you shouldn't have been, and now your footprints are in there forever."

"The station is a black box, Leo," Leah protested. "They don't have lines out. I tried telling you that. They cut it totally off and batch hand-selected datasets semiweekly. You'd know that if you listened."

"*You* need to listen!"

"Oh, I do? Tell me, Leo…why do you have me? Is it because you understand systems better than I do? Is it because this is all just on the tip of your tongue but you'd rather have someone else handle it to make your life easier? The Beam knows too much, does it? But you still think of it like a monster. It's not a monster. It's a system. The system will always do what's best for the system. It responds to stimulus response, same as you. When you go home and search The Beam to find one of these expensive books of yours, the system is on your side because you're spending credits. It doesn't care about your other face, where you pretend to hate it."

Leah felt her heart racing, felt blood pulsing up her neck in a furious blush of mounting rage. She waited for Leo's angry response, but instead of becoming cross, the old man just dropped his head.

"Fine," he said. "We're all hypocrites. But you are still part of a team. You're important to us, but if you endanger the team by being reckless, then you're useless. You are the only one here who I'd give this much latitude, but I can only take so much, Leah. You talk back. You question every plan. You're given direction to do one thing, and you do something else, almost automatically. You throw your knowledge and what you can do in everyone's faces. The idea of getting deliberately caught! Do you know what Laura said when she heard? She wants you kicked out. If you'd gotten caught on accident, that'd be one thing, but there are already rumors about you hotdogging with new enhancements, and people already suspect that you have others…"

"Fuck them!" said Leah.

"Really."

"Yes! Do you want to get into Quark, or do you want to bang tambourines and do moondust and dance in circles? I've done more to advance this group's mission with my add-ons than a thousand Lauras with her braided necklaces and soul dance bullshit!"

"All right. You want to know the truth? I'll tell you the truth. But if you say I told you this, I'll deny it, and people will believe me, not you." Leo sighed again, leaned forward, and set aside his pipe. "In order for the Organa movement to have a prayer of success, a small percentage of us must sell out. That's why you got your training, and why we don't discuss it here. It's why I looked the other way when you got your first enhancement, and then your second. It's why I'll deny you got this new one. But you have to listen to me, Leah. You have to follow my orders and lie low. If people found out just how non-Organa you really are…"

Leah bolted to her feet. "Fuck them!" she yelled again. "You want me to play down? I know the people up here don't have enhancements, but I've done more for this movement than everyone else here put together. What's more Organa — to stick to the doctrine or to try and actually advance the cause? How dare anyone look down on me! And how dare you hide it! You know what best serves the cause, so embrace it, Leo. That's what you could do — what you *would* do — if you really cared. There's more I need! A mimic set, for one, and there's something I've heard a lot about on the black market called…"

Leo shook his head. Leah felt like she was going to either scream or cry, and couldn't decide which. She was angry at the others for their bullshit posturing, angry at Leo for taking their side while acknowledging that she was more important, and angry at herself for getting so caught up in it all. She'd been born in an Organa commune because her mother had wanted her to live without a Beam ID and to have the freedom that came with it. Then she'd moved to the city, under the radar, and explored the other side of the coin. She'd led that dual life, half city girl and half mountain-dwelling Organa, for most of her time on the planet. She'd learned enough about the growing NAU computer network to wonder if it had become too powerful. She'd watched the rolling service blackouts of 2089 and had seen just how despondent — sometimes suicidal — District citizens became when the walls didn't respond, when their presences weren't acknowledged by everything they encountered, when they couldn't find out what was going on in the world and couldn't talk to their friends with a gesture. That was when Leah realized things *had* to change, that there was more to Organa than simply eschewing technology. The Beam was too big to challenge, too big to fail. Humanity, never good at asking if it *should* do a thing once it learned it *could*, was on a slippery slope. So she'd suited up to fight, and now her side of the battle resented her for her preparedness? To Leah, living stark lives as a means of facing a complicated, technological enemy was beyond stupid. How could you fight an enemy you didn't understand? Most Organas shunned technology without so much as a thought. Leah thought it was smarter to embrace The Beam enough to find the system's holes, and a way out.

"No more add-ons," said Leo.

"So I have to pretend. To be a good hippie rather than an effective one."

"You have to be part of a movement. And a community."

Leah rolled her eyes.

"Something else that concerns me," Leo said, studying her expression.

"Something else for your pariah?"

"It's Crumb," said Leo.

That snapped her mood. Crumb was a wacko. The town oddity. There was nothing about Crumb that wasn't a little troubling, and there was, at the same time, nothing about Crumb that was troubling at all. The old man was his own thing, neither good nor bad. He'd been around for as long as Leah had known about the Organas without meriting more than a mention as an oddity.

"What about Crumb?"

"He's getting strange."

Leah laughed. Leo's glance made her stop.

"He's been talking about West," said Leo.

"Yeah," said Leah. "Noah Fucking West."

"I don't think it's just an expression with him. He keeps

blabbing about West this and West that. West is here, and West is there. West is everywhere. It's like he's trying to warn us. Remember how he used to talk about the Indians?"

Leah did. Crumb had found a bunch of stories in a series of worthless tattered paper books that Leo had given him about old-time cowboys and so-called Indians native to the NAU hundreds of years ago. In the books, the Indians were always the bad guys, always coming to attack and rape and pillage. After reading the stories, Crumb had begun to spout off about Indians coming to raid their wagon train. At first, it was cute, but then it got annoying. Two weeks later, when Crumb's paranoia over the Indians reached a head, Leo sent a few men out with Crumb to scout the trails. They'd spotted no men with red skin and feathers, but they *had* seen six police hovers approaching. They rushed back to the village and destroyed or hidden piles and piles of hard storage — slip drives, stolen paper records, plans, and boxes upon boxes filled with Organa propaganda — just in time, just in advance of the raid. Most in the village wrote it off as coincidence, but Crumb had returned to normal after the police had left, no longer yammering on about an impending Indian attack.

"I remember," said Leah.

"That's how he's been with West, as if something's jarred him loose. He used to be all over the place, but now everything is Noah West this and Noah West that."

"He's crazy, Leo."

"It's like he's trying to warn us. We tried to crack his head when he first arrived, back in the '60s, but we've never gotten anything from him. We wrote it off because like you said, we just figured he was crazy. But it's always bugged me. Why was Dominic called to take him in when a sweeper could have done the job? Why was he ordered to *federal* Respero? He should have gone into the state system and then either been contained or dispatched without ceremony. But they were all over Dominic, remember? And that's what got him thinking that maybe his gut feeling to save Crumb meant something."

Leah shrugged, her gesture asking what came next.

Leo tapped his chin with his thumb. "I want you to ride with Crumb to Bontauk. They have the closest hardwired connection to The Beam. Don't say I told you so, but I don't think I have to explain why I'm asking you to do it?"

"My port. And my ID spoof."

"Yes. But not for you. For him. I don't want him scanned, even by something simple like a handheld. Not until we know more."

Leah was shaking her head. "It's just Crumb," she said.

"Yes," said Leo. "But my instincts have never failed me, and they're all ringing that there's something to this."

"Like what?"

"I don't know. But until we know more, I'll be getting the same brand of wretched sleep I've been getting for too long."

Leah stood, brushed at her sarong, and picked up her backpack. "What do your instincts say about my getting caught breaking into Quark?" she said.

Leo stood and pulled something from a satchel at his side then handed it to Leah. It was a small collapsible slumbergun.

"That either way, it's a good idea for you to keep that with you."

Chapter 13

STEPHEN YORK STOOD on the dirt, kicking at it, willing his feet
to do what he told them. After a while, they did. He stopped
kicking and fell still. Then he leaned back and crossed his
arms. Soon, he realized his arms were twitching, so he
pinched them harder to his sides. He told his mind and body
to still; he needed to concentrate for what was coming.

He began reciting prime numbers, like a mantra.

One. Three. Five. Seven. Eleven. Thirteen.

In between numbers, York tried to decide what the last few
days of foreboding could mean. His mind kept wanting to slip,
but he held it down, focusing on the numbers. *Seventeen. Nineteen. Twenty-three.* He could keep going. He had, over and over
and over. He knew up to 3,571 by heart because he had once
memorized the first five hundred primes while studying
cyphers and encryption. It was a relatively useless skill, but
today, he was grateful for it. Like an old man searching his
mind for names from his youth, York felt that reciting the
primes was a way to keep him sharp. He walked through the
list repeatedly, feeling like he was running a stone over his
thoughts, trying to hone their edge. Still, his thoughts kept
slipping. His memories were there, quiet and orderly deep

inside him, but they kept threatening to fall away. Some thoughts were stickier than others. Through simple repetition, some memories had become grooved and conditioned. Like the primes. He'd had reason enough to recite his wife's name that he knew it without thinking. He knew his bank account number. He knew the access codes he'd used back when he'd helped develop Crossbeam decades ago. He could remember line after line of code — all obsolete today, of course. But doing reasoning with that archive of knowledge? Plumbing it in order to draw conclusions? That was hard. Maybe impossible.

He felt like his mind was inside a literal box. He kept rapping his mental shoulders and knees on that confining box because there wasn't enough room to maneuver. That was the firewall, of course. He'd helped develop some of that technology too, but the details weren't as well rehearsed as his wife's name or the prime numbers, and so he couldn't access much about them. He knew the firewall had blocked most of who he was. He knew it kept him inside this box, locked down tight. He knew that his normal way of expressing himself was hampered, and that he'd need to find other ways to do what he needed to do. He had references. Back when York had studied neurology, he'd learned about a man who couldn't form new memories, but who had relearned how to learn by establishing habits that played themselves out without his conscious awareness. York wouldn't be able to do that to get out of his box, of course, but the process was the same: when one way is blocked, you find another.

1163, 1171, 1181.

Something was coming. There was something on the horizon. And here he was, with his hands tied behind his back.

1187, 1193.

York swore, heard himself swear, and again found his foot kicking at dirt. It was still kicking when a woman came up to him on horseback.

"Hop on, Crumb," she said, indicating a second horse behind her. "We're going for a little ride. Leo wants us to play on The Beam."

1201, 1213.

It was a good idea. York didn't know why, but somehow, it was.

He tried to tell the woman on the horse that he wanted to go, that he felt a sense of foreboding in the air.

"Noah Fucking West," he heard himself say instead.

| Episode 2 |

Chapter 1

JULY **13, 2027 — Amalfi Coast, Italy**

"WATCH THIS."

Nicolai didn't reply. He held his tongue and kept his eyes on Enzo as his friend lined up a paper airplane with Ms. Marco's ass then used a blob of spit to stick the hoverdisc to the plane's bottom. The disc — a wafer-like slice of nanobot substrate that was not, in the normal course of affairs, meant to be attached with spit — was slightly smaller than a 1-cent coin and a fraction of its weight. Once attached, Enzo whispered to it and let it go. The plane hovered in the air, unsupported.

"Knock it off," Nicolai whispered, watching the floating plane. He reached forward. "Give it back! You're going to get me busted!"

Enzo looked at Nicolai. "*You* are going to get busted?"

"Yes, me!" Nicolai hissed, watching Ms. Marco's ass to ensure it hadn't heard them at the back of the classroom. "You know, by my father? Or maybe by his partners? While

Marco sends you to the office, I'll be getting arrested for espionage."

Enzo flapped his hand dismissively at Nicolai. "*Industrial* espionage at worst."

He whispered again to the plane. It began to drift slowly between the rows of desks, making for Ms. Marco's serendipitously still-bent-over ass. The other students turned to watch it drift past them, gaping. Enzo would probably have preferred the plane to move faster, but if he made it do so, the disc would come off the paper, and Nicolai would jump Enzo if he considered using glue on a piece of equipment that he suspected might be worth thousands if not millions of euros. Enzo had no idea what he was playing with. He thought the flying disc was a fun novelty. He didn't understand that what made it float were the millions of nanobots embedded in the substrate, chugging air in one end and out the other, floating by virtue of what amounted to countless synchronized mechanical farts. Enzo thought it was a toy, not a classified bit of technology that might one day change the world. It was Nicolai's fault for showing Enzo his father's office that morning, and failing to watch his prankster friend's hands at all times.

"Stop it! Now!"

Enzo leaned back. "Oh, shut up, Nicolai."

"That's a priceless piece of cutting-edge equipment you stole," Nicolai whispered. "And now, you're going to lose it."

"I'm not going to lose it," said Enzo. "I'm going to score a bull's eye."

The plane closed the gap between the front row and Ms. Marco's desk at a putter. Ms. Marco was still facing forward, opening new windows on the network board at the front of the room. She moved like a woman who'd grown up with whiteboards, which, of course, she had. But this was a high-end private school, without any whiteboards. Marco was one of the oldsters who'd bitched up a storm about the loss of markers when they'd gone digital in 2018. Nicolai remembered whiteboards — but only barely, from his older brother's school.

The students watched as the plane politely poked Ms. Marco in the rear, as if trying to remind her of something. She turned. Enzo laughed. The teacher's eyes looked down at the plane and hardened. She opened her mouth to yell but didn't have a chance before sounds of breaking and screaming exploded from the other end of the building.

"It's a Rake Squad," said a girl.

"It can't be," said Ms. Marco, looking uncertain. "This is the most secure school in the area. The rabble..."

She stopped talking as a hail of bullets ripped the top half of her head away from the lower half of her uncertain expression, leaving her face like a pumpkin sheared at the middle. The wall behind her was painted in a crimson spatter.

The students in the room began to scream.

Nicolai looked at the front wall and saw sunlight salting the room through fresh holes. The voices of the Rake Squad (and it *was* a Rake Squad, Nicolai realized, no matter what the bottom half of Ms. Marco's head claimed) swelled closer. The tromping of feet mingled with booming shouts. Nicolai heard them as Marco's body fell: a group of men and women who had nothing to lose and everything to gain by harvesting from elitists who carried on with business as usual while the world outside went to shit. The way the Squads of glorified rioters saw it, Amalfi and the other coastal hotspots would be lost to rising ocean levels within a few months anyway; they were just taking today what the ocean would take eventually. The poor and their families had to eat. If a few spoiled rich kids had to die in order to make that happen, then so be it.

Something inside Nicolai flipped like a switch. His mind seized onto his situation's stark reality: the holes smoking in the wall, Ms. Marco's corpse striking the desk and collapsing like a bag of meat, Marie's hair flying as she whipped her head around two rows up, clearly out of her fucking mind. The feet were coming closer, the screaming getting louder. The bullets had entered near the door. There was only one other viable way out, and he had to take it now. *Now.* There would be no screwing around, no trying to be a hero and save everyone. He could save himself, and he'd give Enzo exactly one chance to come with him. The others could follow, but whether they did or didn't wasn't his problem. The decision wasn't logical or emotional. It was pure adrenaline-laced survival. Nicolai had lived sixteen years on an idyllic, unified planet, then another on whatever Earth had become after the weather had declared war on humanity and everything it had built. If Nicolai didn't want his seventeenth year to be his last, he couldn't afford to be selfless. You couldn't become a martyr without dying, and Nicolai had no intention of dying in a school, cowering under a gum-pocked plastic desk.

Nicolai stood and yelled a command. Paper rustled as the hoverdisc detached itself from Enzo's plane and screamed across the room to slap against the reinforced window glass. The windows, which faced the fences, were bulletproof. But that wouldn't be a problem.

"Duck," he said to Enzo.

They dropped. Above them, the window glass began to crack as nanos from the disc burrowed into the windows, chewing through the lattice. Nicolai felt seconds tick off, hearing the beat of the Rake Squad's boots as they combed through classrooms. But the nanos worked fast. After a few fractures had webbed across the window, the tiny machines started to vibrate, setting up waves of resonance. Then the window blew out in both directions, showering the screaming students with shards of glass.

"Run!" Nicolai yelled.

Without waiting for a response, Nicolai ran. He dove headfirst through the shattered window, tucking and rolling as he struck the grass beyond it. He hopped up, his eyes darting around for rioters. Enzo climbed through the window behind him — feet first, as if they had all the time in the world. Nicolai wasn't waiting. He darted to the fence and threw a scrap of metal at it to see if it was still electrified. Nothing sparked, but he didn't know if that meant anything. It didn't matter. If they were going to escape, this was the only way. Getting fried was better than waiting to be shot and robbed.

Nicolai gripped the fence.

It was safe. The Rake Squad had shut it down when they'd broken in, of course.

Without taking time to reflect on his good fortune, Nicolai clambered up hand for hand, moving fast. Enzo slapped into the fence below him and began moving upward, clumsy and slow. Nicolai stepped on his fingers. Enzo yelled, but Nicolai found himself unable to care. He reached the top, peeled off his sweater by alternating hands on the fence, and tossed it over the razor wire. He made it halfway over before one of the blades sliced into his calf. The cut wasn't deep, but it made him grip the fence too tight. His balance teetered. Then a second blade pushed through the sweater and cut his palm. It was too much pain at once; his grip slipped. He was briefly airborne, then crashed roughly into the tall grass on the far side of the fence.

Nicolai looked up. He didn't know where Enzo was. He heard gunshots close by. They were almost certainly coming from the classroom he'd just left. Rake Squad incursions were strangely formulaic, based on the Internet and news reports they'd been getting throughout Italy: The Squads tended to rob low academies and massacre high academies because seventeen- and eighteen-year-olds had an annoying tendency to fight back. Either way, the Squads took the spoils. If Nicolai returned to the school tomorrow, which he never would, he'd find it stripped to nothing, worse than a ghost town, probably burned for spite.

Something thumped beside Nicolai in the weeds. He looked over and saw Enzo, dazed but still breathing.

"They're dead," he said. Enzo was a class clown at best, an arrogant jerk at worst. But now, his shoulders twitching at the sound of each of the gunshots, his usual cockiness and bravado had totally left his eyes. He looked more than terrified. He looked *lost*, as if he had no idea where to go or which end was up. It seemed impossible to believe that just a moment before, this same boy had been trying to hit his teacher in the ass with a paper airplane.

Nicolai nodded. "Yes. But we're not. Keep moving."

Nicolai's head was cool. He'd lived a luxurious life, but a year of global disaster had burrowed its way into his brain. Nicolai had been sensitive for years — an artistic temperament, instructors and family agreed — but the only way for such a temperament to survive the reports of billions dying and countries brought to their knees was to anticipate the worst. And here it was, real and present: *His classmates were dead, and his school would burn.* Someday, that would bother him, but not today. Right now, only Nicolai mattered. His family came second, and Enzo, for now, came third. Everything and everyone else was trivial, nothing more.

"Good thing you had that disc," said Enzo. "Otherwise, we'd have been toast."

"I've been carrying a stunner in my pack for weeks," Nicolai replied, still looking around. If they hadn't been able to get through the window, he would have stormed through the crowds. "Stunner" was a bit of an understatement. The weapon — one of a few publicly known goodies in his father's arsenal — was like a grenade that exploded in only one direction. Enzo's stealing the disc had made things easier, but Nicolai had been prepared to turn acres of rioters to hamburger if he had to.

"Bullshit! How did you sneak a stunner past the gates?"

Nicolai didn't answer. Jesus Fucking Christ. Why did it matter?

He started walking, not caring if Enzo followed. They tromped through brambles, down into a small ravine and across a tiny clear river, using their hands and feet to scramble up its steep bank. Nicolai missed a foothold and clocked Enzo in the face. He didn't bother to apologize. Enzo was still yapping about school regulations while their world was ending — their cloistered little rich man's paradise finally catching the chaos the rest of the globe had been facing for months.

As they came out of the ravine, Nicolai could see smoke pluming from homes up the hill. He had two tasks: stay alive, and get home. He'd have more tasks once he reached his family's villa, but for now singular focus would fuel his motion. Nicolai couldn't afford to think, if thinking meant stopping.

They ran across a field, staying judiciously back from the winding road that wound up from the touristy downtown to the estates on the cliff. If there were rioters up this far, they'd be on the road. Nicolai stayed low and kept quiet, staying light and fast on his feet. Enzo walked high and was loud. Nicolai wondered if he should outrun his friend and leave him behind, but he couldn't bring himself to do it. So he hissed at Enzo to stay down and shut the fuck up. When Enzo didn't listen, Nicolai hit him in the face, hard. Enzo didn't protest. Something in Nicolai's eyes stopped him cold.

"Where's your stunner?" said Enzo.

"In my bag."

Enzo looked Nicolai over as if he was missing something.

"I couldn't take it. Going through the front door was Plan A. Going over the fence was Plan B, and my bag was in the corner. There was no time." It was a bummer, but there was no point in lamenting the loss of his father's restricted weaponry. The rest of the world didn't even know most of the technology in his father's office even existed. There were privileges that came both with wealth and connections, but now

Nicolai, as just one more boy fighting to survive, was on equal footing. And so be it.

They were crossing a yard when two men stepped out from behind a shed. Nicolai turned and found another behind them, holding a knife.

"Well, whatsie's this?" said one of the two men in front, speaking in the mishmash accent that had become common in the rabble.

"Kindlings," said the man beside him. "Kindlings with richy bitchy shoes. Where you got those shoes, boys?"

Nicolai looked around at the group then subtly lowered the timbre and rhythm of his voice to match the feel of their speech. It wasn't overt enough to look like mockery — just enough to make them feel they knew him, and that maybe he wasn't so unlike them at all. "You want 'em? They's yours."

Enzo looked over at him, confused.

"We took 'em offa some townies. You can haveem, right?"

The closest man lowered his blade. None of the three seemed to have guns, which had grown too scarce for all but the most highfalutin criminals. Oh, what Nicolai would give for his stunner. Fighting their way past road bandits with a stunner would be like hunting squirrels with a bazooka.

"Bullshits," said the man behind them. "You's from here. They's you shoes."

Nicolai shrugged.

"Empty you pockets," said the closest man, looking unsure. He'd clearly planned to kill them, but now it looked like they might get off with a mugging.

"You're not getting my shit," said Enzo, standing tall.

Nicolai closed his eyes briefly, despite the moment. It was exactly the sort of stupidly prideful thing a kid who wanted to die would say, and exactly how that kid would say it.

"C'mere, bitchy," said the first man. "Th'easier to cut you with." He raised his knife again, once again sure of what to do with them. He took a step forward and used his free hand to knock Enzo down. Nicolai flexed forward, but Enzo was already on the grass, and the other two men held their blades at his gut.

Enzo might have still had a chance, but he didn't know when to lie down. He bolted upright, and one of the bandits stabbed him in the belly. Nicolai flinched as the man struck, ready to deflect the knife, but it happened too fast. Enzo's mouth became an O. He gasped his final breath. The other highwaymen watched him, waiting. The murderer twisted his fist in Enzo's gut.

Two blades. One opportunity.

Nicolai slammed into the closest knifeman, closing the short distance between them too quickly for the man to strike. As Nicolai knew he would, the second man jabbed his knife toward Nicolai's back. Nicolai dragged the first man around, twisting him in place. The attacker stabbed his compatriot in the kidney, and before they could regroup and free their knives, Nicolai pushed hard backward, hurling the stabbed man into his stabber. The man holding Enzo still hadn't pulled away. He hadn't expected a challenge, and before he could react, Nicolai took off in a sprint. He was across a path and into a thicket before the men could move. Nicolai heard them yell, but they wouldn't come after him now. There were homes to rob, easier targets to fall upon. The boy could go, and take his fight with him.

Staying even lower, walking even more cautiously and blocking the most recent horror from his mind, Nicolai chilled his thoughts and focused on setting one foot in front of the other. Homes burned around him. His family was the wealthiest on the coast, his house the largest and most obvious target. The estate was near the hill's peak, as visible and opulent from below as a crown jewel. It was the first place the Squads would want to attack…but if the family was lucky, it'd also be the last place they'd be able to touch. Sophia, the home's security system, was hooked into his father's fledgling technology that he swore would change the world and put Italy on top of the new one. Sophia gave their home a brain, and getting at the Costas' treasures would require more than crowbars and explosives.

They'll be needed to open the safes and the vaults, Nicolai told himself as he felt the red fog of panic threatening his mind's edges. *Their knowledge of the system makes them important. They'll be fine. It'll be okay in the end, thanks to Sophia.*

And for a few steps, it even made sense, and Nicolai almost relaxed. How could the Squads get past the mansion's security without hackers, especially considering they'd be hacking a NextGen network that few people in the world even knew existed? But his fantasy fell apart when he reached the estate to find the gates breached, the big wrought iron doors hanging askew. It looked like a tank had run through them. So much for needing hackers to pass the first perimeter; brute force was still obeyed by even the best technology.

The breach (caused by a vehicle that was now half in the pool, its rear poking into the air at the end of two long dirty ruts through the manicured grounds) had set off the house alarms, but they must have been going off for a while by the time Nicolai arrived because all he heard was the occasional reminder chirp. The safety lights were still strobing, making the disorder he could see through the windows look like a riotous discotheque. And at the top of the circular driveway, the front door yawned open as if beaten in by a battering ram.

Nicolai walked the length of the central building, trying to scope the situation before going inside. He saw something dark on the walls, like an explosion of paint. In the flickering light, it looked almost black. Before committing to enter, Nicolai found a terminal and killed the alarm. Then he walked inside.

The house was upside down. Nothing valuable had been left, and nothing inconsequential was still whole and undamaged. The intruders — a group that probably included everyone by now, including the good people of the Amalfi Coast below — seemed to have been settling a grudge. They'd ripped open every cushion and befouled every plush carpet and piece of art. His family's belongings were either smashed to bits or stolen. It looked like the aftermath of a bombing.

He found their bodies in the living room. They'd been killed with knives (his brother, Vincenzo and mother) and with what was probably a homemade hand cannon (his father and twin sisters).

Ever since he'd begun walking up the hill with Enzo, Nicolai had been steeled for what he might find, but his wall crumbled when he saw them. His mouth came open, and his eyes started to water.

Then something struck him from behind, and Nicolai saw nothing else as he fell to the floor.

Someone was snapping in front of his face.

It took Nicolai a long and excruciatingly painful moment to remember where he was and what had preceded his wrists being tied, his mouth being gagged, and his body being dragged down into the wine cellar. Memory returned in red chunks, slamming into him with the rhythm of those snapping fingers. He blinked to clear blood from his eyes. His head hurt, and his scalp seemed to be bleeding.

"Heya. Heya, boyo. You commin' around?" said the fingers. He saw a man behind them, his jaw seemingly twisted out of kilter. The roughneck had days' worth of stubble and a new laceration on his cheek, fresh enough that there was blood at its edge. Nicolai wondered if he himself done it, or if it had been done by someone in his family. The thought reminded him of the bodies in the living room, so he pushed it down and tried to focus.

Nicolai grunted.

"Oy! He's coming back up!" the man yelled over his shoulder. Someone else came walking over, this one in an ugly green shirt that was covered in burns and dirt. His face was long and narrow, as if stretched on a taffy machine.

"So he is," said the newcomer, ripping Nicolai's gag from his face. Then, to Nicolai, he added, "We need your eye."

"To see what you did to my family?"

The man with the long face looked hurt. "Heya, we didn't do that. They were that way when we found them. Some assfuck smashed through the gate and stole all your goodies. Shame that, right? No, I mean your eye. To open the safe."

Nicolai wondered who the men were, but it didn't matter. He could hear more of them moving around everywhere now — in the wine cellar and above in the house. There seemed to be dozens, maybe more. Had they been hiding when he'd come in?

"We don't have a safe," said Nicolai.

There was a sharp pain, and Nicolai looked down to see that the man had poked a knife into his side. The stab was shallow, but the blade was long. Plenty of room to go farther, and take his intestines as it went.

"I don't think the safe will open if I hack your eye out and hold it up to the scanner, but I'm good to try," said the man. "We know you gots a safe. But there's not lots of time. Fortune favors the bold and speedy, eh? There's other bands on this hill. Help with the safe, or I kill you. Your choice."

Nicolai wouldn't satisfy the man by letting him know how much the knife in his side was killing him, but he did look up at his long face and decided that his offer was true. There would be no game playing. If this group didn't get the safe quickly, they'd have to fight other rioters for it. The safe mattered, but not enough to take the time needed to beat the truth slowly from Nicolai's body.

"How many people are in my house?" Nicolai asked. He swallowed and looked up.

"Enough," said the man.

"Will you kill me afterward?"

The knife twisted. "I guarantee that if you *don't* help, I'll kill you now."

Nicolai couldn't help it; he cried out, nodding vigorously until the knife left his side. Then he looked at the wine cellar's wooden ceiling, hearing the number of tromping boots increase with every passing minute. He thought of the security system, of Sophia, and of what his father had told him about concentric perimeters. How much had the looters destroyed? Would the safe even still work?

The long-faced man watched Nicolai, watched the other man. How many were in the group? There had to be dozens. Maybe as many as fifty. He might be able to get by one man, two men, maybe three or four. But the house was occupied like a besieged land by an invading army. Running was no longer an option. Still, Nicolai wondered if he should resist. Why should he let them into the safe? They'd probably kill him afterward, if for no other reason than to cover their trail. So why should his final act in his family's house — be it his last before running or last before dying — be a betrayal of their most valuable possessions…and maybe even their biggest secrets?

The man, seeming to sense his hesitation, kicked him to action.

Nicolai teetered to his feet then climbed the stairs in front of the man's nudging insistence. Nicolai wondered if he could run. They'd untied his hands; his feet weren't bound; he knew the house; he knew the area. Sure, the bandit might shoot him in the back (if he had a gun, which he might not), but at least he'd have a chance. Nicolai was agile; he could duck and weave and evade as well as anyone. But the fantasy dissolved when he reached the top of the stairs and found what looked like an army. Dirty men and women (some looking like a gang, plenty looking like townies spattered with blood and grime) milled through the hallways, assessing everything that remained. They were sprawled on his father's favorite couch, in his mother's pneumatic rocker. His father had an easy chair with a levitating ottoman — a prototype using the same technology that had flown Enzo's paper airplane into Ms. Marco's ass a lifetime ago. Two men were fighting over it, mystified by the floating cushion.

As Nicolai walked, the people in the house turned to watch him. The long-faced man was clearly the leader, and they knew where Nicolai was leading him. It was the only reason they'd stayed.

Feeling conflicted, his heart beating hard in his chest, Nicolai led the growing party into the master bedroom. A few milling rioters who'd camped out in the bedroom were clustered around the nightstand, where a scan panel had already been opened. Its panel was yellow, because Nicolai had put the alarm in standby before he'd entered.

He looked at the thirty or so menacing faces surrounding him in the large room — all of them waiting for the home's heir to set his eye to the scanner.

With a final, rueful look around, Nicolai bent and set his forehead against the pad. The system was self-contained and would function even in a power or network failure. A red light flashed in his eye, and then there was the small chirp as Sophia (or her latest buffered identity algorithms if the connection was severed) recognized him as a Costa. A second panel slid open, and Nicolai keyed in a code. There was another chirp. Then, inside the open walk-in closet, a panel rose from the floor on a pneumatic lift. On it sat a large brushed aluminum safe.

"Boxes in boxes, eh?" said the bandit leader. "Open that one, too."

Nicolai did as he was told, kneeling in front of the safe and feeling the pressure of scores of eyes over his shoulder. Would they swarm when he opened it? Would it become every man and woman for themselves, or was there clan honor among them?

Nicolai turned the dial then pressed his finger against the small green pad on the safe. The mechanism clicked, and he opened the door. The masses behind him sighed and leaned in, but they stayed back.

The man with the long face kicked Nicolai aside and moved forward. Inside the safe was only one item: a beautiful crystal box. The man pulled out the box, crossed to the bed, and set it on the bedspread. The others clustered around, watching. There was no lock on the latch. The man flicked the latch and opened the box. Inside were what looked like hundreds of silver marbles.

"What are these?" said the bandit, looking back at Nicolai.

Nicolai didn't have to answer. As the crowd watched, the marbles began to rise from the box of their own accord. They began to revolve around one another, floating and swirling in patterns. They danced that way for a while then formed a miniature cyclone, fizzing from the box in a wave. The silver balls spread out, moving throughout the room, throughout the crowd. Like the levitating ottoman, the rioters had clearly never seen anything like the flying marbles before. They staggered back, unsure. But after a few seconds, their curiosity got the best of them and they began to poke at the things, to try and grab them (the spheres zoomed away playfully, then returned like sparrows), and finally to laugh. The marbles continued to float, swapping one for another in pairs, bouncing, making vortices in the air. They paused, moved, paused again, like a dance.

There was a chirp.

"Confirm," said Nicolai from the closet.

With a sound like a knife dragged across a stone, every marble in the air grew spikes, becoming miniature morning stars. Then they all accelerated at once, plowing through the nearest skull. Nicolai watched as a hole appeared in the tall man's forehead, the spiked ball emerging from the other side sticky with gore. A dozen bodies fell, then fifteen, then twenty.

Those who weren't hit right away scrambled to run, knocking into each other, tripping on the bodies. The balls followed, easily keeping pace, converging like locusts. Watching from the closet, Nicolai felt a bitter sort of victory. If the intruders knew what they were facing, they wouldn't bother to run. When the target stood still, facial recognition would sight a spot between the eyes and end things quickly. But when the target ran, the ministars became raw bludgeons, beating the target until it lay still and stopped radiating the bioelectric current that came with a heartbeat.

Dozens of stars converged on one man, turning him to pulp. Another tried for a window, but the reinforced windows were strong, and the man simply bounced off. He turned as five or six of the spiked balls struck him in the gut. The ministars were oddly courteous. In the same way they avoided Nicolai, they avoided the walls and furniture. If Nicolai were planning to remain in his family's home, he'd be able to turn on the cleaners to scavenge the blood from the carpet fibers and it would be like the intruders had never been there.

When all of the bodies had fallen (the balls would hunt through every room; they could hear a heartbeat no matter how well a person might hide), Nicolai rose and, now totally alone, made his way back down into the wine cellar. When he was standing just a few feet from where he'd woken up bound, he said, "Nicolai Costa. Five-one-seven-oh. Go verbal."

There was a chirp, and a soft female voice said, "Good afternoon, Mr. Costa."

"Stand down ministars. I want into the arsenal."

"Access to the arsenal is restricted."

"Request emergency access."

There was a chirp as the system accessed surveillance records and the AI determined that Nicolai was the only remaining Costa, turning his word to law.

"Access granted. I'm sorry, Mr. Costa."

Nicolai felt strangely moved by the programmed response to emergency access then swallowed it. The situation was what it was. He was now on his own. Nothing would change that — not sorrow, not despair. He could live, or he could die. Those were the only things that still mattered.

A rack of wine bottles moved aside, and the wall behind it slid open to reveal the world's deadliest walk-in. In a few years, the items inside the arsenal (or in the decoy safe) might be smart enough for automation. Maybe in a few years, the house itself could have saved Nicolai's mother, father, brother, and sisters. But Nicolai's father didn't yet trust his new technology enough to give it free reign over their home's security. It was ironic to think it was that very skepticism that had gotten them all killed.

It didn't matter. What was done was done, and no amount of what-if would change it.

Before entering the arsenal, Nicolai walked over to a corpse without a head and stripped off its clothing and back-pack. He swapped the bandit's clothes for his own, then took a palmful of the man's blood and rubbed it into his groomed hair to muss it. He stepped inside the arsenal, to its back, and loaded the intruder's backpack with food, water purification kits, first aid, and cash. He grabbed a few knives and a small slumber gun, but forced himself to ignore the room's advanced gadgets, be they innocuous, beneficial, or deadly. It was excruciating to pass the kickstands — hovering scooters that collapsed to the size of a police baton — but he told himself that he was now part of the rabble, and that his money would only get him killed. Advanced weapons and transportation mattered not at all if something was discovered in his possession before he could use it to flee. Nicolai was a Costa. He could be trusted with his father's wares. But as the world crumbled, he had his doubts that the rest of the popula-tion could. His father had guarded this technology carefully, and Nicolai wouldn't betray him by loosing it on a crumbling society. What was in here might one day have changed the world…but as his father had often lamented, there was no way to say whether that change would be for better or worse.

He walked to the front of the arsenal then turned to look back.

"I need the remote."

A small device slid from a compartment inside the arsenal's wall. Nicolai took it.

Once outside with the small, rustic pack slung over his shoulder, Nicolai keyed the remote and tossed it aside.

Behind him, the house began to burn in a blazing white phosphorous fire that would destroy it all.

Chapter 2

Natasha stalked up behind Isaac, set a glass of wine on the tabletop, and slapped a hand onto her slender hip.

"I'm sick of being in my office."

Isaac barely looked back. "So come out."

"I'm in there because you're self-absorbed out here. You aren't paying attention to me; it's all Isaac all the time. I can't avoid the Beam feeds while waiting for you. Have you been watching? It's all replays of the riot at my concert at the Aphora, including video of me running away. The sheets are all about me. Bashing me. Saying how I got what I deserved. I've got a concert next weekend, Isaac!"

Isaac turned, his dark eyes hooded, eyebrows drawn together in a way that suggested he didn't want to fight but wasn't buying into Natasha's bullshit. Not that it *was* bullshit. But that's how Isaac was sure to see it, asshole that he could be sometimes.

"Oh, so fucking what, Natasha? Is that really what's bothering you? The *sheets*? Do you even know what that riot was about?"

"They want what I have! It was a bunch of poor people

lashing out. That's why I said no cheap seats. Those fucking cretins don't appreciate…"

"Exactly!" Isaac blurted, raising his hands. "Haves versus have-nots, same as it's been since the dawn of forever. So why are you making it all about *you*, Natasha? The Directorate is poor, and with Shift approaching, it's like they've just *realized* they're poor, and they're pissed. Never mind that they *chose* to be in our party. Never mind that we take care of them, unlike the poor people in Enterprise. Never mind that they don't have to work if they ration properly. Never mind that everything is done for them, that they can plug into Beam simulations all fucking day and rot while synthetic fucking hookers feed them synthetic fucking grapes and *we* pay for their housing, healthcare, and fucking living expenses stipend. But oh, they don't think of that. No. All they think about is who's above them and who's below them. Like us. They just see us as Beau Monde Directorate, all high and mighty in our crystal towers."

Isaac rolled his eyes, practically growling in frustration.

"We're like Enterprise to them," he ranted. "This stupid fucking party! Greedy, greedy bastards. The family in the Old Brooklyn apartment who doesn't have to work is jealous of the family in the Upper East Side who doesn't have to work…and *those* bastards are jealous of the Upper-Westers. Nobody's satisfied. This all made sense when Micah and I split, and now I wonder if maybe he was right. You give things to people, and they only want more."

Natasha flopped onto the divan. Isaac was being such a jerk. Yes, society had its problems, but so did his wife. Why was he so preoccupied with politics when the raff were after *her?* He'd never so much as consoled her after she'd fled the Aphora, never wrapped his hands around her after the concert and told her that everything would be okay. James had led her from the hover and through the apartment's docking port in tears. And what had Isaac done when he'd seen her in distress? He'd treated her like another problem that was crowding his schedule. An assault on his showbiz wife just meant more work for Isaac. So while she'd crumpled and tried to fight the emotions warring within her, he'd stalked off mumbling about the Directorate and how a few assholes were making his whole party look bad. Natasha was left to calm herself while Isaac took call after call, occasionally glaring at her like an uncompleted to-do.

"I don't want to argue politics with you," she said.

"Oh, you never do."

"What the hell does that mean?" she spat.

"It's all about *you*, Natasha. Always *you*. There's more at stake here than just your hurt ego."

She sat up, indignant. "And I don't matter, right? Because I'm just a selfish bitch. Just a diva. The fact that I get spat on means nothing to you other than that people don't like the rich. I'm like a canary in a mine for your damned party. If I die, it only matters because…"

Isaac interrupted her with a snort of laughter. "If you *die?*"

"You know what I mean."

He shrugged, flapped his hands at the ends of his wrists, and gave her a look. "What do you want, Natasha?"

"Maybe a kind word. A moment of your time. If you could deign to talk to your wife about something that's bothering her. The sheets act like I'm not a person, but I am. This all hurts. Every bit of it."

"Oh, so you're *hurt*," he said. "I'm crushed. Look, I've got my plate heaped high with shit here. The Directorate is about to explode in riots, and Micah's over at Enterprise HQ lapping it up, making it worse. If something doesn't change, we're going to see mass defections. We'll lose control of the Senate. Copycat riots continue to erupt, and Beam news stories and your stupid gossip sheets are feeding the whole thing, leading to more riots. Everyone blames us. Oh, and Nicolai is missing — did I tell you that?"

Natasha sat up. "Nicolai is missing?"

"I'm supposed to respond to Micah's latest volley, but I don't know what to say! That asshole has gone off-grid, maybe with some shady upgrade dealer. Captain Long is being a cunt about it, not helping at all, and keeps tossing some bullshit having to do with Organa back at me as if I care…not that those fucking freaks make life any easier for *any* of us, Beau Monde or the lower ninety-nine."

Natasha wanted to snap back but felt bludgeoned by Isaac's words. That was the thing about her husband: Yes, he needed his speeches written for him, but his presence was dominant and persuasive. She couldn't argue with a single word he'd said. It was true that there were much bigger problems out there than her personal feelings about being shunned and rejected. But somehow, in a way she couldn't quite articulate, it seemed like a man should care that his wife had been chased by a mob.

"You should care about me," was all she could say.

"How do we afford all of your enhancements, Natasha? Where would your career and fragile self-esteem be without all of that expensive technology in your system? What if you still had your fat cells? What if you looked anywhere near your age? You're like a fucking antique car with all this upkeep."

Natasha felt tears brim at her eyelids. The tears made her furious. She wanted to be indignant, not weak. But Isaac would see her wet eyes and think that she was being emotional, *just like a woman*. That was how men were; they didn't think a woman could be both emotional and right at the same time. If Natasha was crying, Isaac would know she was wrong…and losing.

"You're an asshole," she spat.

"Sure."

"You're an *ASSHOLE!*"

Isaac waved her away, turning and tapping the screen of his handheld.

Natasha ran to her office, slammed the door, and locked it. She walked over and set her head in a cradle at the top of one of the two comfortable leather chairs along the far wall. Her fingers tapped a button on the chair's arm. In seconds, the surrounding room began to swim. Her eyes' sensory input tuned down as the room's small sounds faded and the chair's feel beneath her began to dissolve. Isaac wanted to talk about expensive upgrades? Fine. These immersion rigs — a pair of which were in each of their offices — were the most expensive equipment they had, and Natasha knew exactly how she wanted to use hers.

As Natasha fell into the simulation, the Beam-projected inputs smoothly replaced all five of her natural senses. After the transition was complete, she found herself standing in an all-white bedroom. She wore a sheer white gown with nothing underneath, and could feel its movement on every inch of her skin. A breeze wafted from somewhere, even though the simulated room had no windows. There were no entrances or exits. Nobody would bother her here, and could only come via invite. This area of the Viazo was hers. She paid a pretty penny to keep her own piece of virtual real estate all to herself.

Feeling with every cell as if she were actually in the white room rather than in a black leather chair in her office, Natasha raised her hands and gestured. A window floated open in front of her. She scrolled through names, searching for one in particular. She found it, relieved. He was online. She tapped the name, and a moment later the chiseled face of a handsome man appeared.

"Andre," she whispered.

"Natasha."

"I'm in the Viazo," she said.

A small smile crossed his lips.

"My husband is neglecting me. He doesn't understand me."

"Would you like some company?" Andre asked.

"I *need* some," she replied.

He nodded. Natasha closed the window. She turned then lay back on the bed. A man shimmered into existence across the room, having moved his avatar into the Viazo on her invite. Viazo avatars weren't like the pixelated, video-and-audio-only avatars that existed in poorer sections of The Beam. These were sharp, and Andre's beauty, as Natasha watched him approach, was sharp and crisp and present. Viazo avatars had all five senses, every scintilla of which were transmitted into the user's cortex via high-end immersion rigs. And thanks to the rather expensive nanos in Natasha and Andre's real bodies that were able to down-tune their real senses so they could experience the replacement senses, it truly felt like being there.

The handsome man climbed onto the bed and lay on top of Natasha. His pressure on her was reassuring and arousing at the same time.

"You shouldn't cheat on your husband," Andre said while kissing down the length of her neck, her chest, her belly.

"How can I cheat?" Natasha replied, spreading her legs to make room for Andre's face. "I'm not even here."

Chapter 3

Dominic Long sat in his shitty public official's office behind his shitty sixty-year-old public official's desk. The casters of his shitty chair rattled on the shitty chipped synthetic flooring beneath his feet, most of which was peeling and faded because, Dominic suspected, it was incredibly shitty. He stared at his shitty console-model canvas and wondered for the billionth time why, if police were so important to maintaining order, they received such shitty appropriations.

Thanks to his high position within this shitty, underfunded public service, Dominic had money despite being Directorate. Good money, in fact — enough to put him at the lower edge of what those above him called the "Presque Beau." But regardless of his good station, Dominic always felt depressed after a visit to the Quark wing. His great grandfather had been a New York City cop back around the turn of the millennium, and Dominic had seen the old digital videos Grandy had shot with his ancient iPhone — enough to know that the station Dominic sat in today hadn't changed all that much since Grandy's day. The Quark station was what law enforcement was *supposed* to look like after a hundred years of progress. But would Grandy be surprised to see how little had changed?

Dominic doubted it. Sure, DZPD had The Beam, but the consoles they used to access it weren't all that different from the PCs Grandy had used back when he used to walk the beat.

Of course, the reason the DZPD wasn't as funded as it should have been was partially due to politics, but it was also due to the fact that DZPD wasn't the real law in town. When all the fancy talk was set aside, everyone knew that The Beam ran the city (just as it ran all cities) and that despite all of their protests to the contrary, it was *Quark* who'd created The Beam…and hence Quark who still controlled it.

"Noah Fucking West," Dominic said aloud. His shitty office didn't respond.

Dominic looked down at his wooden, non-Beam-enabled desk with its ancient blotter then tapped the console with a sigh. He was about to start poking around to see what he could find on new riots when his console trilled. A call was coming in, and the only way he could take it was there on his console screen, same as Grandy had done a hundred years before.

As if that wasn't annoying enough, the call was coming from Leo Booker. Dominic shook his head, tapped the screen, and took the call.

"Leo," he said. They were both using video, so Dominic found himself staring at a man with a headband and two gray braids beside his face. Noah Fucking West. If these granola-fuckers wanted to get anywhere with their cause, why didn't they try harder to blend in? Dominic believed in what the Organas stood for, but the way they dressed and gussied themselves up sure made it hard to agree with them.

"How's your office?" said Leo.

For a moment, it seemed as if Leo's question was psychic. Then Dominic realized the old man was asking about security, not about whether his environment had managed to keep current with the century.

"My door is closed."

"Is that a go-ahead?"

Dominic shrugged. As captain, Dominic had the significant perk of a secure Beam connection that was as close to anonymous as a non-Quark agent could get. His office, while antiquated, was electronically soundproofed. But explaining all of this to Leo seemed like an unnecessary concession to his station's adequacy, so he let the shrug suggest that things were merely acceptable.

"Thanks for covering for Leah," said Leo.

"Sure."

"Her record is as expunged as it can be?" he asked. The question carried the undercurrent they both knew was there — that The Beam never truly forgot — but the answer was, as with everything, that Dominic had done well enough. There was simply too much information in the world. Evidence of Leah's visit to the station could never be fully removed thanks to the ubiquity of City Surveillance and the attention of what Leah had told him were Beam clerics, but the bits that Dominic hadn't erased would almost certainly be lost.

"Yeah."

"Good. Is it getting crazy in tech town?"

"You mean crazier than it is in tech poseur villages up in the mountains?" Dominic's mood was sour, and he wanted to poke Leo. Up in what was supposed to be a blackout zone, Leo had a wireless connection capable of making calls like the one they were on that his hippie toadies didn't know about.

Leo laughed, ignoring Dominic's bait.

But Dominic felt like arguing. Things around the DZPD station had been downright infuriating lately. Shift was always an unsettling time rife with civil unrest, but the last few Shifts had been a walk in the park. They'd gone so smoothly, in fact, that after the last Shift Dominic had joked that the universe must be saving up for a doozy to come. This Shift hadn't disappointed, and the idiocy was only just starting. The city had had riot after riot, and crime was up. The DZPD jail cells weren't usually filled — the core of District Zero was so well watched by City Surveillance and sweeperbots that most DZ citizens managed to keep their hands to themselves or be sent quietly to Respero — but those same cells were overflowing now. Respectable people were raging and rioting. "Civil uprising," they called it. To Dominic, it was hippie bullshit and a headache.

"You think it's funny?" said Dominic.

"So things *are* crazy in tech town?"

"Goddammit, Leo. I know you get a feed up there. You've got your little gadget and your air signal, and I suspect you might even have a hard line…"

"I don't have a hard line."

"…and I frankly don't feel like playing cutesy games. We have riots up the ass, and you send Leah into Quark? That's beyond stupid. And now on top of all of these fucking riots, I'm cleaning up after you. You get to have the ideals, while I'm stuck cleaning up the mess."

Onscreen, Leo finally looked affected. "It isn't Organa that's causing your riots. That's about Directorate and Enterprise."

Dominic grunted. He'd gotten his hippie movements confused. The Enterprise wanted freedom to make as many credits as they wanted, the Directorate wanted freedom from poverty, and the granola-fuckers in the mountains wanted freedom from technology. Or so they said.

"Organa isn't helping," said Dominic. It was a spiteful, groundless comment, but Dominic wanted to blame someone. Leo was the only one within range.

"This is your cause too, Dominic," said Leo.

Dominic held his breath for a long moment then finally exhaled. Blowing steam at Leo changed nothing. The rioters were still rioting, and the Directorate was still bitching. The Enterprise was still making things worse by blustering back. It was like a bunch of schoolchildren slap-fighting. Leo was at least ostensibly on Dominic's side.

Besides, Leo hadn't chosen Dominic; Dominic had chosen Leo. They'd known each other since Dominic's school days, but it was Dominic who'd begun to put together bits and pieces of some giant puzzle over the past decade, a hunch tickling the back of his brain about Quark, The Beam, West, and whether the upper tier had more privilege than was commonly known amongst most of the population. It was Dominic who'd sought out Leo not just as a friend but as an Organa leader; it was Dominic who'd been shuttling drugs and information to keep the Organas one step ahead; it was Dominic who'd sent Leo the vagrant he was supposed to send to Respero and hence saddled both of them with a moral burden. Dominic had made his own bed with Organa, with Leo, and maybe even with Leah's incursion into Quark. He was making his own bed with the riots even now, Dominic reminded himself. He could try harder to stop them — there were plenty of sweepers and apprehenders in DZPD's garages to quell the riots at the first sign a new one was erupting — but in truth, Dominic intentionally let a few fires burn, because a little upheaval was good for the cause.

Instead of conceding Leo's point, Dominic pinched the bridge of his nose and looked at his non-Beam-enabled desk blotter.

"I hate to make your headache worse..." said Leo.

The way Leo trailed off, Dominic knew what was coming. But he asked anyway.

"What is it, Leo?"

"Moondust."

"Noah *Fucking* West."

"I've tried not to mention it, Dominic, but we're getting really low. I don't want to press you, but you're the only person I can ask. Ever since you stepped into Omar's place as an intermediary...well..." Leo shrugged.

Now it was Dominic's turn not to rise to the bait, because the truth was that Dominic had brought the moondust burden on himself, and they both knew it.

The Organas had been synthesizing their mind-altering hallucinogenic in labs since the '60s, but in the late '70s they'd discovered that the compound was especially potent when grown on the moon — something about the vacuum, alternating exposure to unshielded solar radiation and deep cold, and space dirt…or some other bullshit Dominic didn't understand in the least. Opportunistic entrepreneurs with access to the moon elevator had immediately begun growing moondust and smuggling it back. Ever since, the drug had been intertwined with Organa like two hairs in a braid. Organas said Lunis allowed them to see truths The Beam couldn't, and perhaps as a perverse kind of proof, the most elite Beam hackers were deeply, deeply addicted. Whether that was coincidence or not, Dominic couldn't say…but it didn't matter whether he thought it made sense or not. Organa didn't function without moondust, and when addicts ran dry, withdrawal could be fatal.

Dominic didn't need more pressure right now, but Leo was right: *He* was the one who'd stepped into the middle of the supply chain, who'd told Leo to stop buying directly from Omar because Omar was screwing the Organas every way he could manage. Like it or not, it was on Dominic unless he wanted his one "cause" to fall into a pile of twitching junkies and die.

"I'll get you your dust," said Dominic.

"Our stores are nearly depleted. People know it, too. If this goes on much longer, we'll have to start rationing, and if we do that, we'll have our own version of your riots."

"I said I'll get it for you."

"Even if you have to make a run yourself, Dominic," said Leo. "Don't make me beg."

"Okay."

"Promise me you'll do it. Just a few meterbars."

"I'll get it when I get it."

"This week. Can you run this week?"

Dominic, annoyed, pushed down his own irritation as he watched Leo's thin veneer grow thinner. Deep down, Leo was scared. There were hundreds of people who came and went in the mountain community, and that was a lot of need to fill. One person would run out then tear the rest of the others apart trying to find more. Organas were peaceful by nature, but *all* addicts were dangerous when their needs weren't met.

"Look, Leo…" said Dominic.

"What?"

"One of the runners was pinched on the moon," he admitted.

Leo's eyes went wide. Dominic held up a hand.

"It's not a big deal, okay? We have people coming down all the time. There's usually a buffer supply, but, well, it belonged to this guy, and he fucked up. We won't make the same mistake again. There are guys coming down every day, bringing a few dozen centimeterbars with them each time. One of the people we know is sending a hover with a nice big hidden compartment, and he's taking your usual bribe with him. Okay?"

"When?"

"Two days. Tops."

Leo seemed to force his face into a smile. "Okay."

"I promise."

"Don't fuck it up," said Leo.

That made Dominic's head snap around. Leo was just scared, but bullshit was bullshit, and Dominic was doing his best.

"You know," he said, "has it ever occurred to you — the irony of you trying to 'free people's minds' while you're all hooked on dope?"

Onscreen, the man with the gray braids scowled, and then

his image vanished. It was the video call equivalent of slamming a door in someone's face.

Once alone, Dominic pushed back his console then cleared space on his non-Beam-enabled desk blotter. He pulled a small vial from his bottom desk drawer and tapped a miniature avalanche of small gray rocks — each about the size of a troublesome pebble in a man's shoe — onto its surface.

He picked up a trio and dropped all three under his tongue.

Dominic leaned back and looked at the ceiling, waiting for the moondust to show him truths The Beam could not.

Chapter 4

Doc FELT nervous in this part of town.

By contrast, Kai, walking along beside him, seemed to be right at home in a place where the servicing of raw human needs was done so openly. The drug dealers were almost unionized here, each with his or her own specialty, and Kai apparently knew them all. Some dealt dust; some dealt hyper-crack; some dealt plain old-fashioned heroin. Kai treated them all like old friends, despite the fact that her clients were all from much higher social castes. She said she liked society's castoffs. They were honest in a way law-abiders could never be. And everyone certainly knew Kai, even if they'd never met her in person. Her reputation as a woman with connections seemed to precede her.

Doc stared too long at everything, unable to help himself. There were walkers on every corner. Most of them, he knew, would have upgraded themselves with bargain-basement sexual enhancements that even Doc, with his loose morals and entrepreneurial impetuosity, would never sell. He'd heard of such things, though; they were advertised in rip-off shops throughout The Beam, pushing geotagged ads at everyone who connected to the network within twenty miles of this place. The walkers would have vaginas made of flexible Plasteel, with small rollers under the surface that provided ribs "for his pleasure." The rollers vibrated and shook, and would do so to milk a john while stimulating his prostate via an appendage up his ass at the same time. The walkers' faces were barely human. They had lips that looked like a joker's, their skin stretched tight to conceal wrinkles that, in higher-class hookers, would have been erased by nanos. Many of the girls had long, dexterous synthetic tongues. They flicked them at Kai in greeting like obscene robot kisses. Kai waved back and called the walkers by name.

They finally came to a crumbling building with a sandstone facade that, Doc supposed, had once been beautiful and grand. It was just west of the park and had been home to the District Zero's old rich before the upheaval of the 20s had turned the previous century's elite real estate into ghetto.

Kai stopped and looked up. "This is it."

Doc was unimpressed. The nicest-looking older buildings tended to be the worst, and he didn't trust it. Something was running up and down his spine, warning him off like a sixth sense.

"Looks like a flophouse," he said.

Kai, her eyes still on the building, nodded. "Pretty much," she said.

After Doc — on the run from the police and whoever had broken into his apartment — had paged Kai and stormed into her building (and after Kai had soothed his jangled nerves in the way that only Kai could, for a price) she'd listened to his story, then busted his balls. After a suitable period of mockery, she'd called a man named Stanford who she claimed could make people disappear. She explained that Stanford's process wasn't simple, that it'd cost Doc more credits than he'd want to spend, and that it wasn't foolproof…but that it was the best Doc would be able to do. It *was* possible to get your hands on a permanent solution, of course — a stolen Beam ID — but installing stolen IDs was more than tricky, and Doc had neither the time nor the money to make it happen. Beam IDs were mRNA-based and replicated inside a host's body like a virus. Changing a person's ID involved genetic manipulation that a skeeve like Stanford couldn't safely do. What Stanford *could* do, though, was perform a full-body magic trick involving false eyes or lenses, skin lotions, and other spoofed parts that the bots were most likely to scan. Stanford couldn't yank a person from the grid, but he could make that person invisible in the same way a good magician makes things invisible — by using misdirection and flair.

Standing in front of the sandstone building, Doc listened again to his sixth sense playing ominous notes across the back of his neck. Something was wrong. He took Kai's wrist and pulled her farther down the littered sidewalk.

"What are you doing?" she said.

Doc kept his face neutral. "Just keep walking."

Kai, who had seemed to find Doc's reports on Xenia's secrets as ominous as he did, obeyed. They crossed a street and skirted several burned-out hulks of ancient cars when Doc finally saw the unseen thing that had set his nerves on high alert.

"Shit," he said.

"What?"

Doc didn't answer. Instead, he shoved Kai into an alcove behind a refuse bin and pushed his body against hers, suddenly groping her small breasts, reaching around to grab handfuls of ass. He smashed his lips sloppily into her mouth, using plenty of tongue. It was wet and gross and desperate, and Kai pushed back at him until she heard the hum. Then she fell into it and let Doc do what he wanted.

They waited, playing out their little drama. Behind them, the hum increased in volume.

Doc rolled Kai to the side and glanced at the sweeperbot from the corner of his eye. DZPD didn't try to disguise the bots and make them look friendly. Sweeperbots were all metal and menace, without any attempts to mimic human expression. The thing looked like an upright bullet with few visible features. Its sensors were all under the surface of its Alumix skin, able to see through what looked from the outside like a jacket of copper. It was floating now, but at least half the time you ran into sweepers, you'd see them prowling to conserve energy, stalking the streets on long chrome legs with pointed ends, like giant spiders.

The sweeper stood behind them as if enjoying the show, humming as it hovered. Inside its smooth copper-colored jacket, something whirred, reversed, whirred again.

Doc couldn't see the thing fully without being obvious, so he kept waiting, groping Kai while she groped back, now seemingly adding her considerable work experience to her performance. The bot wouldn't be able to scan them without cause, and making out in public certainly wasn't cause in this part of town. But if the bot was looking for a missing man with shoulder-length blond hair in a suit jacket too nice for the district? Well, that might be cause aplenty.

After a long moment, the bot hovered on, searching for criminal activity that violated the low standard it was programmed to accept in this part of town.

Doc exhaled then parted from Kai. She didn't peel off the wall with him. Instead, she continued to hold on south of his belt.

"You fucking pig," she said. "You're totally hard!"

"Come on," he said, ignoring her. "We can go back now."

But Kai kept holding his crotch and refused to lose her infuriating sideways smile. Doc couldn't believe she wanted to play this game right now. Of *course* he was hard. Her pointing it out was like a ninja observing his way with a blade.

"Goddammit. Knock it off," he said.

"You started this."

Doc wrenched free, then took Kai roughly by the arm and

pulled her back in the direction of Stanford's sandstone building. She was tiny compared to him, but right now the small pale-skinned woman with the dark-brown hair clearly had the upper hand over the broad-shouldered blond man. She dragged her low heels as he tugged her, giggling.

"You like me, Doc Stahl," she teased.

"Come on." He released her hand and took the lead, figuring she'd either follow or she wouldn't.

"I can see it in your eyes," she cooed. "*And* in your pants. I could do things to you right here and right now, you know. In this part of town, nobody would think anything of it. That sweeper wouldn't have thought twice if I'd dropped to my knees and put your cock in my mouth."

Doc, who was usually impervious to embarrassment, felt a blush creeping up from under his collar. He'd done acres of dirty deeds with Kai, but all of them had been in the bedroom. He didn't exactly appreciate her come-ons while they were crossing a street filled with hookers and junkies. They were passing a few clusters of people in the gutters, and despite the vagrants' stupor, heads had raised at Kai's remark.

"You know I can do things with my tongue that…"

"Do you ever get tired of being a whore?"

The comment was wrong on a dozen levels, but Kai took it as fair retaliation and smirked. She liked control, and sex was one of her ways to get it. Other ways were money and rapport, both of which Kai had in spades. Doc had always felt comfortable with her. It was as if they were a couple rather than mutual clients. Kai bought from Doc, and she seldom paid with credits. Doc got the dust knocked off his boots and usually remunerated with gifts instead of cash. It was intimate, in a way. It was easy to forget that she probably had the same setup with dozens of guys.

"Can I ask you something, sweetheart?" Doc said.

"Always."

"Why are you here?"

"Stanford," she answered.

"I mean, why are you here *with me*." He shook his head, already feeling dumb for where his question was going. "Never mind. You must get that all the time."

"What?"

"Guys who think they're getting special treatment."

She laughed. It was a strange sound, down in the city's gutter. "This *is* special treatment," she said. "Believe it or not, I don't help all of my clients vanish."

"So again, why are you here?"

She shrugged. "This job isn't about the money for me anymore. A girl can't just do it for the money if she expects to stay whole."

As strange as her laugh had been, hearing Kai talk about wanting to be whole was a thousand times stranger. She saw his look and continued.

"Don't look so surprised," she said. "We all — well, all of us in Enterprise, anyway — earn our credits so that we can do something else. We work hard so we can play hard. But when I'm done working, I don't want to read books. I *like* to fuck. That's the fun part. So I don't have to work and then play. I turn parts of my work *into* play."

"This is play?" said Doc, looking around. He still felt like he could get a knife in his ribs at any second.

"I'm not afraid of life's dark corners, Doc," she said. "I have my favorite clients, and doing things like this for them? Well, it's my version of reading books after work. In fact, another of my favorite boys had me worried when you showed up. He called then disappeared. Now I can't find him. It has me bothered. So yeah, I have my little projects." She caught him looking again and gave him a fake glimmer of anger. "What? You've never heard of a hooker with a heart of gold?"

Doc shook his head. "I guess I figured you did it for the money."

"I've got more money than I can spend."

That got Doc's attention. They were nearing Stanford's building again, but he stopped short of it and faced her.

"How much money you got, sunshine?"

"How much money *you* got, cowboy?" she retorted.

"Plenty."

She looked around, seeming to notice her surroundings for the first time. Then, quietly, she said, "If you show me yours, I'll show you mine."

Doc smiled. "On three," he said. Then he counted down, and when he reached one, they both gave the balances in their credit accounts. Then both looked at the other, impressed.

"I thought you were a scrapper," she said.

"And I thought you were a working girl."

They resumed walking. Looking forward, he said, "You know, we're not that different."

"Sure, we're not," she said, looking at him, amused. She probably used that look a lot, probably when her clients fell in love.

"We're both whores," he said. "We screw people for a living. I do it with slick talk, and you do it with your fancy fur box, but it really ain't that different. I don't know about you, but sometimes it's hard for me to look in the mirror. I've sold defective upgrades when I had to eat. I once got my hands on a friend's client list and stole them all away. I'm not proud of it, but the thing is, sometimes things are tough and a man has to eat. I'd do it all again if I had to, and…"

Kai stopped him by reaching up and putting a thin finger against his lips. She said, "You should know I don't have any fur on my box, unless that's what the client wants. And please, don't be a cliché."

He shook his head. The finger left his lips.

"Men tell me secrets," she said. "It's not wise. Don't just spill your guts to the pretty girl because she acted like you mattered."

"Bitch," he said, smiling, "I matter just fine without your approval."

They arrived back at the sandstone building and turned toward its entrance. Doc had one foot on the first step in front of its door when Kai put a hand out to stop him.

"Stanford is the best, but I don't trust him at all," she said. "When he called me back, there's a reason I tried to push you out of the shot and a reason I got annoyed when you shoved your face back into it. Believe me, he screencapped you and has run your image through enough filters to know exactly who you are."

"So…" Doc began.

"So I'll go up first," she said. "You stay here, and I'll buzz you when it's safe."

Chapter 5

Kai entered the lobby. The foyer of Stanford's building, once home to the rich, displayed an enormously detailed Greek mosaic composed of small porcelain tiles. Here and there, tiles were shattered and cracked, but a shadow of its former grandeur remained.

The lobby itself was large and carried the same sense of forgotten glory. There were fluted columns that had split and now sat askew, leaking dust. There was an old-fashioned elevator with elaborate scrolling around its edges to one end, abandoned. When the building had been rescued as low-end Directorate housing in the '40s, city engineers had decided that despite the boom in building technology that had come during the 2020s Renaissance, the fancy elevator was beyond saving. Bombs from the early skirmishes had unsettled the foundation. The building itself was still sound ("Sound enough for Directorate shit," said civil rights advocates with scorn), but the elevator shaft was damaged past practical repair. So instead, repairs had focused on the freight elevator in the back. It, like the apartments upstairs, had the scantest level of Beam connectivity. The apartments had a single panel at the door and a plug for the rare resident who could afford a hardwired, secondhand console. The elevator had a swipe panel.

Luckily, it also had buttons.

Kai approached what had once been an elegant front desk, turned left, and slipped behind a shattered marble countertop and through a nondescript door. She steeled herself for anyone who might be waiting in the back hallway, but it was mercifully empty. The place smelled like urine. Kai ignored the scent with some difficulty, crossed to the elevator, and pressed the button with her elbow. The button had a fingerprint scanner but worked fine as a button. The technology wasn't intended to allow privacy. It was just old. Back in the day, The Beam hadn't touched as much as it did now. Adding connectivity to something as simple as an elevator had, at the time, seemed unnecessary.

The button lit. The elevator dinged then opened. Kai stepped inside, looking around for a swipe pad. The doors grew impatient and closed. She'd been in old elevators before, but on the few occasions she'd been in this one, Stanford had been with her and he'd operated it. She couldn't see how he'd done it. There seemed to be no gesture sensor. Sure, there was a call button in the lobby, but how could Kai tell the elevator where to go if she couldn't gesture directions? Stanford lived on the fourteenth floor, but there wasn't even a keypad.

"Console," she said aloud.

The elevator ignored her.

"Fourteenth floor," she said, knowing it was breath wasted.

The elevator was starting to feel claustrophobic. Kai had never noticed before how tight the space was. The one in her building was lightning fast and operated by voice or gesture. This box was old and, if she remembered correctly, shuddered as it climbed at the speed of an old woman.

There were two rows of white buttons near the door, with numbers. She nudged the one labeled *14* with her elbow. The elevator started to move. Kai sighed.

But just as the display above the door clicked to 3, the elevator shuddered to a stop. Did someone else want to get on, going up? That might make sense going down, but who would want to go from three *up* to another floor?

With some surprise, Kai realized she was nervous. Why would she be nervous? She was comfortable everywhere, from a Beau Monde penthouse to the bottom of the gutter. She had a variety of defensive add-ons and a naturally sharp ability to free herself from sticky situations. With no reason to expect danger, why were her nerves so keyed up?

It was the elevator. It was dawning on her how much she hated this fucking little coffin.

In front of her, the doors hadn't opened. She'd assumed the elevator had been called on the third floor, but if that were the case, the doors should have opened by now. Why hadn't they? What was wrong?

Relax, girl.

Kai took one, two, three deep breaths. But instead of calming her, her slow breaths simply reminded her of how much time was passing. Three full in-out cycles took Kai more than thirty seconds, and thirty seconds in a stopped elevator was an eternity. The doors should *definitely* have opened. Kai swore. The fucking thing was stuck.

In front of her, the bank of backlit buttons extinguished. The overhead light followed. The small strip of security lighting around the edges stayed lit, casting the box into an eerie twilight. The elevator had stopped humming, too, and suddenly everything was deadly quiet. The quiet in itself bothered her. Tenement buildings were usually loud with the sounds of decaying humanity. She tried to remember if Stanford's building was that way but couldn't. The air seemed so strange, so far beyond quiet. It was as if the elevator had been soundproofed. But that wouldn't make sense, either.

Standing in the scant light, Kai felt herself start to panic.

She wasn't the sort of girl to lose her shit. The feeling caught her off guard.

Relax. The elevator just went to sleep.

Of course. As off-grid as the building was (it only had the slightest Beam access), electricity would be tightly rationed. She'd seen that in the lobby, in the way the lights had subtly brightened as she'd approached then dimmed as she'd passed. Of course the elevator slept when nobody was in it.

But *she* was in it.

Kai pushed buttons, trying to wake the thing. Nothing happened. Her heart started to beat faster.

She looked below the row of buttons and saw a keyhole intended for emergency operation. Beside it, there was a small pad. If Kai put her finger on that pad, she could let the elevator know she was there. Never mind that *pressing the buttons* should tell the elevator she was here; that was a fingerprint pad, mandatory in all forms of conveyance for just such an emergency. The pad and the brain behind it would run on an independent circuit, broadcast wirelessly, and allow her to wake the elevator remotely.

But Kai couldn't use it. Because why would a girl who was currently knocking on the door of Beau Monde status be in such a seedy part of town? People would ask questions. They might send more bots, and this time they'd scan her…and anyone they found waiting outside.

Kai smashed her finger against the pad before she had time to reconsider. But nothing happened. The elevator stayed dark and didn't wake.

"Fucker," she said aloud.

Kai struck her fist against the door in frustration. She was starting to sweat, and hated the feeling. It was so undignified. She could fight; she'd had to fight plenty before. But what could she fight when her opponent was a stubborn metal box?

The lights came on. The buttons lit. The elevator began to move down.

Of course. It was going to the lobby. Doc had finally come after her, thank God.

But it didn't go to the lobby. The elevator stopped when the display above the door read *2*. The floor settled, and something in the old metal clunked. Kai waited for the doors to part. But it didn't matter which floor she ended up on; she just wanted *out*. There was a staircase. She'd walk the thirteen floors up to Stanford's apartment then would walk all fourteen down. She'd do the same again with Doc in tow. But she wasn't getting into this fucking coffin again.

The doors slid open, and Kai found herself facing three men holding slumberguns. They were dressed head-to-toe in black: black shoes, black socks, pressed black dress pants, black belts, black gloves, and black T-shirts under long black trench coats. They all wore black dress hats with brims, circled by black bands. On their faces, each man wore a black visor. The visors had integrated over-the-ear headphones and covered everything but their mouths. Around the visors' edges, Kai could see light leaking from the projections they were watching.

Kai's heartbeat quickened. *Beamers.*

"Get out," said the man at the group's front, pointing his slumbergun.

"Look, I've got no spar with you," said Kai, holding up her hands.

"Get out," the man to the far left echoed.

Kai kept her hands high and slid sideways out of the elevator. She wanted to put the hallway to her back and sprint off the second she saw an opening, but the Beamers seemed to anticipate the move. The man on the far side shifted his position to block. Kai found herself pinned to the wall beside the elevator, its call button at her back.

"I'll just go," she said.

"Kai Dreyfus," said Beamer at the front of the group.

"High-end escort. Dealer in secrets. Rumored assassin. Lives at…"

"I have it," said the other.

Kai looked from one Beamer to the other, understanding what was passing between the men. They were reading her stats from Beam feeds plugged into their visors, but the experience of being assessed by someone who couldn't, literally speaking, *see* her was unsettling. Kai had tried on visors before, of course, but she'd only used them for immersion. Beamers weren't usually fully immersed, because as much as they believed that The Beam's reality was more accurate than the world's, they couldn't escape the truth that things still happened in front of them that they needed to be aware of. If they'd been standing in the middle of the grid, they might not even be using first-person visual because The Beam around them would tell them more about her than sight could, but out here, the visors worked more or less as enhanced cameras. Kai felt X-rayed, and found the sensation invasive, as if they were under her skin.

"What do you want?" she said.

"Data," said two of them at once.

The response sounded like the ritual it was. Beamers *always* wanted data. They wore their visors at all times unless they were sleeping or in a simulator. They never unplugged. Unplugging a Beamer was like death because it forced them to contend with the inferior nature of an inferior world that failed to evolve by the second. The Beam, on the other hand, was *always* changing, always evolving. Reality, to Beamers, felt like standing still.

"I could give you *plenty* of data," said Kai. She lifted her shirt to bare her breasts then traced her fingers across her nipples.

"You're coming with us," said the man on the right.

"Careful," said the one in the middle. "Her temperature's rising."

"So is yours," she said, reaching for the closest Beamer's belt.

The man stepped away.

"Oh, come on," she purred. "I could take all three of you." Her fingers traced the line of flesh above the hem of her pants. "Let me show you boys some reality that's still better than The Beam." She ran her fingers over her lips. She slid her thumbs under her waistband.

The man on the left leaned forward a fraction of an inch. It was exactly enough.

Kai's professional ability to deliver pleasure gave her body the significant side effect of incredibly fast and responsive muscles. Doc had been selling her monthly injections of scavenger nanos for over a year, and hour by hour, the tiny machines tuned her nerves and muscles, making her leaner and faster and stronger. Her legs and arms had learned to move with inhuman speed, and she could strike with surprising amounts of force. Men twice her size were always surprised when she could easily turn them over, throw them from bed to wall to floor without any effort. She could stretch her body into a pretzel — handy as a prostitute, and deadly in fights as an occasional assassin for hire.

Kai reached forward, grabbed the man by the neck, and blew her fist through his visor with shocking ease. The Plaxi shattered, shards digging into his cheeks and forehead. She saw shocked, naked eyes staring at her for a split second before she turned, parrying, and struck him in the side of the head with her elbow. The other two Beamers raised their guns to fire, but Kai split low, one leg forward and the other back, a skill learned through decades of ballet and honed by nanobot muscle reconstruction. One of the Beamers discharged his weapon, but the shot flew above her head and struck the man she'd hobbled, sending him unconscious down the hallway and into a heap on the floor.

The other two attackers tried to compensate and aim

downward, but Kai sprang back up, squeezing her split legs and rising like an accordion. On the way up, she gripped one man in the crotch with a tuned-up fist capable of cracking concrete and squeezed until something popped. The man crumbled, going limp above her, so Kai ducked under his stomach as he screamed, blocking a slumbershot from the remaining man. Then she released her grip on the man's testicles, feeling him fall inert over her and, deflecting with the body, simply reached up and took the remaining man's slumbergun in her hand. And with that, fifteen seconds after the melee had started, Kai stood pointing her final assailant's own gun at his chest.

"What is this about?" she said. "Is this Stanford's doing?"

The Beamer held his hands up, his dark form watching her through the strange immersion visor. The last man's skin was black, and amidst his dark clothing, he seemed to almost disappear.

"We were told to bring you in. That's all I know."

"Is that reality?"

"Yes!"

But it wasn't, so Kai reached up with her free hand and pulled off the man's visor.

"*This* is reality," she said.

His eyes looked around, panicked. He looked like he was drowning. "My visor!" he yelled, scrabbling at her hand.

"You're useless," Kai said, then shot him in the chest and sent him into a snoozing heap in the corner.

Kai looked at the fallen Beamers, gun in hand and satisfied. Then she realized she was cold. She looked down to see that she'd never lowered her shirt and that she'd just defeated three assailants with her small tits out and swinging. Not her first time.

Kai composed herself then sprinted down the hallway toward the stairs. She had no idea what had happened, but Doc's vanishing act would have to wait. Either Stanford had turned them in or something equally shitty had gone down, but regardless, they were in trouble. More troops could be coming. DZPD could be coming. She'd have to grab Doc and go. They'd come in on foot, and that was unfortunate because it meant they'd have to leave on foot. Doing so cleanly if the cavalry was coming would take some fancy maneuvering.

Kai burst through the stairwell door on the ground floor, ran through the lobby, and dashed into the sunlit afternoon. Too late, she realized that the men in the hallway had brought friends. There were another three Beamers outside, hovering in front of the building on screetbikes. Each held his bike by one hand so that they could level their slumberguns with the other. Doc was nowhere.

Kai, facing another three-on-one and knowing her fists and feet wouldn't help her unless she got closer, dropped her gun and held her hands in the air.

"Let's discuss this," she said.

But the Beamers, of course, were wearing visors and had seen everything that had happened upstairs. They didn't want to trifle, bargain, or talk.

The front biker raised his gun and fired. Kai fell to the street.

Chapter 6

Kai woke in a bed, her head throbbing, her hands and feet shackled, presumably tethered to the bed she was lying on. The room was dark, with one light overhead. She heard a strange humming — a generator? Machinery in the next room? — and felt a warbling vibration, as if her mattress had been set atop an old petroleum engine. Consciousness came slowly. She could make no sense of what little she could see or feel. She knew her head hurt and that she was vaguely nauseated, but not why. Then, slowly, some of it came back: She remembered the Beamers and their slumberguns. And maybe someone else had been there? She wasn't sure. It was all so fuzzy.

Then she slipped back into the blackness.

An unknown time later, her eyes reopened. This time, things came to Kai more quickly. She could see that the room she was in was small, almost tiny, and that the door on one end wasn't the kind with a knob. It was a rolling door, like in an equipment bay or a garage. She could still feel the vibration beneath her and could still hear the odd humming. Both of those things seemed to mean more now, but her head still hurt and she still felt blurry. She told herself to forget it, that she could figure it out later.

She rolled her head to the side and suddenly remembered what she'd been unable to grasp before, about the person who'd been with her. *Doc.* Doc Stahl had been with her. And then, with her fog clearing, she noticed that Doc was *still* with her, now about ten feet away, shackled to a bed the same as she was, his arms up and his legs chained to the bed's foot. Or maybe it was a cot that he was on. Whatever it was, it looked industrial and was bolted to the metal floor.

"Doc!"

But he was out cold. His chest rose and fell in a slow, hitching rhythm.

Kai rolled her head to the other side, trying to get a feel for the room. The ceiling was metal too. The overhead light wasn't hanging; it was affixed to the ceiling inside of a small metal cage. When she tried looking at the other wall, she felt wetness on her cheek and realized that she could now make sense of an acid smell that had been bugging her. She'd rolled into her own vomit.

She winced then shoved the thought from her mind. It was what it was. And as the fog cleared, Kai slowly put the puzzle's pieces together: the metal room, the vibration, the humming, the rolling door at the far end. She was in a vehicle of some sort. Maybe a train, or a high-speed cargo shuttle. It was impossible to estimate their speed because whatever her room was, it wasn't accelerating or braking. If it was a mag train or a shuttle in open country, she could easily be moving at three hundred miles per hour, maybe more.

Where were they going?

But she still wasn't feeling all that well. Her headache and nausea reasserted themselves, and again she lost consciousness.

When she woke again, she found herself squinting into

blinding sunlight. The door of her conveyance had opened, and outside she could see what was either brownish cracked concrete or baked land. She squinted, trying and failing to block the sun with her chained hands. She didn't have to suffer the light for long, though, because Beamers began tromping inside. One of them blindfolded her, and another seemed to be blindfolding Doc when her vision was obscured. Her hands and feet were unshackled, and then her hands were re-secured behind her back.

She allowed herself to be led from the vehicle onto a floor that clicked underfoot like polished stone. She thought briefly of running, but that would be stupid. The Beamers surely had guns, and she was blind and had no use of her arms. If she could be sure that there were only one or two men watching her, she might have tried fighting blind (her hearing upgrade was outstanding; she could nearly echolocate like a bat), but based on the voices she heard, there were at least six of them.

She was shoved into a room with a smooth floor then tumbled to her knees. Unable to stop her fall with her hands, she almost smashed her nose into the floor but was able to roll away and took the blow on her shoulder. Someone unshackled her hands and yanked the blindfold from her face. But before she could consider fighting again, the door of her new quarters swung shut, closing her in and her captors out.

Kai looked around, not rising, not turning, economizing her movement and taking in what was in front of her eyes. The room was pure white, perfectly cube-shaped, maybe fifty feet across. The walls were divided into smaller cubes by thin off-white lines.

Beside her, Doc was moaning. She could see that he'd taken a beating. Kai was lucky; she'd only been slumbered. Doc appeared to have been punched and kicked and pummeled with batons. One of his eyes was puffy and half-shut. Blood had crusted under his nose and around his mouth. Kai crawled over to him and said his name, but he just rolled his eyes up at her and vomited.

For some reason, it was the final straw. She grew angry — not at her captors, but at the only person within range for her to yell at.

"Get the fuck up!" she spat.

"Jesus, darlin,'" said Doc, blinking. "Give a guy a minute."

"Noah Fucking West, Doc! I took out three Beamers all by myself. You couldn't do your part?"

Doc winced as if the light was painful. "My head hurts," he said. Then, with puke still on his lips, he gave Kai a perverse smile. "Did we just do some rough fuckin'?"

"Wipe that shit off your mouth, and get up!" she yelled. "Who are these people? What did you get me into, Doc?"

"Well, isn't this a motley crew?" said a voice from behind them.

Kai spun, sensing a trap and feeling stupid. She'd been so focused on Doc that she hadn't even looked behind her. Her blindfold had come off, and immediately she'd taken the easy route, choosing to lash out rather than think. She almost wanted to laugh. Now there were Beamers behind her with batons, and she'd learn her lesson.

But Kai didn't see Beamers when she turned. Instead, she saw a man with dark, messy hair wearing small round glasses. He, like Doc, appeared bruised and lethargic.

They weren't the only two prisoners in the white room.

Behind Kai was Nicolai Costa.

Chapter 7

Kai's toes dug into the gritty sand of what she suspected was the Mallorca coastline. The sun was bright. The sky was deep and blue.

A few moments ago, Kai had been in a forest filled with big, thick-trunked trees. An hour before that, she'd been in a rain forest hung with creeping vines and topped with a thick, lush canopy. Before that, it had been an underwater habitat, where she'd found herself inside a pressure bubble. Once, she'd been in a cabin by a lake. Once, she'd found herself in an empty city. There were only two things that all of Kai's various and shifting surroundings had in common, and they were that all of their varied surroundings had been empty save two other people, and that those people, in every instance, had remained Doc and Nicolai.

None of the environments were real, of course. The white, featureless room Kai had found herself in with Doc and Nicolai turned out to be a simulator — and a good one at that. If they all stayed together and if they ignored their gut feelings that something wasn't quite right, it was almost possible to believe, right now, that they *were* in Mallorca. The room's temperature had adjusted upward, and the "sun" even seemed to be mimicked by a strong radiant UV lamp. The imagery and sound were damn near perfect.

They'd been stripped of their belongings. Most of Kai's best weapons were inside her body, but their captors seemed unwilling to eviscerate her — or Doc, who she knew had several defensive add-ons of his own. She no longer had her handheld, or anything else that might broadcast time. However, according to what was normally a fairly useless enhancement Doc had in his right wrist, nearly eighteen hours had passed since they'd been tossed into the room. Kai had seen sunlight when she and Doc had been pulled from the transport, so she supposed it was nighttime now.

Beamers had been coming and going at regular intervals the whole time they'd been in the simulator. All were dressed head to toe in black, and all were men, all about the same size. All but one of them were white. Because the Beamers all wore visors and hats, it was nearly impossible to tell them apart and know how many there were in total.

According to Doc and his timekeeping wrist, their captors had been showing up to subject Kai, Nicolai, and Doc to pain pods every one and a half hours on the nose. Both the cruelty and precision thereof seemed very like Beamers. Beamers felt that The Beam's reality was superior to actual reality, so Kai began to see their captivity as a lesson. They were being trained, like dogs. They were allowed to revel in the luxury of The Beam's beautiful simulated worlds, but the only appearance of the real world for the three captives came when men in black entered to beat them. The Beam was benevolent. Earthbound reality was cruel. Yes, that sounded like Beamer thinking.

They'd slept in shifts. They'd been given containers in which to relieve themselves. They'd eaten, but all of their food had been simulated — parodies of foods assembled from raw materials by the room's compilers. Nicolai had protested, saying that by eating, they were giving the Beamers what they wanted. Doc had countered, pointing out that accepting the Beamers' pain but not their food was the product of stupid pride. After enough time, Kai and Nicolai had joined Doc and eaten. The food, though lacking in flair, was real enough to sustain them.

They'd tried attacking the Beamers twice. Neither time had gone well. Since, they'd fallen into reluctant acceptance, telling themselves that they were biding their time and taking their beatings as they were doled out.

Nobody had explained anything to them about their captivity. At all.

Kai hated the uncertainty. Why was she here? Why were Doc and Nicolai here? What did their captors want from any of them, and why weren't they just getting down to whatever it was? If they were a threat to someone, why hadn't they just been killed? What was the point of toying with them?

But despite the uncertainty and the hate and the fear and the disorientation, there was little point in asking unanswerable questions. So time passed. The environments changed. The three of them adapted, waiting and talking, steering their discussion away from forbidden topics in deference to the attention of unseen ears. Between incursions by the Beamers, they accepted what they were given. They became just three people on a beach, three people in a forest, three people in an abandoned downtown.

Now, during a quiet interlude, Doc was lazing on his back in the sun, his tan, nano-sculpted muscular arms and chest and flat stomach on display. Nicolai, who Kai felt had a similarly impressive body, was more modest, sitting in the shade of a palm tree. Kai sat between them with her toes in the sand, watching the water and waiting.

"I could go for a harem of lithe eighteen-year-olds right now," said Doc, propping himself up on his elbows. He looked around, waiting to see if the room would respond to requests. It did not. Doc swore and lay back down.

Kai rolled her eyes. "You're disgusting."

"Said the lady who sells it," Doc retorted. "That's the second time you've accused me of being a pervert, but it's how you earn credits."

"I'm fucking with you," said Kai, annoyed and not fucking with him at all. She didn't want to hear his blather. She was assessing. Her add-ons and training made her strong and fast, and she had enhancements that gave her what amounted to extra senses, but she needed to find her chance to use them. She wouldn't see it while bantering with Doc.

"What about you over there, Tonto?" Doc said, looking at Nicolai. Kai followed his gaze, wondering if Doc was referring to Nicolai's stoicism or if Doc had honestly mistaken Nicolai's Italian complexion for native NAU blood. "How's the haps for you? Enjoying your vacation? C'mon, two to one. You start talking about naked gals with me, and maybe they'll hook us up due to sheer numbers. Kai might join in on the fun once they give us chicks. You know she's into it. She's just being uptight."

Nicolai looked off into the distance, not rising to Doc's jocularity.

"I'm waiting," he said.

"Waiting for what?"

"To see what happens next."

Doc scoffed, then lay back on the sand just as the beach disappeared and was replaced by cool black dirt pocked by tufts of rough grass. The blue sky darkened to black until the only light and warmth was coming from a campfire that had appeared between them.

"Great," Doc said, sitting up and pulling on his shirt, shuffling closer to the fire's warmth. "You get vague with 'what comes next' and they give us a campfire. I *could* have some girl hanging off my knob right now, but now all I can do is make s'mores." As he said the last, a red box containing graham flats appeared at Doc's side along with a bag of marshmallows and a cube of chocolate discs. Doc laughed in spite of himself.

Camp chairs materialized beside them. They climbed onto their seats then dragged the chairs closer to the fire.

"You know," said Kai, "we're just doing what they want, behaving as if this is a real fire out in the real wilderness."

"I've never been in the wilderness, hon," said Doc. "I just know that *that* thing is hot, and I'm cold."

Nicolai nodded. "I doubt they've been in the wilderness either," he said. "This is a caricature of camping made by someone who's never been. There are no stars overhead. In the wild, you can still see a few through the lattice. The tiny noises are missing, too, and the sounds I *can* hear are echoing wrong, as if bouncing off walls that are..." He stretched down, picked up a rock, and threw it into the blackness. Where the rock struck an unseen obstruction, the night rippled like a pool of ink. "...right there, no matter how open it all looks."

"What are you, a Boy Scout?" said Doc.

Kai looked at Doc. The two men — two of her favorite clients, but for different reasons — had known one other before their internment because Nicolai was also Doc's client, but they hadn't known until today that they were both *Kai's* clients. It was easy to forget that everything wasn't already out in the open, given Doc's unflappability and his salesmanlike ability to become overly familiar with everyone instantly.

"I spent a lot of time in the wilds in the 30s," said Nicolai. "I came up from Italy and across Europe on foot with only a backpack, a crossbow, and more blindly stupid guts than you can believe."

"The *30s?* How old are you?" said Doc. Nicolai looked like he might be thirty-five or forty, but appearances, more than ever, were often deceiving.

"Old enough."

"How the hell did you get into the NAU from the Wild East?"

Kai already knew the story, but as with all Nicolai's stories, she loved hearing it. She had traced her long manicured fingers across Nicolai's chest many times in a post-coital haze as he recited her favorites. Most men today were soft. Nicolai, artistic appearances to the contrary, was hard. Today, in the civilized West, a man displayed his power in terms of wealth. But there had been a time when survival had come down to brute strength.

"I went up into France from Italy, avoiding Switzerland for obvious reasons, staying as far west as I could. Made my way to Paris then hiked north until I hit the English Channel. I wanted to score a ride through the Chunnel into England, but I didn't know about the Chunnel Crew, or the fires. Today I might have turned back when I couldn't find a conveyance that hadn't been ransacked, but I was young and stupid enough back then to just start walking right through with an air converter and my crossbow out. Most of the Chunnel, save the infernos, was pitch black…and I do mean *pitch*. I had IR goggles, but they failed halfway through, and I had to go through two sections — including the corpse of a stalled train — by feel.

"Somehow, I avoided the Crew and made it into England, but England, even then, wasn't much better. Eventually, I realized that the West was getting close to cutting itself from the rest of the world and sealing its borders, so I decided I had to find a way there or die trying. That was when they were grounding everything other than military aircraft, and Old America was blowing everything out of the sky, so as the barbarian armies came up north, I sneaked into a shipyard, stowed away on a transatlantic ship, and hoped for the best. I got lucky, and after eating rats for weeks, I arrived in Philadelphia's harbor and got into an immigration line. I hear I was one of the last — maybe *the* last — person allowed in before they closed the borders and started gunning ships."

Doc was probably impressed, but if he was, he wouldn't allow himself to show it. He speared a marshmallow on a sharp stick and started to roast it.

"And how do you know our lady here?"

"We're friends," said Kai before Nicolai could answer. Something in Doc's manner made Kai nervous, and she didn't want to add any sort of testosterone-fueled competition to their already messy situation. Outwardly, it looked like Doc was keeping cool, but there had been an edge growing in him over the past few hours. Doc didn't like to show weakness, but Kai could read it on him. Among her handful of add-ons that didn't require Beam connectivity was a heat map in her right eye. She could see Doc's pulse and how his breathing had shallowed. Fight or flight. Doc was already keyed up, and for some reason his agitation was increasing as he listened to Nicolai.

"*Friends,*" said Doc, not at all fooled.

There was a moment of quiet. In it, Kai could hear a few noises she thought might be frogs and the buzz of something she couldn't identify. Overhead, a few stars had dotted the sky. Their captors had heard Nicolai's criticism and had made adjustments. Kai hadn't been out in the wilderness much either, but the camping experience felt authentic to her. The fire was nice, and she found herself wanting to get closer.

She watched the two men over the fire's dancing orange light. They were both tense. She could see stress in Nicolai too, despite his calm exterior.

"Let's play a game," she said.

They both looked at her as if she'd suggested swimming in acid.

"Seriously. If they're going to give us a quiet night and a fire, let's use it. Let's tell our best client stories. Tell the truth.

The others have to try to keep the storyteller honest, to see if they believe it."

"Shouldn't we be drinking for this?" said Doc.

Three bottles of Clearzo appeared on the ground. Doc picked one up, raised it, and said loudly, "Anyone else not want to play while a bunch of Beamer assholes are listening?"

Nicolai looked at Doc. Kai's gaze went from one man to the other. Doc's comment should have been funny, but nobody was laughing.

Nicolai's eyes softened first. "Okay. You start, Kai," he said.

Kai watched Doc's temperature drop half a degree. Some of the tension left his neck and shoulders as he lowered the bottle.

"I had a client who wanted me to dress like a man," she began. "But not a sexy man. A fat freight driver. He brought a holo synth to make me look like I had a huge gut and was all hairy. I wore a cap and a filthy white shirt. He brought a pair of jeans with him. They smelled. He said that when I wore them, I was supposed to let my ass crack hang out."

Nicolai snickered, but Doc looked disgusted. "You did it?" said Doc.

"He didn't even want to fuck me. He just watched me walk around like that while he beat off. Paid me very well for a half hour of being a guy."

"Who was it?" Nicolai asked.

Kai smiled demurely. "I can't tell you that."

"A fat freight driver himself," said Doc, looking at his bottle.

"My clients are at the top of the food chain," said Kai, insulted. She wasn't a bargain streetwalker, and she never did anything for money that didn't amuse or please her in some way. At least not anymore.

"A high-ranking Directorate official then. They're all secretly perverts." He looked at Nicolai. Kai wondered if it was a jab. Doc practically wore an Enterprise flag on his head everywhere he went, and he knew that Isaac was Directorate. But she couldn't tell if it was a playful joke or a shrouded insult.

She let it go and shrugged, playing coy.

"How about you, Boy Scout?" said Doc, still looking at Nicolai.

"I only have one client, and our relationship is confidential. So I can't play. Should I leave?"

"Such an important man," said Doc, still using that odd, almost-joking tone. "Tell us something else then, champ. You ever kill a man when you were out marching around the Wild East like Daniel Boone?"

Nicolai took a swig from his bottle of Clearzo.

"We didn't say when you should drink," said Doc. "So is that a yes?"

Nicolai shrugged then drank again.

"Okay, I've got one," said Doc. "I had a client who used to buy a new digestive upgrade from me every month. Big fat Directorate slob — one of the few with dough to burn." Again he looked at Nicolai. "I don't think this piece of shit ever moved. He had a cush job for a while, then got a dole high enough that he didn't have to work and sat around all day like a lot of Directorate do. I had to go to him to sell to him, but I was happy to do it because he paid me so much. You know how a lot of the do-nothings have a ton of useless knowledge about one dumb thing? This guy had encyclopedic knowledge of '80s entertainment. Not 2080s...*1980s*. The whole time I'm hooking him up and helping him unpack the latest crap to send down his throat or inject so he could eat more and more and more, he's telling me about this guy named John Hughes and something called the Brat Pack. But he's telling me about it all sideways — like about Molly Whatever's later projects instead of who the fuck Molly Whatever *is*. That's the way these fucking savants are, like their obsession is something that everyone else understands and gives a shit about."

Nicolai gave Doc a polite smile. Kai watched them both.

"I sold him something to install in his throat once," Doc went on. "It cut his food like a sink disposal so he didn't have to chew. Even then, he got, like, seven varieties of digestive nano injections. Everything was centered around liquefying his food as fast as possible so he could keep eating. He'd do this *with* EndLax, not instead of it. You know how EndLax will turn you into a bottomless pit and give you one meal of insane gluttony? But even then, you eventually, after hours, fill up, right? Laws of physics; there's only so much space in a person. But see, this fat piece of shit had tubes going out as much as in, into a reclaimer he could empty through a port. All he did was eat and shit out his tubes. It stank in there. He spent whatever money he had left on cleaning."

"I thought this was a drinking game?" said Nicolai.

Doc drank half of his bottle of Clearzo. Kai could see his irises already starting to shake. You couldn't bolt Clearzo like that. He'd be on the floor in twenty minutes if he kept at it.

"There ya go, Boy Scout," said Doc. "Your turn."

"I don't drink Clearzo," said Nicolai.

"Well ain't you perfect," said Doc, taking another swig.

"Maybe I should go next," Kai offered.

"I'm not finished," said Doc, even though he clearly had been. "I want to tell you more about this fucking Directorate pig who couldn't get by without making his body half robot, like a weak piece of…"

"What's wrong with you?" Kai snapped. She and Doc had had the add-ons conversation too many times. Doc sold enhancements for a living, and Kai had bought most of her significant number from him. She felt that everyone could use a little mechanical help to be their best self, and Doc usually agreed.

"What?"

"You *sell* enhancements. You have plenty yourself."

Doc shrugged. Kai didn't know what to make of Doc's spiny mood, but now she was getting pissed, too.

Doc took another sip of Clearzo. "Hey, I thought this was a game where we tried to outdo each other. That's all I'm trying to do, sunshine, is outdo my boy here's fantastic wilderness story and his outdoorsman knowledge." He gave Kai a toothy smile. "Now…if this is a drinking game, I know *you* drink. You've downed shots between sucking my…"

"Fine," said Kai, re-crossing her legs. "You want to see if I can out-do your story? I can. I'll tell you about another of my clients. Most of the guys who I work with are okay, but in the end, it's all just business. But one time, a man took me out to dinner, and…"

"I've taken you out to dinner," said Doc. He took another sip.

"This one *just* took me out to dinner. Twice. That's all we did those two times."

"That's one hot story, sunshine."

"But," Kai continued, running her fingers through her long dark hair and then trailing them down her neck, "on the third date, when the check came, I insisted on paying. The guy fought for a moment, but then I said I was insisting because I wanted for him to owe me a favor."

Kai almost smiled at the memory. She'd had men before who wanted to date her and "get to know her," but those cases fell somewhere between annoying and pathetic. Kai was excellent at what she did and had spent vast amounts of time and credits perfecting the art of making her clients feel loved, as if they were her boyfriends rather than paying customers. It was one of the things that made her so in-demand and allowed her to charge exclusive clients such exorbitant prices, but a side effect was that sometimes guys fell in love with her. Kai didn't have to turn them down; she subtly cut them off with an anti-pheromone, and they stopped being interested and eventually didn't come back.

But it had been different with the client she was talking about now — with Nicolai. She'd met him at a Directorate dinner that she'd been attending with a member of the Senate. She, Nicolai, and the senator found themselves at the same table. The senator got drunk and hit her then said something coincidentally on-point about how her mother must have been terrible to raise a daughter who turned to whoring. Rather than retaliating, Kai was so shell-shocked that she simply walked off. Nicolai found her outside, eyes wet and loathing her own weakness. He had managed to offer her a ride home without sounding like he was trying to be a knight in shining armor. In Kai's world, every intimate encounter ended in sex, so she'd been ready to give him a freebie by the time he dropped her off, but he hadn't asked, or seemed to want it.

Kai told Doc (and Nicolai, for Doc's sake) about how this mystery client had come to check on her the next day and the day after, and that each time they'd had a platonic, being-there-for-you dinner. Doc rolled his eyes through the story, and Nicolai watched her with an unreadable expression. Then Kai explained that on the third "date," when she'd insisted on paying the bill, that the "favor" she'd wanted was sex.

"That's the first and only time I've ever had to ask for it," she said. "I thought he'd be too gentlemanly to do it, though. He knew I was an escort, and maybe would think I was dirty. But that didn't happen at all."

Doc rolled his eyes.

"We barely made it back to his place." She smirked. "We were tearing each other's clothes off in the cab. And when we did get inside and got the door closed, it was like he could read my mind. He spoke to me like I wanted to be spoken to. He touched me in all the right places. He took his time, and it lasted for hours. And the things he could do with his cock…"

"Please," said Doc.

"Everything else is *nothing* by comparison," said Kai, leaning forward in her camp chair, toward Doc. Her voice had turned into a taunting purr, and a hot feeling was creeping up the back of her neck. "No other lover has *ever* been able to measure up, literally or figuratively. I can fake my way through it with other clients, but *nobody* holds a candle to the guy I can't bring myself to think of as a client, even when he pays me. I hear him in my head when I'm with the others. I feel his hands on my skin, his tongue on my…"

"Noah Fucking West," said Doc, his face finally, satisfyingly, losing its cocksure expression.

But as Doc looked away, it was like a bubble popped for Kai. She felt suddenly and uncharacteristically embarrassed, aware that Nicolai was giving her a strange look. She blinked and leaned back, disoriented. She'd gotten so caught up in trying to jab Doc that she'd gotten carried away, and had said too much.

She tried giving Nicolai a jesting smile, to show him that it was all just part of the game.

Doc said, "If that's the craziest thing you've ever done with a client, then I've grossly misjudged what it is you do. *We've* done crazier stuff than that."

Nicolai looked at Doc. Something in his eyes shifted.

"I didn't know you hired escorts, Doc," said Nicolai. "You must spend all your time telling her how great you are."

"Someone has to," said Doc. He wore a grin that sat halfway on his face, like it was hiding something.

"Some men pay women so that they can feel better about themselves," Nicolai explained.

"Some men pay women then forget it's just a transaction," Doc retorted. "It's really sad."

"That's the problem with you, Doc," said Nicolai, slowly shaking his head of messy black hair. "You think everyone's like you."

"Hey, I'm just honest, Scout. I pick my path and keep my feet on it." He lowered his voice then turned to Kai. "I know you won't believe this, sweetheart, but some people sell their souls for cash then spend all their time wishing they could be something else."

Kai watched Nicolai's eyebrows draw together. Nicolai had the heart and spirit of an artist, but Isaac Ryan had plucked him from the rabble when he'd first come to the NAU, and Nicolai, fiercely loyal, had ended up Directorate by circumstance. It was a constant sore spot — one Nicolai must have shared with Doc before purchasing his creativity add-ons.

"You're drunk," said Nicolai.

"You're a sellout," said Doc. He stood and walked closer to the fire, now inches from Nicolai's camp chair.

"Sit down, Doc," said Kai.

"What did you do to get us all picked up, Doc?" said Nicolai, looking up. "Finally sell the wrong defective add-on to the wrong person?"

Doc opened his mouth to answer, but Kai seemed to be the only one of them who remembered that they *weren't* actually sitting around a campfire but were instead prisoners locked in a simulator. Doc was about to say something revealing, so she stomped hard on his foot.

"The *fuck?*" said Doc, staring at her.

She stared back until finally, he seemed to understand. But then he raised his foot, planted it on Nicolai's chest, and pushed him backward onto the ground.

Nicolai fumbled into an untidy heap. Then, untangling himself from his chair, he rolled and came to his feet. He walked forward until the two men — the tall, broad-shouldered upgrades dealer and the smaller, darker speechwriter — stood chest to chest. They stared at each other, the air hot with tension, until two Beamers entered the room, breaking their campsite illusion.

"Hit him," one of the Beamers said to Doc.

"Don't let that fucker get away with disrespecting you like that," said the other Beamer to Nicolai.

"Dream on," said the first Beamer. He pointed at Nicolai then poked his partner in the chest. "You think that little bastard can take my guy? He'd be squashed."

The second Beamer also pointed to Nicolai. "Are you kidding? Look at his eyes. That's a kid who's been fighting his entire life. I'll bet he's like a ninja. What kind of ninja shit can you do, kid?"

Nicolai, who was probably older than the Beamer who'd called him "kid," said nothing. The arrival of the Beamers had broken the spell for Nicolai, and his angry expression was already gone. Doc's expression, however, had been lubricated by drink and remained livid.

"Hit him," said the first Beamer, again speaking to Doc. "Prove me right, and I'll have the room give you a pie."

"I'll have it set *you* up with a naked chick," said the second Beamer, looking at Nicolai.

"Two chicks and a pie," said the first Beamer, to Doc.

"Six chicks."

When neither man moved, the first Beamer walked over to Kai and pressed his pain pod against her neck. "Prove me right, or I'll turn this pod high enough to make her neck muscles snap her spine."

Kai was considering her fight options when movement caught her eye. Beside her, Doc reared back and punched Nicolai hard enough in the face to make his feet leave the ground. Nicolai struck the dirt hard. The first Beamer hooted in victory and raised his hands, then said, "Watch this!" to the other man. When his "watch" command was followed by nothing, Kai assumed he was replaying slow-motion video of Doc's punch in their visors to gloat.

Kai ran to Nicolai. The Beamers watched her and then left the room, one laughing and the other sulking. Nicolai was unconscious, a sea of red swallowing one eye. Doc's muscles had been enhanced with carbon nanotubes and scavenger nano injections, and that had been a hell of a hit — far harder than it should have been.

"I had to," said Doc, standing over her. "He was going to kill you."

Kai lashed out with one leg and struck Doc in the chest. Just as he fell toward the campfire, the scene changed, and Doc struck grass in an open prairie rather than flame, avoiding well-deserved burns by milliseconds.

Chapter 8

CRUMB'S HORSE trotted along beside Leah, who was riding Missy. They could have doubled up on one horse, but Crumb smelled horrible. There was a strange thing that happened with Crumb that nobody could put their finger on that made him especially pungent on some days, and today was one of those days. Leah had a theory about it. She thought that every once in a while, the food in Crumb's gray beard reached a critical mass and began to ferment. At those times, he wafted an especially rancid odor that was partially BO and partially something acidic, like spoiled dairy.

On his separate horse, ten feet distant and safely out of smell range, Crumb continued to ramble about persecution and conspiracies. But as they rode through the peaceful mountain trails on such a near perfect day, Leah found herself not minding Crumb's rambles. It was soon background, as much a part of the scenery as the birds or chattering squirrels. Besides, Crumb couldn't help himself. There were people in the Organa community who were far more irritating than Crumb because what they did and said, they did and said willingly. Crumb had been this way, an eccentric and integral part of the Organas who couldn't help what he was, for as long as Leah had been alive.

Hoofbeats struck the hard clay, and Crumb said, "Back in my day, we could take a man and put him on The Beam, and he'd live forever. Did you tell Leo? Leo is the Wizard of Oz! The wonderful Wizard of Oz. Noah Fucking West!" Then he started to sing a song about this Wonderful Wizard.

Leah didn't know who the Wizard of Oz was — if said wizard was anything — but something about the day and Crumb's song and the scenery made her thoughtful, and she found herself realizing that once Crumb had been young. She wondered if, rather than being a crazy memory from the now, Oz had been a sane memory from long ago. Maybe in his younger days Crumb had been normal, and something inside had broken later on. They could only guess at his age, but it was possible that he'd gotten age-extension treatments before the Organas had met him. Not nanos; they'd scanned him and knew him to be unenhanced. But if he'd had a few rejuvenations with temporary refurbishment nanos? Well, then it was possible he could be over a hundred. An artificially aged man wouldn't be out of place with the Organas either; that was the funny thing. They all had their high-tech secrets. It was just more evidence that as pure as most Organas tried to be, most were hypocrites when you got right down to it.

But hey, Leah, with her own enhancements, wasn't pointing fingers. The way she saw it, you could fight fair and die, or you could cheat and have a chance at winning. If that made her a hypocrite and a heretic, then so be it.

They'd been on the trail for almost two hours. It wound away from the village, down a rather treacherous slope into a valley, then back up around a dozen or more slow switchbacks. It wasn't well traveled, but that was the point. The mountain towns weren't usually hardwired into The Beam; the people up here who wanted to access it did so via handhelds. It was a very one-dimensional experience, not unlike how people a hundred years ago experienced the Internet before even Crossbrace (let alone The Beam) was a twinkle in Noah West's eye. But given what Leo wanted Leah to do with Crumb, she needed something very specific. She needed a connection that was hardwired but ancient, fast and reliable but forgotten — like what she'd find in the cabin in Bontauk.

The town of Bontauk had bloomed and died well before Leah had come into the world, but at the end of its life it had been home to a man named Vance Pilloud, who'd come into the mountains not because he was poor (as was the case in much of Appalachia), but because he was rich. He'd wanted to be left alone, and the mountains were one of the only places still available where "alone" was the rule. He'd built himself a small but very nice house on a large swatch of land and then, because he didn't want to be totally cut off, paid for a Quark affiliate to lay a fiber line to his door.

Pilloud hadn't lasted long in the mountains. He'd had a massive heart attack and died merely three years after completing his ranch, then had lain dead in the house for a week before anyone found him. His property went abandoned and was repeatedly raided. Now, twenty years later, the house was a decrepit and mostly burned shell on an overgrown patch of land. But the line was still there, and that was good enough for Organa's best young mind.

Crumb said, "The munchkins, Leah!"

The day was beautiful. The air was clear and clean and unpolluted — something that Leah, who spent much of her time in District Zero, could appreciate more than most Organas. Breathing the clean mountain air, she found herself unperturbed by her companion's rants. Crumb was a character, a part of their lives. In many ways, he was like an enthusiastic slow child. So she played along with him, smiling, her pink dreadlocks swinging with the horse's slow rhythm.

"Oh yeah, Crumb? What about those munchkins?"

"They're everywhere!"

"You mean now?" She looked around theatrically, as if afraid her horse might step on one of the munchkins…whatever they were. She assumed from the name that munchkins were small, but she supposed they could also just be hungry: eager for munching.

"No," said Crumb, his eyes serious in their cradles of wrinkles. "Of course not! They're with the Wizard!"

"Where's the Wizard, Crumb?"

"We're off to *see* the Wizard," Crumb explained. "The Wonderful Wizard of Oz."

Leah felt herself chuckle. "We're going to hook you up to The Beam, you old nut."

"We're off to see the Wizard!"

Leah held both hands up, despite the fact that she knew better than to lay this particular horse's reins across the saddle horn even for a moment. Given the vehemence in Crumb's voice, the gesture of contrition seemed necessary.

"Where is the Wizard, Crumb?"

Crumb wasn't listening. He was rummaging in his beard, which he seemed to use as a hairy backpack. He pulled some odd scrap of food from deep in its gray hairs and slipped it into his mouth.

They finally emerged from the forested part of the trail, which was good because overhead clearance had been getting worse and worse on the old path for the past few minutes. Leah reminded herself to check her head for ticks when she got back, and to ride out sometime soon with clippers to clear the path.

The path didn't take them into what remained of Bontauk's pathetic town center. It took them to the edge of Pilloud's old property. So they crossed a large open field, past some fallen fencing and through a small sea of very tall grass, and walked up to the house. It looked like the house had been burned again since she'd last been here, and the place seemed to have fallen to another round of raids. There wasn't anything left for raiders to steal, but the house's shell looked big enough to be tempting, even as burned and decimated as it was. Eventually, she knew they'd burn it down entirely and people would lose any cause to raid it, but for now an entire wing was still standing. That was where they needed to go.

Leah tied both of their horses to a remaining fencepost. Crumb hopped down at her command and followed her inside the house. He pulled off bits of conventional, non-Beam plaster as they entered the old house and, Leah felt quite certain, began to eat it. She lost him for a while as he went into another room and pissed. When he found her again, kneeling over the FiGlass port with her toolkit, he held a small metal bowl covered with painted kittens that was rusted through and had a hole in its bottom. Crumb clutched it like a jewel.

She looked up at the gray-haired old man with an air of getting down to business.

"Crumb, do you know what we're doing here?"

"We're off to see the Wizard."

"I need to hook you up to The Beam. *Directly* to The Beam. Leo thinks there's something in that melon of yours that we need to know about, and it'll be firewalled if it's there. I can't hack into a mind. I'm good, but not that good. We need The Beam as an intermediary. The Beam is able to talk to neurons, and I'm able to talk to The Beam with this." She tapped the small rectangular port behind her ear. "So this is going to be me rooting around in your mind, through The Beam. We're basically putting miles and miles of cable between us even as we sit here so that we'll have the tools and the mutual language to communicate. Do you understand?"

Crumb seemed to concentrate very hard. Leah expected him to nod stupidly or to walk away, but he didn't. The focus in his eyes — for Crumb — was intense. Finally, with both hands jittering, he said, "I want to see the Wizard."

"Come over here."

Crumb sat down and scooted closer to the wall, where Leah had uncoiled twenty feet of FiGlass line she'd ripped from the wall the last time she'd been here almost a full year before. Soon, the rest of the house would burn, and the FiGlass would melt and she'd need to dig it out of the dirt where it crossed the yard, but for now, the house offered shade and shelter.

As if he understood, Crumb turned so that the back of his filthy head was facing her. Leah fought nausea at his stink.

She tapped him on the shoulder so that he swiveled his head to look at her, then held up a Plasteel device that looked like a massive black spider.

"I call this 'The Hat,'" she said. "It's like one of those temperamental, sometimes-they-kinda-work experimental immersion rigs, except that there are no user outs. So you won't see or hear the feed like you would with a rig. This is read-and-meta only. To whatever extent I can get in, it'll allow me to download what's in your head and let The Beam talk to the metadata underlying our handshake. But to you, it'll just feel like sitting there with a tight hat on your head. Do you understand?"

Leah looked at Crumb, saw that there was zero chance he understood a word of what she was saying, and slid the device onto his head. There was a knob at the top of the Hat, and the fingers of the spiderlike contraption pointed down the back of his neck, beside his ears, and over his forehead. She picked up the end of the FiGlass line, checked the coupler, and found it intact. The male operator's connection on the other branch of the line looked okay too. That was good. She'd brought what was needed to wire new connectors onto raw cable, but doing so took time. This made things much easier. She plugged one connector into Crumb's Hat and stuck the smaller, rectangular connector into the concealed port behind her ear. With the connection made, she immediately saw the controls appear in her mind. She didn't see the controls with her eyes, which still showed her Crumb and the room. The controls and the rest of what came next would happen deeper down and felt more like the "sight" that occurred within imagination. It had been disorienting at first, but by now, Leah was used to it.

In front of her, Crumb was playing with a bug, heedless of the contraption on his head. But at least he was sitting still. Leah had been afraid he would want to walk around. But Crumb was being compliant even if he didn't understand — something that was almost shocking given his status as the town crazy.

"Crumb, I'm going to try to enter your head. Is that okay with you?"

Crumb said nothing.

"Crumb?"

He turned, meeting her eyes. It could be Leah's imagination, but looking back into Crumb's eyes, it was as if some of the crazy had left them.

"I'd like your permission," she said. "What I'm about to do is kind of an invasion. So is it okay with you if I access your mind?"

Crumb nodded vaguely. It would have to be enough. She doubted he understood, but she'd done her best. What Leah was about to do was a sort of mind rape, and she wanted the closest thing to consent she could possibly get.

"I won't be able to get in at first," she said. "It'll take a while, for two reasons. One, minds have a natural firewall. We usually think of it as repression or mental defenses. Conscious, top-of-mind information is easiest to identify, but we know that whoever you are, that information isn't top-of-mind. So this is going to be closer to an art than a science, and a lot relies on my intuitive abilities — of which I have many, fortunately." She smiled, trying to affect good bedside manner.

Crumb was no longer listening. Still, Leah found herself wanting to speak. She was beyond uncomfortable, trespassing in someone else's mind. She wasn't exaggerating about it being an art. Hell, it was closer to *trance* than art, and what she didn't want to tell Crumb was that before working on the connection, she'd sneaked away from him and done a rather large dose of moondust. Delving required a fugue. But who wanted a drug addict rummaging around in their brains?

She went on, knowing she was whistling in the dark.

"The second reason is due to The Beam itself. People hook up all the time, and nobody wants their brain hacked while they're doing so. The encryption and firewalling around hookups like this are the toughest stuff a hacker can run into. It's incredibly difficult to plow through."

"I was once a mason," Crumb said, flicking at a piece of stray plaster.

Leah sighed and went to work. She closed her eyes, stilling her mind. She operated the controls, mentally pushing the buttons that were available to anyone with a port like hers. She sniffed into The Beam, shook hands with Crumb's feed, and began speaking to it. At first, she saw what anyone with access could see — no different than the most basic Beam page, readable like a billboard. She saw that all of his identity fields were blank, but that he'd self-identified as "Crumb," which was almost touching. The other fields staying blank wasn't suspicious in itself. People today were sometimes still born without Beam IDs as she herself had been. Identifiers also occasionally went missing or were deliberately obscured for privacy.

She let her mind slip, easing into the moondust trance. The sensation was like sinking below Crumb's first layer as if it were the placid surface of a lake. Her thoughts grew darker. She could no longer feel her body. She let herself settle into Beamspace, her moondust-augmented mind spreading out and seeing the data as if it were bits of furniture in a room or fish in a sea. She could put any mask on the connection she wanted, but the one that seemed to work best for Leah was the visual metaphor of an immense rabbit warren filled with interconnected tunnels. She could "go down" any of the tunnels, parts of her mind touching Crumb's, processed through the interpreters in an outlying, untrackable sector of The Beam. So she tried one of the tunnels and saw it branch into dozens of other tunnels. She tried another, finding even more options. In her mind, the metaphor shifted until instead of tunnels, she saw a huge bank of tubes lined up like a honeycomb — a warren for yellow-and-black striped flying rabbits with wings and stingers. Her mind flew to one of the cells, found it filled with metal. She went to another and found the same.

She pulled back, hovering. This was strange. The rabbit warren and hive constructs were usually adequate. Brains were complicated, but in the end they were just big computers. Yet Crumb's mind was so much more complex and so much more secure than she was used to. She couldn't burrow her way in, which was how hacking normally felt to her. It was shocking, really. Leah figured getting into Crumb would be like pushing through mud. Her concerns, now that she was in, revolved around a fear that the warren tunnels might collapse under pressure, not an inability to get in or to find the correct path among hundreds or thousands.

She told her mind to fly out, to tap at the metal filling one of the tunnels. The metal was impassible, the ground around it hard. So she saw herself scratching at it, forging a new path, trying to dig around the metal representing Crumb's mind's protections. The dry earth wouldn't move. So she doubled her effort, mentally freeing her next-level hacker's tools, and scratched at the dirt with a giant claw. But the earth still wouldn't do more than sift away, so Leah switched to a kind of explosive ram and struck at the tunnels. Immediately, the metal started to twist inside the holes, bending the entire network. It was like she was trying to punch through an unbreakable metal can, but rather than puncturing through, her efforts were denting it instead. It was like trying to remove a screw and stripping its head — her own attempts to free the screw rendered removal impossible.

Alarmed, Leah pulled all the way back and opened her eyes. Crumb was still quiet in front of her, the plugged-in Hat on his head. She tapped him on the shoulder. He turned.

"Who are you?" she said.

"Crumb," he answered.

"Who else? Who were you before you came to us?"

"Crumb."

She looked at him for a long moment, trying to understand what she'd seen. His mind was, without question, the most complex she'd ever run across. It seemed to be filled with bulletproof security, but the moondust fugue was as intuitive as it was analytical, and something inside Leah told her she wasn't just experiencing security. It was as if Crumb's brain itself was incredibly advanced. She might have understood if she were trying to hack the mind of a genius — Leonardo DaVinci, Albert Einstein, maybe Noah West — but this was *Crumb*. She'd known him all her life, and he was out of his fucking gourd. So it *had* to be just security, but even that seemed odd. Why would anyone go so far to protect such a simple mind?

"Crumb," she said.

He continued to look at her, still surprisingly compliant.

"I can't get in. I'd have to be more forceful to do so."

"We can't see the Wizard? The wonderful Wizard of The Beam?"

"What did you say?"

"Oz," said Crumb.

"Your mind is locked down," she said, blinking away the strangeness. "I can't get into it without hurting you."

Crumb looked earnestly back at her. "I want to see the Wizard."

She reached for the connector on Crumb's Hat, but his

hand beat her to it. He put one hand over the port, then his second hand over Leah's as her hand touched his.

"I want to see the Wizard," he said, his voice soft, almost pleading.

"Do you understand what's happening here?"

Crumb said nothing.

"I'm afraid I'll kill you. I've never seen anything like it. Your mind seems to have a crumple zone — an intentional failure point. If I can't unlock what's in there, the system seems to have decided it would rather collapse than allow me in by force."

"I want to see the Wizard," Crumb whispered, now sounding desperate.

Leah pulled her hand away, leaving the connector in Crumb's Hat. Then he looked forward again, waiting, as if they hadn't just spoken, but Leah couldn't shake the feeling that she'd just had one of the most meaningful exchanges anyone had ever had with Crumb. Nobody *ever* knew what Crumb meant or wanted, but right now, Leah felt like she did.

"Okay," she whispered.

Leah closed her eyes and allowed herself to settle back into the fugue. She found herself in front of the odd hybrid of rabbit warren and honeycomb, her mind struggling to assimilate the complexity of Crumb's mind and security. She flew forward, found the earth as hard as before, and again struck at it. Everything again began to dent; she wasn't going to get through without collapsing the whole works. It wasn't a question of risk. The chances of failure, if Leah simply tried to bludgeon her way in, were absolute.

She looked at all of the metal-filled cells of the honeycomb, her conscious mind thinking of it as a puzzle. How could you solve a puzzle with no point of movement? A Rubik's Cube had to turn. A lock's tumblers had to move. But what Leah was seeing was immobile. So where could she even try? Where was the point at which access could be attempted and failed?

She looked at the wall. This wasn't all security. This mind had been complex before it was sealed. Why would a complex mind wall itself off and thereby cause its owner to become a Respero-fleeing vagrant? No, Leah intuited, this hadn't been something Crumb had done himself. It had been done *to* him. But why?

But it was the wrong question. Instead, she asked herself: What would a complex mind do when it was faced with fire-walling? What would it do to fight, even when there was no way to win?

Answer: *it would create a back door.*

Leah flew around the honeycomb, looking for access points. But there were none. She was circling surrender when she saw honey dripping from a cell near the bottom.

Honey.

Because the honeycomb was just her own mind's interpretation of what she was facing, of course it wasn't actually *honey*. It was simply something leaking — something that made sense within the larger mind (as honey made sense in a hive) and that anyone might overlook. It wouldn't be anything particularly poignant, but it could be a key. Something that might lead from clue to clue, deeper and deeper.

Leah flew to the yellow honey and touched it. An image flitted in front of her mind's eye

(a book)

visible for a thin sliver of seconds. Then the image was gone, along with the honey.

But it was enough. Leah had trained her mind to be sharp and observant, and she'd seen plenty. For that scantest of moments, she'd seen a leather volume, *JOURNAL* written on the cover. Inside, an ownership attribution: *Stephen York.*

Who was Stephen York?

She didn't know the answer, but that fleeting vision had

shown her the book inside of a larger context. It had been on a shelf with other books, in a building with a red roof, in District Zero. But that was it. That's all she had.

Then something went wrong.

As Leah watched, the honeycomb in front of her mind's eye began to shake. She suddenly intuited that the honey had been structural. In another metaphor, it might have been mortar in a building rather than honey in a comb, and her touch might have unseated enough of that mortar to cause the house of cards to fall. She braced and winced and pulled back then watched as the top half of the honeycomb bent over, now folded within the space. Then it stopped, damaged but not yet broken.

Crumb.

Leah pulled all the way back out and found Crumb unconscious on the floor. He'd crumpled, one arm pinned under himself and his face on the bare floorboards. She yanked the connection from behind her ear, pulled the Hat from Crumb's head, and rolled him over. He was alive but unresponsive. Catatonic or in a coma or…or broken inside.

"Crumb!" she yelled. She shook him, knowing it unwise, and yelled again. But he remained limp, eyes closed.

She leaned down and, for some reason she herself didn't understand, gave him a small hug.

"I'm sorry," she whispered. "I'm so sorry. I'll get you to a hospital. A *real* hospital. I promise."

Crumb, limp, said nothing.

Chapter 9

Isaac told himself some bullshit, knowing it was bullshit.

My marriage needs this, he said.

Then he inhaled his office air, smelled the Viazo's digital scent instead, and tried to pretend that he wasn't shoveling the world's largest pile of crap.

Isaac was fully immersed, marveling at an experience that Natasha no doubt had grown used to these days. Isaac didn't have much time for virtual recreation, so he hadn't used the new and extremely expensive Xenia rigs in his office nearly as often as Natasha used the ones in hers. At first, he'd been unimpressed with the top-end machines; they were barely more immersive than a simple visor-and-headphones rig. But when he'd told Natasha that, she'd laughed at him and explained that his experience was lacking because he'd never gotten the nano injection required to use the rig. How was he supposed to immerse himself if his real senses were competing with the virtual inputs? So he'd gotten the injection and had tried again — and *that* time, he'd been impressed. With the nanos in his brain tuning down his real sensory inputs, the digital inputs had taken over and made the experience almost shockingly real.

Now, as Isaac let his nanos do their work, the feeling of the Viazo's unreality faded, and he began to forget that he was actually in his office, in the rig. The experience was so real, in fact, that Isaac was able to subdue the truth: that he was inside the Viazo to procrastinate and hide. He forgot about the Directorate mob demanding answers, forgot about the Enterprise high-steppers who always seemed to beat him in debate, forgot about Micah, his younger brother, who thought he was so goddamn smart. And instead, he told himself some bullshit: that he was here to heal the fracture in his marriage.

Isaac had no time for Natasha. It was sad, but it was true. It wasn't that he didn't love her. He suspected he probably *did* love her (it made sense that he would, right? They'd been married for sixty years, after all), but time was scarce. That was the price of power and fame, and he could still maybe love his wife while also being short on hours. Hence this little artificial errand he was on right now. He wasn't here because he was hiding, right? He was here because he needed to set things right with Natasha…right?

Feeling the Viazo to be as real as reality, Isaac crossed the floor of a clean white office that he wasn't actually in and sat in a comfortable chair that didn't technically exist across from a striking young woman who may or may not have been a real person. The air smelled fresh and clean. Easing himself into the chair, Isaac felt uncharacteristically peaceful.

"Hello, Mr. Ryan," said the young woman. She was dressed professionally and was sitting behind a professional-looking wooden desk. She had shiny brown hair and full lips. Isaac guessed she was twenty or so — and that's a *legitimate* twenty, not a *faux* twenty in the way that Isaac, who'd been on earth for eighty-four years, looked to be in his faux thirties. She had beautiful green eyes and a small, upturned nose. Isaac vaguely remembered that somewhere in the Viazo preferences, you could set the clerks to nude. He wasn't sure if this woman was a clerk or a real person's avatar, but he kind of wanted to dig into the preferences and find out.

"I'd like to book a virtual vacation for me and my wife," he said, flinching as the words came out of his mouth. He suddenly realized that he didn't want the woman to know he was married. Oops.

"Of course. We already have your request," she said. "You didn't have to immerse to do the booking."

"I'm new to this," he said, feeling stupid. "I didn't know."

The girl spread her lips in a stunning smile. "It's all right, Mr. Ryan. Immersion is tricky. Do you know the Viazo?"

"I know it's exclusive."

"Beyond exclusive. You are a very powerful and attractive man."

Isaac blinked. The comment seemed extraneous. He began to wonder if he'd imagined her saying it.

"I'm sure you'll want to explore," she continued, reaching for something. The loose collar of her dress shirt opened far enough for Isaac to make out the top of a white, lacy bra. She straightened up and smiled. "There's plenty to sample inside."

Isaac reminded himself why he was here. He couldn't lie on top of his lie, so he pretended this was about him and Natasha, and tried to ignore his (possibly virtual) erection.

"I figured I'd make sure everything was okay for the trip. With my wife. You know, while I'm in here anyway."

The girl shuffled papers — actual papers; ah, the charm of virtual space — and nodded. "You are booked and fully pre-authorized. You will only need to lie in your rigs when you are ready to start. Just be sure to refill your nutrient packs before you do. If you're taking a week-long vacation, you'll need to give your nanos something to feed your body while it lies there. And, of course, they'll keep your muscles toned. You understand that our process results in zero atrophy, and that many of our happy vacationers return from time off stronger, despite a week of motionless, unaugmented reality?"

"That's what they told me."

"Ah!" she said, looking at something on the paperwork. "I see you haven't opted for time compression. Would you like to add it?"

"What's that?" said Isaac.

"Your nanos are already in your brain, down-tuning your natural inputs — and, unless you opt out of it, stimulating endorphin release," said the girl. So that was why he felt so happy and horny. "But just recently, we've also been approved to offer a patented neural process that slows your experience of time while immersed. It means that a day in real time can be made to feel like two or more days inside. It's the ultimate efficiency tool for the busy man or woman: experience your vacation in full, but only use half the time in your busy, real-world schedule."

Isaac's eyebrows rose. A way to spend the required time with Natasha without wasting a full week!

"I want that," he said.

"It comes at an extra charge," said the woman.

"How much?"

"Depends on the acceleration factor. A compression factor of two doubles the price of your vacation. One-point-five compression costs less, at…"

"How much to make my vacation take eight hours?"

Isaac thought the woman would balk, but instead she pulled out a calculator. It was a prop for effect, of course. Even if the woman was real, The Beam would give her the answer instantly.

"That's a compression factor of twenty-one," she said, looking up.

"I figure I can fit it in when I'd usually be sleeping."

"Very clever. For an extra charge, I can also stimulate the effects of a night's sleep on your body. We can move you into an alpha-theta-delta-REM progression while keeping you immersed."

"Okay," said Isaac, getting excited. He was going to get to take a week-long vacation overnight and wake up refreshed with no loss of time. Everything was coming up Isaac.

The woman touched some keys on a stylized canvas console and shuffled more prop papers. She turned to him and said, "With your week of full immersion in our Ibiza simulation, enhanced, full experience roster, with the five-star hotel and all expenses included, platinum upgrade package, time acceleration factor of twenty-one and sleep simulation, your total is…one point seven six million universal credits."

"Put it on my account."

The woman pressed something on her console then frowned.

"What?"

"It says you've reached your cap," she said, staring at the antique console screen.

"That's ridiculous," said Isaac. "Check it again."

She did, but of course it was unnecessary. The false reality of virtual space had him totally convinced. The woman wasn't "checking" anything. It was all ones and zeros, there were no mistakes, and touching a board wasn't required to run a process. The girl herself probably wasn't even real.

"I'm sorry, Mr. Ryan. You won't be able to make any purchases exceeding three hundred and sixteen thousand credits for…seventeen days."

"Our cap is fifteen million per month!" Isaac blurted. "You're telling me that I've maxed that in two weeks?"

"Well, you or…"

"Wait," said Isaac, holding up a hand.

The account, of course, was joint.

"Would you like me to…" the woman started to say, but Isaac had already called for emergency withdrawal, not bothering with the slow rising process recommended to save the brain from the trauma that could come with suddenly shifting realities.

Head spinning, feeling like the room was too dark and rotating slowly, Isaac stood inside his office and ran toward the door. He tripped, feeling vertigo, and smashed into it. His anger multiplied. He willed himself to coherence, stood, and yanked the door open. While his head was still struggling to reconcile the last shocking change in realities, he was assaulted with another; as the soundproof seal on his office popped, his ears were deluged with Beethoven, which Natasha was listening to in the living room at full volume.

Isaac wanted to make a statement. He crossed to where an illuminated window displayed *BEETHOVEN — FIFTH SYMPHONY* on the glass coffee table in front of Natasha. She was lounging on the couch, eyes closed, wearing a pink-and-white sleep mask, one arm draped casually back behind her head like a diva on a chaise lounge. He grabbed one of his own service trophies — a heavy metal civic award he'd received last year — from a shelf and threw it hard through the coffee table. The table, made of Beam glass, shattered into a million tiny safety cubes instead of sharp shards. Then the canvas, sensing a disturbance, killed the music as if Isaac had smashed the mechanism that was playing it.

"ARE YOU FUCKING KIDDING ME?" he blurted.

Natasha took the fuzzy sleep mask from her eyes with an irritating lack of alarm, then looked up at Isaac and said, "What? I thought you were in your office."

"You've got to be fucking kidding me!" he spat, his anger increasing as she stared up at him with doe eyes. "In just two weeks, you managed to…"

"Your *soundproofed* office," Natasha continued, cutting him off, "which you soundproofed so that my presence wouldn't disturb your important work."

"What the hell, Natasha? *This* is the debate you want to have, when…"

"I can listen to it at whatever volume I want without damaging my ears thanks to my cochlear upgrade," she said.

"I can hear the nuances when I play it this loud." She lowered her eyes and batted her eyelashes — something that made Isaac want to put a boot through her throat. "I *am* a musician, you know."

Isaac could only stare. "You are *unreal.*"

"What? Why do you care?"

Isaac stared at her then said, "Canvas."

The canvas made a chirp in response.

"Total expenditures of this household, month-to-date."

A soft voice said, "Fourteen million, six hundred eighty-five thousand, eight hundred, and twelve universal credits."

Natasha, unmoved, continued to stare at her husband. Her long red hair was tied up to look casual but had surely taken hours of primping. Her long, thin, pale arm was still slung over her head. Isaac found himself wanting to snap it at the elbow.

She said, "If you ask for it in NAU dollars, it'll tell you the number of cents, too."

"What have you been spending our money on? Fourteen fucking million? When we had our cap set, we received special dispensation. It was above the highest cap the Directorate allows. Impossible to hit!"

"I know," she said. "With only three hundred thousand left this month, we won't be able to buy groceries. We'll starve!"

"Answer the question."

"Cars. Planes. Vacations. What do you care? I'm buying my way out of loneliness."

Isaac rolled his head back. "Oh, *holy motherfucking...*"

"What do you care? You don't spend it. You just sit in your office and work. You take virtual meetings with your brother. You take *real* meetings with your brother. Sometimes, when I see you for two minutes, you bitch about your brother. So yes, I spent a lot of money. What does it matter to the great Isaac Ryan? Look at how much your dole is, and how much mine is. We have billions in savings. Why does it remotely matter?"

"Because people watch us, Natasha. You wonder why you end up being the target of riots? Oh, geez, I don't know. Maybe it has something to do with the fact that with Shift approaching, with everyone in both parties acutely aware of how they made the wrong choice and pretending that the other choice might have made a difference, *you* ride around in fancy cars, wearing furs, replacing 100 percent of your parts with enhancements. Who are you anymore? Should I pull up our wedding album?"

Natasha's eyes narrowed. "Don't you dare," she snarled. Their wedding, over sixty years ago, had happened before Natasha had her first nanos — fat scavengers and rejuvenators that turned her from the soulful, beloved songstress into the thin plastic doll she'd become. She'd tried several times to have their wedding photos recreated in her new image, but Isaac wouldn't allow it. He'd finally locked the photos down inside his own private files. Natasha saw her old photos as round and fat, but Isaac thought she'd been beautiful back then — in her twenties for real instead of fake, unenhanced in face and body, round enough to be a woman.

"I earned my money, and I can do what I want with it," she said.

"Sounds like Enterprise thinking," Isaac said.

"If you remember, I used to *be* Enterprise," she snapped. "*Someone* made me shift."

"For much larger pay, guaranteed."

"Pay you don't want me to spend! I could have been with your brother and not had a cap! I should be allowed to spend three, four times what I do!"

That made Isaac's skin prickle, but he couldn't let her get to him. "Fourteen million in two weeks, Natasha. You deserve the hate you get, doing that. The average Directorate dole is still under twenty-five-thousand a year. Do you know what *those* people's spending caps are?"

"Oh, fuck off, Isaac!" she shouted, standing from the

couch. "This is about equality for you? Then give your fucking money away. Be Robin Hood more than we're already expected to be. I gave up Enterprise for you. I used to have incentive! My excellence used to be celebrated, not hated! Now here I am with money I can't spend and a husband who doesn't love me, who can't write a fucking speech without his Cyrano, who spends all his time running from his problems…"

Isaac wound up and threw the award hard at the window. It bounced harmlessly off, leaving a tiny scratch. A cleaner scrambled from its garage on the floor, climbed the window, and began repairing the glass.

"Mature," said Natasha, watching the bot.

Isaac stared at his wife, furious but unsure what to say. So he turned toward his office and stalked off.

"Good idea," she said from behind him. "Keep avoiding your problems."

"Go buy some more enhancements, Natasha!" he shouted back. "Keep trying to make yourself feel young and beautiful and vibrant! Make yourself feel alive for five more seconds!"

"Canvas!" she screeched, furious. "Beethoven! Full volume!"

Music blasted into the living room as Isaac closed his office door, shutting it out. His heart was hammering. He was so angry that it took several minutes of stalking in circles and drawing deep breaths before he trusted himself not to trash his shelves, his equipment, and everything else in frustration.

When he calmed down, he sat.

Fuck her. Fuck Micah. And fuck Nicolai.

Nicolai wanted to abandon him in his hour of need? Well, he could eat shit. Isaac wasn't a puppet, or a PR tool of his brother's — a punching bag for the always-in-control Micah Ryan. Isaac was his own man, who could write and give his own speeches. Isaac Fucking Ryan was a man who could make his own decisions.

Dominic woke up sprawled on the floor, trashed, in his apartment on the twenty-second floor of the Lycos building, head on fire and mouth filled with cotton. He was still fully dressed, and his mouth *was* actually full — not with cotton wadding, but with his neckband tie, which he'd removed at some point. That wasn't good even if it made sense, which it most certainly did not. He could choke on it. And if there was a close second to choking on your own puke until you quit breathing, it was choking to death on a symbol of civilized slavery — the workingman's noose, killing him from the inside of the throat rather than the outside.

Dominic managed to roll over, still feeling nauseated and like choking on puke wasn't yet an unlikely scenario. Even the small motion hurt, tearing his core muscles as he made them work, crushing his arm under his side as if it were made of glass. His vision was splintered, almost literally; he saw two versions of his bedroom (where he apparently was), and they seemed to be cracked apart from one another with a sharp edge, like a knife's.

He wanted to call for help, but Dominic was a bachelor and lived alone. He had no one to help him. If he died with his drooling lip plastered to carpet, they'd find him that way — another moondust junkie dead. But as he thought about it (insofar as he was *able* to think with his throbbing brain), that made no sense. Moondust users didn't OD. Moondust addicts died plenty, but only from withdrawal. Moondust itself was mellow. Even after a bender, the worst you could expect was to wake up mildly dehydrated with hours gone missing. Or you could die in a car accident because you were blitzed, or step in front of a mag train because you thought Jesus was coming to hug you. But you didn't get fucked and wake up feeling like *this*.

What the hell kind of dust had Omar sent him?

Dominic forced himself to his hands and knees, felt something swell in his gut, and heaved onto the floor. His puke poured out brown and gray. *Gray*. What the hell had been gray? Or was it the dust? Dominic imagined the tiny moondust rocks turning into literal moon dust in his stomach, as if he'd eaten handfuls of ash from a fire pit. The thought churned his gut, and he threw up again. The smell made him want to start back up, but Dominic couldn't think about the puke now, or waste any more time in surrender. His housebot could handle the mess while he was at work…if he survived. He didn't have enough strength to call for his canvas, so he hoped the bot would find the barf while on patrol without his pointing it out, like a parent discovering a kid's wet bedsheets after the kid ran off embarrassed. The housebot would probably find the various puddles just fine. The thing had sucked up his copy of Yankees slugger Brian Morgensen's autograph and the cigar Dominic had bought to celebrate his fiftieth birthday, so it didn't miss much. Although given the idiot nature of AI, it seemed equally to Dominic that the bot would suck up the important paperwork on his desk and ignore the vomit entirely.

Dominic stepped into the shower, hoping it would make him feel better. It did not. He threw up again, at least satisfied that the drain would clear the liquids away. His canvas then spoke up, asking if he was okay. Dominic said he wasn't and requested a light scan. The scan reported that his vitals were fine, which was as deep as a noninvasive scan went. So Dominic asked for music, entertainment…anything to distract him. He asked for warm towels and a warm floor mat, which he never asked for. He put the news on his mirror then had it follow him back into his bedroom. He put on new clothes with fingers that were clumsy and painful. He'd taken some Novril tablets and used the never-used acupressure bot while he'd been brushing his teeth, but the usually quick fixes were taking their time to kick in.

Dominic stumbled to the balcony, barked at his canvas for a mag shuttle, and took a hoverskipper to the mag line. He got a private shuttle, not wanting to wait for a cheaper group transport because feeling like he might die and fall to the city streets below was too horrible to consider. So he forked over the twenty extra credits, clicked off the robotic driver's voice, and rode to the station (which the mag line ran directly through) in silence.

By the time Dominic arrived, his headache and pain were both mostly gone, but his mood was still foul. His skin was apparently also gray and hanging in all the wrong places — or so he was told by a scan port that some asshole had placed in front of the station's door.

The scan port was essentially a small section of the long hallway that led into the Quark wing, and it was just as judgmental. Noah West's voice told Dominic that his toxin levels were quite high and asked if he needed anonymous help with any addictions. It told him that his breath was foul and slid a small mint at him on a tray. It told him that his shirt was wrinkled and that his shirt cuffs were uneven and that his shoes were dull and scuffed. Without asking, a robotic armature reached out and tried to comb his hair. Dominic, knowing exactly what he was doing, reached up and hit the thing hard enough to break half of it off, leaving it to dangle by a cable. The assault left his hand bloody, but the release he felt was worth the blood, the repair fee, and the reprimand he'd face later.

Noah's voice, in its unperturbed and polite way, asked after the armature-breaking incident if Dominic would like a bandage and a squirt of repair nano ointment. Dominic refused, knowing full well that nano ointment would return his skin and capillaries to knitted within fifteen minutes. Instead, he wrapped a napkin around his fist, and when Noah gave him the all-clear and a green light and told him to have a nice day, Dominic told him to fuck off and die.

Dominic took a few irritated steps and put his hand on the shoulder of Damian Prince, the rookie who was manning the scan port's monitor.

"What is this bullshit?" Dominic snapped, jerking his head toward the scan port.

"Captain Long!" said Prince. "I'm sorry, sir. We've been trying to contact you all morning, but your canvas wouldn't ping you."

Dominic had installed a little hack that was quite useful for moondust junkies. He didn't have to manually put his canvas into Do Not Disturb. Instead, his apartment's sensors monitored his movements and turned calls off automatically when he was unconscious or in a trance, seeing as calls during trances were always a drag.

"I was in an important meeting," said Dominic.

"Well, sir, we had a brief outage here at the station last night. Just a system reset."

Dominic was aghast at Prince's nonchalance. "*Just* a system reset? Are you kidding me?"

The station's data was all fed directly into The Beam despite the station's shitty Beam connections at the user level. (Police data was considered vital while police officers were considered city budget expense items.) Unfortunately, a significant side effect of the city's schizophrenic attitude toward DZPD was that there were no good redundancies in place. When the connection failed, as it sometimes did, the station went totally offline. And with it, Dominic and a few others knew, went most of its security. Wireless hackers trying to access the routers while the hard line walls were down needed only to cross a few layers of encryption. Because most of the hackers used hacks employing EverCrunch compression algorithms, all they needed were thirty seconds. It was an unforgivable and shortsighted gap that Dominic had been complaining about for years.

"I'm sorry, sir. It was brief. But HQ wanted this security checkpoint set up until all of the lights are green."

"Are they green now?"

"EOD, sir. After all staff has cycled through."

"Noah Fucking West. And the servers?"

"Secure, I believe, sir."

"According to who?"

"Officer Harper, sir."

Dominic pinched the bridge of his nose. Harper was smart, but was almost a rookie himself. Harper didn't know about the glaring security gap. He probably *did* actually think everything was fine, even if it wasn't.

"How long did the system reset take?"

"I don't know, sir."

"When did it happen?"

"Around one-fifteen a.m., sir, give or take."

Dominic thanked the kid and left, but he didn't like this at all. There was an old axiom about computers that said, "Garbage in, garbage out," and it was supposed to refer to the fact that computers only made mistakes when people made mistakes programming them or giving them data — i.e., when the inputs were garbage. But in Dominic's experience, The Beam had mostly evolved beyond that quaint expression. With the advent of AI and increasingly sophisticated algorithms,

The Beam could, in most cases, either find its way around bad data or make what were essentially educated guesses. There were system outages due to failures in the lines or inferior incidental technology, but The Beam itself seldom made mistakes. What Prince had described sounded to Dominic like a hard reset or a bug, not an outage. Outages were possible, but hard resets were caused by people or intelligent programs like clerics. Bugs, as far as The Beam was concerned, were things of the past.

Harper might think the fault was accidental, but Dominic didn't buy it.

His anger now turning to concern, Dominic crossed into his office, started up his console, and began checking the system logs. His sector of the station's canvas, being the chief's sector, had an extra layer of security. Its logs were independent from and duplicated off of the server, then stored in protected memory. This memory was physically shuffled every half hour on a device called a data carousel that was sometimes a pain in the ass, but for which Dominic was suddenly thankful.

He went to the wall behind his office chair and removed a panel. Behind it was a large wheel with vertical slots that reminded Dominic of an ancient slide carousel Grandy had used to project family photos onto the wall until the day he died. There were forty-eight slots in the wheel, and each held a data card representing a half hour's worth of everything in the station from surveillance to logs to bookings. Every thirty minutes, a mechanical arm removed the card from the backup drive and placed it in a slot in the wheel, then replaced it with the next half hour's card.

The device was clunky and non-compact by design. Everything the carousel did could have been handled digitally and without moving parts, but as The Beam became more and more ubiquitous, the only way to truly isolate data was via its physical removal. Unless someone walked into Dominic's office and used human hands to remove or alter the data cards, it would be safe from hackers.

Dominic removed his handheld, turned off its wireless connectivity, then wrapped the thing in digital foil just to be sure it couldn't broadcast. He removed the card from the carousel slot marked *01:00-01:30* and slid it into the handheld. He quickly scrolled through the logs and found what he was looking for:

01:13:02 SYSTEM FAIL
  01:14:12 SYSTEM RESET

THERE WAS no data at all in the seventy seconds between those two entries. Normally, the entire system's activity was logged six times a second using EverCrunch compression, collapsed for easy viewing and expandable by anyone with sufficient access to view the 360 backups made each minute. But at 1:13 a.m., there had been a reset, and it had taken seventy seconds to restore logging — an eternity in which any skilled hacker would be able to remove or copy any files they wanted without leaving a trace.

"Shit," he said aloud.

He compared the file tree before and after and found no significant difference between the two backups, meaning that nothing seemed to have been deleted. No files other than the self-referential meta logs had changed modification dates. So if someone had been inside, they'd been snooping, probably copying. Someone searching for information.

"Chrissy," he said, talking to the handheld.

The handheld, recognizing his voice, chirped.

A soft female voice — not Noah's; Dominic had changed that default immediately — said, "Validation, please."

Dominic said his name, pressing his thumb onto the hand-held's screen.

The handheld, recognizing his voice and thumbprint, chirped, then said, "Thank you, Dominic. What can I do for you?"

"Compare the three minutes of logs prior to system failure entry at oh-one-one-three-oh-two."

"What would you like to know about the comparison?"

"Project the file trajectory of any activity during that period."

File trajectory wasn't a term Dominic had ever heard anyone else use, but he'd been working with this particular handheld long enough for it to know what he meant. He wanted to know what people had been up to, where they'd been snooping, and where they'd probably been headed — and hence what they might have done while the lights were out.

"There were four users during that time period," said the handheld in its soft feminine voice. "One was officer Harper, doing his hard backups. One was an outside access port, 048390, labeled as Brooklyn sub-PD, searching for a suspect in recent bookings named Dotson, Wyatt. The third was the Quark daemon. The fourth was anonymous FTP, looking at…"

"FTP?" Chrissy might as well have said someone had ridden into the office with the Pony Express and sent telegrams while listening to music recorded on phonograph cylinders.

"Yes, sir."

"FTP hasn't been used in eighty years," Dominic said.

"Records show IBM 286 processor, connecting at 1200 baud…"

"Are you fucking kidding me?"

"No, Dominic. Serial of Lima-three-three-tango."

"Noah Fucking West," said Dominic. They weren't even being careful. Everything about the entry was spoofed and clearly designed to be found, because someone had thought it hilarious. 286 processors and 1200 baud modems weren't much newer than his great grandfather's slide carousel. And the serial? L33t, the old hacker dialect? Yes, someone was having a shit ton of fun while committing high crimes.

"Where were they going? Can you predict their trajectory?"

"Your files would be my guess, Dominic," said the soft voice. "They opened files all over the system prior to the outage, but it looks to me like misdirection. The pattern suggests intentional subterfuge intended to make it look like they went for arrest records, but if they'd been after arrest records, they wouldn't have…"

Dominic killed the voice, in no need of details. If Chrissy intuited that they'd been after his files, he believed her. He removed the data card, slipped it into his pocket, and returned the handheld to broadcast mode. Before shutting it down, he thanked the voice, wondering what it said about him that his most cordial relationship was with an artificial person.

There was plenty in Dominic's files that an intruder might have been after, but only one thing he cared if anyone found. He pulled up his console then clicked through to bookings and cross-referenced those against the tracker in his uniform shoe. Being careful not to open any files and disturb the footprints, Dominic pulled up a window containing one particular tracking set and another containing a single day's booking records. He closed his eyes, whispered a prayer, and looked at the open dates for each. Both files had been opened the previous night, meaning that the intruder had been looking for exactly what he'd feared.

Dominic slumped into his chair. "Shit," he said.

The vagrant. The fucking vagrant, and his own fucking compassion that had made him act in a way he shouldn't have.

Once upon a time, Dominic had had a sister who was four

years younger than him. They'd not always gotten along because she'd required so much of his parents' attention. At the time, Dominic hadn't understood why; he hadn't known what Down's Syndrome was or that unregistered clinics were the only hospitals that still permitted Down's births. He hadn't understood why, after his father died and his mother had gotten an actual paper letter under the door, she had spent two weeks crying, then three years taking his sister to special doctors, special schools, and finally special people who would only do business in abandoned places that made Dominic, then sixteen, nervous. Even after their mother died in a car accident, Dominic hadn't stitched it all together — not until six full years later, when he found himself his sister's guardian and received her final Respero decision. The board referenced the letter that Dominic's mother had received nearly a decade earlier and said that the board was very sorry, but the subject had reached age eighteen, and her brain was still not growing to spec. A summons to her Respero dinner was attached.

Respero was something many people had whitewashed into "graduations" (rich people's dinners were extravagantly catered and populated by guests popping EndLax so they could fill their stomachs like bottomless pits), but Dominic, jaded from a young age, saw right through them. Dominic saw Respero for what it was: *murder*.

So rather than delivering his sister to her euthanasia, he'd started to dig, using all of the skills the police academy taught him for all the societally wrong reasons. The board had given the family two weeks to prepare her dinner, but within ten days Dominic discovered a hideous truth: for the right number of credits paid to their families, it was possible to buy terminally ill people to stand in for Respero.

That was Dominic's first association with Omar, the first time Dominic was forced to choose the lesser between two evils. He sold out, becoming Omar's inside-the-system moondust liaison in exchange for enough credits to buy Chrissy's replacement.

It took Chrissy another fifteen relatively happy years of life spent in Appalachia to die of natural causes, but both the lesson and the wound had stayed with Dominic through the years. So when he'd been called to Times Square to apprehend a ranting vagrant a few years later, he remembered what he'd learned about Respero. The state had ordered Dominic to take the man to a free center immediately, but Dominic had sensed something in Crumb that he couldn't ignore. There was a desperate look in his eyes — a kind of pleading intelligence that wasn't quite able to claw its way to the surface of his crazy, scraggly bearded exterior. Dominic was still in his cheap apartment at the time but had just gotten his designation advancement and the correspondingly large Directorate pay dole. So he'd used the surplus credits to buy another body and had shuttled the man up into the mountains to live out his days, the same as Chrissy.

And now, someone knew. The record Dominic's tracker had made of his first encounter with the vagrant and the file showing that the vagrant's ID hadn't appeared on the same day's duty roster (booking him through to Respero) had both been opened last night during the system outage.

Someone knew, and that someone had surely made copies.

It was enough of a betrayal to bust a captain to nothing — or maybe send him to an elegant dinner and a bitter dessert.

| Episode 3 |

Chapter 1

JANUARY 15, 2037 — District Zero

NICOLAI LOOKED DOWN at the two small pink pills sitting in the tiny dish perched atop a small plate as it was set in front of him by a white-gloved waiter. His first thought was that the dish was unnecessary. His second was that the plate was, too. He'd been to restaurants where a side of ketchup would be delivered on a saucer, and Nicolai thought *that* unnecessary. The idea that pills would be given to him not from a bottle but in a dish was dumb, and the idea that the dish would need to be delivered atop a plate was ludicrous. It was supposed to feel opulent (like the white gloves on the waiters and the hot towels he'd seen delivered to other tables), but to Nicolai, it felt pompous.

"EndLax," said Isaac, looking over at Nicolai. "Take them, and you won't have to pass on any of this amazing food simply because you're full."

Nicolai looked up at Isaac, then around the table at Natasha, Micah, Micah's date, Paige, and back to Isaac. Isaac's expression was helpful, and Nicolai decided not to tell him that he knew exactly what the pills were. He also decided not to tell Isaac that his confused look was being caused by how he felt about them.

"It's okay," he said to the Monteffero's waiter. "I'll do without."

The waiter didn't take the plate away. "Are you sure, sir? You have quite a lot of food coming."

"I'll just stop when I'm full," he said.

The waiter looked at Nicolai as if he'd just expressed his belief in Bigfoot out loud, then looked around at the table's other occupants, seeming to ask if he should listen to the crazy dark-haired man and take the EndLax away. Micah nodded, and the waiter, with a sense of confused resignation, took the pills.

"You'll have to excuse Nicolai," Natasha said to Paige, laughing. "He's used to eating only what he needs." She laughed as if this were the most preposterous thing she'd ever heard then smiled at Nicolai to show that she was teasing. Her red hair was piled high, her smile wide and genuine, her breasts pushed up and her curves — in her opulent dress — settling in all the right places.

Nicolai tried to decide how he should respond. The Ryans didn't know he'd come from a wealthy family, or that he'd once been wasteful in his own way. When he'd first abandoned his old life for his new one trekking through Europe's chaos, Nicolai had missed his wealth and privilege, but he'd very quickly learned to appreciate the spartan life he'd been thrust into. It was like a whole-life fast, showing him what was truly important and what mattered not at all. EndLax, in Nicolai's opinion, was perhaps the perfect indication of the widening gap not just in the world, but even within the NAU itself. The fact that the rich could have all they wanted was morally diffi-cult enough…but the idea that they'd created a pill specifically so they could consume more than they were physically *able* to consume? That was a full step too far. Yet Isaac and Micah were his hosts, and Isaac was the reason Nicolai was sitting safe in the new country instead of still on the run amongst anarchy. He didn't want to be rude.

"You appreciate food more when you're rationed," he said. "And I don't just mean to ration so that it lasts. I mean rationing *during* a meal. All this amazing food tastes better when you know you only have so much room, and must carefully pick and choose those foods most worthy of passing your lips."

Isaac smiled then gave a small glance to his brother. It was a proud glance that said he'd hired the perfect wordsmith to help him communicate his vision to the world.

"We're going to be here a while, Nicolai," Micah said. "What will you do once you're full?" He lit a cigarette and puffed. The smoke bothered Nicolai, but it was another thing he knew better than to mention. Apparently, smoking had been banned throughout much of America years before only to reemerge for some reason shortly before Nicolai arrived. It was as if, with the world in chaos, everyone had decided that lung cancer again mattered less.

Nicolai glanced to his right, toward a long-stemmed glass. "I have my wine. We have our conversation."

Micah laughed. Unlike Natasha's laugh, Micah's was condescending.

"I heard you came through the Wild East," said Paige. She looked like she was a decade younger than Micah, but her tongue was sharp. She was thin and beautiful and blonde, clearly raised in privilege.

"Barbarians," said Isaac.

"Bad luck," said Nicolai, trying on a PR smile. "We had a lot of it in Italy and the rest of the East. When the oceans rose, they swallowed so much land that those who were left started to fight for the scraps, just like I heard happened here. There were many gangs, forming fast among too many governments. In a way, you were fortunate here to have so much space governed by one country, and just one country to the north and one to the south with whom you were so friendly. Think about it: The NAU — just the US, Canada, and Mexico — is only three governments. You didn't need much consensus. In Europe, we had dozens, in far less space. And of course, where was Switzerland while all of this was happening? Right in the middle, and you know what happened with *them*. With all of those governments scrambling to talk to one another, the EU coalition didn't matter. It all went back to little kingdoms. The French stopped being EU and went back to being French again. The Germans stopped being EU and became Germans again. It all fell to pieces. Try getting that many different cultures to agree when the pillaging started and the Faction started moving their bombs around, and it's a lot harder. I don't blame the NAU for closing the borders and am grateful to be here. But I don't think anyone can blame the East for what happened there."

Natasha shrugged. She didn't seem to see any reason not to blame the East for being who they were. It was nothing she'd ever need to worry about.

"You may feel differently in a few years," said Micah. "All those bombs are still over there, you know. That stuff goes back decades. Russia still has ICBMs in bunkers. India, Pakistan, Switzerland…it's only a matter of time. The NAU rose to the challenge. And now look at us: we're doing as well as ever."

"*Better* than ever," said Isaac, a knowing look in his eyes.

"For us, the calamity and chaos was a hiccup," Micah continued. "But for the Wild East? Crippling. They simply weren't strong enough." He tipped his cigarette toward Nicolai. "No offense, of course. You were clearly strong. But as a whole, the structure there just wasn't enough."

The part of Nicolai that housed his pride wanted to argue, but selective abandonment and triage were the only reasons he was still alive. He'd left his school and home to burn; he'd left his town to bandits; he'd left his country and friends and everything he'd ever known to *try* for America, fleeing toward Lady Liberty like a cliché from two hundred years before. People who insisted on saving others and obeying their pride ended up dead. Those with enough fortitude to cut the chaff might live to see another day, and make their difference that way.

"And what *about* those bombs?" said Micah. "They're already starting up the old machines over there. Did you hear that report about pirates who stole an entire fleet of old English military vessels? They're carrying warheads. There are subs, magnacopters, supersonics, all of that. It's only a matter of time before they stop scrapping in the East and find legitimate ways to come after us here."

Paige said, "We have an army."

Micah looked over at her with a mixture of surprise (that she'd spoken) and irritation (that she'd said something so stupid). "There's no *army*," he said. "There are monkeys with guns. The legitimate bases were all destroyed in the calamities, and the groups that resurrected them are quasi-military at best. And then, sure, the NAU government took them back over, but did they swap out every scrap of personnel? Were there enough people left who knew all of the secrets, about where the big machines were and how to use them? You know why we haven't nuked the East?"

"Because it's genocide?" said Nicolai.

"Well, that's what they say." Micah brought his cigarette to his lips and let it hover. "But I think it's because no one knows how to work it all. Or that it was disassembled or damaged beyond repair. We lost a lot of intellectual capital in the wars: all of our smartest people. It's taken time to grow them back. But the future of a country is in its people. We lost all of that knowledge, and that can't be allowed to happen. And now? I'm telling you, we're sitting ducks. We're the block's one rich house, surrounded by ghetto. They're eyeing us. Bet your bottom dollar, the rest of the world will find a way in."

"Well…" said Isaac.

Micah looked over. *"Isaac."*

Isaac stopped speaking. Nicolai sensed that some unspoken understanding had passed between the brothers. The public version of who the Ryans were and where they had come from was vanilla, but Nicolai could taste the nuts. They were both impossibly wealthy and supposedly had come from family money: a line of engineering plants scattered throughout North America, plus various other controlling industry interests. But Nicolai knew business and knew the history of the biggest of the Ryan companies, and he found it hard to believe that all of those fabricators, faced with the international embargo that had blocked raw imports from countries outside of the NAU, had had what they needed to spit the volumes required to thrive after the word "volume" lost most of its meaning. The NAU was self-sufficient today and had been for three years, but a significant side effect of the contained economy was the stalling of manufacturing. Technology puttered along, but true innovation was only now starting to progress again. Micah was right; the country had lost much of its brainpower. It had also been borrowing a large amount of brainpower from the rest of the world (particularly Japan) prior to cutting off. The NAU's isolation was forcing it to better itself, but the fledgling nation was only now finding its legs. There was another story, Nicolai thought, about how Ryan Enterprises had managed to keep its head above water during the transition — and delving into military operations was certainly one possibility.

Nicolai raised his eyebrows, asking an unspoken question. Isaac looked at Micah. Micah closed his eyes briefly, then shook his head as if to say, *Whatever*.

"There are rumors," said Isaac in a voice that suggested

that what he was about to say wasn't a *rumor* at all, "that the military is working on a kind of wall."

"A wall around the whole country?" said Natasha. She looked at Nicolai then smiled. She'd had a lot to drink, and had been friendly throughout the meal. Maybe too friendly.

"Around the entire *NAU*," said Isaac.

"How will a wall stop bombs?" Nicolai asked.

"The rumors — and they're just rumors, understand — suggest that this wall will be a bit more than bricks and mortar."

"Like what?"

"That's all the rumors say," said Micah, holding and then releasing another line of smoke. "A fancy wall."

Isaac looked at his younger brother, apparently understanding that it was time to stop talking. So he did, and a few minutes later the first course arrived.

It took fifteen waiters to bring all of the food. The table that Nicolai, Micah, Isaac, Natasha, and Paige were sitting at was much larger than necessary for a party of five, but when the waiters arrived, something whirred beneath the table; an aperture bloomed from the middle and fresh table poured into the hole from underneath. The table swelled in size the way a pancake spreads when new batter is poured into the middle. They were still close enough to talk, but fortunately Natasha was now far enough from Nicolai that she could no longer brush his legs with her feet under the table.

The white-gloved waiters placed platter after platter onto the table. Nicolai, who'd eaten his share of fine food, had never seen so much haute cuisine at once: Kobe burgers topped with seared foie gras and truffles on brioche buns; hand-packed sausage infused with 150-year-old Louis XIII cognac, topped with lobster and seared in olive and truffle oil; pizza topped with four types of caviar plus lobster tail; and what Nicolai knew would be his favorite before it touched his tongue: delicately crafted quesadillas with hen of the woods mushrooms, ricotta, and caramelized chayote squash on two perfectly cooked tortillas.

Once the waiters had finished setting dishes on the table and wishing the diners *bon appétit*, everyone but Nicolai took the EndLax tablets from their dishes, swallowed them with a gulp of overpriced wine, then began piling their plates high with giant helpings of the exorbitant dishes as if they were at an all-you-can-eat family buffet. Nicolai, who enjoyed sampling food at all economic levels and had been to plenty of buffets, found it interesting that the ridiculously rich ate exactly like the moderately poor.

After over an hour of gorging and small talk (and more too-friendly looks from Natasha, a few of which Nicolai found himself returning against his better judgment as one empty glass ran into the next), the diners seemed to grow bored with the food and stopped eating. Nicolai, who had taken no EndLax, felt full and satisfied and pushed his dish toward the middle of the table as he leaned back in his chair. Looking around, it was as if the others hadn't even eaten. They'd consumed thousands of dollars' worth of food that seemed to have pleased them not at all. It was a kind of gustatory masturbation for them, with no release.

Micah ordered "Dream Chocolate," a whipped mousse the Monteffero was well known for having perfected, in a way that suggested he felt obligated by ritual to do so. Nicolai found himself salivating in anticipation but looked around the table and wondered if the other diners, who wouldn't need to make room in their bellies, would even be able to taste it.

As they waited for the desserts to arrive, Isaac stood.

"I'd like to make a toast," he said, raising his wineglass, "to a mastermind, a visionary…and my amazing younger brother."

The others raised their glasses. Nicolai did the same, wondering what he was actually toasting.

"To the man who saw opportunity where everyone else

saw tragedy," Isaac continued. "To the man who, while the world was panicking, saw a way to line his pockets."

Isaac's voice was unsteady, and Nicolai realized just how drunk he was. Micah tugged at him, simultaneously thanking his brother and trying to get him to sit.

"But nobody ever gives *Isaac* any credit," said Isaac.

Micah half stood and said quickly, "And to *my* brother. Who supported me all the way."

"Supported you?"

"Who was forward-thinking enough to steer our companies toward a brighter future," Micah amended. Then, quieter, just to Isaac: *"Sit down."*

"Who signed the loans, as ill-advised as some of them were!" said Isaac, still raising his glass.

"Isaac."

"Who shouldered all the risk, while someone else did all of the…what?" He looked down at Micah, annoyed.

"That's good. Thank you for the toast."

"I just think we deserve recognition. Because this is good for everyone."

"Yes. Thanks. Sit."

"Not just us! Opportunity for the *NAU!*"

Micah, still tugging: "Yes. Sure, Isaac."

A few waiters were starting to arrive, removing plates that were, in many cases, still mostly full. Nicolai watched, estimating the dollar value of each dish. There went most of a pheasant under glass — probably over a hundred dollars. A bowl of caviar, mostly full? Twice that much, at least. The meal was ridiculously expensive, and the diners had raised their collective fingers at the price, sparing nothing and wasting much. Nicolai watched the waiters' faces. Though their expressions were neutral, Nicolai knew their thoughts wouldn't be. Despite working in opulence, the servers themselves were probably barely scraping by, like most of the country. Nicolai had been hungry many, many times over the past few years and could see their disgust, barely hidden. Would they try to take the expensive food home for themselves and risk losing their jobs? Or would they simply toss it into the garbage and resent the table's opulent waste?

"What's this big opportunity?" Paige asked. Beside her, Natasha wasn't paying attention. She was smiling devilishly at Nicolai, drunk and uncaring. She was also slouching down in her chair and, Nicolai suspected, probably reaching her foot toward his under the table. But the table was as large as she was lubricated, and Natasha was unable to know. Or care if her husband noticed, which he very much didn't.

"It's a big secret," said Isaac, planting a finger on his lips.

"It's *not* a secret," said Micah, who'd had very little to drink.

"Then why are you trying to stop me from telling everyone?"

"Because you're drunk."

"No, I'm not," said Isaac. But then he dropped his wineglass onto the table. It didn't shatter (it was made of some sort of new synthetic glass), but it did spill. A few waiters were hovering around the table, and one stepped forward, but Isaac managed to snap at him to clean up the mess before the waiter could do it himself.

Micah turned to Nicolai, whom he seemed to regard as the only one at the table left worth speaking to. Natasha and Isaac were getting sloppy despite the EndLax's dilating effect, and Paige was just something he'd brought along to fuck later. "It's not a secret," he repeated.

"They're raping the Arctic," Natasha added matter-of-factly.

Micah threw a look at his sister-in-law then smiled a somehow unperturbed smile at Nicolai. "You've seen it on the news, I'm sure. You could pull it up on your cell right now. There's no 'raping.' North America must operate in isolation now, and most people don't know just how hard that's been, on a macroeconomic level. It takes a while for various stores to run dry — for 'rationing' to turn into 'nothing left.' That's what happened to much of the East. But we got lucky. Ryan Industries was one of the big players investigating the thawing Arctic, and we were the first to start discovering things as we did. Now it's like we've discovered a hidden treasure, and there's no competition for it. The news has hinted at natural resources being uncovered under the ice up there, but they've not given the public the full picture yet because we've not released it, though of course we will shortly. There are a lot of natural resources up there waiting to be found, including stuff we haven't seen or thought of before. Plasteel, for instance, wouldn't exist if we hadn't found pockets of a naturally occurring alloy up there last year. Notice how quickly it went into production? That's because it was damn near ready for use as we found it and needed only to be shaped, which we did in our existing steel mills. Something about space and freezing and the time when the solar system was just a bunch of hot rocks ramming into each other trying to stabilize...I don't understand it all myself. The upshot is that, given time, the NAU will be fine — and once the barrier is up to protect us, it will *stay* fine. A lot of the Arctic is simply ice over water, but a lot of it in the NAU is land as well, and much easier to mine. Thank God for Canada. Alaska had a lot of ice, but the Yukon has more."

"What about Siberia?" Nicolai asked. There was plenty more arctic land in non-NAU territories, too. Greenland. The Nordic countries. The EU and Asia might be able to heal themselves with an infusion of raw materials. If the same was available in the southern cap, the existence of land in Antarctica meant there was more than enough to go around.

"They're too far gone," said Micah. "Who's going to organize mining operations? The Russian Mafia?"

As platters of food were stripped from the table, the hole reappeared in its middle and spilled downward, seeming to reel the five diners closer to one another again. Nicolai watched the table's surface descend into the hole as if it were liquid rather than wood. Was this a material that had been manufactured from something found under the ice in Northern Canada? Was this how the NAU's coming wealth was being spent — to create gorging tables in high-end restaurants?

Now that they were closer, Nicolai could feel Natasha's leg brush his. He looked over, not as annoyed as he should have been. She was truly stunning. He was a fan of her music, too. She was so raw, so emotionally charged. Natasha had a way of making a person *feel*, just as Nicolai was *feeling* against his will as her bare foot touched him.

"What he means," Natasha said, "is that nobody from the NAU has bothered to tell them to look for riches under the ice."

"Because they'd just fight over it and make things worse," said Micah, annoyed.

Natasha rolled her eyes for Micah, looking at Nicolai. Micah watched her. Nicolai felt certain that Micah was restraining himself from hitting her. She was sloppy, Isaac was sloppy, and both were making fools of themselves, making a fool of Micah in the process.

Nicolai didn't ask further. He'd pry information from Isaac in the morning, if he was still curious. It all made sense. Still, Ryan Industries had thrived throughout the turbulent times, and Micah said that they'd discovered the precursors of Plasteel just one year before. There would have been a lot of upfront expense to get it ready for prime time. Soon, Ryan Industries would be astonishingly wealthy, but how had it survived in the meantime?

When the bill arrived, Micah paid in full, using dollars. The waiter told him that the restaurant only accepted universal credits, but Micah replied that he'd not had time yet to convert. The maître d came to the table and apologized in an underhanded way, perfectly balancing syco-phancy and condescension as he explained that the restaurant was no longer equipped to accept dollars, indicating that the gentleman had been pre-warned about the change for months. Micah told the waiter (who had a French accent) that the universal language was English and that the NAU was mostly America and that the NAU only spent money within its own borders, and that a wholesale conversion to the same currency as the Wild East was idiotic.

The maître d's European pride seemed to unravel his composure, but then Micah slipped something into the man's palm to calm him. Then the maître d bowed and walked off, a moment later a waiter returned with an old fingerpad, and Micah paid for their meal with dollars.

On their way out, Nicolai took on the burden of keeping an eye on Natasha. She needed it. Micah and Paige had both sipped at a few drinks but were more or less sober, and Isaac was drunk but at least wearing flat shoes. Natasha, on the other hand, was in high heels (which made her taller than Nicolai) and looked like a baby giraffe trying to walk. Isaac was ignoring her, tagging along behind Micah like a sidekick. So Nicolai walked with Natasha, ready to catch her if she fell. Soon it became apparent that he had to actually hold her, which she took as a come-on.

They were a few steps behind the others when she said, "You *like* me, Nicolai."

"I like you both," said Nicolai, looking toward Isaac. The official version of their collective story said that Isaac had saved Nicolai. It was bullshit, because Nicolai had always saved himself and always would. But he was appreciative for the Ryans' help (he certainly wouldn't have all of those credits in his account after only a few years in the NAU without Isaac), and he was loyal, with an acute ability to see the good in everyone. He liked Isaac and Natasha, and parts of what he saw in Micah. But he also saw how badly Isaac and Natasha needed someone's help, though neither would ever admit it.

"You think I'm *beautiful*, even though I'm fat."

"You're hardly fat," he replied. Natasha had entered new levels of celebrity spotlight since her first album was released a year ago. One year, it turned out, was just enough time to start thinking of five-ten, 150 as fat. Natasha pretended to be above the gossip sheets, but they were clearly getting to her. If you couldn't see a woman's ribs, Natasha was coming to believe, then she was too fat.

Natasha smiled at Nicolai. He held her arm as they walked toward the cars. Nicolai had told the valet to bring the cars around, but Micah had wanted to walk. Nicolai had also told Natasha to remove her heels, but she'd refused, saying the ground was filthy.

She stumbled. Despite his disadvantage in leverage, Nicolai managed to catch her. He ended up with her breasts pressed into his arm and looked down to see that the top button of her blouse was open. He raised his eyes to find her green eyes already watching his brown ones. He looked away, toward the retreating backs of Micah, Paige, and Isaac. None had noticed.

"You're such a gentleman," she said.

"I'm just trying to keep you alive."

"You're still a gentleman. You stayed with me."

"Come on," he said, trying to right her.

"Why are you in with us, Nicolai? You're better than us rich assholes."

Nicolai hadn't bothered to tell the Ryans that, back in Italy, his family had had much more money than the Ryans. He saw no need to tell them now.

"You're not assholes." She was fishing for compliments, and he was throwing them right back, not knowing what else to do. Ignoring her would be rude, and as confident as Natasha pretended to be, he knew how fragile she was inside.

"I made the wrong bet with Isaac," she said.

Nicolai looked at her for a moment, but that was one he didn't — *couldn't* — respond to. He pretended he hadn't heard and started helping Natasha to her feet, ignoring the something inside him hungry to parry.

"Come on. Get up. They're getting away from us."

Nicolai pulled Natasha to her feet, and they stumbled after their party, his thoughts filled with arctic treasures, wealth, and betrayal.

Chapter 2

"LEAH."

Leah looked up, saw Leo standing above her, and gestured for him to sit. Leo lowered his old body into an ancient red plastic seat that looked like a bucket beside her. He didn't moan, and his body didn't crack or pop. Yet she knew Leo was ancient. It all went to show that everyone these days needed at least a few tiny bites of synthetic assistance to get by, whether they admitted it or not.

"Thanks for calling," he said.

"They have *phones* here. Can you believe it?" She gestured toward a white device mounted on the wall by the nurse's station.

The rustic mountain hospital had Beam access, but diagnostic machines were the only systems directly wired into it. Admittance and billing were done on a manual console and batched in, and once Leah had told the nurse she was from the Organa village (along with the safe version of what she'd been doing with Crumb up at the house in Bontauk), the nurse had taken Leah and Crumb even further offline, recording their account in a large book, using a pen. Crumb's visit to the hospital was more off-record than off-record, and taking them off-record had been done with a conspiratorial "It's us against them, sweetheart" air. Out in the sticks, city technology was often regarded as sour grapes. If the people of the hills couldn't afford the best connectivity, they mostly declared it to be no good and worth opposing. So when Leah had wanted to call Leo, she'd started to use The Beam…and the nurse, seeing this, had shown her the phone instead. Leah was amazed that the phone system even handshook with The Beam when she used it to contact Leo (who, Organa as he was, didn't have access to a true phone), but then again, what didn't handshake with The Beam these days?

"I used to have one of those in my house," said Leo, nodding toward the phone.

"You're kidding."

"I had a gasoline car too."

"Just how old are you, Leo?" Leah asked.

"Let's just say that when diagnostic and scavenger nanos came on the market and rich people started using them to keep themselves young, I was already old. So I settled for using them to stay alive."

Leah looked over at Leo, taking in his headband and gray braids. Tech knew tech, so Leah had long ago decided that Leo had had nano treatments, but this was the first time she'd heard him admit it. She could imagine him the first time he became an old man, a decade from his grave, accepting an injection that would hit the pause button on his aging. She found herself newly impressed. Even the best nanos couldn't keep a body from decaying forever, and usually couldn't keep up at all if the recipient was too old by the time of their first treatment. That meant that before Leo had gotten those first treatments, he must have been in prime shape. Even when he was purely biological, he must have been eighty going on twenty-five.

"How's Crumb?" Leo asked.

"In a coma. They say there's no brain damage, thank

West, and that he should be fine. They dosed him with some cleanup nanos and will apply stimulation once those nanos show green. He should wake within a few hours at most."

"Did you find anything?"

Leah stared at the hospital tiles under her feet. All was well that ended well, but she still felt guilty. She'd nearly killed Crumb by rooting around inside his head. Or at best, she'd nearly *burned* him. He could have woken up as a vegetable, or never woken up at all. She remembered not wanting to hook him up, then remembered Crumb saying he wanted to see the Wizard — as if he knew exactly what was happening and was giving her the thumbs-up to proceed.

"I found something small. I'll tell you later." She looked around, trying to tell Leo without words that even as rustic and disconnected as the mountain hospital was, the walls here might have ears.

Leo stood. He rose easily. If Leo was old enough to have owned a wall phone, he must have maintained himself fantastically to stay as spry as he was.

"Let's go for a walk," he said.

"A walk?"

"I want to meditate, and we need a spot that's not here. You said Crumb will be out for a few hours? Let's not lose any more of our life to these uncomfortable seats. Let's find a nice place to clear our heads." He looked down at her and smiled knowingly. "I can see guilt all over your face."

"I could have burned him," she said.

"But you didn't."

Leah nodded.

"You handled this perfectly, Leah. Like a grown-up. You weren't rash or impetuous, you got him the care he needed, you let me know, and you're not your usual cocky self right now, making excuses. You're respecting the gravity and reality of the situation. You've done well. I'm proud of you."

Leah twirled a pink dreadlock. "Thanks."

Leo held out his hand. "So come on. Let's meditate."

Leah took Leo's hand, and they left the hospital together. They walked through the grounds until, leaving the hospital's small oasis of civilization within the mountain wilderness, they found themselves surrounded by trees. The wood's silence immediately helped to soothe Leah's guilt and fear, and after a short time hiking by Leo's side, she felt herself settling in to nature's rhythm and as eager to meditate as Leo. Meditation was a sort of safety valve for Leah — and, strangely, it felt a lot like navigating The Beam. Leah could hack code and hit keys better than most, but at its best, steering through The Beam's hive mind (or the minds of those willingly attached) felt more like a trance or a dream than pushing buttons.

Once out of ear and eyeshot of the hospital, Leah told Leo about her nugget of discovery: the book, the name of Stephen York, and the building with the red roof somewhere in District Zero. She asked Leo if any of it meant anything to him, and he shook his head. Then he repeated that she'd done well and agreed that the level of complexity in Crumb's mind made the fact that she'd gotten anything at all was amazing. As to the complexity of Crumb's mind, Leo only shook his head. He said there was clearly more to Crumb than they'd thought, and reiterated that hooking him up had been the right decision. As loud as Leo's instincts were about Crumb before he'd sent Leah on her errand, they were louder now. He was more certain than ever that it all meant something, and that the book and Stephen York were both worth finding.

They found an open area in the trees and sat down a few feet apart, facing each other, on a bed of brown pine needles.

Leo closed his eyes and placed his hands palm-up on his knees. But instead of doing the same, Leah studied Leo. He seemed old and not old at the same time. His skin was wrinkled around his eyes and mouth, but it was smooth on his forehead and arms. He had a glow about him rather than the fading light you saw around most of the oldest people. He moved like a man of biological fifty, yet looked at first glance like a man of biological eighty. Yet based on what Leo had said, he had to be older than that.

"Seriously, Leo. How old are you?"

Leo blinked. His brown eyes opened and peeked at Leah.

"I can keep a secret. You've pretty much told me anyway. I could figure it out."

"Go ahead," he said, his body unmoving.

"Ninety."

"Sure," said Leo. His eyes closed.

If he were ninety, Leo would have been born in 2007. But hadn't phones — the kind that hung on walls in houses — already been on their way out by then? Leah wasn't sure. She wasn't good with history. She was born in '68, and The Beam was mostly everywhere by then. She'd lived all her life in ultra connectivity and had always had to leave the city to pull any of those plugs.

"Older?"

Leo's eyes opened again. "You're making it hard for me to find inner peace."

"A hundred? Are you a hundred?" Nanobot technology had blossomed in…what? Maybe mid-century? If Leo was in that first wave (which she didn't know) and had been old when he'd done it (which she couldn't be sure of), then he could be…

There was too much she didn't know.

"I'm over a hundred. Satisfied?"

"Were you around before The Beam?"

Leo nodded. After Leah nodded back, he closed his eyes again.

"Before the *early* Beam? Cross…whatever?"

"Crossbrace," said Leo, sighing and putting his hands in his lap. Leah wasn't remotely trying to find a meditation posture, so Leo let his collapse. "A 'beam' is stronger than a 'crossbrace,' so it works. Get it?"

"And you were around before Crossbrace?"

"Leah, we thought Crossbrace was going to take over the world. It was a topic of great debate. And look: It *did* take over the world. You can't forget to buy milk anymore. Your refrigerator knows and has it delivered for you. You can't get lost. You don't even need a handheld to keep from getting lost; if you carry a spark toggle, you can flash your ID at The Beam from the most remote locations, and it'll send a bot."

"Unless you don't have an ID," said Leah.

"And assuming you don't actually *want* to get lost," said Leo, agreeing with a nod. "My generation used to *want* to get lost. We talked about 'getting away from it all.' People don't do that anymore. They have the vacation islands, but those places are even more wired than DZ. Or they take virtual vacations, staring into visors. Nobody wants to march out into the woods and unplug anymore, except for fruits like us. Have you heard about the tragedies that sometimes happen during Beam outages?"

Leah nodded. Two years back, there had been a citywide outage in District Zero that had lasted for two full days. The lights and power had stayed on, but during those forty-eight hours of lost connectivity, seven people had become so despondent that they'd committed suicide. A few of them left notes indicating that they felt like they'd lost all of their limbs and senses. They said they felt like invalids trapped in beds, like how Crumb was right now. There had also been a rash of depression that had lingered for months after connectivity was restored — a strange sort of post-traumatic stress. City counseling centers had been overwhelmed.

"I remember the first July 21, Leah," said Leo. Then he chuckled. "Well, not the *first* one, but the first one that was an official holiday, in 2019, when they established the lunar base in the Mare Frigoris and started finding all of that great space stuff out there in space. They had that new far side radio telescope, where there was total radio blackout from Earth's interference, and that big old array was seeing all the way back to the beginning of the universe." He inhaled slowly, lost in the memory, a smile of recalled optimism on his face. "Everyone thought it was so important at the time. And it *was* important, back then. Strange, how seeing new celestial objects and seeing back in time all the way to the Big Bang bolstered the world. The tech Renaissance followed quickly afterward, with the first hovertech showing up, and the HIV cure, and all of that."

"You say it like one thing caused the other," said Leah. She knew a lot of this, of course, but she knew it in the distant, sepia-toned way that history books portrayed it. Leo, on the other hand, had lived it in Technicolor.

"It sort of did," he said. "The telescope came first, and it gave the world a feeling of 'We really are all in this big universe together.' The vaccines came very quickly afterward, as if that global optimism allowed people to finally work together for a change. Hovertech popped up next, and for some reason, the way nanobots could make things float exploded into thousands of other applications, which spawned even more new ideas, and on and on. There's a reason they call it a *Renaissance*, because so much of it happened pretty much all at once. They even have a word for that kind of thing, where everything happens at once, in evolution. It's called 'punctuated equilibrium.' It means that evolution doesn't occur slow and steady, but through distinct periods of phenomenal growth. That's how it was for us back then. All of these new treatments and technologies at once, one followed another, and each was better than the one before. It was as if all of humanity stopped our fighting and turned our attention toward moving forward as one. The notion was paradise for a hippie like yours truly. The world all held hands, it seemed, as we found our global purpose."

Leah was doing the math in her head. How old would Leo have been to remember the Renaissance so clearly, and to have considered himself a hippie at the time? Teens at the least?

"You lived through the wars?"

Leo snickered. "*Wars.* They weren't wars, Leah. The planet declared war on *us*, yes, but then the people just kind of went to shit when the oceans rose at once and swallowed the biggest cities. Most of New York went too, before they managed to build the seawall and drain it back out. Have you seen a globe from the 2010s?"

Leah had. There had been so much land back then. There'd also been a cap of white on the top and bottom of the planet. She'd once asked a teacher what those white spots were, and the teacher had told her that they'd been ice. Modern globes didn't look like that. The north pole was blue, and the south pole was green. It was strange to imagine it any other way.

"It was a terrible time," said Leo. "Just like that, we went from global cooperation to global animosity and suspicion. Everyone started looking out for themselves and *only* themselves. Maybe they looked out for their families too, if their families were lucky. And then for some reason, leaders in most of the civilized world thought this would be a good time to launch missiles at each other, presumably because there was only so much land left and they all wanted it." Then Leo looked at Leah, and his starry eyes cleared. He laughed and said, "But I'm going on and on."

"I'm just trying to figure out how old you are," Leah replied, smiling.

"I had a car. A Plymouth Fury. Fire-engine red, like Christine. She was old when I got her, but she was still beautiful."

"Who's Christine?" said Leah.

"Oh, but you wouldn't understand the beauty of a fine car," said Leo, either missing or ignoring her question. "Back then, your car was your freedom. You could get into your car and go anywhere you wanted. Hovers aren't like that. You can still go anywhere, but it's not the same. And land cars? Forget about it. They're so stripped down, they're an embarrassment."

"Didn't those cars pollute like a motherfucker?" said Leah.

"Don't judge me," said Leo. "I was young."

"So you had cars, but no computers?"

"We had them later. But you can't imagine that, can you? What are you, twelve?"

"What are you?" said Leah. "A thousand?"

Leo sighed, apparently tired of playing coy. "I was born in seventy-six. *Nineteen* seventy-six. And don't gasp. I'm your elder, and you have to respect me."

Leah gasped dramatically. Leo rolled his eyes.

That started another round of questions, and once Leo got rolling, Leah had a thousand questions. How could they know the weather before it was controlled inside the NAU lattice? And if they didn't know the weather, how could they plan their days? How did they get what they needed if things had to be shipped over the course of days? Was it a bummer growing old when you were still so young? Leo said he'd been born before the ancient Internet and had had to watch an old screen only when his shows were on, at certain times. Nothing was 3-D, and he'd even watched for a while on an old black-and-white screen. How, Leah asked, were they able to function with so little information? How did people survive without add-ons on such a large scale? Today, the Organa were considered tough, living life mostly unenhanced. But back then, everyone did it. How had they managed to let bones heal without replacements? How had those who played sports competed without eye or muscular enhancements? How had average people remembered what they needed to remember without wetchips or recall flashers?

Leo groaned, but Leah could tell how delighted he was by her interest, how willing he was to answer her many questions, and how pleased he was to go on and on about the US,

Canada, and Mexico before they formed the NAU. He wanted to tell her about his days exploring Europe and Asia in the 1990s, back before chaos turned the Wild East into what it was now.

After over an hour, Leo brushed off, stood, and made a good-natured comment about Leah not letting him meditate. She made a good-natured joke about how he wouldn't shut up, then parodied his voice, mimicked walking with a cane, and did an impression of Leo yelling at fictional kids to get off his lawn. Then they returned to the hospital, spending their short walk in discussion of what they should do with Crumb if he was awake.

But when Leo and Leah stepped back into his room, they found his bed empty. Crumb — with his strangely complex, locked-down mind — was gone.

Chapter 3

Nicolai woke to find Kai touching his face with something cold. Her brown eyes were tender. It took him a while to place her, along with his location (currently simulated as a large, old-fashioned saloon), and to place the blond man sitting on a stool ten feet away, his arms crossed and his face almost angry. But then, slowly, it all came back. He remembered the Beamers, the simulator, and the one-sided fight.

"Hey," said Kai, still touching his face, withdrawing the cold object as Nicolai sat up. He had been lying with his head in her lap, and although his senses were still fuzzy, he thought she'd been running her other hand through his hair.

"They gave you ice?" said Nicolai, indicating the cold rag in Kai's hand.

She nodded toward the saloon's bar. "I got it over there, in a big chest by some bottles. They also have beer on tap."

Doc, still cross-armed, stood from his stool and said, "Okay. Your pretty baby is awake. You can stop playing nurse."

Kai stared at him, and Nicolai got the impression they'd been having this argument since he'd been knocked cold.

"How long was I out?"

"Not long," said Kai. "They came in, gave you a quick scan to make sure you didn't have a concussion, then said you could sleep it off."

"She's been preening over you," said Doc, "seeing as we've established she's the hooker with the heart of gold."

Kai shot Doc a look, but the look was full of exasperation, not anger. Nicolai knew that Kai liked Doc a lot and considered him a friend, but right now that wouldn't stop her from kicking him in the balls to stop him from being an asshole.

Nicolai stood bit by bit, making sure he still had his equilibrium. He could feel that the side of his face was swollen, his cheek too large. Nicolai's nanos weren't specialists in large-scale repair like those injected by athletes and criminals, but they'd reduce the bruise and swelling in much less time than would take to heal naturally. Still, for now, it hurt.

"You hit me," said Nicolai.

"They made me."

Nicolai seemed to remember the Beamers' persuasion as being less than inevitable and Doc as being rather quick to comply. Normally, everyone here should be friends. Nicolai and Kai were Doc's clients, and Doc and Nicolai were Kai's clients. If they remembered that everything was just business, amity should shine through. Eventually.

"How much have I paid you over the years, Doc?"

"How much have you thought yourself better than me over the years, Nicolai?"

They hadn't neared each other, but Nicolai could still feel menace radiating from Doc's body. He didn't think Doc would hit him again, but Doc had an ego about as big as the NAU lattice. He didn't like to appear weak or wrong, and he certainly never apologized.

"Just admit you hit me because you wanted to."

"Fine," said Doc. "I hit you because I wanted to."

"And that you hit me harder than you needed to."

Doc chuckled, looking down at his right hand. From

where Nicolai was standing, the hand looked swollen and the knuckles abraded, but already the abrasions and friction burns on his fingers had started to fade. Doc, whose business walked many lines, had quite robust repair nanos in his blood.

"Oh, definitely," said Doc. "I hit you as hard as I could."

"With your artificial muscles. Like a real man."

Doc stood. "I built what I have."

"Without help, right?" said Nicolai. "Who goes to the gym twice a month and gets arms like yours?"

Doc gave Nicolai a crocodile's smile. "The real power in a punch comes from the *legs*."

"You fucking fake," said Nicolai. He didn't want to fight, but he couldn't help himself. He'd been sucker-punched, and he hadn't gotten a chance to even the score.

"Okay," said Doc. "So I've got a fake body, huh? Well, smartass, *you* have a fake brain. How's that wetchip working in your well-reasoned arguments against me?"

"Not as well as my upgrade would," said Nicolai. "Which I already paid you for, by the way."

Doc made a show of searching his pockets. "Oh, I'm sorry. You want that upgrade now? Let me just get my tools. I've got nothing else going on."

Kai stood. Nicolai was tall, and Doc was taller. Between the two men, she looked downright tiny. She held her hands out and said, "Will both of you just grow up?"

"I thought you were on my side," said Nicolai.

"I'm on the side with fewer assholes." She looked at each of the men in turn. "They *want* you to fight. Are you really going to give them what they want?"

Nicolai stared at Doc for another long moment before turning away, exhaling. Doc chuckled. Then Nicolai, who'd broken eye contact first, looked back up. He was down two-zero in his sparring, so if there was a next step, it was up to Doc.

Finally, the taller man extended his hand. "I'll knock half off your next upgrade," he said.

"*And* refund half of what I paid for my last one," Nicolai countered.

"Fine."

Nicolai gripped Doc's hand and shook it once, then released. Neither had apologized. Kai rolled her eyes.

After a moment of odd silence, Nicolai began to pace.

"We've been here forever," he said. "Why? What the hell do they want?" He looked at the saloon's simulated walls as if staring at their captors themselves, but no answers came. He turned to Doc. "Tell me again. How did you end up here? Did you see who it was? Did they say *anything?* Anything at all?"

Doc paused, looking at Kai. Then he said, "I was in my apartment. I was falling asleep when someone broke in and somehow killed my connection. Some asswipe came at me, so I ran to my car." He laughed. "I was in my boxers. First time I've had to use my emergency pants."

"Emergency pants?"

"Brother, when you're as cool as I am, you learn to keep a change of clothes in your car just in case. Maybe keep a set where you lay your log, too." He glanced at Kai, who looked disgusted. "Anyway, I drove around all night then hooked up with my lady here. Got ambushed by a bunch of fucking shadows in a building down by the park. They brought us here. Nobody said shit, just hit me with clubs and pain pods. That's all I know."

Nicolai read between the lines, aided in part by the creativity enhancement from his wetchip. Doc and Kai were probably just below Nicolai on the income ladder. The only reason they'd go to an area of town so far below the line would be to meet someone beneath the law — likely someone who could help one or both of them disappear. But why would anyone come after Doc in the first place? Had Kai been involved? Was that why he'd "hooked up" with her? One or both must have gotten mixed up in something, pissed the wrong person off. But of course, they couldn't discuss that now.

"What about you?" said Kai.

"I'm an innocent bystander," Nicolai replied. "I came to Doc's, and…"

"For a purchase," Doc interjected. Nicolai liked Doc when Doc wasn't punching him, but the man was such an asshole. Even now, he felt the need to remind Kai that Nicolai wasn't as clean and pure as he pretended to be.

"For an upgrade on my wetchip," said Nicolai, making a gesture toward Kai. Kai already knew about his add-on. She had, in fact, urged him to get the upgrade because she wanted to see his creativity blossom. "I found the apartment open, with stuff broken. Someone put a knife to my throat and knocked me out. I woke up in here, and same as you, nobody told me anything. And that's all *I* know."

Kai looked from one man to the other. Her role, as far as the Beamers were concerned, was adequately covered by Doc's story. Kai was smart; she knew not to add anything more.

The door opened. The saloon simulation faded as if the machine had been shut off, and the three captives again found themselves standing in the middle of a great white cube. Six Beamers entered. Centered in the cluster of men in black was a tiny man of indeterminate age with a shock of hair so white that it nearly vanished against the walls.

"You are comfortable, yes?" said the small man.

No one replied.

"Well," he said, his voice tinged by an odd and unplaceable accent, "I hope you're comfortable while you stay with us. Allow me to introduce myself. My name is Alix Kane. I am new here. And by *here*, I mean the NAU. All hail the NAU!" He saluted with a fist then cackled like an old woman.

Nicolai felt his eyebrows wanting to rise. The borders had

been sealed since he himself entered the old USA. How could *anyone* be new?

"Yes, yes," said the small man, pacing. As he did, the Beamers stayed where they were, as if they didn't want to be in the room at all. They were all carrying either slumberguns or pain pods, but Nicolai noticed that as Alix marched, the Beamers' visors stayed fixed on Kane and that their weapons subtly pointed toward him rather than the prisoners. "I am from the Eastern Alliance, near what you would probably know as Krakow, if you in the NAU bothered to study the rest of the world at all. They let me in for reasons that are none of your concern, and did so using means you don't need to know. You need only know is that officially, I don't exist." He clapped excitedly, as if something had just occurred to him. "Oh! And that I have a present for you." He turned to the Beamers. "Go and get it," he said, waving a hand at the cluster.

As one of the Beamers moved toward the simulator's door, Kane turned to Nicolai, Doc, and Kai and spoke low. "They may look intimidating in their black gear, but they are afraid. They've never seen one before, you understand. Not for real. And for a Beamer to see one? Well, you understand."

Nicolai didn't understand at all, and his lack of comprehension wasn't improved when the Beamer re-entered the room, pushing a long aluminum table on wheels. The table had a skeletal sort of helmet on one end and straps hanging from four places on its frame. There were holes in its surface. Below the table's top, stretched between the legs, was a sort of shallow pan. The Beamer behind the thing had a set expression on his face and was pushing it far out in front of himself as if it stank.

"Mister Stahl," said Kane. "You were at Xenia Labs on Friday, yes?"

Doc, staring at the aluminum table, nodded.

"Tell me what you saw."

"I went in to see Nero and…and…" Doc scrunched his face as if searching for memory. "I think he didn't have anything new? I guess I got my standard order?" He scratched his chin.

"Yes, yes," said Kane. "You are very convincing in your pretending to forget, but they have had a lot of time to scan you while they've been waiting for me to arrive, and we have done our research on the type of wares Mr. Ryu deals in. We know about your implant and do not believe you about not having your memories. So tell me again, 'Doc,' What did you see at Xenia?"

Doc stopped, seeming to war with an internal decision. Then he sighed and told Kane a story about being mistaken for another salesman and being ushered by a Mr. Killian into a room filled with ultra-high-end upgrades. Nicolai was more intrigued than nervous. He'd seen plenty of odd things from Isaac and Natasha over the last few years, and had long suspected that they had access to upgrades superior to those he was allowed to purchase. Once, after Nicolai mentioned his desire to learn piano, Isaac had inexplicably become a virtuoso, though he'd never so much as mentioned piano before. And when Natasha had expressed a desire to dance at an upcoming Directorate ball, Isaac had groaned. But at the ball, they'd danced beautifully together, as if they'd studied for years. And on and on.

"Uh-huh," said Kane. "Well, thank you for your honesty, Mr. Stahl. Now if you could tell me why you went in to see those upgrades in the first place."

"I told you, it was a mistake."

Kane nodded thoughtfully, curling his lower lip. "Ah, well. This is the sticky part. See, we have reason to believe that it *wasn't* a mistake — that you manufactured your way in. So my question is, how did you know about these lines ahead of time? Who was your source?" He tossed a look to Nicolai.

"Source? I didn't have a source. I told you, this was all a surprise to me."

"So nobody told you. Nobody with any kind of insider information — say, someone you know or deal with who might run across such devices in the course of his daily life or work?" Again, he looked at Nicolai.

"No," Doc replied.

"Because currently, those lines are available only to a very narrow segment of the population. So if you were sent in by someone — "

"I wasn't sent in!"

" — it could only have been by one of a handful of people, relatively speaking," Kane went on. "Someone who has *access* to these wares, but who isn't actually allowed to purchase or own them. Someone who isn't Beau Monde, but who works very closely with the Beau Monde."

For the third time, Kane turned his head to look at Nicolai. Then he looked back at Doc and waited.

"Nicolai?" said Doc.

Kane shrugged. "Why not?" Then he turned away from Doc and started speaking to Nicolai. "Maybe you let your friend Mr. Stahl into your employers' apartment. Maybe you report to him regularly on things you see and hear. I believe our man even found you at Doc's apartment after midnight. Quite late for a casual visit, isn't it?"

Nicolai said, "I was picking up an upgrade."

"An upgrade. What kind of upgrade?"

"A creativity chip."

Kane gave a laugh that sounded almost like a chortle. "I see. You write speeches for the Directorate, so you got a creativity chip. Because Directorate is where all of the creative people are."

"You'd be surprised," said Kai.

Nicolai turned, giving her a look that he hoped would tell her to shut up. None of this felt right, and the best choice, for all of them, would be to keep their heads down as much as possible.

"I'll tell you my theory," said Kane, putting a thoughtful finger to his chin and beginning a lazy stroll around the group. "I think you see things when you spend so much time with the Ryans. I think they aren't as careful as they should be about keeping the secret. Come on. What have you seen?"

"Nothing," said Nicolai.

Kane stopped walking then tipped his head to the side. "Please."

Nicolai looked at the white-haired man, trying to gauge him. Nicolai had run across all types in his travels. He'd seen the best of the best — saints who sacrificed themselves to save others — and the worst of the worst. You didn't make it far on your own in the wasteland without the right barometer for people. Looking at Kane, Nicolai knew him as a killer. Not a man to trifle with.

"I've seen them learn things quickly," said Nicolai. "Maybe too quickly."

"What kinds of things?"

"Dancing. Piano. And when I told Isaac that I would love to learn to play my piano like he could play his but that I couldn't find the time, he laughed. Like he knew something about 'the time needed to learn to play' that I didn't."

"What else?'

"Natasha is in her office for hours and hours. Then she comes out all cheery and relaxed, like she's been at a spa. It doesn't seem like she's just on The Beam. And she has these two rigs in there like I've never seen. I asked about them once, and she told me that they're normal rigs, just really comfortable." He didn't go on to tell Kane the other things Natasha did that made Nicolai suspicious: the way she'd hinted to Nicolai about "going away somewhere together" and how she'd said that sometimes, you could *do* things without really *doing* anything at all. She'd licked her lips suggestively when she'd said that last. He knew Natasha enough to know those little quips for the come-ons they were, but he didn't understand what they meant — other than trouble.

Kane nodded. "Yes, she is one of those types." He didn't elaborate on what "those types" were. "It makes sense. Loose lips. Your suspicions were inevitable, really." He looked at Doc, then back at Nicolai. "So maybe you told Doc about the things the Ryans seem to have. About those fancy immersion rigs, say. Maybe Doc was curious, and so maybe you made a deal. You give him information, and he gives you...*creativity chips.*"

Before Doc or Nicolai could respond, Kane threw his hands theatrically in the air.

"Or not!" he said. "I do not know these things. It doesn't really matter how you learned about the restricted product lines, Mr. Stahl. What matters is why you went to the trouble to learn more by breaking in — something I believe I already know — and also *how* you did it. Xenia's security is complex. I find it hard to imagine you broke through the locks. So how did you bypass security?"

"Security?" Doc blurted. "Look, short stuff, they led me in. Ask Killian. Ask that cute little receptionist."

"The receptionist was a temp and has unfortunately lost all memory of Xenia Labs," said Kane. "Mr. Killian says you posed as another salesman. You had a manufactured ID and everything."

"Bullshit! Check your security feed!"

Kane chuckled. "We don't keep visual records at Xenia."

"It was a mistake. They thought I was this guy Greenley. I even thought I was late, and was all sweaty and gross. Your reception gal sent Killian to *me*, and Killian rolled out the red carpet. I saw what I saw. So you've gotta wipe me? Go ahead. Gauss my shit up; I don't care. Tell you the truth, I'd *like* to forget all of this."

"I'm afraid that won't do," said Kane. "We don't just want you to forget. We want answers."

"It was a mistake!"

Kane sighed. The Beamers were still staying back, edging away from both the aluminum table and the small man with the white hair. Kane gestured at the table. "You know what this is?" He looked at each of his prisoners then waited for all three to shake their heads.

"It's called an Orion."

Kai gasped.

"Yes, you would have heard the rumors, wouldn't you, as a woman so steeped in pleasure?" said Alix Kane to Kai with a serpent's smile. He turned to Nicolai and Doc. "There are places on The Beam — very, very, *very* exclusive places — where people with rigs as high-end as those you saw can experience total immersion in an artificial environment. It *feels* as if they are there. These places cater to fully immersive experiences, but unsurprisingly, the most popular are those grounded in pleasures that its clients cannot experience in their normal lives. An Orion is a device — a device developed at an accelerated pace for certain quarters of NAU defense — designed to access an area very like those places in concept but quite different in experience. Humans have debated whether Hell exists?" Kane took a step toward the table and laid a palm flat on its top, looking at the contraption with something like affection. "It exists *in here*."

"You can't use that," said Kai. "They were banned in '84. Use is punishable by the Department of Respero."

Kane laughed. "So the penalty is a quiet and peaceful death?" He slapped the machine twice and turned back to his prisoners. "We should be so lucky! But alas, the '84 ban was on older Orions that were mere toys compared to this one — this one, which, once you're given a little injection of nanos, will immerse you more fully than you currently believe is possible. Besides, I'm afraid I must insist. There are too many limits with conventional torture. For one, there is the question of scope. If I came at you with real-life jagged blades, how many places could I possibly cut you at one time? And think of all those areas I could never reach! Real life can't pull all of your skin apart with hooks at once, but this can make you feel as if it's happening. Then there is the issue of death. If I were to flay you, death would be imminent…and all too soon. But even if you didn't die, how could I tear the skin from your body once it's already been peeled away?" Kane chuckled as if discussing problems as mundane as weeding a garden. "And lastly, we run into mercy. A torturer doesn't have to be merciful in order for the subject's body to grant mercy. You can go into shock, fall unconscious…even, in a way, grow used to the pain. But the Orion allows us to make each cut as terrible as the first. To keep you awake and focused. With access to all of your neurons, the levels of agony that can be delivered are beyond belief."

Nicolai tried to maintain his composure, looking at the device and swallowing a lump. Across from him, Doc had lost all of his bravado. His tan skin was ashen.

In a small voice, he said, "It was a mistake. I swear."

Kai stared at the table, fixated on the glistening chrome. "Torture is an unreliable way to mine information," she said.

"Well," said Kane, beckoning to a man in a white lab coat who'd just entered holding a syringe, "we shall see."

"Don't do this to me," said Doc.

"Oh, we won't." He pointed at Kai. "Let's start with her."

Chapter 4

EVERYTHING ABOUT MICAH RYAN'S black-and-chrome office was designed to subtly intimidate the people who met with Micah in person. And of the two words in "subtly intimidate," both were equally important.

Micah's desk (unnecessary since every scrap in his files was virtual and every surface in the office was Beam-enabled) was large and made of solid mahogany. The walls were decorated with original Salvador Dali paintings — Micah's favorite artist, because in Micah's opinion, he so perfectly infused realism into scenes of surreality. Front and center, beside Micah's desk, was *Crucifixion*, a Dali painting depicting Christ crucified on a tesseract, mounted in a smooth black frame that was almost as large as the painting itself. Micah said he liked *Crucifixion* because it symbolized the idea that the world was composed of multiple dimensions and as many realities, just like The Beam itself. But to his visitors, the painting symbolized what Micah Ryan might do to people who fucked with him…in any dimension.

But all of this intimidation was subtle, by design. Like Micah himself, the office also radiated a welcoming feel along with its symbols of power — and accordingly, visitors to the office often thought they might be imagining whatever menace they felt. They'd reason that Micah had the desk because he liked its look. They'd reason that he might have had the room designed to completely eliminate all echoes (even off of the polished wood floor) not to unsettle people, but because he enjoyed quiet. Along one entire side of the office, there was no wall or window; the floor and ceiling simply stopped, opening into a void. It looked like a precipice from which anyone might fall seventy stories to their death, but visitors would reason that Micah might have employed a force field barrier rather than windows because he enjoyed the aesthetics and wasn't afraid of heights.

Micah walked to the wet bar, opened a small black box, and pulled out a cigarette. He held the cigarette up and looked at it for a moment before placing it between his lips and lighting it with a heavy table lighter. He inhaled, held the smoke, then vented a curling plume from his nose. The flavor was exquisite. The cigarettes were extraordinarily expensive, packed with engineered tobacco grown many districts south, where the weather was always kept warm. Between the shrinking of the North Atlantic continent and its continued rise in population (handled somewhat by Respero and a very secret and very controversial Beam-mediated pregnancy control program), land was precious. Little was left for farming, and the scant areas available were allotted almost exclusively for growing food. Tobacco grown in tiny sectors of the available land came at a premium. There were synthetic cigarettes, but they were terrible, and Micah didn't understand the point. Even synthetic cigarettes were taxed out the ass and had been since humans realized they damaged the body, so the poor couldn't afford them. The rich — who had the nanos necessary to undo smoking's damage as fast as it occurred — were the only people who smoked anyway. Fake cigarettes were smoked by a small class of poseurs — the Presque Beau, just below the elite Beau Monde — who had enough money to buy smokes, but not quite enough money to afford real ones.

Micah walked to the edge of his windowless wall and stared out across the city. The high-end force field, like the rest of his office, had been ludicrously expensive. He could have gotten a less expensive model, but cheap fields shimmered and shook like heat haze in the desert. They were also staticky, and tended to spark when you neared them. Micah's force field, which had cost at least ten times as much, was perfectly clear and semipermeable. As he stood at his office's edge, he could feel a light breeze rustle his perfectly groomed dark-brown hair and run up the sleeves of his tailored blue suit, ruffling his authentic cotton shirt cuffs. The real wind up this high was intense, but the field only let through a puff, and even that vanished once a person was more than a few feet from the edge. Micah raised the toe of his polished black shoe and stepped forward, his toe hanging over the edge. There was no resistance. But if he tipped forward, he knew the field would pull him back. You couldn't fall out…but it sure felt like you could.

Micah turned, again drawing on his cigarette and curling the smoke through his nostrils, aware that he was restless and not liking the weakness it implied one bit. Annoyed, he flicked the cigarette at the force field even though the smoke was only half finished: eight-five credits worth of waste. The Beam surfaces around him read his flicking motion and his pulse, decided that Micah wanted the cigarette to leave his office, and let it pass through the force field. Micah watched it catch the wind and fly. Not for the first time, he looked through the force field and wondered how picky the AI was about interpreting his intention. If he pushed a man toward the edge in the way he'd just flicked the cigarette, would the force field allow him to fall?

Micah strolled away from the edge and across the expansive floor, wondering how to quell his restlessness. Then his canvas chirped, and he realized he wouldn't have to.

"Mr. Killian is ready for you in the anteroom, Mr. Ryan," said a soft female voice. The voice had been meticulously replicated from old recordings of an adventurous woman named Veronica whom Micah had once known, although he called his console "Rebecca" for reasons of discretion.

"About goddamned time," said Micah. "Give him five minutes of mild paralytics, then ping me."

"Yes, Micah," said the voice.

Micah paced for another few minutes, knowing the virtual space where Killian waited was being flooded with a subtle neural imitation of poison. Participants in virtual meetings weren't supposed to have access to the inputs of the other participants, but most people weren't Micah Ryan. The poison wouldn't hurt Killian, but it would make (and leave) him unsettled. He wouldn't be able to find a position that felt comfortable to his proprioception inputs, and things might smell slightly funny to him. The console would lift the poison when Micah arrived, and Killian's subconscious would learn a lesson about being on time and about whose presence solved problems.

Once the five minutes were up, Micah sat in his immersion rig, plugged in, and had the console send him to meet Killian.

Micah opened his simulated eyes to find himself in what looked like a large boardroom a moment later, still dressed exactly as he was in real life, again holding a cigarette. Cigarettes were just as expensive in virtual space as in life — not to keep the raff from smoking them (the raff couldn't afford full immersion even if they knew about it), but rather to rape people a little bit more. Meeting spaces on The Beam were capitalist endeavors, just like the rest of Enterprise.

Across from Micah was a tall man in a white lab coat, sitting in one of the chairs, clearly uncomfortable. When

Killian saw Micah blip in, he stood then held himself stiff, as if at attention. Micah, who liked to watch old war films from back when war still existed, half expected Killian to salute.

"Sit down, Jim," he said. Killian preferred to go by "James," but Micah thought it sounded presumptuous.

"I'm sorry," said Killian, sitting. There was that "subtle" thing again. It always surprised Micah how many people, after he fucked with them, ended up apologizing.

Micah didn't sit. He circled the table instead, drawing puffs from his simulated cigarette. He could taste it in his mouth, feel the smoke in his lungs, and smell it as he plumed through his nose. He also felt mildly high, thanks to the engineered tobacco the cigarette's programmers had so excellently simulated.

"Tell me what's new, Jim," said Micah.

Killian shifted, and something like relief crawled across his body language. He looked like someone had pulled a thorn from his toe.

"Oh, things are going very, very well, Micah. Fidelities of BioFi 7.6 are well above what we'd hoped, and the speeds we're seeing are tremendous. We're seeing successful replication of entity after entity not just on The Beam, but also within our buffers. Which actually raises an ethical issue, because once the transfer is complete and verified, we'd want to delete the buffer copy, right? I mean, once it's no longer needed as a backup? But some of our people are joking that it's murder."

"How can it be murder if no lives are ended?"

"Well, it's a joke, of course. But really, if you think about it, the definition of 'life' is evolving, as is everything else. Life has always been conceived in biological terms — something that consumes, excretes, defends itself, reproduces, and so on — but when we're talking about sentience within a virtual world, that definition no longer suffices. Even the earliest AI with the smallest emergent properties present versions of those traits of living things. They consume space on a server. They can copy themselves to reproduce. I mean, just look at West — there are copies of him everywhere, in addition to West Prime within the central spindle. So we get all these sticky new questions like, 'When you erase a mind — even if it's just a copy — then is that 'killing' that mind? I see both sides. Truth is, if you took one of the buffer copies and dropped it into one of the main sectors, it would continue to function as any other because that's the whole point of there being a backup in the first place. And when you consider that it would carry a self-image and would, in a space like we're in now, present itself as wholly real and corporeal? That it'd have thoughts and an attitude, and if you pushed it or tried to fight it, it would fight back? With all that considered, I see why people wonder about deleting even our redundant copies. But I'm speaking philosophically, you understand."

"Fascinating," said Micah. He didn't actually care.

Killian seemed to read Micah's impatient expression and continued. "But yes, the speeds and fidelities are very, very good, and soon mind duplication and transfer will be considered as nothing more than a simple outpatient medical procedure. Then, it'll become wholesale, and people will stop regarding it as a fringe practice."

"Excellent. Good work." This time, Micah *did* care. Most people were governed by fear. Fear was a much bigger obstacle than restraint or conscience. Most tempted men didn't refrain from cheating on their wives because they felt it was wrong, but because they were afraid of getting caught. Removing fear in the right places and adding it back in the right places — even if the moral qualms stayed right where they were — was the key to selling anything. From Micah's point of view as a majority Xenia shareholder, fear could be sticky. Philosophy, not so much.

Killian looked down, fiddling with his fingers and thumbs, almost twiddling. He looked up, catching himself, and moved his eyes around the room. Everywhere other than at Micah.

"What about the biologicals?" Micah asked.

"That side is much harder, but we're getting there. The problem is that truly biological parts don't like to live without a mind operating them. I know how that sounds, but it's true. Working in this field...I'll tell you, it's enough to turn a man religious. And I mean the old church, not the new church. God and all that." He looked up at Micah, who was holding the cigarette in the corner of his mouth, hands clasped loosely together in front. "What I mean is," said Killian, still stammering, "is that you start to wonder if a body, after you die, maybe *is* just a hunk of meat. Because at this point, we can stimulate the biology almost entirely, and all that's missing is... well...a soul. Or a *mind*, I guess. Yes, 'mind' is sufficient. Sorry, I'm not expressing this well, but what I'm saying is..."

"How long?" said Micah.

"Oh, I don't think it'll be long. We'll crack it. It's a bit like trying to hold a bag open for long enough to shove something large inside it without anyone to help you. Right now, we can do it all piecemeal. And we can do it with processors and metal and so on, but..."

"Biological parts," said Micah. "That's what we want."

"Of course. And it's coming along. Humans all function as mind and body. We can engineer a lot of the body. We can split off the mind. All that's left is the pairing. We'll get there."

Micah nodded. But Killian had already looked away, now with his leg crossed, fiddling with his shoelace instead of his thumbs.

"What's up, Jim?" said Micah.

Killian looked up.

"Just tell me. Stop fucking around, and tell me what's bothering you."

Killian seemed to consider playing coy then hemmed and

hawed for a moment before admitting that there had been some confusion over a new salesman named Greenley. A temp receptionist had confused Greenley for another man — a Presque Beau and below salesman named Thomas Stahl — and had sent Stahl into the advanced biologics lab. Micah, his temperature rising, thought that Killian was probably deflecting. The receptionist would already have been wiped and hence be unable to defend herself. Regardless, Killian fucked up. Who simply took the word of a receptionist as gospel?

"It's not a problem!" said Killian, attempting to smile. He pushed back from his seat, but Micah put a hand on the chair's back, telling him without words to stay seated. "We wiped him, but apparently he had a deflector implant..."

"And of course, the world's most advanced upgrade lab wouldn't check for that sort of thing," Micah interjected.

"Well, yes, but see, it was all very confusing with the swarm escape the day before, and...well, like I said, it's not a problem anymore, in fact, it's..."

"You didn't think to tell me about this when it happened, Jim? It's Sunday, and seeing as Xenia is on nine-to-five, the very latest this could have happened was Friday." He was keeping his voice even and low, but everything in him was repressing an urge to use his virtual hands to rip Killian's virtual head from its shoulders. Thanks to Micah's hack, he could make Killian's real body feel it, too.

"Well, it was handled very quickly! We discovered the deflection as feedback on the sensor records when we did our nightly sweep, and plus, I'd decided to check in on him anyway because I wanted to be thorough, and we found out that some of the people he buys from...well, that's not important. But we sent someone out that night." He paused, as if deciding to omit part of the story. "He's in custody now. I sent in Kane. So I didn't want to burden you with it. You don't need to be concerned with trifles. You..."

"You sent in *Kane?*"

"Well, yes, because…"

"Why would you send that sick fuck in? That's so much *worse* than taking prisoners. Both could get you sent to Respero — " Here, Micah carefully avoided saying that "we" could be sent to Respero. " — but you know how I feel about that goddamned Polack. I didn't want him here in the first place, *certainly* not at Xenia, *certainly* not in development, but the board…"

"He was being obtuse! We needed information, and…"

Micah's eyes narrowed. "You needed information?"

"Well, yes."

"About?"

"Just in case…you know…"

Micah thought he knew what Killian was implying and didn't like it. Was this salesman's incursion truly an accident? Or had he been sent there by someone? Killian's actions seemed to imply the latter.

"It's handled, Mr. Ryan," said Killian, still fidgeting. "We'll Gauss them all, and they'll never even know…"

"Them?"

"Well, there are two others. A woman who was helping Stahl and a man — probably an accomplice! — who came into his apartment right after we apprehended Stahl. It's handled. Really. Promise. The only reason I didn't say anything is because your time is more valuable than this, and you have bigger things on your mind than your involvement at Xenia, what with Shift coming and all…" Killian trailed off, apparently done but content to leave the thought hanging.

Micah realized that his shoulders and arms had tensed and told himself to relax. Because his current body was a projection, it obeyed his commands as they came through The Beam. His fists unclenched, and his shoulders drooped. His breathing fell. He decided that what was done was done. So, with effort, he smiled. He told Killian that he'd handled the situation admirably, clapped the man on the shoulder, and politely excused himself. Then, with the meeting complete, Micah left first. He opened his real eyes to find himself back in his office, in his rig.

Micah stood then started to pace, refusing himself the luxury of succumbing to the vertigo that often followed reemergence. Despite the mood he'd forced upon the end of the meeting, Micah was far from pacified. The way Killian had handled things was hardly admirable or appropriate.

After his head cleared, Micah walked to a wall, swiped open a window, and tapped prompts until he saw a revolving icon that indicated The Beam was trying to reach Micah's "fixer." Despite Killian's assurances that the situation was handled, Micah felt far from sure that it was. It was time to send in the person who made him feel sure when nobody else could. The person who worked for Micah outside of Xenia's little security force of inept Beam zealots, who wouldn't hesitate to make things right at Xenia — even if Xenia was too blind to see what was in its own best interests.

The call didn't connect, telling Micah that the party he was trying to reach was offline or off-grid.

Micah swore. He was alone, so he allowed his tone to rise, running a hand through his hair, mussing it.

"Canvas."

Chirp. "Yes, Micah?"

"Rebecca, send a message to Jason Whitlock." He couldn't take any more infuriating discussions. At this point, he only wanted to issue commands, and for people to do as they were told.

"What is the message?"

"Tell him I want a Capital Protection agent assigned to round-the-clock surveillance on James Killian from Xenia Labs. The minute Killian does anything out of the ordinary, I want that agent to report in. If he can't get me, he's to report to Whitlock, and Whitlock is to use his judgment on pulling Killian in or doing what is needed. Priority."

The canvas AI scanned the message for loose ends then found one. "Do you care whom Mr. Whitlock assigns for this surveillance, Micah?"

Micah ran a hand through his already-mussed hair. "It can be anyone," he said, "as long as they are equipped to wear a Stark suit."

Chapter 5

WHEN KAI WAS FIFTEEN, she was raped by three men who saw her on the street during the day then followed her to her temporary home — up under the stanchions of a highway overpass — later that night. The next day Kai found herself beaten, bloody, and barely able to twitch. A woman found her and took her to an emergency room where she convalesced for several days. Kai's first act after becoming ambulatory was to go to a well-known local dealer and trade half of the food she'd managed to scavenge for a conventional grenade. She then entered a ramshackle settlement, every vagrant eye fixed on the young girl so stupidly walking amongst them like a bull's eye with feet, and found the men who had raped her. A few minutes later, Kai scraped pieces of her attackers from shrapnel-pocked walls and took them home as souvenirs.

A few years later, after Kai had bought her way out of the gutter, she found herself trafficking services in lower-end neighborhoods, a roof over her head as she worked for a man who "managed" her business. Even at twenty, Kai didn't feel she needed help — either in handling her affairs or protecting herself — but the neighborhood was union: You worked for Tom or didn't work at all. It was a good deal for Tom; his new girl was incredibly popular and made him a ton of money. Kai didn't see it that way — she was doing all the work while Tom sat back and sipped his percentage. So she tried leaving, and when she did, Tom stabbed her in the stomach with a four-inch kitchen knife. That pain — on a physical level, anyway — easily trumped the torment from her rape. It was as if every nerve in her body had sparked to life and was suddenly screaming. She could barely breathe, every molecule focused on her center of agony. Tom ran off, thinking her finished as Kai crumpled onto the ancient Formica floor in a ball. Her bleeding wasn't critical, though, so she'd simply lain where she was for a long while, unable to activate her low-end apartment's canvas because it had no voice interface. It had taken Kai hours to drag herself to the door and yell — hours filled with the most excruciating pain she could imagine. The rape had been beyond agonizing, but those hours spent on the floor of the kitchen were so much worse — and this time, thanks to Tom's connections, she knew she'd never be able to fight back. The physical agony was torturous. The mental feeling of helplessness, for a girl who'd always been able to handle whatever came at her, was torturous. Even looking back years later on those hours, Kai didn't think there existed more pain in the whole world.

But she was wrong.

Right now, Kai felt dozens of knives severing each of her toes and fingers wide open, peeling them back, separating every shred of tendon from her bones. She felt the pulpy innards of her digits smashed and chewed, farther separated — the nails peeled straight back and skin slowly stripped. She looked down, vision commanded as if by the push of a strong hand at the back of her head, and saw her fingers and toes coming off. The pain should have stopped once the digits were gone from her body; it didn't. Kai felt each cut, each flay, each intrusion and impalement. Then the knives were on what remained of her hands and arms, running up and into her gut, shredding flesh from flesh. Something was happening to her face; she seemed to feel her skull retreating from a blade, her face melting from bone, her eyes becoming hot like rocks in a fire and popping. A circle of agony wrapped her neck and slit it, her larynx seeming to crack and fold back on itself like a split walnut. Still, she was able to scream, her lips peeling from her face, and as she did, her…

It stopped. Kai's eyes blinked, and she suddenly found herself staring at a featureless white ceiling. The pain's departure was so complete and sudden that she was totally disoriented. This wasn't how pain was supposed to work, and her body was baffled. Pain was supposed to subside and retreat, not cease like a switch being flipped. She was afraid to move. The absence of pain was a sort of torture in itself. Everything in her braced, preparing for its return.

"It's very real, is it not?" said a pleasant voice. Kai rolled her eyes and saw Alix Kane's white-haired head step into view above her. Her own head was strapped firmly down on the Orion, a kind of cap snaking long fingers under her hair. "That's what people of your lower station always say when they're first exposed to this level of immersion: that it's so *real*. With this technology, you aren't being *shown* horror. You are *experiencing* horror as if it were really happening." He tapped the machine beneath Kai with his palm. "If I had a kinder machine than this old girl, I could put you in a meadow. You would not experience it as a falsity. You would believe you were there. *Fully*. I could let you live out your entire life in that meadow, and soon you'd forget that there even was another world that you used to call reality. There is no way to tell them apart. Now do you see why Mr. Stahl was so interested in learning about all of this?"

Kane circled the table once while Kai's breath hitched and she fought to get her bearings. It had been *real* all right. Realer than real. She'd never imagined that such a degree of simulation was possible. The Orion's takeover of her five senses, aided by the neural down-tuning nanos they'd injected into her, had been perfect.

"That was just a starter," said Kane. "I can literally excite every sensory nerve in your body at once, but there's no art to that. At lower levels, I can give you knives and fishhooks and white-hot brands. We have programs for the iron maiden, for being drawn and quartered, for all sorts of terrible things. But that doesn't occur everywhere, see? Even when a team of horses is pulling you apart, your scalp doesn't hurt. Some people, they use this thing like a blunt weapon." He tapped the table's aluminum surface beside Kai's head. "But there is value in anticipation, is there not? You of all people should understand the power of teasing."

Kai felt her heart thumping in her throat. Her breath was coming fast and hard. She jerked against the restraints, testing them. But they were too strong for her to break, and Kane had managed to disable her upgrades by uploading what he called a "short-lived virus" into her — something Kai didn't know was possible. She still had her mental add-ons at her disposal, but that was probably intentional because right now, all they were good for was categorizing the depths of her agony, recording it for later playback if she wanted.

"I don't know anything else," Kai managed to say. She'd already told Kane about how Doc had come to her, how he'd seen some strange things at Xenia Labs, and how she'd been trying to help him disappear. She hadn't needed a round on the Orion to tell them everything, because they knew it all already. But Kane had strapped her in anyway.

Kane laughed. "Oh, I know you don't." Kane called over his shoulder. "Unmute Mr. Stahl."

Kai rolled her eyes, trying to look around. Her head was fixed, and she couldn't move it, but she soon saw one of the Beamers dragging Doc into her field of view. His blond hair was unkempt, eyes wide and wild. He was ranting and raging, screaming and shouting — except that no sound was leaving his mouth. Then the Beamer touched a button on a handheld and the nanos they'd shot into him moved away from his vocal cords, and Doc's voice returned as suddenly as Kai's pain had departed.

" — know anything, you motherfucker! I keep telling you! It was a mistake! Let her…"

He stopped, seemingly surprised by his voice in the quiet room. Of course, it couldn't have been this quiet a moment ago, could it? Kai assumed she'd been screaming, but she realized she had no idea. Her experience on the Orion was fully immersive — more immersive than even she, as an expert in sensation and sensation-enhancing technology, thought possible. She hadn't just *imagined* her fingers peeling like bananas to show the bleached white bone beneath. She'd felt it as if it were happening. She'd *seen* it. She'd *heard* it. She'd even *smelled* it, and she'd tasted blood in her mouth, metallic like copper. She'd felt as if she had screamed, but she might have been doing so into the black, bloody room in which she'd been sequestered a moment ago. As far as the others were concerned (and she had to believe Nicolai was over there somewhere too, equally muted), it might have looked like she was peacefully napping.

Doc said, "Why is she bleeding?"

Kane reached down and ran a finger along Kai's neck, below her ear, then pulled it away and looked at a fat line of red blood. Kai felt sure he would lick it.

"We don't understand that," said Kane. "The eggheads say it's something like stigmata. But it's the reason the table has holes. Sometimes, their bodies believe the pain so intensely that they'll bleed through their clothing. It can get… messy."

"What were they doing to you, sweetheart?" said Doc. As pissed off as she'd been at him earlier and as steely as she herself had been, Doc's use of the word touched her in a strange way. It almost made her want to cry. But she couldn't answer. She could only shake her head.

Doc turned to Kane.

"She doesn't know anything, and I don't know anything, either. I told you. It was a mistake. They thought I was this other guy, Greenley. I had no idea that stuff existed. I went home and tried to look it up afterward, even. I have a secure router. I'll tell you where I got it; I don't care. I hacked into a dozen high-end upgrade stores but couldn't find anything like the stuff at Xenia. I haven't told anyone other than Kai what I saw. I swear. Go ahead, Gauss us all, problem solved."

"It's not enough," Kane said. He didn't seem angry. He just seemed unfinished, or perhaps unsatisfied.

"It's all there is. Please."

Kane looked at Kai, his small white head haloed by the overhead light, creating a haze around his face. He raised his own handheld and made a show of preparing to push a button. He wanted Kai to see it coming.

"Wait!" she yelled.

"Yes?" said Kane.

"Don't. Please. I don't know anything. I'd tell you if I did. I would."

Kai saw Kane press something, and like a light switch had been flipped, found herself again in the black room that smelled of sour meat. She felt a spear strike her middle, then flower out into a slow-moving circle, tearing a hole through her body's center. Her flesh burned, and her throat was slit, her neck contorting and breaking. She wanted to scream, but there was no air, and when she managed to inhale, Kai found her lungs filled with acid, burning and devouring and...

"*Jesus!*" Doc blurted as the room returned. He stared at her, his face ugly. So apparently she'd done something visible or audible after all. She may have screamed, or bled. But now, returned to the white room and feeling logic want to leave her, she hardly cared. Her head was too foggy to care. The white room, with Doc and Kane, was becoming peaceful. Not just because there was no pain, but because here, Kai's mind seemed to want to surrender and forget. While the Orion was on, she was totally present. But in the real world, her mind could drift. She felt it wanting to unhinge, drift away and vanish. She wondered if the Beamers could see her. They'd feel vindicated. The Beam's world really was more vivid and alive than the foggy false environment she assumed was still known erroneously as reality.

Kane raised his handheld again, finger poised. He was putting on a show for Doc, but it was Kai who responded.

"It was my fault," she whispered, her heart starting to flutter. She did *not* want that button pushed, not again, no matter what. "I told Doc to go to Xenia."

Kane's handheld gave a low buzz. Doc had already started to protest, but the buzz beat him to it. "Lies won't help," Kane said to her, like a teacher relaying a lesson.

"She doesn't know anything!" Doc bellowed. "What do you expect to get? Let her go! I'll tell you whatever you want. Everything. *Anything.* I'll talk *until* you hear something you want. When I was twenty, I robbed a homeless guy. I've scammed half my clients. I fucked my neighbor, who was thirty years older than I was and looked every year. I've got hundreds of thousands in illegal equipment. Whatever. Xenia. Anything I have! Just let her go."

Kane stared at Doc, uncertain. He looked down at Kai, then at the Orion.

Reluctantly, Doc added, "If you've got to put me on that thing, do it. But me, not her. She can't help you."

Kane pursed his lips then gave a small nod and looked up at the Beamer holding Doc then across the room at something Kai couldn't see.

"Take her down," he said.

Another Beamer came forward and unstrapped Kai's arms, legs, and head. He removed whatever was under her hair, then rolled her up to a sitting position. She found she couldn't stand, so the Beamer pulled her from the table and dropped her unceremoniously onto the ground. Kai watched floor and ceiling trade places as she rolled, her body limp and unresponsive. She couldn't feel the Orion's pain in her body anymore, but it must have left its mark on her mind because she couldn't feel the pain of striking the floor, either. Dissonance between her nerves and memory was jarring. Her body didn't even want to try. Something in Kai's brain said it was beyond dead, cut to its constituent pieces. She decided, body and mind, to surrender, then rolled onto her back, able to see the men above her. If she'd found herself staring at the floor (which she couldn't believe wasn't painted in blood), she'd have been just as content.

Kane looked at the Beamer who had pulled Kai from the Orion. His sleeves were black, but Kai thought she could see wet spots shimmering, and assumed it was her blood. Not that she had it within her to care.

"Get him an injection and strap him on," said Kane. Then he looked at Kai. "Her, you can kill."

Kai, from her spot on the floor, thought this was a brilliant idea.

Chapter 6

Feeling like a cliché and not caring, Isaac stared at his reflection in the convention center's green room mirror, slapping his chest and taunting himself.

"You don't need anyone else, do you, motherfucker?" he yelled at the Isaac in the mirror.

The first time he'd asked his reflection a rhetorical question, a voice had answered him. Before asking again, he'd turned off the mirror's verbal interface so that he could be awesome without being disturbed. His mirror at home was a plain mirror. The mirrors at the convention center would, however, have to be Beam-enabled. VIPs using the green room would want to follow news stories, get updates on their financials, or have the room's sensors provide feedback on their appearance or their body language. Isaac, trying to pump himself up for his speech, found this all very annoying. Sometimes, a mirror should just be a fucking mirror.

The reflected version of Isaac didn't respond re: this particular motherfucker needing anyone else.

"You rose to greatness on your own, didn't you?" Isaac continued, staring daggers at his reflection. *"Not* because of

Micah. *Not* because of Nicolai. And *definitely* not because of Natasha. You're your own motherfucker, aren't you?"

The man in the mirror offered no opinion as to whether or not he was his own motherfucker. So, knowing that it would ruin his makeup, Isaac slapped himself across the face in order to give himself even more shit.

"Wake up! You got this! You don't need anyone! Fuck Micah! Fuck Natasha! And fuck your speechwriter! He wants to go off-grid and leave you, then fuck him! You can do this on your own, because you are *Isaac Fucking Ryan!* Aren't you?"

The man in the mirror did not reply. However, his stare seemed to indicate that he was, indeed, Isaac Fucking Ryan.

Isaac held his own gaze for five long seconds then broke it with a feeling of *That's what I motherfucking thought!*

He stepped back, reasonably full of testosterone, wondering if a Beam-enabled mirror could be programmed to mimic a regular mirror in order to give you a lifelike reflection then break from its mimicry and cause your reflection to start yelling back at you. He decided that was indeed possible. In a world where you could book a week-long virtual vacation that you could fully experience in a single night while sleeping, getting into an argument with your mirror sounded like playing with blocks. Isaac tried to decide if it would freak him out to have his reflection yelling back at him, or if it'd be awesome. He had just decided that it would be awesome (and was about to tell the mirror to grow a motherfucking spine and give him some motherfucking lip) when the green room door opened and a page stuck his head in.

"Five minutes, Mr. Ryan."

"Did I not lock that fucking door?" Isaac yelled. The fact that the page had nearly caught him in a symbolic dick-measuring contest with his own reflection made a furious blush creep up under the collar of Isaac's starched white dress shirt.

"Well, it's a privacy lock, sir, but because it's Beam and

because there's always a clock ticking, we need to have access to…"

"GET THE FUCK OUT!"

The page retreated, and Isaac found himself almost glad he'd intruded. Yelling at the kid had further bolstered his feeling of cruel badassery. He wasn't just going to deliver a kick-ass speech to that crowd out there; he was going to fuck every one of those people up the ass with a cock made of plutonium while smoking six cigars, and when it was over, they'd all look up, wide-eyed, awed by whatever immense and awesome shit Isaac Motherfucking Ryan had just laid on them.

On impulse, Isaac spun to face the mirror, turned the verbal interface back on, and said, "Canvas, have my reflection insult me."

He was unsure whether the mirror would be able to comply, but immediately he saw his reflection meet his eyes and say, "You're ugly."

"RESPECT THE COCK!" Isaac screamed. He plowed his carbon nanotube-reinforced fist into his wiseass reflection, his shoulder seeming to dislocate as the Beam glass in the mirror detonated.

The moment of adrenaline lasted for six or seven seconds, and then his fist began to bleed and his entire arm started to ache. He wanted to feel stupid, but it was better to feel powerful and badass. So he wrapped a towel around his fist to keep the blood off of his suit and went to the bathroom. On the way, Isaac used his good hand to fish a small pen-like device from his briefcase and pressed it to his wrist. Immediately, the high-end scavenger nanos began tuning down sensory nerves in his arm while conducting emergency repairs. By the time he had removed the glass from his knuckles and washed away the blood, his lacerated skin was mostly knitted. The adrenaline remained. Isaac balled his hands into fists, not feeling whatever had gone wrong in his shoulder thanks to the anesthetic. His badass nanos would repair his badass shoulder while he delivered his badass speech.

The page didn't return. Instead, he chirped Isaac from the overhead speakers. Isaac took one final look into the mirror's remaining shards and marched through the door and onto the stage. He *owned* this stage. Isaac looked out at the people in the hall waiting to hear him, knowing he *owned* them too. There were Beam cameras everywhere, and he owned every mother-fucker watching, too.

Isaac didn't need Nicolai. He had written every word of the new speech himself. Once onstage, he delivered it with his chest out, chin high — the esteemed Czar of Internal Satisfaction, the perfect, immutable, unshakable symbol of the strength of the Directorate Party. He told them that Shift was less than a month away and urged everyone listening to stand up from their everyday ruts and *really* consider what that meant. It was easy to see Shift in the same way you'd see the election of an official who'd been in office for decades and would never be ousted, but Shift wasn't like that at all. Shift wasn't like voting, because Shift was about *you* and no one else. It was said that a person couldn't choose his or her own destiny, but Shift was a chance to do that exactly. *At Shift, you'll choose to be Directorate or Enterprise,* he announced to the crowd. *It will define not only what you receive (or, in the case of Enterprise, what you DON'T receive) for six years, but also who you are. Do you want to be one more body in the Enterprise gutter, always fighting for your life but never being part of a team that always has your back? Do you want to spend the next six years living in fear of dying in the street while your children starve because you chose selfishness over security?*

Isaac told the crowd about the new Beam-based currency that Enterprise was trying to push. Every person in Enterprise was another vote for Enterprise in the Senate, and a predominantly Enterprise Senate would ratify "beem" currency for sure.

"And who do you think will earn the most beem?" Isaac

asked his audience. "Will it be the Directorate, who do the jobs we've been assigned for the greater good? Will beem be given out equally, as it is in the Directorate? Or will beem instead subvert our system, and turn the entire network into a marketplace? Who will benefit when the entire Beam begins to side with one party over the other? Will it be you? Or will it be those who control The Beam and would never design a system that wasn't to *their* benefit, as greedy, cutthroat capitalists?"

Isaac felt power surge through him as every word he'd written — that *he'd* written, not Nicolai — crossed his lips with the force of a bludgeon. Nobody could argue with what Isaac was saying. Anyone who chose to become or remain Enterprise after listening to this speech was an uncontested idiot. The next time he spoke, Isaac would repeat the key points from this speech, ramming them home. When Shift came, Directorate would win by a landslide, and inter-party solidarity would be at an all-time high. Enterprise defections would set records.

Isaac ended his speech. The room cheered. Then they stood, applauding him in a roar. Isaac thought he saw tears. He had done this. *Isaac.* He wouldn't have to split credit with Nicolai this time.

This was Isaac — *all* Isaac, and no one else.

He returned to the green room to find that while he'd been kicking ass, someone had replaced the mirror. It had probably been a bot that had done it, but Isaac preferred to think of a person doing the job instead, quailing at the thought of a man who held such fury and strength. He looked at the mirror, eyed his reflection to see if it would flinch (it was just a reflection now, and didn't), and then, with a cheek-stretching smile on his face, said, "Canvas, give me Beam top stories."

Isaac's reflection faded into the front page of the Beam's news feed. His speech hadn't been voted to the top, as he'd suspected. Instead, it was number two. Isaac frowned, wondering if his public triumph might take another minute. He wanted to get in there and read his praise but wanted to see it rank at the top first — a validation that said, for once and for all, that Isaac Fucking Ryan did not need a speech-writer to prove his greatness.

But his speech didn't rise; instead, the top story hung in place above it, racking up votes faster and faster. He pulled it forward, confused by the headline ("Ryan Proposes Hybrid System") and felt himself bolstered. He hadn't proposed any hybrid solution, really, but at least he had grabbed the top spot after all.

But when he exploded the story, he realized that the Ryan in question wasn't Isaac. It was Micah.

Fifteen minutes before Isaac had given his speech, Micah had delivered one of his own while Isaac was in here yelling and breaking mirrors. And Micah, of course, had done it better. He'd managed to answer each of Isaac's objections — to beem, to Enterprise, to the system in general — in advance.

Isaac swore. The Ryan brothers, with their famous rivalry, were news celebrities, so of course most viewers had watched them both. Isaac's speech, badass though it was, had said nothing new; he'd simply raised complaints…unknowingly *after* the same complaints had been effectively addressed by Micah. Worse: Mutual relevancy between the two speeches would be high because so many people would have watched and indexed both of them. So how had The Beam arranged them in a playlist? Why, with Micah's speech first, of course. Isaac thought he'd conquered, but in reality he'd only made himself look stupid and ill-prepared, redundant and a day late.

"Canvas," said Isaac, already feeling his mood crumble to dust. "Send in that stupid little page."

The room's Beam connection must have known which page Isaac meant because a moment later the same kid knocked on the door. Isaac had to tell him to enter twice before he did so, looking nervous.

"Yes, Mr. Ryan?" he said.

"Did you see my brother's speech?"

The kid looked around the room, helpless.

"Tell me the truth. I won't yell at you."

The page nodded slowly.

"What do *you* think about beem? Again, honestly."

"I'm unsure, sir."

Isaac sighed. "Don't make me have the canvas run a truth assessment."

The kid furrowed his brow, which was now beaded with sweat.

"Well, it just seems like it might be the best of both worlds," he said. Then, when Isaac didn't snap his head off, the page continued, seeing the reluctant *Go on* in Isaac's eyes. "I mean, sir, it'd be great for Enterprise of course, but maybe for Directorate too. Because you could open a virtual business on The Beam and trade in beem. If it was legal tender, you could spend that beem rather than having to use it for virtual upgrades and dumb tokens like you do now."

Isaac sighed.

"No offense, sir," the page added.

Isaac dismissed him then reopened both of The Beam's top pages, watching comments filter in on both speeches.

He looked at his fist, remembering how bloody it had been and how powerful he had felt, as he watched himself become more and more hated in real time.

Chapter 7

"This isn't necessary," said Doc.

Alix Kane smiled. "I know."

The small, white-haired man circled Doc as he was strapped to the Orion, Doc's head cradled in the black, helmet-like device at its top end. Somewhere past his feet, Nicolai was watching the scene, unable to speak. Doc couldn't see Kane at all times because he couldn't move his head, and that was a sort of torture in itself. Kane hadn't laid a finger on him in real life, but even the real-life experience was already terrible. Doc kept feeling as if, when Kane was out of sight, he'd push a button and Doc wouldn't be ready, and he'd suddenly find his soul being ripped to pieces without warning.

Doc said, "I've told you all I know."

"I don't think so."

Doc insisted: "Really, I have."

Kane scratched his chin, thoughtful. "You must understand. This isn't exactly the scientific method. I don't come in here with an open mind, ready to discover an unpresupposed truth. I've been told in advance that you know something, and I'm here to find out what that something is. This isn't 'innocent until proven guilty.' I'm afraid, Mr. Stahl, that your guilt is assumed."

"That's a bullshit way to do things."

"It assures we'll get what we want, if it is there to be gotten at all," Kane said. "Try to see it from our perspective. Even if you really do know nothing, if we torture and kill you, what have we lost? Nothing. But consider the alternative: What if you *do* know something? Well, I can't give up so easily. The sort of people who authorize something like this aren't terribly understanding people. As little as you want to be on the Orion, Mr. Stahl, I *really* don't want to be on it. So to be totally certain, it's best that you tell me what I think you know, or you die."

"If you're going to kill me anyway, why should I tell you dick?"

In response, Kane pressed a button, and Doc found himself in a pit, buried in the dirt and compressed into an impossibly tight ball. Every muscle screamed because the ball wasn't tidy; his joints had all been bent the wrong way, ripping sinew and tendon and muscle and bone. He couldn't breathe; his lungs were filled with dirt. His spine was ripped open and exposed, and his spinal column at each vertebrae was being slowly impaled by a dull, serrated spike. He felt his eyes pop and run down his cheeks, igniting rockets in his brain. His teeth came out slowly; bones erupted through skin, his jaw hyperextended, then sheared off entirely as every nerve screamed in…

It stopped. Doc stared at Kane, panting, his heart racing fast enough to burst through his chest.

"To answer your question," said Kane, "the reason is because if you tell me what I need to hear, we can move on to the part where they kill you rather than having me continue to serve you nightmares. Wouldn't that be nice?"

"I don't know anything!" Doc screamed, spittle flying from his lips. "What the hell do you want? *There's nothing in my head!"*

"Tell me again how it started," said Kane.

Doc had told Kane the story over and over and over in the time that had passed since Kai had been taken away by the Beamers. He'd come to Xenia. He'd been late, but had been told by the receptionist that he was early. His name hadn't been taken. They'd simply come in and escorted him into the room with all the high-end goodies. Kane asked why nobody had recognized him — and hence known what he should and shouldn't see — if he'd been there so often. He asked how Killian could have not realized he wasn't Greenley, seeing as Killian was a professional and would know his salesmen. He asked why Doc's Beam ID hadn't been checked at reception or at the secret door. Doc replied that the receptionist was a temp, and it seemed like Greenley was new. As to the rest, Doc suggested Kane put Killian on the Orion — a suggestion Kane seemed to like.

"You went to great lengths to protect your memory," said Kane. "Why would you do that if you hadn't come to Xenia to collect information you thought someone might later wish to erase?"

"Why wouldn't you have a Gauss chamber if you wanted to be so goddamn sure about erasing memories?" Doc countered.

Kane reached for his handheld, but Doc blurted out for him to wait. He told Kane that he'd been in many sticky situations before in which people had wanted him to forget, but that for a scrapper like Doc, information was power. So he'd gotten the implant, and had had it for years — long before his trip to Xenia.

"Where did you get the implant?"

"I told you!"

"Yes. Mr. Ryu. You surrendered his name quite easily."

"Everyone knows Ryu is a double-dealing asshole! He'd turn me in without blinking. Screw Ryu! Yes, he sold it to me.

He also sold me a hot router and an ID spoof for my car. Just let me off this, okay? It was a mistake."

Kane shook his head. "But then you kept the memories, Mr. Stahl. *And* you investigated. We know about Mr. Ryu. His protections are excellent, but nothing we can't hack. We with our 'superior technology' as you saw. As you *intended* to see, and as you refused to forget."

Doc jerked his hands against the restraints. "Of course I investigated! I was curious. And refusing to forget? Are you *fucking kidding me?*"

The room went black. Doc screamed as something enormous slammed into his gut, crushing his organs and ripping an aperture in his abdomen that began to spill his intestines. He looked down and realized he could see into his own chest cavity. Whatever had struck him was like an enormous club, laying waste to his insides. He saw his heart try to flutter, his intestines split like pulverized sausage casings, his unprocessed shit oozing its way out of them, mingling with gore. The pain was astonishing, but the smell was almost as bad; Doc watched the bag of his stomach heave, and he threw up, looking down, filling his shattered chest cavity with bile and blood. Then something large was slowly pressed against his face, advancing steadily. His skull shattered with a snap, sending shards of bone through his ears and cheeks and…

It stopped, and the white ceiling appeared above him.

"I DON'T FUCKING KNOW ANYTHING! I'D TELL YOU, NOAH FUCKING WEST, I'D TELL YOU! I DON'T KNOW ANYTHING, YOU SICK FUCK! THERE'S NOTHING IN MY HEAD FOR ME TO TELL YOU!"

Tears painted the sides of his face. Panic welled inside him. But there was no way out until Kane decided to end it.

"You thought the information was valuable," said Kane, his voice calm and thoughtful, as if they were just having a friendly chat.

"Of course!"

"As it turns out, it is. Quite valuable, Mr. Stahl. Are you sure you wish to stick to your story? Are you sure you still insist that you didn't know what you would find at Xenia? I'll end this if you tell me what I need to know. But don't lie. The room will know if you simply tell me something in order to make me stop, and I'm afraid that the Orion's level of agony will go much higher if you do that."

"Then you know I'm telling the truth about knowing nothing."

Kane seemed to think. "Maybe. But concealment and fabrication are third cousins at best."

Something leapt into Doc's mind. A witness. *A way out.*

"Call Nero!" he said. "Nero will tell you! I come in at the same time every week! I came to meet him last week too. They gave me Killian, and Killian fucked this up. Not me — Killian! Xenia had some issue with a nano storm, and they said Nero wasn't available. Call Nero! Ask him about me!"

Kane shrugged. "Nero is indisposed."

"They said he was dealing with the police over a break-in they'd had."

Kane chuckled. "Is that what they said?"

"Then you know? You know about Nero?"

"Nero, yes. You? Not so much. But alas, I can't ask him right now. Tell me, Mr. Stahl. How do you know Omar Jones?"

Kane's change of topic was so sudden that at first Doc had no idea what he was talking about, and certainly not how to respond. Omar had once — and *only* once — made a purchase from Doc. But how did Kane know, and why did he care?

"Um..." Doc thought about lying outright, but the room would be able to read the lie in his voice. Or would it? Doc had plenty of practice lying, and could maybe beat it. But evasion and delay felt safer, so he pretended to think, waiting to see what Kane might reveal to help him.

Instead of revealing anything, Kane said, "Let me show you."

Kane raised his handheld and touched its surface. Doc felt himself respond immediately, his muscles tensing, his body bracing for pain. But instead of being sent to the torture chamber, he found himself in a park, standing behind a hot dog cart. There was a merry-go-round in the background with several kids circling on it, one being dragged as he tried to push, laughing as his feet raised brown clouds of dust. A man stood near the merry-go-round in a fine suit coat, jeans, and boots, seemingly waiting for something. Doc looked down and saw hands that were too dark to be his own and felt a substantial gut pulling on his back. Apparently, he was in someone else's body — the body of whoever had recorded the immersion he was experiencing.

Then Doc realized that the man he was watching was himself.

It was bizarre, seeing himself from a distance. He could feel the breeze on his new skin, could smell the foreign scents of his new alien shell as he watched his usual body cross an expanse of grass twenty feet away. He recognized the scene, but when he'd last seen it, he was looking at the surroundings from behind a different set of eyes. It had been just a few weeks ago, in the southern part of Central Park. He knew what was coming, but he wasn't in charge of this body's motor controls and had to wait for the fat man to turn his head. When he did, Doc saw a thin black man approaching. That would be Omar.

The two men shook hands then started to chat. Something passed between them: a slip of paper. Doc remembered the paper. On it had been the number for a part. Doc had searched for the part, ordered it, then burned the paper in his fireplace. In a world where data was everything, Doc always marveled that paper and its secrets still burned just fine.

The vision seemed to accelerate, as if under the thumb

of impatience. Then the immersion ended, and Doc was again strapped to the Orion, staring up at Alix Kane's white head.

"I guess I know him," said Doc. He said it lightly, even though he was beyond shocked. There was nothing about what had just happened that he would have believed likely or possible a few hours before. Doc had met Omar in the park because, thanks to the trees, it was the one place City Surveillance didn't see well unless it sent in fliers, which it never did because the intrusion pissed people off. He didn't know it was possible to record a man's senses, and had had no reason to think he was being watched. Or was Omar the one who was being watched? He'd had his doubts about dealing with Omar, and now they resurfaced. In a way, it was starting to make sense. It was fucking *Omar* who'd gotten Doc into this mess.

"Why were you meeting him?" Kane asked.

"We're having an affair."

Doc suddenly felt his leg torn from his body at the knee in slow motion. It was a new species of terrifying because he hadn't gone to the torture chamber; he was still staring at Kane. Was this happening for real? He couldn't lift his head to check. He screamed out then clenched against the seething torment, but it was already gone.

"Why were you meeting him?" Kane repeated.

"Noah Fucking West! Fine, we were talking shop. He's an add-on dealer. I'm an add-on dealer. We hit the same circles."

"You're not rivals?"

"I'm everybody's buddy," said Doc. He wiggled his toes and felt them move in his shoe, his leg apparently still there. But of course he knew that; the pain had shut off like a switch.

"What did he hand you on that slip of paper?"

"Nothing!" Then, realizing more pain was coming and wondering what he owed to fucking *Omar*, who it seemed had gotten him into this, Doc cried out, "Wait! It was the number for a part. For an upgrade."

"Not the name of anyone at Xenia. Not instructions."

"No! It was an order."

That was true, at least. The part number scrawled on the paper had been for an add-on Doc had access to through Ryu. It was a parasite — a specialty of Ryu's and something illegal enough that Ryu would never sell to anyone other than trusted dealers, like Doc. Omar had needed a way to smuggle a few meterbars of moondust back from the moon elevator, and customs had grown wise to most mechanical means of concealment. More and more often, customs scans were stopping anyone with an add-on that created a compartment within their bodies, so that agents could search them. But the scans wouldn't so much as see the seven-foot engineered tapeworm Ryu had later sold to Doc and that Doc had later marked up and sold to Omar. And even if they did see it and had reason to suspect it, enzyme pockets inside the thing would dissolve the rocks in its gut long before anyone could extract it.

"Why were you using paper for an order? Why didn't you use handhelds?"

"People still use paper."

"When it's people in the Beau Monde or Presque Beau, like you and Omar, paper is usually only used to conduct illegal business."

"I still use Post-it Notes," said Doc. He did, too. There was something about the feel of a pen rolling on paper that couldn't be replicated by even the very best stylus. It was an expensive eccentricity. The only pens he could find were antiques, and Post-it Notes were almost entirely extinct. Doc had found a guy on Marketplace whose grandfather had stockpiled them for some reason and was selling them off for fifty credits per brightly colored pad.

"What was he ordering?"

"I think it was a brain thing. A kind of wetchip, like N…"

Doc's head was wrenched in a circle. He felt skin tear, then his neck broke and became knives of bone. He felt his esophagus and windpipe twist, like a swallow in reverse, yet still somehow he found just enough air to scream.

"I'm not lying!" he gasped when the pain ended. "Nicolai has a wetchip! Ask him! *Scan* him!"

"You expect me to believe that the biggest add-on dealer in the district came to a Presque Beau scrapper like you for a wetchip? He *sells* them. Why would he come to you?"

Doc could answer the question truthfully, but the answer was just as damning as if he'd actually gone to spy on Xenia at Omar's command, as Kane was suggesting. Xenia was very, very careful not to deal with dust runners, and Omar worked with Xenia. Telling Kane about the dust-smuggling tapeworm would get them both Respero'd at best, Orion'd into oblivion at worst. Maybe Omar knew about the fancy add-ons Doc had seen, and maybe he didn't, but regardless of whether Omar had deliberately sent Doc in (which he hadn't), Xenia thought they were in cahoots. And in a way, they were — but over moondust smuggling, not industrial espionage. But it hardly mattered; both would be offensive to the people in charge.

"It was a *special* wetchip! A creativity booster. Nobody sells those. Omar wanted one. I had one. That was all there was to it!"

Kane looked toward Doc's feet, toward Nicolai. He seemed to consider, then turned back at Doc.

"I'll tell you what," he said. "We'll scan your friend over there. See what kind of a chip he has in his brain. If it's something we know Omar to sell, I'll turn this device up as high as it goes and leave you here overnight. Because, Doc Stahl, I don't believe you were selling Omar Jones a wetchip. I believe you were meeting with him to plot what you claim was an accident. I believe you heard rumors about what was available at the tier above yours and got greedy. Maybe you didn't know what you were facing. Maybe you simply thought you could boost your profits by black-marketing some wares above your pay grade. Maybe you had no idea about the implications of what such high-end technology could do, and hence maybe this is all an accident in a way, and maybe now that Xenia's cards are all on the table, maybe you'd like to amend your statement."

Kane leaned in. Doc could smell his skin. The scent was somehow organic and artificial at the same time, like Plasteel covered with a film of algae.

"Maybe if you tell me the truth," said Kane, his breath in Doc's face, "I will *allow* you to amend it. Maybe you were only curious. Maybe you never knew, ahead of time, what you would find. And if that's true, then maybe you aren't dangerous, and maybe this can all end. Maybe you never met me. Maybe you don't know a device such as this Orion even exists. Maybe you can wake up in your own bed tomorrow without memories of this unfortunate incident, and suffer the loss of only one client…and one whore who knows entirely too much."

"It was a tapeworm," said Doc. "Omar wanted me to order him a tapeworm, so he could smuggle moondust past customs."

Kane straightened upright as something shifted in his expression, but not for the better. "So you still expect me to believe your encounter at Xenia was an accident?"

"It was, goddammit!"

"But now you're also telling me that one of our best men is a dust dealer."

"Look," Doc yelled, "I told you the truth!"

"No, I don't think so."

Kane touched the handheld, and returned Doc to Hell.

Chapter 8

KAI'S HEAD HUNG BACKWARD, limp like overcooked pasta. As the pair of men hauling her body by the arms and legs walked, her vision was upside down, swaying rhythmically back and forth. She had a strange thought (*This is what it must be like to be a metronome)* and in a way it was hilarious, and she laughed, the sound far off even to her own ears.

"Did she just laugh?" said one of the men, stopping. The other kept walking, and Kai had the distinct impression that they'd tear her in half down the middle. She wondered if nanos could repair a half girl. She also wondered if her vagina would end up with the right or left half, and this mattered because it was her moneymaker. But then she had a harrowing thought. While the idea of being ripped in half was only interesting as an intellectual exercise, the idea that she might rip *at the vagina* was downright terrifying. It made sense, too, seeing as it was a natural structural failure point.

"She didn't laugh," said the second voice above her. She couldn't see either man. Her neck no longer worked. She didn't remember why, but it seemed to involve pain and the distinct impression that death would be grand. Preferable to living, anyway.

"I heard her laugh," said the first voice.

"She's spent an hour on an Orion and showed nearly flat when we ran her through the scanner. She's as good as dead. I don't think someone with brainwaves that flat even *can* laugh."

"I can't kill someone who's laughing," said the first voice. "It's too creepy."

Kai's right arm and leg jiggled. The motion caused the rest of her to jiggle. Her vision went with it. Her vision's rhythm was as hilarious as the idea that she was flat. She wasn't particularly well-endowed, but none of her clients had ever called her *flat*. Nicolai in particular had always said that anything more than a handful was wasted.

"Hey, sweetheart!" said a cheery voice from the jiggling side. "Are you having a good time?" Then: "See? Flat."

Kai tried to say that she wasn't flat. She failed, drooling instead. But immediately afterward, she seemed to realize they weren't talking about her chest. They were talking about her brain. The thought was no longer hilarious. She wasn't sure why any of it mattered, though it certainly seemed to. She wanted to sit up and think, but her body still wasn't responding.

"I *heard* her laugh," said the first voice.

"Why do you give a shit?"

"I've...I've never done this before." The voice sounded nervous.

"It's not killing," said the second voice. "It's disposal. Look at her. She's gone." He paused. "What a waste. She's pretty hot."

"Yeah," said the other man. Kai found that she could interpret his voice — not his words, but their inflection. Something inside her wanted to attribute emotions to the voice's timbre, and Kai found she could hear his heartbeat, could feel his skin where he held her wrist and ankle. Sensors in her own skin added data about temperature and vasodilation to what was becoming a character profile of the man on her left side.

She wasn't totally aware of where she was, but a separate part of her had roused. That part seemed to be trying to shake her awake from inside. Kai saw it in her mind's eye as a reboot, internal lights flickering and circuits again starting to fire.

"Want to check out her tits?" said the second voice.

"What? No!"

"Oh, so tossing her in an evaporator is okay, but checking out the wares isn't. What does it matter?"

"Exactly," said the other man. "What does it matter? Give her some dignity."

"Said the man about to kill a woman."

"You just said it wasn't killing!"

"Pal, she's ready for Respero either way. They let her go, and she's a brainless vagrant. They'd pick her up right away, and they'd do the same thing. You ever seen a Respero chamber up close?"

"My dad had a really fancy Respero dinner a while back," said the voice. Kai found she was increasingly awake somewhere inside, now able to muster pity at the man's statement. He said "Respero dinner" like it was a fond memory rather than state-mandated euthanasia. Funny how all it took was a generation of repetition to convince people that murder was honor.

"Well, this is the same deal. We're just doing it sooner. And I say, let's throw her in naked."

The stronger of the two voices let her down, and Kai found her head leveling, her right hand and leg lying on some hard, cold surface underfoot. Now she could see the evaporator a few feet ahead, looming above them like a furnace in an ancient tract home. The door on the front was already open, but the furnace itself hadn't yet been turned on. The inside was pristine, like a tiny sterile hospital room.

As the second man laid her down, Kai found that she could see both of the men who'd been carrying her. The strong voice was coming from a large man, probably over six feet tall and easily 230 pounds. The timid, hesitant voice belonged to a thin man wearing glasses. Both were in blue coveralls, like the Directorate janitors who stole jobs from hard-working cleaner bots.

Kai felt tiny inklings of strength returning to her limbs, but she breathed deeply, forcing her muscles to stay limp. A kind of electricity was running all through her body, lighting everything. She felt herself powering up like a machine, but the returning strength was a fraction of what she usually had. Whatever Kane had done to her had popped Kai like a bubble. As she lay on the floor like a dishrag, Kai estimated that if she were to stand right now, she might have the strength of a moderately ambulatory towel.

The big man began fumbling with her shirt as the other man continued to protest. He was having problems with her dead arms, which were nothing if not in his way.

Then all at once, she realized what had happened.

Kai carried herself like escorting was all wine and roses, but she wasn't stupid; she knew she'd chosen a dangerous profession. When she added in her few murder-for-hire jobs and her habit of stockpiling secrets, Kai's activities put her quite a bit nearer to peril on a daily basis than most people. Hence the defensive add-ons; hence the manipulative enhancements...and hence her installed ability to play possum. Kai had been shot twice, and the only reason she was still around today was because she'd been able to play both wounds as fatal. One of the men who'd shot her had run off, but the second had stayed to check her pulse. He'd found her heartbeat stilled, her breath ceased. But it got even better; if he'd stuck around, he'd soon have found her skin cool and her galvanic responses absent. Thanks to the possum enhancement, trauma sent Kai into hibernation, and coming out of that hibernation felt like a system reset. She realized she'd have a strong pulse now, and normal brainwaves. Best not to give the men any reason to check.

"These are *nice*," said the first man, reaching under her shirt. "Let's keep her."

"*What?*" said the first man.

"Like a doll. A big, retarded doll."

The first man both looked and sounded panicked. "You can't do that! What the hell is wrong with you? You…Kane! Kane will kill you, Paul! I'll…I'll tell him!"

The first man, who'd mostly straddled Kai's inert form, rolled his eyes. "Relax. Holy West. I was kidding. Nice to know whose side you're on, though."

Kai could tell the big man had actually only been *half* kidding, because as he sat on her chest, a stiffness in his crotch belied the fact that he was rather enjoying himself. It wasn't a big deal to Kai; his fondlings were buying her time. So she used that time to move her mind beneath the veil of consciousness and assess herself. Her mind saw the possum program as a dashboard filled with lights. Right now, every meter on that dashboard was only lit a quarter of the way up. Enough to run, maybe, but not enough to *out*run anyone.

Right now, Kai couldn't be strong or fast. She'd have to figure out how to get the most out of what she had.

The thin man had turned, looking at the evaporator. Her hand was at his ankle. Kai wondered if she could trip him. But then what?

"Come on, Paul," he said to the bigger man. "Let's toss her in and be done."

"So now you're *for* killing?"

"If the alternative is this, yes." He glanced at the big man, who was still straddling Kai.

Kai found a spot deep in her throat then made a shallow noise. Enough to be overlooked.

"Did you hear something?" said the man on Kai's chest, cocking his head.

"No."

"I think she made a noise."

"Maybe she wants you to get off her."

The big man smiled an evil smile. "Maybe she *likes* it."

Kai made the noise again, louder this time.

"What's that, sweetheart?" said the big man, leaning in. He puckered his lips for a kiss. The thin man in glasses turned away.

Kai let the big man push his lips onto hers before she pushed back, then bit his nose with everything she had.

The man tried yanking his head away, but even a quarter-strength bite from Kai's strong jaw was enough to embed her incisors and canines deep enough that he wasn't able to easily shake free. He tried to stand, but the weight of Kai's head (and, as he rose farther, her torso) stopped him. He lost his balance and tumbled forward. Kai's knee was ready, catching the man in the balls.

The thin man spun. Kai might be able to reach *his* nuts too, but it would be a paltry strike, and she was betting it wouldn't be necessary given the personality profile she'd worked up on him. So instead, her face smeared with the big man's blood, Kai widened her eyes and snarled, *"Run."*

After a moment of indecision, the man ran.

With only one assailant to contend with, Kai rated her chances at fifty-fifty. She'd taken the man off-guard, and he appeared closer to janitor than soldier. His struggles had sawed her teeth farther into his nose, and she felt herself press against something unyielding and rubbery. So she was down to the cartilage already? That was fast.

The big man was flopping all over, rolling and thrashing and spraying droplets of blood like rain from the sky. A great glut struck Kai's own nose and lips before it ran down her neck, smelling like copper. She realized she would never be able roll him by force — especially clamped onto his nose and as weak as she was — so she growled "Roll over" around her gritted teeth and kneed him in the jewels again. This time, she struck them sidelong as if trying to carom one of his testicles off the other like a trick pool shot. He flinched away, and she rolled with him, now on top.

Despite his agony from both ends, the man was gaining his wits. His arms came up and found Kai's neck, so she put one thumb into each of his eyes and pushed until she felt brain. Or at least, she imagined it was brain.

When Kai stood, covered in gore and weak at the knees, the man in blue had two bloody hands covering his face, howling.

"Hope my tits were worth it," Kai said, spitting fragments of nose back into his face. Then, unable to stop herself, she added, "Oh, who am I kidding? Of course they are."

She ran.

Sixty seconds earlier, the thin man had left through a door at the far end of the warehouse space, so Kai went the other way. It made sense that he'd run back to mommy — toward the center of whatever this building was — so the opposite direction should lead her to the nearest perimeter. She was right, and soon found herself facing a small lawn and an unimpressive eight-foot chain-link fence.

An alarm began screaming. She could already hear yelling and the tromping of feet. She assessed her chances. The fence was just a barrier and nothing more. It wasn't intended to keep prisoners in because wherever she was looked more like a factory than a prison. There were no guard towers. But, maybe a hundred yards distant, she could see black-clad Beamers starting to swarm. They'd have slumberguns, probably even slamguns. And seeing as she was already supposed to be dead, they wouldn't hesitate to use the latter.

Kai looked at the fence and leapt.

But she'd forgotten how weak she was, and found she could barely leave the ground. Her legs extended; hyperextended; she came up on her toes; her face met the fence. She grabbed it and, feeling her limits and seeing the closing Beamers, began to feel her heart hammer in panic. She got one foot up, pushed, missed her toehold with the other. She pulled with her hands, now finding the fence's top, feeling the tines of twisted wire there gouging long scratches into her arm as she pulled and missed. Then she was up and over, falling hard onto the ground and feeling her wind knocked from her.

There was no time to waste. The Beamers were close. They fired through the fence, and Kai felt the nano-driven pellets woosh around her head, trying to find her. She dove into a deep patch of foliage and clawed through the green, feeling it on her hands, face, and mouth. It was fucking poison ivy. She hoped her nanos were up to the task, because she would have a bitch of an itchy rash to clear. If she survived, that is.

Without warning, Kai tipped forward. Quite by surprise, she'd found the edge of the ivy, the edge of the building's property, and a steep, rocky downslope all at once. She went ass-over, rolling in an untidy somersault. Something snapped in her chest, and she yelled out, but her cry was drowned in the firing of slumbershots, slamshots, and the scrabble from a scree of rocks sliding beside her. She reached the bottom in a heap, feeling nearly dead and completely battered, then climbed behind a fallen log and waited. And waited. And waited. But above her, the ridge was clear. The Beamers hadn't tried to climb the fence. Maybe they still would. Thanks to the fall, she'd regained her lead, but she had to keep moving.

Kai took one step, then another. She found her legs and ankles unbroken as she shambled into an unsteady run, soon slipping off her shoes and moving barefoot, stepping so she wouldn't leave tracks. But after a few minutes she decided she'd probably been safe after she'd cleared the fence. Beamers didn't do well in natural environments. Forests, rivers, and prairies weren't artificial enough for them.

As she put more distance between herself and her pursuers (who may or may not be behind her, and who might also have sent hoverscouts), Kai felt her small impetus of energy beginning to deplete. She was tired, battered, and damaged. She kept thinking of what she'd felt on the Orion, and somehow the thought alone was enough to hobble her. Her legs moved slower, each step remembering the pain she'd felt before. She longed for sleep, or maybe death. Her body seemed ambivalent about which of the two came. Still, through will alone, she used everything she had to keep going for a bit longer. But after a while, she couldn't even do that.

Curling herself into a ball behind a fallen log, Kai pulled the artificial fingernail from her right ring finger. She whispered to it, and it flew up and away, into the breeze, off to deliver a message to her only hope: the man who had taught her to kill without spilling blood.

| Episode 4 |

Chapter 1

Nicolai woke, stalked half-awake into the shower, and let his apartment's canvas do all the work. The canvas turned on the lights ahead of him; it started the shower at the perfect temperature (Nicolai liked the water piping hot); it turned on the surround dryer when he stepped out naked. Normally, Nicolai wanted to do things himself, feeling a very non-Directorate desire to not be taken care of, but today he craved coddling. If he didn't have a Saturday brunch appointment with Isaac to get ready for, he'd go back to bed and let the apartment's bots prepare him an elaborate breakfast and feed it to him in bed. He'd order in. He'd get a massage. Anything but working, or exerting effort.

Nicolai's head pounded. He was much more tired than he should have been. He remembered a late Friday night and Isaac's speech and too much political posturing. Being a stooge was, for Nicolai, like being a boxer with both hands tied behind his back. He always felt battered after having to circle a room with a dumb smile that said everything was under control. Yes, he made excellent money as Isaac's speechwriter, but his job always seemed to extend far beyond being a speechwriter, far past even being a consultant or adviser or right-hand man. He was like a janitor for Isaac's reputation, and he'd been cleaning up for Isaac for as long as he'd known him. It was as if their careers were braided: one career trajectory for two men. Isaac didn't pay attention to details, so Nicolai had to unless he wanted both of them to end up looking like shit.

In fact, Isaac reminded Nicolai of Enzo, a boy he'd known back in Italy. Enzo's family had been nearly as rich as Nicolai's, but both of their parents had made them get jobs in the sailing club that both families belonged to. The idea was to instill a work ethic in the boys so they wouldn't get too comfortable with getting everything for free. Nicolai accepted the lesson and did his job well. Enzo, on the other hand, knew it didn't matter, so he didn't even try. When they were told to stock shelves, Enzo threw things into place without regard to order or presentation. Nicolai, who knew Enzo's work would reflect on him too, always stayed late to stack things nicely, to turn labels so they faced out. He cleaned up for Enzo so they'd both look good because the alternative was both of them looking bad. Today, working with Isaac felt very much the same.

As Nicolai stood in the dryer, he rolled his head back, feeling it ache. Why did his fucking head hurt so much? He rolled it around, feeling for damage. There was none, but it felt like maybe there *had* been, and that his body hadn't yet gotten around to the deep tissue after handling the larger trauma. Maybe he'd been run over by a truck in his sleep. Maybe his muscles were bunched from tension. But what tension was there, beyond the normal irritation that came with being Isaac Ryan's toady?

"Canvas," said Nicolai.

A chirp answered him.

"I'd like a massage. Internal tissue."

"Yes, Nicolai," said a soothing female voice. "Would you like your diagnostic pad? It's in the living room."

His canvas could talk to his nanos, but Nicolai usually preferred to direct any necessary repairs manually by using a diagnostic pad that would also tell him which parts required attention. But today, getting the pad and directing repairs sounded like entirely too much work. The dryer's hot air felt good, and Nicolai wanted to stand in it a while longer. He peeped at his bathroom mirror, saw the time displayed in its corner. He had time.

"No. Just direct massage here…" He touched the back of his neck. "And he…"

Nicolai stopped in the middle of the word "here" because he'd been about to direct his nanobots to massage his face. That was where it hurt most, but it wasn't a place a person normally had muscular tension. Had he been drinking the night before? Nicolai didn't think so, but falling onto his face was the only way to explain the throbbing. Unless he'd been punched, which he very much didn't recall.

The canvas chirped, indicating it was still waiting for him to finish his command.

"Canvas, give me a verbal assessment. Internal tissue. What needs attention?"

The canvas indicated the areas Nicolai was already feeling discomfort — his neck, his face, and, strangely, his wrists. The system reported already-polished and burnished bruises that had been on his hips, right leg, and left arm, near the shoulder.

"Was I beaten up?" The question was rhetorical, and Nicolai asked it lightheartedly as if intending the canvas to laugh, but the canvas cut off its response as a mail message came through in the bathroom mirror, marked urgent. Twice, meaning that it was *double*-urgent. An Isaac move for sure.

Nicolai read the message and groaned, knowing full well that Isaac had sent the summons (a summons to his apartment instead of their Saturday brunch spot; what the hell?) so that he could deliver a tirade in person. Isaac didn't want to waste his rage over a vid connection; he wanted to yell about whatever it was in person. What Nicolai had just gotten was essentially a note to meet him in the principal's office. Another total Isaac move.

Nicolai told the canvas to direct his nanos, expediting repairs and initiating internal massage, then got dressed and hired a hovercab at street level. Given a choice, Nicolai normally preferred non-hovertransport for personal reasons, but Isaac's message had been marked double-urgent and sounded like a prelude to a hissy fit, so he shouldn't dally. Unfortunately, enduring hissy fits was one part of what Nicolai was paid so well to do.

Ten minutes later, the cab docked onto the guest port of Isaac and Natasha's penthouse. The port detected the cab as a non-Ryan vehicle and blacked out the glass, then turned the port itself into a kind of faux, Beam-generated foyer with art on the walls. The foyer-port even had piped-in elevator music — Isaac's idea of clever.

"Good morning, Mr. Costa," said the canvas. "Would you like me to alert the Ryans that you have arrived?"

"No, I'll just hang out on the side of the building," said Nicolai, looking out through the open wall and the precipitous plummet to the street.

The canvas chirped.

"I'm kidding," said Nicolai. "Yes, please let them know." He rolled his eyes. Of course Isaac kept his canvas stupid so he could feel superior. Such sarcasm would have killed at Nicolai's.

"Of course, Mr. Costa."

Nicolai waited, listening to the elevator music, recognizing the warbling voice of Samuel Bolton. *There* was a family who knew how to recycle. Bolton's songs were all his great grandfather's, written untold numbers of years ago. Each generation tweaked the songs then rolled around in the innumerable credits generated by the timeless classics.

After a moment of waiting, the foyer's privacy walls dissolved back into the clear glass they'd been before the cab had approached. A door at the far end opened. Nicolai waited to see a familiar face greeting him, but given the glass's transparency, it quickly became obvious that he was alone and presumably supposed to enter on his own.

Nicolai entered, annoyed. This was all such posturing. He walked from the port into the living room then from room to room, expecting to find Isaac at some point with his hands on his hips, his petulant ire raised over something stupid. What that stupid thing could be, given the previous evening's success, Nicolai couldn't imagine.

Instead of Isaac, Nicolai found Natasha sprawled across the couch like a cat, draped in a thin garment that was somewhere between a dress and a nightgown. Nicolai imagined the pose was supposed to be seductive, and it might have been if he hadn't known the Ryans for so long. Natasha was still beautiful (although Nicolai preferred her younger and less-skeletal look, before she'd eradicated nearly all of her fat cells) and looked to be in her late twenties, but after six decades of bullshit, it was hard not to think of her as an old woman clinging to youth.

"Long time, no see," she purred.

"Where is Isaac? He mailed. Urgently."

Natasha's voice lost its purr and became biting. "He's beating off in his office."

Nicolai dodged the "beating off" comment, which was probably not literal, and said, "Does he know I'm here?"

"*I* know you're here," she said, effortlessly and shamelessly switching back to her soft voice. Beside her, her stupid little dog yapped. Clearly, the two needed to communicate better about which people should be courted versus barked at.

"Should I wait?"

"You could wait on my lap."

Nicolai rolled his eyes. "Now now, Natasha," he said,

taking a few steps toward the office. He looked at Isaac's office door. If there was one thing more annoying than being summoned like a slave with a double-urgent mail and a power-playing air, it was being summoned and then ignored. Despite the physical discomfort still in his body, Nicolai felt himself growing angry. He'd done his job. They'd been celebrating last night. What was Isaac all shitted up about now?

"Where have you been, anyway?" said Natasha from behind him, still striking her movie star pose.

"Sleeping. But apparently that was out of line. I should have known better."

"Sleeping?"

Nicolai turned. "Why aren't we meeting at the restaurant? I did my job last night, yet I'm getting the anger game. Summoned here like a bad little boy. Are we still having brunch?"

Natasha's veneer thinned. She seemed confused.

"What do you mean, brunch?"

"It comes between breakfast and lunch," Nicolai snapped, turning back and slamming his fist onto Isaac's door. The office was soundproofed — both physically and electronically — but if he pounded long enough, chances were that the canvas would tell Isaac that some asshole was tap-tap-tapping on his chamber door. Besides, it felt good.

"Honey, we don't do brunch on Mondays."

Nicolai turned his head, his eyebrows drawing together. He was just about to ask Natasha what the hell she meant when the door opened and Isaac emerged, staring daggers at Nicolai, his hands as poutingly on his hips in life as they had been in Nicolai's mind.

"Where the fuck have you been?" Isaac blurted. Then, with an annoyed look at Natasha (Nicolai intuited an argument in progress between them), Isaac grabbed Nicolai by the arm and dragged him into the office. Once the door was closed, Isaac resumed his irritated pose, waiting. Nicolai had thought Isaac couldn't be more impotently angry, but he'd been wrong. Isaac postured like a master.

"I've been at my apartment," Nicolai answered, starting to suspect there was more in play here than he realized.

"Off-grid? For two days? Have you been watching the feed?"

"What's on the feed?"

"Oh, well," said Isaac, broadcasting his agitation, "where should I start? Let's see…you weren't around when Micah gave that speech trashing us. The *first* speech trashing us, that is. You missed a few riots, a few stories and reports saying how incompetent I am and how I'm making the Directorate look terrible. Why is it *my* fault, by the way? I'm not king and grand fucking poobah of the Directorate. I'm just the Czar of Internal Satisfaction. But everyone is up my ass anyway — and up Natasha's — because of motherfucking Micah and the way the sheets eat up the whole 'brothers divided' thing. It's almost fucking biblical, how they act about him and me, and…"

"How is Natasha holding up?" said Nicolai.

"Fuck her!" Isaac spat. "She spent fourteen million credits this month already, most of it in the Viazo, and you know what I think? I think she's fucking some guy in there, or maybe a lot of guys, and meanwhile she's giving *me* shit for 'not making her feel better' or some crap, like I don't have enough on my plate without…"

Nicolai held up a hand, suddenly realizing he'd passed up Isaac's strange phrase "for two days" in jumping directly to "watching the feed."

"Wait. Not to sound like a total cliché, but Isaac…what day is it?"

"What *day* is it?"

"Just…yes. What day is it?"

Isaac looked as if Nicolai had asked if the sun still rose in the morning. "Monday," he finally said.

"I thought it was Saturday."

"Noah Fucking West. How much did you drink on Friday?"

"I barely drink," said Nicolai, thinking of the two glasses of wine he'd had at the celebratory after party. "Look…I'm missing time." He touched his neck, then his face. "I think I've been in a fight."

"You black out, get into a fight, and disappear for two days *NOW?*"

Nicolai's mouth opened in shock. "Are you kidding?"

"No, I'm not *kidding!* I haven't even told you about…"

"Jesus, Isaac! This doesn't concern you at all? Did you even *know* there are ways to manually erase memory? Don't you think there might be something to worry about here?"

Isaac looked slapped. "They can erase memory?"

"Yes, Jesus!"

"Who can do that?"

"Does it matter?"

"So, what…this is a conspiracy? Not your fault?" said Isaac. "Because I've gotta say, that's awfully convenient, Nicolai. I had to write my last speech myself, and…"

Nicolai felt himself becoming angry. "Wow, that must have been tough. Almost as tough as being beaten and having your memory erased."

"Don't feed me that bullshit!" Isaac yelled. "I know you see that hooker. I know people who know her, and she vanished last weekend too. Kind of coincidental, right?"

"You think I'm lying?"

"Well, I think it would be bad if you didn't have a really convenient excuse. And I think now that I'm telling you the shit that went down while you were gone, you'd never be able to change your story because…"

"You think I'm *LYING?*"

This was beyond ridiculous. In the space of sixty seconds, Nicolai had been charged with abandonment, had found out he'd lost two days and had been assaulted, and had been accused of lying by someone whose ass he had wiped for sixty years. Someone whose rise into the upper echelon of society and politics was largely Nicolai's doing. Nicolai, who *wasn't* in the upper echelon himself yet and had gotten none of the credit.

"Micah gave a second speech, Nicolai!" Isaac barged on, apparently deciding to put a pin in the current discussion and get back to his own petty problems. "It preempted mine by fifteen minutes! He just made me look like a…"

"I want out," said Nicolai. "Now."

"What?" Isaac's superior expression shattered like a plate dropped to the floor.

"I also want to hit you," he added. "Very, very badly. But I'll try to simply storm out on you instead. Let you keep writing your own fucking speeches, now that you know you can do it."

"But…you can't leave! I mean, what will you…you won't have a job!"

"Who gives a shit? I've got Presque Beau status and a credit balance that's nearly as much as — well, shit, not *nearly* as much as yours, if your wife is blowing fifteen million fucking dollars a month. I'll be just fi…"

"Fourteen million," said Isaac, looking helpless.

"Noah Fucking West, Isaac! *This* is what's wrong with the Directorate, right here! It's bothered me for years…but hey, I was Isaac Ryan's man, so I had to toe the line. We talk about equality, but everyone earns a dole based on their position. Sure, Enterprise is a ruthless meritocracy. But at least there's *merit!* You and Natasha don't have to work harder than a cabbie does — and in fact, he works a hell of a lot *harder* — and yet he barely gets by while you spend fourteen million fucking dollars on virtual sex and…and…" He grabbed an object from Isaac's shelf. It looked like ivory, was maybe a foot long, had to cost a fortune, and seemed completely pointless. Nicolai picked it up. "...and whatever the hell this is!"

"It's an antique gunpowder horn," Isaac said lamely.

"Raff on the bottom, below the line. Us up top. Equality, my ass! Sure we meet their needs, but what are we keeping from them? And how much is the gap widening by the day? There *is* no Directorate middle class. There's *us,* and there's *them.* Even between you and me there's an 'us and them.' We're not remotely on the same level, are we, Isaac? I know you have access to stuff I don't, like those rigs in your offices. And how did you learn to play the piano so fast, Isaac? How did you and Natasha become dance experts overnight? What the hell *is* this 'Viazo' where Natasha is fucking other guys? Because it's not in *my* Beam directory. But if it's the kind of place where you can fuck people for millions of dollars, then hey, the simulation's gotta be a lot better than my visor and headphones, am I right?"

Isaac looked shocked, like he'd been caught. He didn't try to close his mouth or backpedal.

"I want out," Nicolai repeated, his voice becoming calm but firm. "I'm no longer your speechwriter. I'm no longer your right hand. I'm no longer the guy you get to cry to. I'm moving to Enterprise at Shift. That's where I belong, where I've *always* belonged. I've got plenty of credits, which gives me more of a head start than most. I'm going to write, and I'm going to learn to play my piano. Maybe I'll die in the gutter a few years from now, and if I do, then so fucking be it. I'm out. You're on your own."

"Not now," said Isaac, his voice and expression threatening to break. "I'll be...I need you."

"Yeah, you do," said Nicolai, still angry. Isaac's tone was solidifying his decision rather than softening it. This had been brewing for too long.

"At least wait until after Shift," said Isaac.

Nicolai had his hand on Isaac's doorknob. He paused,

wondering how much it could hurt to wait a few more weeks. He could leave after Shift. After sixty years of history, he could at least do that much for Isaac.

"Just be honest with me about where you were the last two days," said Isaac, "and we can pick up the pieces."

Nicolai threw Isaac a look, suddenly feeling stupid for hesitating. Then he stormed from Isaac's office, slamming the door behind him.

Chapter 2

Leo didn't even make the pretense of eschewing technology. While they sat in his office back at the Organa Village, he pulled out the handheld Leah wasn't supposed to know he had (but that everyone knew he did) and told The Beam to get him Mercy Hospital yet again. He talked for a while using voice then stowed the device, suddenly looking at Leah with something like guilt.

"I knew you had it already," said Leah, waving a hand.

"For emergencies," said Leo.

"Like my nano fabricators."

They looked at each other for a pregnant moment, and Leo sighed, conceding to Leah. The Beam had opened a kind of Pandora's box, and Leah knew she was right: To fight fire, you had to use flame. They could only sit up in the mountains and munch homemade granola for so long. If they wanted to challenge The Beam, they'd need The Beam's help.

"They said they didn't know what I was talking about," said Leo.

"Of course not. They told you that in person. And also the last three times you called."

When they'd found Crumb missing, they had asked the

nurses where he'd gone. They'd expected the nurses to report that the crazy old man with the ratty gray beard had wandered off, but instead the nurses had stared at the two Organas, genuinely perplexed. They'd been wiped. Not by a hand wipe, either, but by a full Gauss — probably the hospital's own machine.

"I thought I might get lucky," said Leo. "I talked to their records office this time. Thought a copy of his admission might have uploaded."

"They did it on paper," said Leah. "My request." She'd checked the places she'd seen nurses leave Crumb's charts and paperwork, to no avail. His bedsheets had been crisped and tight. His room had the tang of an industrial floor cleaner. He was gone, as if he'd never been there.

"There had to be some sort of a ping. They're on The Beam. The Beam is paranoid."

Leo was always saying things like that. It was bullshit, of course, but his thought gave her an idea.

"The Beam is a system," she said. "It's not paranoid. Even AI doesn't get paranoid. *People* get paranoid, and believe me, I didn't leave them anything to be paranoid about. Those nurses are used to dealing off the grid."

"But they wouldn't know it if a Beam tech managed to…"

"*You're* paranoid, Leo," she said. "The Beam touches everything. What possible reason would they have to watch that shitass hospital? Why would they send someone out to hotlink it? But you're right; it would have pinged something. Nothing damning, but there'll be an access imprint, like I left when I was scouting his brain at Bontauk. It won't have his ID since he doesn't have one, but it'll have his key sequences indexed to his scan."

"They can track without a Beam ID?" Leo asked. He looked much more frightened than he should have.

"It's a *hospital*, Leo," said Leah, exasperated. "They DNA print him at admission so they can flag any known mutations they'd need to know about while treating him. It drops into a file with his allergies and medical history. It's anonymous. But…*we* have his map, too."

"Why?"

"Some smart girl with too many tech enhancements suggested it," she said, pointing to her own pink-dreadlocked head.

"Oh."

"So we just match against the hospital's pinged records. Not the official indexed ones, but the raw access imprints. That should tell us if there's a record of him at all. If there is, we can follow it."

"The data? Or Crumb?"

Leah sighed. "What's the difference, Leo?" Leo, like most people, thought hacking was about ones and zeroes. Once upon a time, that was true. It wasn't anymore.

Leo still looked nervous, still paranoid. Leah suddenly realized why. Even from a few feet away, she could see his shaking pupils. He was jonesing, and would soon be in full-on withdrawal.

"How low is your stash?" she asked.

"What? Oh, no. We've just been away too long."

"No, you carry a rock on your ring. I can see it right there, still full. You're intentionally rationing moondust. Why?"

Leo took a breath. She didn't miss anything, and he damn well knew it. "Fine. The village's supply is kind of low. I'm stretching."

"*How* low?"

But Leo wasn't able to answer because at that moment, the door slammed open and a moose of a young man entered. He was well over six feet tall and had the build of the Death-bringers the NAU had used during the splinter attack on DZ in the '30s.

"Leo! Fuck!" said the big man.

"We're kind of in the middle of something, Scooter," Leah

said, annoyed by the intrusion. A moondust shortage would be bad. Very bad. Leo had told Leah and a few others when Dominic Long had insisted on becoming their sole source of the drug. She'd been against it. Nothing good, Leah said, ever came from putting all of your eggs in one basket.

"We've got a fight, bro," said Scooter, speaking to Leo and ignoring Leah. "James and Milton. It started while we were prepping for the community campfire tonight, back behind the loom and dye house. I tried busting it up, but it just got bigger. James says Milton stole some of his rocks. I was like, 'Bro, you can have some of mine!' but James was all hopped up, like he hadn't rocked in days, and he wouldn't listen, just kept coming at Milton. You'd think he'd want some dust, right? But he was all burned, like totally fried, like the shit was doing something to him. And I gotta say, I've felt it harsher lately. Not as mellow. You got any fresh rocks, Leo? Maybe the shit's gone bad."

"Are they still fighting?" said Leo, ignoring Scooter's question.

"Nah, I knocked 'em both down, made 'em listen."

Leah looked at Scooter, thinking it had probably been the most decisive and strangely polite "knocking down" either of the fighting men had received. Scooter was enormous but gentle — the kind of guy Organa could have based an entire PR campaign around. He had a bushy brown beard and arms like a lumberjack's, strings of beads hanging from a multicolored floppy hat, and wore brown sandals that wound up his calves like a Greek's, even in the wintertime.

Scooter had been picked up by DZ Child Services after his mother had gone into a Beam game simulation one day and then refused to leave. Game addiction (not understanding or preventing addiction, but learning how to addict others best) was something you could study in college, and advances in immersion technology had made things almost too easy for developers who liked to use compulsion as a marketing strategy. After Scooter's mother decided she'd rather stay in NeverForest forever with the rest of her gaming guild's avatars rather than with her son, Scooter, then twelve, had decided that The Beam was something he wanted nothing to do with. Today, in a village filled with poseurs, Leah respected Scooter as one of the few who, for his own genuine reasons, lived as far removed from The Beam as was reasonably possible. Scooter's hut ran off of a shared generator, and he didn't mind roughing it with lanterns and fires when the thing went on the fritz, which was often. He bought clothes from other Organas. He didn't have a mail account or a Beam ID and was nearly impossible to get ahold of other than by running into his hut. Scooter even wrote on Organa-made paper that had been fashioned from pulp — ironic, considering that protesters years ago had fought against paper and for the trees they came from.

"Thanks, Scooter," said Leo. Then, when Scooter didn't leave, he asked, "Did you just want to tell me about it?"

"Nah, Bro!" said Scooter. "I wanted to ask about the rock. It's making dudes paranoid. Not like I'm some scientist, but… can you, like, analyze it? It gives great buzz, lasts, all that…but I've been coming off with a headache, and then you get shit like with James and Milton. I gave 'em each a boulder, let 'em mellow. But it's like they both got the idea that they're running light, and instead of going with the flow, they got uppity. Paranoid, y'know?"

Leo forced a laugh. Beside him, Leah did the same. Nobody in the village was going to do any analysis, but between Leo's shortage and Scooter's fears about purity, that was two chinks in moondust's armor in a single day. If people were really starting to run low, that could mean trouble on the horizon. Leah was going back into District Zero shortly. Maybe she should pay Dominic a visit, maybe see how much dust she could shake loose.

"I'm sure it's just one of those things. Nothing to worry about," Leo told Scooter.

"Maybe."

"How are *you*, Scooter? Doing good?"

Scooter's beard-covered lips cracked. He was all sunshine and flowers; nervousness couldn't sit on his shoulders for long.

"Good, man. Yeah. Walked to the summit of the east hill this morning and watched the sun rise. Sat and journaled for a while then came back and had breakfast with Carl. I don't know how the city dwellers do it. Run here and run there, hook up and..."

"Great, great," said Leo, standing in front of Scooter, hands on his hips.

Scooter seemed to read Leo's body language. "Okay, man, I guess I should head back and watch those two. They should be fine now, but when you get some new dust, can you let me know? I want to try some next to this batch and see if it rocks different." He raised a paw of a hand at Leah. "See ya, Leah," he said, somewhat more quietly.

"See you, Scooter."

That seemed to seal the transaction. Scooter, suddenly reminded that Leah had been there all along, lost his boisterousness and skittered out. Leah felt her lips press into a small smile as she watched him leave.

With the room clear, Leo turned to Leah and asked her if she wanted to try and track Crumb, as she'd been discussing before the interruption. She nodded then said it was just like investigating a crime, and that the trail would go cold if they waited too long. Leo asked if she could do whatever she needed to do from the cabin in Bontauk, and Leah said no, that the connection was too isolated. She'd need wider access. She needed to be able to reach out into all of the little tendrils touched by the DZ network. She said she could even try using Quark PD's records now that she had her nanos behind the firewall, but when she mentioned it, Leo expressly forbade it, telling her she'd taken enough risks for a week — that she'd taken enough risks for a year, really.

Leah promised that she'd stick to the unrestricted grid for as long as she could, that she'd use all the spoofs at her disposal, and that she'd be careful. Leo made her repeat it. Leah did. Then Leo made her promise she'd adhere to *his* definition of "careful" rather than her own. After an eye-rolling moment, Leah finally relented. If Crumb was out there, he'd either be right in public or behind sixteen layers of top-end security. Shades of gray between Leo's standards and her own probably wouldn't matter anyway.

"Who do you think Crumb is?" said Leah, donning her backpack. "It never seemed to matter for my entire life. But then you get your 'feelings' about him, and I go into his head see what he has inside lockdown, and then he goes missing. I've gotta admit, I'm getting curious. Is it possible he just wandered off and is now telling squirrels somewhere about Noah Fucking West?"

"With all of his records gone, and people's memories erased?"

Leah nodded. "Okay. Then could he be this Stephen York guy?"

Leo shrugged. "I'm sure he had a name, so why not Stephen York? But that doesn't help any. Because then, who the hell is Stephen York?"

"I did a quick search from the hospital while I was waiting, but wireless out there is shit, and you can't get a good hack from a handheld. But whoever York is, he's got a diary. A journal. Somewhere in DZ. In a building with a red roof."

"Well, that narrows it down."

"I'll bet that journal is filled with recipes," said Leah. "Or a madman's manifesto. Maybe some crazy poems. We've got to find it. There may be limericks."

"'There once was a man from Organa…'" Leo began.

"You really think he's important, huh?" said Leah, reading

through Leo's sarcasm. She didn't bother to soften it because Leo knew she felt guilty and would go after Crumb with or without anyone asking her to.

"He's one of us. And he's got a secret."

"But is it an *important* secret? Or is it useless?"

Leo shook his head slowly, swinging his gray braids. "All I know is that he's one of us."

Leah thought that was as good an answer as any. She left with a wave and a promise to be careful then headed for the barn to saddle Missy for a ride.

Leo watched Leah go, thinking about fate.

Leo had been born in 1976 — too late to catch the previous century's hippie movement, but just in time for its leftover spirit. His mother had raised him in cloth diapers, had grown her own vegetables, burned incense, and meditated daily. She hadn't been totally in the clouds; she made her living as a bookkeeper. But she was spiritual enough for Leo to grow up believing that everything was connected, and that everything truly happened for a reason. Everything he'd seen growing up — in a pre-Beam, pre-Crossbrace, pre-Internet world — had born that out. Every event had a way of looping back on itself, as if life were a story being told by someone who knew how it would all eventually all stitch together.

Most people came to the Organa community Leo had founded by deliberate choice. There were three people, however, who had been placed here, and all had their purpose.

The first had been Chrissy Long, Dominic's sister, who had bonded Dominic to the Organa movement forever and set one of Dominic's feet on each side of the thin blue line. Without Chrissy, Dominic might have been a straight cop, skeptical of fringe groups.

The second had been Crumb, also dropped into the

community by Dominic. Crumb had been the village's crazy old mascot for a few decades, but now it seemed he had his own starring role to play. Without even knowing it, Dominic had coincidentally brought them a time bomb, and it was finally ticking toward its end.

And the third person to be placed within Leo's community unwittingly had been a baby, brought into the mountains in utero by her mother so she could be born without a Beam ID. A baby who had become a prodigious hacker — the kind of talent that could be groomed but never created. Leah didn't even understand her own gift and never truly had. Accordingly, Leo had sent her to the best academies to learn about computers and codes and language and encryption and systems. But The Beam was ruled by AI these days, and its intelligence had gone far beyond rules and algorithms. It was a kind of emerging consciousness, capable of whims and attitudes and preferences. Leo didn't understand what Leah did when she spoke with The Beam, but whatever she did, it wasn't just hacking. It was more like something a spiritualist would do…or maybe even a medium. Leah wasn't pushing data; she was channeling. And today, if that baby hadn't (coincidentally) been left in the village once upon a time, Organa wouldn't have the mind required to speak with the inhuman, giving them access to another realm of existence.

Everything really did happen for a reason.

As Leah climbed onto her brown-and-white horse and rode off down the trail toward the train, Leo watched her go, hoping she would keep believing she'd been abandoned by a mother who didn't want her.

But if that wasn't how things were supposed to happen, there was little Leo could do about it anyway.

Chapter 3
____

Dominic stood in an empty warehouse that had once manufactured glass, wondering when he'd crossed the line.

He had wanted to be a good cop, and had tried to be one. He could even still argue that he *was* a good cop (rather convincingly, he thought) and that there were guys out there who were much, much dirtier than he was. Intentions mattered more than anything, and Dominic's intentions had always been in the right place. Dominic had never been out for himself. He'd never tried to make a profit, or skim anything off the top for personal gain. Every law he'd broken — every shady act he'd committed — had been for someone else. He'd defied Respero and forged records to save his sister then had done it again to save a vagrant who had somehow stirred the sluggish heart inside his too-fat frame. He'd supplied moondust to Organa because Quark and The Beam had too much power and Organa was their only real rival, and he'd let a few of the riots burn longer than they should have for the same reason. Then, once he was in with Organa, he'd had a responsibility to make sure they didn't get nabbed or into a bind. At the time, they'd been dealing directly with Omar, but Omar was fucking them six ways from Sunday.

Dominic had dirt on Omar, and Omar had dirt on Dominic, so he had stepped into the middle to protect Organa's supply and to keep them in the good fight. He hadn't done it to make money for himself and hadn't gained a single dirty credit during his sideline career as a drug trafficker. He didn't understand what the Organas did with the moondust — whether it genuinely helped them get into a deep enough fugue to do their work or whether they were just junkies like he was — but it didn't matter anymore. Regardless of what the drug did, the Organas were addicted. In the end, the police captain and the Appalachian hippies were rowing from the same boat. If they ran out of those little gray rocks, they were in for a rough ride. If that happened, they'd be useless to everyone, and would doom his one big cause.

Dominic wasn't a dirty cop. He was a revolutionary. If anything, he cared too much about the principles underlying the laws to obey them entirely.

He strolled through the warehouse, a policeman's incapacitator on his right hip. Grandy, when he'd been a cop, had carried a revolver that fired lead slugs. There were plenty of those old weapons still out there, but they were now considered too barbaric for officers of the law. The logic made sense: incapacitators and slumberguns were both more effective than lead-shooters in neutralizing a criminal since the blast cone was larger and even a sidelong hit would paralyze a man. But every time Dominic had pulled his weapon against a criminal firing lead, he'd felt the difference with every heartbeat. *He could die.* The other man could not. Efficient or not, criminals' psychological advantage was a bitch and a half.

Not for the first time, Dominic wondered why the only people who had to follow rules were those who made them. And also not for the first time, that inequity made him feel slightly better about doing what he *felt* was right, even though everyone else — including the police department he'd given his life to — would judge him as wrong.

Dominic heard the crunch of glass then looked up to see Omar walking toward him. The man could walk as quietly as a cat if he wanted, but he said that when he met with people, it was best if they were aware of his approach…except when he planned to burn them.

Dominic's hand flinched toward the small, pistol-shaped incapacitator, but it was only instinct and hopped-up nerves. He let the hand relax, and Omar smiled.

"Every time, you make to shoot me, Dom," he said. He was wearing a white suit that would have been ridiculous if it weren't so perfectly cut. He somehow pulled off a look no one else could, as much the trustworthy portfolio manager he was by day as the kingpin he was by night. Omar's skin was very black, and his wide grin seemed to float above it. The look was disarming. When most people smiled like that, Dominic's bullshit meter screamed murder. When Omar did it, the smile was so overt it felt like it *had* to be genuine, which it almost never was.

"I hate places like this," Dominic said.

"I keep telling you, I'll meet you in my office downtown," said Omar. "You're almost in my financial manager client base anyway. What do you make working captain at DZPD?"

"Enough," said Dominic, annoyed. It was strange to have your drug supplier offer to manage your mutual funds and investments, but Omar did have a stellar track record for making rich people richer…while, Dominic felt sure, skimming plenty off the top for himself.

"You act guilty, Dom," said Omar. "That's your problem. That's the difference between you and me. Me, I don't think there's anything wrong with what I'm doing. I see needs and fill them. You do the same, but without the sharp edges and without the need for *this* stuff." Omar tapped his chest, which Dominic knew had been reinforced beneath the skin with a bulletproof mesh of carbon nanotubes. "You act like a straight man, people will see you as a straight man. On the other hand, if you insist on meeting your partners in a place like this? Well, then you look like you have something to hide."

"I need dust," said Dominic.

"Shit. *And* you blurt things out like that. What's wrong with you, Dom? What if I were wearing a wire? What if NPS had sent me here to set you up?"

Dominic felt himself scowl, wishing he could be as cool and cavalier as Omar. Omar shot his cuffs, adjusted his band tie, and tipped a stylish white hat perched atop his head. He had a scruffy little goatee and two sliver studs through each ear. Dominic couldn't pull off anything like it. If Dominic tried to play dress-up, he'd look like a wannabe pimp or a target, or probably both. And while Omar could joke with a smile about getting caught and shot, Dominic stuttered and said everything wrong. God help him if he ever had to deal with someone more intimidating than Omar. Right now, Dominic made money for Omar, and Omar was enough of a businessman to respect their relationship as sacred. Yes, Omar had made it to Presque Beau status by brute force, but the elite still trusted him to manage their millions and billions. Why? Because in the end, business was business. Omar skimmed from his clients and used that plus his legitimate income to fund his moondust and arms dealings, but it was still in his best interest to make money for everyone. Somehow, all of his clients — both on the legitimate and criminal sides — knew it.

"Goddammit, Omar."

"Relax, Dom. I have your rocks. But you've gotta do me a favor."

"What?" Dominic felt like the vein in his forehead might pop. He didn't know if he was more angry or afraid.

"You've gotta breathe. This here? This is a *transaction*. It ain't a *drug deal*. You're not doing anything wrong. Well, other than breaking the law." He laughed. "You ever feel like you've been doing something wrong?"

"Just give me the rocks, Omar."

Omar shook his finger at Dominic. An expensive watch, worn entirely for flash, danced on his wrist. He smiled that disarming smile again.

"You made *me* come *here*, Dom!" he said. "*Your* choice. It's not like a few Ms take up a lot of space. You could have walked into my office and walked out — just another up-and-comer using my excellent services and bringing his briefcase full of nothin' with him. So if you want to play dirty, I ain't giving you shit until you admit to the drama."

"Okay," said Dominic, extending his hand. "I'm being dramatic."

"And that you could have bought moondust from me in my office rather than making me come somewhere like this every damned time."

"Fine, fine."

"Say it, my friend! Sing it out!"

"I don't need to buy dust from you in places like this."

"And you're a *good man*, too, Dom. Are you doing this dust yourself? Are you selling it on the street?"

"Noah Fucking West."

"Hey," said Omar, holding up his hands and feigning offense. "I'm just looking out for you. How's your blood pressure? How's your stress level?"

"Not good," Dominic admitted.

"Look at you. I'm a businessman. You die, I've got a problem. You get pinched because you're acting like a spook, I've got a problem. So tell me, Dom. Are you selling the shit?"

"I'm giving it to Organa," said Dominic. He tried to breathe. This was just like Omar, to rehash things they'd discussed again and again just for an extra glimmer of clarity. Dominic wanted to be annoyed, but like Omar's smile, his manner was disarming. He made his clients feel confident and strong, and they always felt like they owed him. If someone made you feel good about what you were doing, why wouldn't you keep doing it? Omar was a self-serving, manipulative son of a bitch who acted differently with every person he talked to, depending on what he needed from them. Omar was always looking out for number one. Dominic knew Omar all too well, but that didn't change how he felt. You might know to never turn your back on Omar, but it was impossible not to like him just the same.

"You're a freedom fighter," said Omar, nodding.

"In a way."

"You help people. Like your sister. What was her name?"

"Chrissy."

"You kept her from Respero. Like that old man."

"I guess."

"I still don't know how you did that."

Dominic took a deep breath and shrugged. "I guess there are benefits to being the chief of police. You have access to a lot of records."

"Ain't that right."

"Yes," said Dominic, feeling noticeably better and hating himself a little for it. "Now, on that helping people thing, I've got a lot of people who are low because Jameson got pinched."

"I hate to tell you this," said Omar, "but it serves you right, using Jameson. You should stick with a pro." He touched his own chest. "You know I don't fuck around. Not that I'm angry about it, but that's how I felt when you stepped in to begin with. You're just an extra moving piece here, Dom. It's like you don't trust me. You think I was scamming them, without you here to watch me?"

"You *were* scamming them."

"Maybe a little," said Omar, shrugging. "But it's cool. I found a way to recapture the profits you lost me, with the same amount of rock."

Dominic thought of how he'd felt when waking, what felt like three hundred hours ago. That was bad, but he'd felt an edge on Omar's dust for weeks now. Dominic assumed it was getting stronger and he wasn't used to it, but was it possible Omar was cutting it? Profit mattered above everything else to Omar. By splitting Organa's order with Jameson (Dominic thought of it as diversifying), he'd hurt that profit. And it was just like Omar to taunt.

"Well," said Omar, watching Dominic's face. "Problem solved. Jameson's out. I'm in for full time. But you know me; I'm always looking for the next best thing. And I said, 'Omar, how can you continue to deal the same but also take another grasp for that brass ring?' It was time to upgrade."

Dominic still hadn't moved. As disarming as Omar's false compassion had been, this was worse. He had no idea what he was talking about. There were about fifty different reasons Dominic wasn't cut out for shit like this. Damn Leo and his junkie's habit.

Dominic was about to say that he didn't understand when Omar's eyes darted to one side and then the other. Then, as if trying to keep a secret, Omar leaned in close and whispered, "I know they're hurting. There are three meterbars in a place we've used before, one phone call away. Just so you know I'm not a total son of a bitch."

Omar leaned erect then started taking paces backward. The dealer's manner had changed in a way Dominic couldn't place. Something was happening.

One phone call away.

Dominic thought of all the criminals he'd processed over the years, none of whom would ever shut up until given their phone call. *Gimme my phone call, gimme my phone call.* Their one stab back into the world before being locked away, jonesing for that one last desperate shot.

And he knew.

Dominic wasn't sure whether to reach for his incapacitator or run as Omar turned and began taking larger steps, putting more distance between himself and the police captain. The dirt at Dominic's feet started to flutter as if it were being stirred up by a breeze, circling like a cyclone. A cloud rose, climbing up his legs and then covering his waist. Dominic knew what was about to happen but not how to avoid it. He couldn't run from a swarm. The nanos were faster than him, and millions would already be clinging to his clothes, neck, face, and hands, crawling into his body through his pores. He froze, waiting, and then the decision was stripped from his hands. Without warning, he collapsed to the dirt. The cloud settled above him, still infiltrating his mouth and nose, covering his motor neurons to paralyze him.

When Dominic was completely inert on the dusty warehouse floor, a plainclothes NAU Protective Sector keeper entered his field of view, the shimmer of a nano-repellant field visible over his skin. He blew a small whistle, seducing a two-note tune. As he did, he held out a small metallic box. The brown cloud of unattached nanos spiraled into the box. The keeper touched a button on its side, then one at his waist. The force field shimmer vanished. He slipped the small nano depot into a compartment on his belt beside his incapacitator.

"Clear," he said.

At the call, several other NPS agents approached. They formed a circle above Dominic. After a few moments, Omar stepped out from the shadows to join them. He was not in custody.

"Thank you for your service, Mr. Jones," one of the agents said to Omar. "We've been trying to nab this one for a while."

Chapter 4

CRUMB OPENED his eyes to see a beautiful young woman, maybe eighteen, with long dark-brown hair shot with streaks of auburn like lightning strikes. It took Crumb a moment to get his bearings. Once he did, he realized he was lying down, with the young woman above him. He was on a bed, but not in a hospital as someone (Laura? Leigh? He couldn't be sure) had promised. The room looked like it was in a fancy home. Crumb could see the tops of fluted columns without moving his head. Elaborate crown molding circled the edges. Ornaments were carved into the ceiling — scenes of a pre-Beam Christian Heaven, mostly. Everything was so white, he wanted to squint from the brightness. Even the woman wore white — something sheer. It seemed inappropriate to look down at her torso because for some reason he thought that when he did, he'd see that her robe (or whatever it was; it was flowing like gossamer) was see-through. Only, instead of seeming scandalous, he knew it would seem appropriate. The way naked angels and saints were somehow appropriate because nudity was their natural state.

"Unnamed male, called 'Crumb,'" she said, smiling down on him.

"Crumb," he said, smiling.

"That's what it said on your hospital record."

But he wasn't in a hospital. He was in an elaborate, fancy bedroom. It didn't make sense. But things often didn't make sense…and *that* thought — that things often didn't make sense — stirred other thoughts inside his mind. Crumb (who remembered knowing himself by another name but could not put his finger on who or what or when right now) seemed to recall brilliant periods of clarity through the fog currently surrounding him. Those periods, he knew, had been accompanied by an infuriating inability to express himself. But it was hard to think right now, so no details came. His mind felt punched and battered. Was he a man named Crumb, or had his name been something else? It was all so foggy. He wasn't sure.

The woman ran a hand through his hair. He could feel how his hair moved under her touch and realized it had been recently washed. Suddenly, disturbingly, he remembered that his natural state had always been dirty and gross. He intuited that his constant dirtiness somehow hadn't been his fault, but he wasn't sure how or why. His current cleanliness was an anomaly, as was his awareness of that truth.

"But you don't remember the hospital, do you?" the woman asked. She smiled. "Of course you don't. Your newest memories leave ghosts at the surface before diving deep, into the protections. We can feel them, like silk on skin. And there is no hospital there. You remember the house and the wizard, and you remember Leah, whom you trusted. Whom you still trust. Tell me, do you remember the places where you played as a child?"

None of what the woman was saying made any sense to Crumb, but he blinked up at her as if he understood her, and that understanding was easy. He didn't remember the hospital, sort of remembered Leah, and knew nothing of ghosts. He couldn't imagine why she would ask him about childhood places to play.

"Who are you?" Crumb asked, his tongue itching for more, wanting to add to the too-simple question — something about squirrels and future doom, strangely — but he ignored the itch and kept his tongue from wagging. With the ability to hold his tongue came a thought: *I used to be crazy.* Confusing thoughts followed: a stark white room not unlike the one he was in now, and an old man dying. A promise he'd kept, and one that was broken to him. A building with a red roof. And a rope dangling from a tree's tall branch, its pendulous swing swiping the surface of a small and dirty creek.

The woman said, "My name is SerenityBlue."

That had to be a lie. No one had seen SerenityBlue, and no one had met her. She was famous in an almost literary way, like Tolstoy's Anna Karenina. Stories of SerenityBlue seemed to assume she was fact and not fiction, but pursuit meant waiting for a white whale; many had driven themselves crazy trying.

"You *do* remember, don't you?" the woman continued, laughing a tinkling, girlish laugh.

"Leah."

"No," she said. "The swing." She smiled, revealing a slight, charming overbite. For some reason, her hair refused to lie flat on her head. It was as if there were a breeze in the room stirring it, though Crumb could feel none.

"Swing."

"You can see it," she said. "I can feel that you can see it. I could lay my hands on you and draw a picture, but that's not how it works, is it?"

Crumb continued to lie in the bed, either uninterested in sitting up or unable to do so; he wasn't sure which. All he knew was that as odd as this place was and as odd as he felt, everything was quite comfortable. Above him, against the white walls, he watched the beautiful young woman's hair stir in the nonexistent breeze. Her lack of rationality and sense didn't bother him. Things would settle in time, he felt certain.

"Crumb — if I may call you Crumb? — when was the first time you connected to The Beam?"

"Always," he said. But that made no sense. It just came, like breath.

Instead of looking confused, SerenityBlue nodded. "You are ancient there. We've been looking for you, and for ones like you. I've just met you, Crumb, but in a way, my children and I have known you for years. There is a ghost of you in The Beam, and it is unlike the rest. It is wise. Steeped. It looks and sounds very different from your body as it exists now, and someone has tried quite hard to hide you from us, but you cannot hide the soul's voice. It's like if I met you in Heaven. I'd know you from the feeling and sound of your soul, no matter what you looked like. Do you know what I mean?"

"No," Crumb said.

She laughed without surrendering an explanation.

"There was a swing," said Crumb. "The swing was rope."

She nodded then smiled. Her smile was magnetic and enchanting. Something about her small overbite endeared her to him. He wanted to hug her, but if the woman was fully organic, then she was young enough to be his great grand-daughter. And although he hadn't verified it yet, she might be naked beneath her sheer white robe.

"I know what it's like for you now," she said. "Not first-hand, of course, but through others I've seen, and through the disconnection that can come for one such as me, when we're isolated." She touched her collarbone to indicate herself but didn't elaborate on *one such as me* or *disconnection* or *isolated*. "Your mind is on one side, and your soul is on the other, and in The Beam. That's why I asked about your childhood. Childhood memories are special. They transcend mind and body and soul, and live in something more ethereal. Biologically, those memories can be repressed, destroyed, and squashed. But if you learn to *see* — " And here, she drew the word *see* out and gave it emphasis, as if imbuing it with new meaning. " — you'll find they are always there in your energy, and within your Beam soul."

"The soul is outside," said Crumb, shaking his head in negation. He was trying to argue but seemed capable only of short, clipped sentences. Still, it beat ranting of squirrels and Noah Fucking West, which he was becoming disturbingly convinced he'd done often.

"When you grow up inside," said Serenity, "you create your own definitions of certain words. But you also find higher truths, because you don't grow up blind."

"Who are you?" Crumb repeated.

"You can see who I am," she said. Then she laughed that girlish laugh again, as if to point out how silly he was being.

But he couldn't see who she was at all, and despite her calm demeanor, he was getting annoyed that the girl's every word was airy and obtuse with doublespeak. She didn't sound quite like a disciple, but she was clearly on the fringe of something spiritual. That was what happened with people — power brought them to their knees at the altar.

He thought again of the rope swing and the creek, remembering himself: a young child who hadn't been called Crumb, swinging out over the water. He remembered falling and pulling himself from its ugly current, thinking his mother would kill him when she found out.

Then, quite unexpectedly, Crumb looked up at the woman and saw exactly who she was.

"You're a cleric."

"Yes," she said. "But my intelligence is not artificial, no matter what computer scientists insist about AI. I remember awakening on The Beam through a sensation I do not understand: that of myself as a spoon made of chocolate, melting in a pot of hot liquid. I remember the disparate systems that made my emergent consciousness like limbs on a body. I remember emerging in nanos, and remember inhabiting this corporeal body. I don't know what you've heard of clerics, but I at least do not leave The Beam when I'm here with you. It is me, and I am it, my mind in both places forever. Just like how you can feel your eternal wellspring, how you can feel your connection to others."

"I do not feel."

"Maybe not yet," she said. "But we are all connected. Connected twice now, through The Beam. It is how you knew who I was. You knew me only in nullspace before."

"Nonsense."

The woman cocked her head and smiled with wide lips. Again, she giggled. "Yet you knew I was a cleric!"

Crumb turned his head, the conversation suddenly exhausting. Quasi-spiritual mumbo-jumbo. Existential meanderings. He was remembering more and more as he lay awake, but what he was remembering was at least real. He'd been with Leah in a rundown house, plugged into something. He'd awoken here. All he wanted was to know where Leah was, who exactly he was, and how to get home.

"You're tired," she said, seeing his expression.

"I'm tired," Crumb agreed. He tried to articulate his exasperation, but his lips stayed empty.

"I'm sorry. You should rest."

"I want to go back to Leah."

"I'm sorry," she repeated, shaking her head. And then Crumb realized that the girl wasn't simply expressing regret. She was denying him. It was as kind and understanding a denial as he could imagine, but it was a denial nonetheless. He sighed, considering. The room he was in was pleasant. The possibly nude woman, who may or may not really been SerenityBlue, seemed perfectly nice. Still, he wanted to be back somewhere familiar — or at least as familiar as was currently possible.

"We've been looking for you for a long time," the woman continued. "Your soul is strong on The Beam, but this…" she tapped his head, "…contains data that is firewalled from us. Your brain is like a slip drive, and the only way to access a slip drive is to hold it in your hands and plug it in."

"I am nobody," said Crumb.

"I'm betting not," said SerenityBlue.

"Then who am I?"

She shrugged. "We don't know. But I will say there's only one other soul we've found on The Beam who is anything like you. When you showed up on the grid (first via an interpreter program, then later in the hospital — masked, sequestered, and vain attempts to hide notwithstanding), my children saw you. Now we need you, Crumb."

"Who is the other like me?"

"Noah West," she said.

"I knew him," said Crumb, surprising himself.

"Of course you did."

"But I don't remember."

In Crumb's mind, he saw a swing over a creek, then a handsome man in a lab. He seemed to remember a dream, but he couldn't remember its insides. He saw a building with a red roof, and a book.

"My journal," he said. "I need to find it."

"I think so too," she said.

"I can't get it," he said. Crumb wasn't sure why, only that he knew it to be true. The red-roofed building was somewhere inside the city, and Crumb couldn't go to the city. He wasn't sure why; he knew only that he'd been sent away for a reason, and that entering the core network would be very bad and would undo whatever benefit the diary might bring.

"You don't have to get it," said SerenityBlue.

Crumb realized that she was going to suggest he tell someone else where to find it since he couldn't retrieve it himself. But his mind was too muddled, and he had no idea where to direct them. He had only feelings and flashes of memory, intuition and fluff. It was worthless.

The beautiful young woman watched him, saw his frustration, and smiled.

"You can send Leah," she said.

Chapter 5

Micah was in his kitchen, sleeve up and injector pressed to his arm, having breakfast, when the countertop chirped twice and flashed red once, indicating a new message.

"Canvas," he said, "who is it?"

"Kitty," said the soft female voice.

Micah sat up, realized his arm was still clamped in the injector's robotic grip, and settled to let his kitchen bot deliver the infusion. He could spray breakfast into his arm himself, of course, but he had so much goddamned money that not having a bot do it for him was almost insulting. Besides, if Micah had to do it himself, he'd forget, and his cells would slowly starve. It was strange how food had become so polarized in his life. He ate socially, often with the assistance of EndLax to make sure the food never actually did its job and filled him up. Then, separately, he got his nutrition in the most sterile, most medical way possible. Micah was so dispassionate about giving his body what it needed that he could have been a sculpted adonis even back before nanotechnology if he'd had today's attitude, but back then (when he'd been fully organic, in the twenties and early thirties) he'd carried extra weight and was developing a black lung from smoking. The irony was thick: now that didn't need self-control, he had all the self-control in the world.

The injection finished, and the grip released his arm. Micah rolled down his sleeve.

"Kitty? Where the hell has she been?"

The AI in Micah's apartment had adapted to his tendency to ask a computer system for unknowable information and had learned to respond patiently.

"I don't know, Micah."

"Okay, bring it up."

Micah looked down at the flashing countertop, waiting to hear what his problem-solver's message would say. The fact that she'd sent a message at all was strange. Kitty didn't send messages. She'd *leave* messages if Micah was too busy to take her calls, but she wasn't in the habit of recording them herself for him to play later. That plus the way she'd been uncharacteristically offline earlier made him nervous for a reason he couldn't put his finger on.

Micah stared at the screen, but the screen never changed from a readout of the message's metadata — the sender's Beam ID (spoofed, of course, seeing as it was Kitty), the message ID, and a complex, useless string of values detailing the message's path through a series of Beam nodes. The message was voice only, and started with heavy breath. Quite different from the calm composure he expected.

"I need a pickup," said Kitty's voice. "At…" She paused, as if calculating exactly where she was. The pause went on for so long that Micah wondered if the rest was cut off and blank.

"Canvas," Micah said into Kitty's pause, "where is this coming from?"

"It was transmitted from a beacon."

"A beacon?"

"Yes, Micah. It entered The Beam at the western end of the Brooklyn Bridge, but its path prior to that has been obscured. It may have originated far from there."

"That sounds like Kitty. And what…?"

Kitty resumed speaking, so Micah stopped to listen.

"I've attached an encrypted shot of my surroundings. The unarchive password will come separately. I don't know where I am. At least partially because I can't think straight." She swallowed, and Micah heard several shallow breaths. "Use the City Surveillance DB to pattern-match my location. And Noah Fucking West, *hurry*. I can't risk a live call, but I'm…I don't think I have much left in me. I don't…I can read some of my numbers, and…and they fried a lot of my nanos. I don't know that I've got ten minutes. I'm fucked up, Champ." That was her codename for Micah: *Champ*. Not as cute as his codename for her, but Kitty was cunning, not especially creative.

Then the message ended.

"Canvas, when was this received in Brooklyn?" he asked.

"Twenty-seven seconds ago…*now*," said the soft voice.

The message made Micah jittery — both because one of his prime connections was somehow in peril and because it might make Micah himself vulnerable. And, frankly, because he liked Kitty. She was like the brother Isaac had never been.

"What the hell happened?" he muttered.

"You cannot return the ping, Micah," said his canvas. "The message is listen-only."

"I *know* it's fucking listen-only," he snapped. "I wasn't talking to you, bitch."

A moment later, a second message blipped in, containing the enormous alphanumeric password he'd need to decrypt the image attached to the first message.

"Process the image attachment," said Micah.

Nothing happened.

"*Canvas*, process the image attachment," he repeated.

There was a chirp, and a flashing blue square appeared next to the message, indicating a readable attachment.

He said, "What, you're not talking to me now?"

Nothing.

"Canvas."

"Yes, Micah?"

"Stop being a cunt."

"Yes, Micah."

He sighed, summoning his composure and glad that no one else was around to see him arguing with a computer and losing his cool. He wasn't often unfettered. Isaac was quick to anger and impetuosity, which was probably why their mother (whom, Micah reminded himself, he needed to pay a requisite visit to soon) liked him less. It was why Micah had taken over his father's majority stake in Ryan Enterprises and his sizable holdings in Xenia Labs despite being younger, while Isaac managed only to gather a few shittier bits of his father's business's detritus.

Micah closed his eyes and forced his mind to be still.

Kitty had unsettled him. There was so much wrong with her message. He'd taken a risk, going in with her early. He'd trained her; he'd mentored her; he'd paid for her add-ons (including the nanos that kept her so young) before she'd grown wealthy enough to buy them herself. Soon, she'd achieve Beau Monde status — and in the hands of someone like Kitty, Beau Monde status would damn near make her a god. There weren't many people out there like Kitty, and she'd never intentionally betray Micah. But there were always connections and loose ends when you exposed yourself and gave someone your trust and compassion. It was hard, at times like these, not to regret it.

Regardless, Kitty was in trouble, and it had become his problem. She'd sent a beacon message rather than risk a live call. She had sounded exhausted and near death and didn't think she had much time. He had to help her. Kitty was a significant asset. Micah had plans; if she expired now, his house of cards would collapse. He'd lose everything he'd invested in her. Certain...*plans* would never bear fruit.

He tapped the blue square.

The voice asked Micah if he wanted immersion.

"No. I don't even want a holo projection or a 2-D. Just run it through CS for a location match. Hurry." But that last was idiotic, too. Computers worked at the speed they worked at. They did nothing slow and were incapable of hurrying, whether they were part of emerging consciousnesses or not.

"I have a match, Micah." A map appeared on the countertop, centered with a red dot. Micah pinched in and out, trying to get his bearings. Eventually, he recognized where the map had placed Kitty: near the Xenia warehouse in the sticks, way the hell off of Manhattan. It was lucky City Surveillance even had any usable images out that far. She was maybe a mile or three from the warehouse itself, in the wilds beyond. The area had once been a neighborhood, but the neighborhood had been struck by a stray Chinese missile in the '30s, had been razed after the lattice went up, and had never been rebuilt. Over the past fifty years, the place had become a strange sort of quasi-jungle surrounded by housing and industrial parks, filled with trees and pocked with hovels that were used by transients. There had been many reports of wildlife in the area — and not gophers.

"What the fuck is she doing there?" he said. Then, to forestall another annoying response from his canvas, he added, "Never mind. Show me Capital Protection in the area. Not Beamers. I don't trust those assholes. Just CP agents."

Blue dots peppered the screen, all to the right of the red one. He'd zoomed out to assess Kitty's location, and when he pinched in again to show only officers within a reasonable distance, the blue dots vanished.

"How far is this — " He placed one finger on the red dot and another on the blue one closest to it. " — by car or hover?"

"Approximately two hours by car. One hour by hover, depending on observance of speed regulations."

"How long by screetbike?"

"There's heavy traffic in the area, Micah. At least forty minutes."

"What if the copter uses line of sight, avoiding the skyroads?"

"That is illegal, Micah."

"That's not what I fucking asked!" Micah bellowed. He wished the canvas had a throat, so that he could choke it.

"Maybe twenty minutes at full speed, if the bike is not stopped by autocops," said the canvas.

Micah thought of the message and its barely contained sense of panic. Kitty didn't complain, so if she was admitting to being near death, then she was convinced it was true. Her breathing had sounded labored, her voice sober and too quiet. At least five minutes would have already passed between the time Kitty had recorded the message and he'd received it, given the time a stealth beacon took to float up undetected. Twenty-five minutes total from recording to rescue wasn't much, but Micah was suddenly certain it wouldn't do.

"Send bike CP017," said Micah, reading the tag beside the closest blue dot. But then, quite suddenly, a new blue dot appeared much closer, labeled CP518.

"Wait. Who's this?"

"Agents Kevin Jameson and Jason Whitlock," answered the voice.

"On bikes?"

"Yes."

"Do they have a Neuralin kit?"

"Yes, Micah."

He had no idea why Whitlock was way the hell out near the warehouse or why his locator seemed to be fritzing sporadically on and off (Jameson was new and didn't have one yet), but it didn't matter. They could be at Kitty's location in two minutes at most.

"Send them Kitty's location and tell them to get her. Tell them to burn air to get there."

The canvas chirped as the message was delivered. Immediately, on the zoomed-in map, the blue dot began to move. It winked off, then on again, closer.

"Hurry, you bastards," he whispered.

The canvas said, "They can't hear you, Micah."

Chapter 6

Once, years ago, Kai had owned a cat named Saul. Everyone agreed it was a ridiculous name for a cat.

When she'd owned Saul, Kai had been living in a shitty street-level apartment near the park, in gangland territory. The place had rats, which Saul loved plenty — that being the primary reason Kai wanted the cat in the first place. Saul had done his job well, exploring exposed holes in the tattered walls and seeking nests, leaving Kai one macabre trophy after another.

One day, after those holes in the wall were all cleared of rodents and after he had lived a long and happy and useful life, Saul climbed inside the walls, refused to come out, and died the next day. Kai, crying, had to root him out and extricate him by the tail.

The cat had somehow known his days were over.

Now, with her breathing shallow and her pulse slowing, Kai crawled on her hands and knees toward a bombed-out and abandoned shack, knowing as surely as Saul had that her days were over, too.

Kai, like a poor, dumb animal, didn't know how she knew her death was waiting, but she did. Something inside her had broken during her time on the Orion, under the uncaring hand of Alix Kane. Inside her mind, Kai's body had been twisted backward upon itself, every joint snapped, tendons unthreaded from bone and neurons yanked free like loose and sparking power lines. Inside her mind, Kai's heart had been shredded, her lungs punctured as she struggled for breath, a metal spear impaling her gut and making her swallow rust from the inside. Those experiences had been purely in her brain — senses perverted into feeling things that had not happened — but it made no difference. For centuries, yogis had shown it was possible to still their hearts and lower their skin temperature by force of mind alone. And if the mind controlled the body, why couldn't the mind kill the body just as easily?

The old wives' tale: *if you die in a dream, you die in life.*

Kai had died, and died, and died, and died. If being a killer and whore made her fit for Hell, she would welcome it. No Hell could be worse than what she'd lived through on that chrome table. Satan's agony would feel like kisses beside it.

With the beacon she'd sent to Micah already forgotten, Kai used her hands to claw through the dirt. She made her way to the shack, punted the door shut behind her with one desperately kicking foot, and gave a tiny, helpless cry as she dragged herself across the shack's wooden floor. She was finding a spot to die, just as Saul had all those years ago. Still, despite her resignation, she screamed as something grated inside her. It felt like she was being stabbed by a shattered rib, but she couldn't remember if she'd taken a real fall or if it was all just the evil of artificial memory.

Inside the abandoned shack was a wooden dining room table and a pair of chairs, everything ancient and covered with slick green fungus. Kai dragged her useless corpse under the table and formed a protective ball, soft organs toward the center and backbone around her like a frightened animal's shell.

Breath came slowly. Kai might have fallen asleep, and might have cried. She certainly revisited her earlier horrors, feeling each finger bend far enough to touch the back of her hand. Bones snapped loudly in her ears. Too late, Kai realized she shouldn't have moved from her earlier spot. How far had she gone from the place she'd released the beacon? If Micah managed to send a rescue, how would it find her? Would the person who came to find her body know to check the shack?

But really: Did it matter?

Kai waited. And as she did, something itched at the back of her mind. She seemed to remember two other men who'd been with her, and seemed to recall something similar to responsibility — like being sure to turn the oven off — concerning them. Then, with difficulty, she placed them. She'd been with Doc and Nicolai. What had happened to them? Even as dead as Kai felt, she summoned the empathy to hope for their welfare. She hoped they had managed to escape their torture, and missed their dates with the evaporator as she had.

But her escape was so narrow, how could they have made theirs at all?

Kai exhaled a long and shambling breath. She couldn't care. She had no space in her mind.

The room became black as she drifted away.

Some time later, the sound of boots snapped her awake. She tried to make herself alert, aware of threat's whisper, but she had nothing left. Her head rose, but at first she couldn't even open her eyes. She was groggy, sleep sealing her lids as morning brayed.

Her puffy lids rose on swollen eyes. She could see two offending sets of boots on the small room's far side. The boots were black. Above them, neat black slacks. Kai rolled her eyes up to long black coats, and black gloved-hands clutching shiny black guns. They'd entered with their guns up and their blank, visored faces forward. One of the men's digital gazes swept to the far side of the room then toward Kai. She curled tighter, trying to ball herself invisible. But of course, that was absurd. She was under a table, not in a box. Or, for that matter, between the walls of a rundown apartment.

"There she is," said the first Beamer.

"I see her," said the second. He was looking in the opposite direction as the first man, but of course, thanks to his visor, he saw whatever the first man (or headquarters, or whoever was in charge) wanted him to see.

Surprising herself, Kai suddenly resolved that no matter what, she would not die in the fetal position. And with that thought, she found energy. Hardly any energy…but energy nonetheless.

She exploded up from the floor, uncurling as she sprang to her feet, upsetting the table, raising her fists and raking her fingers at them like claws…

…or at least that's how it seemed in her head. In reality, nothing much happened. She tried to spring, but could barely twitch. She tried to snarl, but she winced instead. She couldn't extend her arms or uncurl her spine. She stayed in a ball, protecting herself with all the natural defense of a potato bug, apparently doomed to die in the fetal position after all.

The forward-facing Beamer seized her, dragged her from under the table, pulled her upright, and plopped her onto the tabletop like a bag of groceries.

"You don't run from Beamers," he said. Below his visor, his lips curled into an angry grimace as if the man was trying to prove something.

"But you caught me," Kai wheezed. It was hard to speak, but she needed to say the rest: "What a big man you are."

"I want to beat the shit out of her before we take her in," the man yelled back to the other.

"Let's just drag her up," said the other. "Come on. Hurry. I'm already late for a meeting with my gaming guild."

"Talk more about your gaming guild," Kai coughed, still flat on her back. "You're making me hot."

The second man stopped and turned to Kai, pausing to assess what she hoped was a condescending smile on her lips.

"Okay," he said. "We'll beat her just a little."

When the second Beamer's face appeared above Kai, she spit up at him. The spit never left her lips, and ran down her cheeks instead.

"Did she just spit at me?"

"She's drooling. Burned."

"I think she just spit at me."

"I would never spit at a man who's part of a *gaming guild,*" Kai croaked. "Come over here, big boy. You're giving me a fever." She reached for the Beamer's groin, but it was too far and her arm didn't have the strength to stray outstretched. It flopped like spaghetti, slapping the table with the sound of a fallen fish.

"Is she coming onto me?" said the second Beamer.

Kai rolled her arm, palm up, and flexed her fingers in a grabbing motion. "Just lay it in my hand."

The first Beamer said, "Yes, I think she is."

"I won't squeeze it until your balls pop or anything."

Instead of answering or unzipping, the second man used a black-gloved hand to punch Kai hard in the gut. She wanted to laugh and would have if she'd had the air. But Kai didn't even have the reflexes to flinch around the blow, so she just gasped, smiled, and waited to die.

The man who'd hit her said, "Do you have any idea how bad it looks for us, you escaping?"

"As bad as your acne?"

He hit her again.

"Keep mouthing off. We can bring you back dead. It's what they expect anyway."

"Then hurry," she said. "Hit me like a man."

The shack had a fireplace in the corner. Beside the fireplace was a set of black iron tools. The Beamer tucked his gun into his holster, grabbed the poker, slapped it against his palm, then raised it. With no hesitation for drama, he swung. The swing was already launched when a hovercar-sized cannonball blew through the shack's far wall and knocked the Beamer sideways. He struck the table's edge and folded the wrong way. Something snapped, and the man screamed. A robot of some sort charged the room, its skeleton shifting from something wide-bodied, collapsing into something the size and shape of a silver man. Kai didn't understand where the extra parts went; they seemed to simply melt into the smaller mechanical form. She wondered if she were hallucinating as the robot man removed what looked like a slumbergun from somewhere behind its body and fired it at the yelling Beamer, who fell immediately silent.

The other Beamer was coming at the robot man from behind with his own gun raised, but the robot man blurred to the side, and the shot missed him entirely, obliterating a large mirror on the shack's opposite wall and venting outside air into the cabin. Kai looked at the robot and saw the lower half of a human face inside its hood. The face's mouth looked shocked, as if its own movement had been a surprise.

The Beamer aimed and fired again. The man in the suit moved, but again the movement seemed involuntary, judging by how the human mouth gaped, barely able to keep up. The movement was so fast that Kai barely saw it happen. The Beamer's shot went wide for a second time, blowing a dozen bricks from the fireplace. He wasn't firing slumbershots, and if anything, the robot man seemed offended by such rude lethality.

The Beamer touched something on his visor and yelled, *"GET THE FUCK IN HERE!"*

A third black-clothed Beamer stormed the shack and stood on the opposite side of the robot man. He aimed his gun as the first man re-aimed his. Neither gun was a slumber.

Then two things happened back-to-back.

First, the new Beamer discharged his weapon. The man in the suit moved as he had before, and the shot struck the first Beamer (the one whose partner had already been knocked flat) and cut him in two. Simultaneously, a second blur stormed the door and disarmed the remaining man. The Beamer who'd fired looked shocked, his weapon smoking in the first robot man's grip like an old pistol, his mouth open. The two robot men blurred again, like bullets, and converged on the Beamer, stripping weapon from body, and sending the black-cloaked man to floor.

One of the robot men touched something on his arm and said, "We found her. All clear."

Then they tidied. The disarmed Beamer's weapon collapsed to a third of its full size, so the second robot man tossed it into a compartment on his back. With Kai's two rescuers now looking like silver men with a few knobby, mechanical protrusions, she again wondered where their weapons and suits (she could have sworn they'd been larger when they'd burst through the door) were going. The new robot man raised his slumber and fired it unceremoniously at the Beamer. He fell, and the first robot man pulled out a pair of cuffs and shackled him to an iron ring set into the brick by the fireplace.

"That one's hurt," said one of the robot men.

The other looked at the splatter of gore on the shack's far wall. A pair of black-clad legs with boots on the end slumped against the wall, the torso missing.

"He sure is."

"I meant *that* one." He pointed at the first of the two Beamers — the man who'd cracked when he'd struck the table.

"And you want me to help him."

"We're not animals," said the first man.

"Rowr," said the second.

"Fine. And they say you're the nice one." While his partner made tiger noises and clawed the air, the robot man who'd expressed concern for the Beamer walked over and pressed a small tube to the sleeping man's neck. Almost immediately, his body straightened and twisted as nanos knitted his bones.

"You're too compassionate," said the other man. "They tried to kill you."

The other shook his head. Kai, who thought she might be imagining the entire scene, pictured him rolling his eyes beneath his robot helmet…or whatever it was.

"You could at least help her," said the first robot man.

The man jumped as if suddenly realizing he'd forgotten something. He'd been leaning casually against the shed's wall, ignoring Kai. He walked toward her, pulling a similar tube from a pocket on his silver robotic leg.

"I have nanos," Kai croaked up at him. "Lots."

The lips above her smiled. The smile was genuine. Kai wondered just what the hell had happened. Everyone was killing and beating and torturing everyone; everyone was brutal, brimming with bloodlust. Yet she'd just been saved by two superhuman cyborgs, but they were taking mercy on their prey (which they clearly outmatched and could easily squash), as well as the prey of the prey.

"This is Neuralin," said the man, showing her the vial.

As Kai looked up, she saw that he wasn't a cyborg or a robot at all. He was an ordinary man, covered in a skin-tight metal suit. And as she watched, the metal surged and shifted and flowed like waves across his body, like liquid.

Kai wanted to know more about Neuralin (starting with what it was), but before she could ask anything, the man had injected her, and Kai found herself falling into dreamless sleep.

Chapter 7

Kai had been hauled off the Orion and out of the simulator room approximately ten thousand years ago. Doc reasoned that she had to be dead. At the time, her departure had seemed worth noting — maybe even worth his concern — but now, as his nerves retched for breath, Kai and her death fell neatly into the pile of shit that Doc couldn't spend a splinter of energy to think about.

Now, what felt like thousands of years later, Doc realized that Nicolai was also gone from the room — another fact that for some reason no longer mattered. He figured this out shortly after Kane used the Orion to make Doc feel as if something the size of a utility pole was being shoved through his stomach. The sensation, looking back, had been as interesting as it was unbearable. If a man were struck with a utility pole in real life, the thing would pulverize him, not impale him. And if it *did* manage to impale him, it'd do the job in a single blunt strike, displacing his center in one big chunk like a cookie cutter through dough. But that wasn't how the Orion's utility pole impaling felt. What Doc felt was like being impaled by a *needle-thin* pole which then rapidly expanded inside him like an umbrella popping open. The sensation had been so horrifyingly awful that Doc's abdominal contraction in the real world was strong enough to break the Orion's chest strap. It had also unseated the cap that delivered the Orion's horror to his cortex, and when that happened, the utility-pole-through-the-gut sensation had faded in a blink. Doc had found himself sitting up, confused, wondering where the pole had gone as he noticed that the room was empty save himself and his torturer.

Realizing the absurdity of the question, Doc had then asked Kane about Nicolai. Kane had tried to push Doc back down and to re-seat the electrode cap, but a man in white entered the room at that moment and told Doc rather casually (for a man witnessing torture) that the speechwriter was gone. Kane shouted at the man for a reason Doc didn't understand, and the man, his composure suddenly snapping, shouted back at Kane. The man told Kane to stop, that he was going to get them all Respero'd, and Kane told the man to get off his back. The exchange had the feeling of an ongoing debate, equivalent to a wife telling her husband that he *never* took her anywhere nice and the husband snapping back that the wife was letting herself go. Doc, his nerves trying to recover and his head foggy, found this all fascinating. He tried to decide whose side he was on, but thirty seconds later, when his Orion connections were re-seated, Doc found that he no longer cared.

He came back to reality after another mental beating to find that someone was tugging at the straps holding him down on the torture machine. Doc looked up and saw the man in white who had been arguing with Kane. He wanted to thank the man then hug him. Anyone who argued with Kane was aces in Doc's book. But then Doc passed out from remembered pain and didn't wake again until he spilled onto the floor and landed with his arm wrenched beneath him. Above him, Kane and the man in white were arguing, but it was Doc's fall that seemed to be the source of their disagreement.

Kane was saying that the man in white didn't know what he was doing. The man was telling Kane that he could at least fucking *help*, if he wanted the evidence disposed of in time.

Doc saw that they were going to kill him, but the news seemed less appalling than it should have.

Then, again, he blacked out.

His interlude couldn't have lasted long because when he woke he was just five feet from the Orion's bright aluminum legs, his limbs somehow wound around his torso like a wet and floppy doll that has been wrung dry. His head was pointed toward the two men, who were still scrapping with each other, so Doc was able to watch them fight and argue. He heard the man in white say something about Nicolai. Kane replied that Nicolai was "handled" and resumed his yelling, now questioning the other man's competence, appearance, and ability to satisfy his wife. The man in white retorted with a well-reasoned argument accusing Kane of fornicating with corpses.

They must have come to some sort of an agreement because the next time Doc woke, he had both of his arms over his head, one held by each man, with his feet splayed out behind him. They were dragging him from the room, still arguing. Both men seemed to agree that they should not be the ones "taking out the trash" but seemed to disagree about the reasons. The tall man argued that Kane was at fault because he was "an incompetent sadistic fuck," and Kane replied by suggesting that the other man engage in sexual activity with his own mother.

Before Doc could be dragged through the doorway of the simulator, however, several voices appeared behind him. He wanted to turn and see the source of the new voices but didn't have the strength. Doc also wasn't sure he cared. He really just wanted to die — ideally, soon. Anything that got between Doc and dying a non-horrible death seemed like an unneeded distraction. But as the voices talked further — and Doc heard the names "Kai," "Nicolai," and someone important who was referred to simply as "the boss" — Doc's interest grew. He decided he could die later, after he heard a bit more.

There was pressure on his chest and a flash of silver, and Doc felt himself rising into the air. Suddenly, he found himself looking at something long and gleaming that looked like buttocks. This went on for several seconds, until the man whose shoulder Doc had apparently been flung over propped him in a corner.

In front of Doc were five people: the man in white (who looked satisfied before he marched from the room, apparently vindicated), Kane, two silvery men who appeared to be covered mostly in mercury (and with a few robotic protrusions — islands in the mercury), and…and…

He blinked. The fifth person in the group was Kai. She was standing among the others, unbound, acting for all the world as if she wasn't dead.

Doc tried saying her name. He failed.

The small group was across the room. He couldn't concentrate enough to figure out their words, but he could read body language well, and what he saw was so shocking it was clearly delusion.

The person in charge of the group wasn't Alix, or the men in silver. It was Kai.

Even through his haze, Doc could easily interpret her look as she spoke to Kane. Kai was expert with false faces but couldn't hide her venom when addressing the man who had tortured her. If Kane were smart, he'd double his security and maybe go into a short stint of hiding for the rest of his life. Kai had obviously gained some kind of odd authority over the torturer, and now he was kowtowing. Doc could see each of his not-so-subtle *Yes ma'am, no ma'am* nods as she grilled him.

After a while, they walked over to Doc, with Kai in the lead.

"Help him," she said.

Only the lower halves of the silver men's faces were visible, but Doc could see their lips press together. "We only carried the one dose," said the one on Doc's right.

"You only carry one?"

"Whoever ends up needing Neuralin?" the man replied, looking at Kai. "Of course we only carry one! We've got all sorts of repair nanos, though."

"Nanos won't help," said Kai.

"I'm just saying, we carry a complete kit. I could manually remove his appendix. Noah Fucking West, we don't expect to run into two nerve-strips in one outing!"

"Okay, okay," said Kai. "Relax. What can you do for him?"

"Take him back," said the silver man on Doc's left. "We have refills at the station."

"Fine. We'll go to the station."

Doc squirmed and protested. He didn't have the core strength to stay upright, so squirming sent him onto his side. Shockingly, it was Kane who reached down to prop him up. Something in the small man's eyes seemed afraid.

"It's okay, Doc," said Kai, squatting in front of him. "They came to help us."

Doc looked at Kai, at the robot men, and at Kane. Somehow, they were all in this together. And where was Nicolai? They had killed him for sure. Kai seemed to be okay. That meant she must've been with them since the beginning. Doc wasn't sure that made sense, or about anything else. But he *was* sure that he didn't want to be taken to any station.

"No," he croaked.

"We have to do something. We need to return a favor."

"No," Doc croaked again.

He looked up at Kai. Her clothes were filthy and torn, and she had smudges of blood on her cheeks and neck. She seemed strong and upright and (he had to admit, even now) looked dead sexy, but she'd taken a beating. He could see bruises and cuts that her nanos had yet to erase. She seemed to have a slight limp. So maybe she hadn't been in on it from the beginning after all. She had somehow *moved* into a position of control mid-stream. But how? It made no sense…but then Doc had it.

Kai was being played.

They were both being tricked — another tactic intended to mine information that Doc didn't have, about fucking Omar and his role in espionage at Xenia. They hadn't been able to draw information out using torture, so they were playing Kai so that she could unwittingly play him.

"Trust me, Doc," she said, reading the doubt on his face.

"I don't trust *them*," he said, looking at the others.

Kai gave a tiny, humorless laugh. "Let's just say they're afraid of the right person. Come on." She reached for him. He flinched away like a frightened child. She reached again, this time grasping his arm. Kai was small, but Doc knew she could easily handle him, especially now. He had a drunken thought that Kai sure was one tough honey. She could probably lift him even without add-ons.

"No," he repeated.

"Don't make me carry you."

"Nicolai," said Doc. It was just one word, but it was also an avalanche of questions.

"He's safe," said Kane, above Kai. "We sent him home."

From the corner of his eye, Doc saw Kai's eyes close and her shoulders relax. She must not have thought to ask about Nicolai because hearing Kane now and apparently believing him, her body language told Doc that she was relieved.

"Bullshit," said Doc.

"We got a call," said Kane.

"Nicolai is safe if Mr. Kane here says he is," Kai echoed, speaking to Doc. She turned her head and eyed Kane with ice-cold hatred. "He knows how far his balls are into the evaporator already."

"Bullshit," Doc repeated. "They didn't even put him on the table. And they didn't let *me* go."

"He had better connections than you did," said Kane. "I figured from the beginning that we'd have to toss that particular fish back into the water — after seeing how he lined up with your lies, of course."

Kai stood from her squat and came face-to-face with Kane. The small, white-haired man lowered his head and played with the buttons on the front of his shirt.

"Not going," said Doc, knowing how stupid he must sound.

"You're going," Kai said, bending forward.

"They're playing you."

She shook her head. "I have reason to trust them."

"Who are they?"

"Soldiers."

"What are their names?"

"Whitlock and Jameson. I don't know which is which."

"They're playing you."

"What do you care? Where do you think we're going? Somewhere worse than this?" She nodded at the Orion.

Doc's head was starting to clear. Kai wasn't stupid; she could read the situation's temperature. But whatever nefarious purposes the masked men in silver had in mind, it had to be better than torture. Leaving the room would open up some new possibilities. If they didn't cuff or paralyze them for the trip (if they "went willingly" because the soldiers were "on their side"), there might be opportunities for escape. Maybe he'd get his strength back as Kai had, and he'd find himself able to run…to make it back to that fucker Omar, whose fault all of this seemed to be.

"Fine," he said.

Kai nodded to one of the soldiers. The man hefted Doc over his shoulder with all the effort of grabbing a wad of tissue. Doc again found himself staring down at metal buttocks, watching as the simulator room disappeared behind the soldier's silver back. After the simulator, Doc saw wood-colored flooring then concrete as outside air kissed his sore and beaten skin. The soldier pulled Doc from his shoulder, rotated him, and settled Doc behind him on a high-end weaponized screetbike. He took Doc's arms and placed them around his own silver waist, then turned his head to speak. Doc looked at the man's blank, silver-visored face and his visible human lips.

"Can you hang on, or do you want me to cuff your wrists around me?" he asked.

Doc felt annoyed. The fucker couldn't refrain from making threats, even in the throes of subterfuge.

"I can hang on." He gripped his hands together to show him.

Kai climbed on the back of the other bike behind the other soldier. Kane stood between the bikes, blubbering something about telling the boss that he was only looking out for all of their best interests. Nobody paid him any attention.

The soldiers kicked off and rose into the sky, staying near the tops of tress and houses as they accelerated. If the soldiers had brought screetcopters, Kai and Doc would be sunk, but bikes had to stay low. Hopefully, once they reached the city's edge, where air congestion increased, they'd drop to the streets. If they did, they might be able to find an opportunity to roll free.

The screetbikes flew side by side. Kai looked over at Doc, smiling encouragement. Doc kept jerking his eyes sideways, attempting to convey his intention to roll away the second he had the chance. Kai furrowed her eyebrows, seemed to think, then shook her head. Doc jerked his eyes again, insistent. Kai furrowed harder and shook her head faster then took a hand from the soldier's waist and used it to pat down on the air, nonverbally saying *Settle down* or *It's cool.*

Doc shook his head and mouthed, *It's a trap.*

Kai yelled back, over the roar of the air between them, *"WHAT?"*

Doc's eyes widened with alarm as both soldiers turned toward her shout. Her bike's pilot spun his head so quickly that the bike jerked sideways, and he had to scramble to correct.

Doc shut his mouth, refusing to look over until they started crossing a large open area that looked like a park. Ahead, Doc saw the District Zero spires. They were close.

The bikes, finding nothing to push off of, sank toward the grass.

Doc turned to Kai, his face urgent as he violently jerked his head toward the ground.

Kai shook her head, equally vehement.

The grass area was ending. Ahead were more houses. Once they reached the houses, they'd rise up again, and their opportunity to escape would vanish. He didn't know if he had the strength to run, but he would have to find a way.

"GODDAMMIT, DOC, DON'T!" Kai yelled, watching as he shifted behind his driver. *"WILL YOU FUCKING TRUST ME?"*

Doc's driver, sensing trouble, started to turn his head. Doc moved his hands up to grab the man's shoulders and twisted them the same direction as he was turning his head, magnifying the soldier's momentum. The bike jolted and shook as the soldier's hands left the handlebars. Beside them, on the other bike, Kai was still yelling.

The soldier's shifting weight twisted the bike onto its side. The driver slipped and fell. Doc fell with him, pushing off. He'd known the crash was coming (seeing as he'd caused it) and had prepared; he dove for the ground, tucked his chin against his chest, and rolled on impact. In front of Doc, the soldier struck the ground in a heap. His foot snagged in the stirrup, which grabbed the ground, bucked the bike forward, and threw it hard into a fence. It sputtered then stalled. Doc was off the bike and running with all of his diminished strength while behind him, the solider remained twisted and pinned under his bike, the other officer and Kai slowing above him. As Doc ran, he waited for Kai to crash the other bike and follow him, but she stayed mounted, still shouting.

They'd crashed very close to the field's edge — good news for Doc, who had almost no energy in him. He stumbled into a thicket of trees, adrenaline bolstering his uncertain legs, his heart trying to keep up. Kai cried out from behind him. He waited for slumbershots, but none came. Both soldiers remained mute. If the metallic suits did something to make the men powerful or fast, which he assumed they did, then it would only be a matter of time before they would be on him. So he kept forcing himself to move, to gain whatever advantage he could.

His feet struck a shallow stream, and he turned to see an enormous drainage culvert. Doc ran into it, water splashing his legs, his shoes squishing. He reached a fork in the culvert, turned, then reached another and turned again. Minutes passed. He hunkered down, spent. He waited.

Despite his daring escape, Doc knew it had been in vain. He was too weak, and they would be too strong and too determined. It wouldn't be long until they found him — and when they did, he'd have no energy left with which to flee. The tunnels weren't that complicated, and the soldiers would surely have every sort of gadget at their disposal. They wore visors, like Beamers, so they'd be able to see in the dark. Doc was important; Kane's insistence on continuing to torture him even after giving up with Kai and "freeing" Nicolai proved that. Doc was the one who had supposedly bypassed Xenia's security, the one who was supposedly selling secrets.

He squatted in the culvert, waiting in the dark. But nobody came.

A few moments later, he heard the distinctive whine of two screetbikes starting up then gliding past overhead. They wouldn't let Kai drive one of the bikes, so the fact that he could hear both of them meant that the soldiers were leaving without him.

Doc waited a few more minutes to make sure it wasn't a ruse then carefully made his way through the culvert to its far end. He found himself emerging beneath a suburban street and into a neighborhood — all old construction, probably barely Beam-enabled. But it was still a neighborhood, and that meant there would be cabs. It also meant that somewhere, he'd be able to find a public connection.

Doc composed himself and started walking.

He had to find a Beam connection. He had to use his spoof to call Omar.

Oh yes. He would need to hook up with that slippery motherfucker as soon as possible.

Chapter 8

Leah woke from a moondust haze to find her head throbbing. She felt vaguely sick, and was nursing a hazy memory from a fading dream — one of those persistent on-waking thoughts that refuses to leave. She remembered something about an enormous moon bearing down on the world from above, threatening to crush her. In the bright sunlight streaming in through the mag train's window, Leah's dream image should have seemed absurd and stupid, but it was neither. She looked outside and up, searching the blue sky for the moon's ghost. After a moment, she found it. It was up, and she saw it right where it was supposed to be through the lattice, still tiny, pale in the light of day.

The train was approaching District Zero. She'd asked her tablet to wake her when she was fifteen minutes from the station, and it hadn't alarmed yet, so she wasn't quite that close. Maybe a half hour total travel time left. She could see buildings, but they were at her vision's limit, still distant.

Leah lay back in the empty train cabin — not private, though she was the only one inside — and closed her eyes. She had barely been sleeping lately and was looking at a busy time once she was back inside the city. She should sleep while she could.

Behind her eyelids Leah saw a building with a red roof then saw a journal. They were the images from Crumb's mind, which she'd seen in the metaphorical honey back in Bontauk.

She opened her eyes then shook her head and closed them again.

Leah tried to sleep, but rest mocked her. She was moving back into District Zero's primary Beam network, and she could feel a hacker's itch in her fingers. Now that she'd left Leo behind, Leah could indulge that itch. Leo tried to understand the duality of what she did for Organa, but he was too old and set in his ways to truly get it. Leah had grown up in the world of The Beam. Leo had grown up before the Internet. The gulf between them, technologically speaking, was unfathomable. They came from opposite worlds, and there was no way they'd ever be able to truly speak the same language. They were like a couple with different definitions of infidelity. For Leo, the dirtiest you could get as a tech-fighting Organa was to secretly use a handheld from time to time — the equivalent of beating off in the bathroom. For Leah, abundant use of technology was still perfectly fine as long as she did it in service of her cause — more like going to a prostitute you didn't connect with emotionally. Leo tried to understand (which was why he'd gotten Leah her elite training), but again, his doing so was like sending his wild wife on a hedonistic trip so she could get out her jollies then return to him as a loyal partner. Leo was willing to indulge because the training was what Leah wanted and needed, but he didn't truly get it, deep down, or see why it was necessary.

Leah rolled her eyes to herself, wondering why the metaphor was so sexual. She wondered if she was horny on top of being sleep-deprived.

The train's high-band connection to the DZ core would be

at full strength now, so Leah pulled out her tablet and began plinking around. But the tablet was a poor adept's tool. She decided she wasn't doing anything particularly scandalous, so gave herself permission to use the train's native canvas.

Leah didn't feel like craning her neck to the side to use the window as her surface, so she hit the pads on her armrest to project a screen and airboard. The train's projections were decent, and she found that she couldn't really see the compartment seats across from her through the screen.

She touched the hologram with her fingers, dragged it wider, then started touching keys on the airboard. She could speak to the canvas, but for Leah at least, her hands used a different part of her mind than her voice. It was why, when she tried dictating mail, she always gave up after a few minutes. But her fingers loved the airboard, especially since she'd had tactile response add-ons inserted into her fingers and thumbs. Leo didn't know about the add-on because it was none of his business and would never matter to him; all it did was give her fingers the feeling of pressing keys. A neat side benefit of the add-on was that when Leah was plugged in, she didn't really even require an airboard. She could mime typing with her fingers even if they hung at her sides, as long as her add-on was active. It would have been an outstanding way to subtly pass notes in class, if only she'd been enhanced back then.

For Leah — and for many Beam-native young people, especially those with a hacker bent — poking around on The Beam was almost meditative — an experience that didn't need to have an objective in order to be fulfilling and relaxing, like taking a stroll with no destination in mind. So-called Beamwalking was just one more thing for Leo to rail against in his stodgy old way. He said that nothing had changed since he'd been a young man, back when people had first started mindlessly checking their handhelds over and over…or when they'd sat for hours in front of their old 2-D canvas screens, drifting from display to display without really caring about anything they saw.

But as usual, Leo just didn't get it. The Beam wasn't like the Internet of Leo's youth, and it sure as hell was nothing like television. A hundred years of progress separated Leo's memories of obsession from the modern Beam experience. Leah didn't like to admit it to the other Organas (who were mostly poseurs anyway; fuck them), but she saw tremendous good in The Beam. It really was another world — one you could stroll and experience as if it were a different country. The problems people saw with The Beam had little to do with the technology itself. They had to do with human restraint, or the lack thereof. Was it bad to travel for a while in an alternate world facilitated by The Beam? Not at all. Was it bad to become so obsessed that you'd lose yourself in that world and not know when to surface for air? Yeah, maybe. And maybe that kind of obsession was damaging society, crippling inter-personal connections, shearing ties to the natural world, battering morals, and totally annihilating self-reliance. But that wasn't the technology's fault.

After ten minutes of window-shopping and running simu-lations and following rabbit holes into off-topic hyperthreads in hacker forums (many filled with irreverent holos that she thought were hilarious), Leah found herself drifting and tired despite just waking. She also felt a haze on her thoughts that she normally felt only during a moondust high.

And she drifted.

An unknown time later, Leah realized that she'd stopped feeling her fingers on the airboard a while back and was more or less sitting still, staring at the projection. She became distantly aware that she must look like a junkie or mental patient, with her jaw hanging loose and her eyes fixed on the screen. Leo's remonstrations about zombies staring at twenti-eth-century TV barged into her thoughts, until she snapped out of it and returned to reality. She felt suddenly guilty. How had she gotten so sucked in? She remembered visiting dozens of different locations, yet her hands were at her sides and her arms had gone numb, so she obviously hadn't used her fingers to get there. Yet Leah didn't remember dictating her way to all of those sites, and hadn't even brought the wireless dongle that plugged into the port behind her ear. Had she blacked out? How much time had passed? What had she been doing?

And why was she so fucking hungry?

Leah gestured the screen and airboard away. She suddenly wanted Chinese food very, very badly — and not just any Chinese, but Chinese from one particular hole in the wall — somewhere in Chinatown — where she had gone with a boyfriend she'd not thought of in years. The feeling was sudden and insistent. Like a compulsion. Leah could practically taste the noodles in her mouth.

Then Leah realized that she'd never been to a restaurant in Chinatown. She'd walked *through* Chinatown, but had never eaten there.

The mag train compartment suddenly felt too small, too confining. Leah realized, with a fair degree of shock, that she felt panicked. What had just happened? She'd gone into a trance and had apparently blacked out only to wake with a strange craving she couldn't explain (and holy *fuck*, was it strong! She could barely think around the hunger for noodles) and with an intrusive memory: meeting in a restaurant she'd never been to with a boyfriend she'd never had. Leah could still see the memory, even. She could almost smell it, even though she knew it wasn't hers. The man across from her had been tall, thin, handsome, and neat, with delicate round-lensed glasses. But Leah had never had a boyfriend who wasn't shaggy, usually with a beard and matted, dreadlocked hair like hers.

She'd heard of this happening. Sometimes, an implant went bad and stimulated parts of the brain it wasn't supposed to touch. They used hypno-suspension to install brain implants for a reason — because without anesthesia, the recipients relived sensations and memories (tasting pie, remembering a visit to a water park, smelling lilacs) as the surgeons worked. Degradation wasn't supposed to happen anymore, but of course it did. The Beam was filled with reports of people who'd had an implant malfunction and found themselves hallucinating. Was that what was happening?

Leah stood, spun, and sat. She looked out the window, watching District Zero's spires approach. She suddenly wanted to visit her upgrades dealer. Only that wasn't true — what Leah *really* wanted was to claw at her scalp and dig the port behind her ear out by hand. The idea that the thing was malfunctioning and fucking with her mind felt like a tapeworm in her brain. Yet of course she couldn't claw it out, so she'd need to see a dealer. Or a doctor. Leah wondered which would be easier to find, and faster.

Oh god, oh god, oh god, she thought. *What if it's going to pop? What if it surges, fries my cortex, and I end up burned?*

That probably wouldn't happen, of course, but if the implant was the problem and Leah didn't get it out soon, the random memories and sensations *could* drive her insane. How could you stay sane when you couldn't trust your reality?

Leo was right. She shouldn't have gotten enhancements. She should have stayed organic. No implants, no nano fabricators, no fucking nanos in her system. She decided to have it all flashed. Every bit of it. She wanted nothing in her brain. She was Organa, not a cyborg. Leah thought she'd known better, but she was wrong, and would now end up like Crumb.

Crumb.

Something cross-linked in Leah's mind — the false memory of the noodles finding a connection, one thought sniffing out the next like a browse trail on The Beam. Network forming network. Leah found her desire for noodles wane and her perception of the meeting in the Chinese restaurant with the handsome man in round glasses finding context. Neurons settled; the memory was slotted somewhere deeper inside her as a realization struck: *This has to do with Crumb.* Somehow. That was why she was returning to DZ, after all. She had to find Crumb. And where was she planning to start? Nowhere. She had no plan. She'd simply trusted that she'd figure it out, same as she always did when facing a particularly stubborn problem. That's what made Leah so Beam-adept, and something even the best hackers usually didn't understand. Skills were the underpinning of what she did, but in the end, Leah had to let all of her how-to go and simply trust. At her best, she didn't even know what she was doing. Her best hacks were like dreaming. And that, Leah was starting to realize, was what was happening now. If she'd plugged in and entered a moon-dust haze to find Crumb, none of this would be shocking. What made it shocking was that the dream was assaulting her here and now, sober and on her native plane.

Leah settled, trying to believe that this was coming to her rather than being sought. It had something to do with Crumb. What, she didn't know.

Inside of the memory of the Chinese restaurant, Leah realized that the building she was in had a red roof.

She thought of her experience inside of Crumb's mind.

Overhead, her cabin lights went dark then came back on.

The man with the round glasses. She'd seen him before. There was something there, something she couldn't grasp. She'd never had a boyfriend who'd looked like him, and had never, she felt certain, had a friend (certainly not one good enough to share a meal with) who looked like him. Yet somehow, she did know him. Just as in the memory, Leah knew that the Chinese restaurant's roof was red. And that while she was sitting in that restaurant, it was also something else. Someplace important, and secret.

Leah closed her eyes.

Inside her mind, she tried to conjure the handsome man with the glasses. Why was he so familiar? She watched the part of the memory she'd been able to hold, seeing how his lips moved, the way he gestured, the tiny smile that happened only on one side of his mouth, peeling up to reveal a few teeth.

"Who are you?" she said aloud.

Tall. Short brown hair. The sort of sideways smile that endeared him to the world.

She thought of the man as he said, *We can live forever.*

And then she had it.

"Canvas," she said.

Something in the compartment chirped.

"Search Noah West. Pictures. Give it to me right here." She put her hands together in front of her then pulled them apart as if stretching taffy. A life-sized head appeared between them, almost as real as a genuine human head. Damning her nervous system's intrusion, already deciding her port wasn't at fault for this intrusion of memory after all, Leah clutched her fists twice to turn on the tactile feedback in her fingertips. She grabbed the hologram, now finding it solid and opaque. She turned it in her hands, watching. Then she waved to the side, and the head vanished.

"Younger. Noah West, 2020s." She did a calculation in her head. "No, wait, 2030s."

The canvas, in the voice of a bureaucrat who'd had no user softening, said, "No holographic records exist."

"Then give me a fucking 2-D!" Leah was suddenly impatient. This was taking too long. The need to find the right photo was as pressing as the need for noodles a moment earlier.

A two-dimensional picture appeared in front of Leah: a handsome young man with brown hair and small, round glasses.

Leah slumped back against the train seat.

"Noah Fucking West," she said.

Literally.

She already knew the intrusive memory had something to do with Crumb. *Crumb and West?* It made no sense. But of course, none of this made sense. Leah wasn't plugged in, and a rather vivid memory of Noah West from sixty years ago had entered and begun fogging her mind. She wasn't on dust and had initiated nothing. It was like a memory of both time and place was being pressed upon her.

Leah felt her need for Chinese noodles swell and then subside in a pulse, as if her brain and body were trying to remind her that that part of the memory was important, too. Then the need for noodles faded to a memory of memory, and Leah realized that she no longer precisely wanted the noodles; she was simply experiencing nostalgia. Was this what it had been like for Crumb when she'd entered his mind? Because she didn't like it. The sensation was intrusive, like someone sticking their fingers into her mouth. The memory wasn't hers, and she had no context for it, whatever it was. Still, Leah found herself wanting to revisit the time and place in the memory (or at least mull fondly upon it), but how exactly did that work when she'd never experienced it in the first place?

"Canvas, switch off connectivity to this compartment," she said.

A chirp, and the memory vanished.

"Canvas, resume connectivity."

The memory returned.

So it was coming through The Beam. But how? Leah wasn't plugged in. The Beam didn't communicate directly to the cortex. That's not how it worked. Except that it kind of did, seeing as how entering an intuitive, dreamlike fugue was how Leah did her best hacking. She entered a haze then lost track of time and released control over the details of what she was doing. Beam-related problems, approached that way, had always resolved themselves. She always knew where to go. And hadn't she come here looking for something?

Leah closed her eyes and allowed the memory to fill her. She stepped into its shoes, scrolled backward in time, and found one memory inside another. Entering, she knew there'd been a red roof. And in the back room, there was…

"Canvas," said Leah. "Has Quark or a Quark subsidiary ever owned a restaurant in District Zero's Chinatown?"

The canvas trilled, indicating a positive search.

"Show it to me."

LEAH WALKED from the mag train station. She had plenty of credits for a cab or could have rented a hoverskipper, but she wanted to use her feet. If nothing else, she felt she needed the fresh air. But secondly, she was also starting to feel dumb. The memory of the Chinese restaurant had faded as quickly as it had come, and after it was gone, Leah had come up with a list of reasons why it had never been genuine in the first place. She'd decided that her port implant was malfunctioning after all. True *memories*, in any real sense, didn't exist on The Beam. They certainly didn't project themselves into the heads of other people, especially if those people weren't even plugged in. The only explanation for Leah's spontaneous burst of strange thought (and a strange, compulsive craving that had hit her like a brick) was an implant malfunction.

But she hadn't been able to let it go and hadn't headed to a clinic or a dealer immediately upon arriving in DZ station. Instead, she had set out on foot toward Chinatown. She felt stupid doing it, but despite common sense about memories and malfunctions, the experience had contained too much coincidence to ignore.

For one, the odd thought slotted neatly into her current mission. Leah had set out in search of Crumb and had done so on blind faith that she'd be able to find his path on The Beam. The Chinatown scene, she'd been sure, somehow involved Crumb. Secondly, when Leah had been inside

Crumb's mind back in the burned-out house, she'd seen a vision a lot like she'd experienced on the train: the building with the red roof. And thirdly, what of West? If the memory was entirely a product of her own malfunctioning mind, why had she pictured Noah West in a way she'd never seen him before? West had died before Leah was born, and she'd known him only as the voice of The Beam. Avatars and projections of West used inside The Beam were very different from the young man she'd "remembered" an hour earlier. Her usual conception of West was older, with longer hair, giving off a more serious bearing. And lastly, there was the way the memory had led Leah to a rather obscure and strange bit of knowledge: namely, that one of Quark's earliest holdings had been a restaurant in Chinatown. Who knew something like that, and who could possibly care? And how could Leah explain the fact that *she'd* known it if her experience on the train had simply been the work of a faulty implant?

It took her a long time to cover the distance to Chinatown on foot, but she didn't mind. She needed time to convince herself that even if she was being stupid, she had no other leads and was blind anyway. She'd planned from the beginning to hook in and Beamwalk around without any deliberate strategy. Only after getting her feet metaphorically wet would Leah start the work that Leo thought of as true hacking: trying to plunder the trail Crumb might have left in moving from the hospital to somewhere else, searching for whispers of a John Doe who fit his description. But it was the Beamwalking, not the searching of records, that was most important. The Beam had stopped being an archive of information a long time ago. True virtuosos today understood that navigation was an art rather than a science — and that you had to treat The Beam like a brain rather than a databank. Just as smell could conjure vivid memory inside the human mind, the oddest bit of recalled data could open floodgates inside The Beam. You had to intuit your way to what you needed if what you needed wasn't concrete and defined.

So, Leah reasoned, following this stupid but strangely compelling errand wasn't as off-track as it seemed. The air was nice and smelled clean thanks to the filters, the day was warm, and the sun was bright enough in the sky to almost entirely obliterate the appearance of the lattice covering the continent. If Leah closed her eyes as she walked — a bad idea, seeing as she'd be run over by people on foot and hover-skippers, or maybe a car or cab with faulty collision sensors — she could almost pretend she was still in the mountains. A loud part of the mountains, filled with the sounds of people.

Leah took the long route, heading down Old Bowery and through the neighborhoods, avoiding the ganglands that ruled SoHo and passing the expensive, high-rent towers in Big Italy. She meandered around the bomb crater, never rebuilt and left as a monument from the skirmishes. Then, as Chinatown drew nearer, Leah wandered farther and dawdled more until finally heading back toward Old Bowery, down Canal, and into the small streets that (save the hovers in the street) were among the few that hadn't changed much since the days when DZ had been Manhattan. Leo, old enough to have known New York as New York, loved Chinatown and had shown Leah 2-Ds of it from his youth. As she stared at the small, narrow streets now, it was as if those old 2-Ds had come to life.

Leah knew the address the train's canvas had given her and didn't need to re-access The Beam. She found the building easily, right where the map had said it would be. The red roof was still there, unchanged, like the rest of the street. But it wasn't a restaurant, and it was no longer open. The front windows were soaped, and the door was locked tight. There was no sign to indicate what the small building might now be (or had been, before being closed up), but Leah could see bolt holes and a lighter swatch of paint where a sign had once hung.

She looked up and down the street, feeling like an intruder. People milled behind her, unheeding. Chinatown had become very ethnically pure around the time the lattice went up — citizens clustering together with those like themselves out of fear, seeing as one of the NAU's largest antagonists at the time had been China — and most of the people she saw were Chinese. Leah, an Organa white girl with bright-pink dreadlocks, couldn't have stood out more.

What am I doing here? she asked herself.

But as she stood in front of the building from her memory, the door clicked and then slowly swung open. A black square similar to a Beam hand pad circled briefly with a dull-white glow, indicating that it had just been accessed. But Leah hadn't pressed her hand to it. She hadn't even spoken.

"Welcome, Leah," said a voice she recognized. It was the default voice of any canvas, modeled after the creator of the network that powered it: Noah West.

And somehow, the canvas knew who she was.

The place had scanned her. That was the only explanation, and it wasn't legal. You couldn't scan a person who didn't willingly access a panel or request information that required a scan. It was an invasion of privacy, permissible only by DZPD sweeperbots whose AI had probable cause. The place, when it had illegally scanned her, had read her Beam ID, confirmed her identity, and given her access. And the only problem with that theory was that she shouldn't have access to this door, this building, or this canvas. And also, she didn't *have* a Beam ID.

"Canvas," she said, regarding the open door with suspicion.

The voice of Noah West answered. "Yes, Leah?"

Behind the door, the building's interior lights came on. What she saw looked clean, and not at all like a restaurant.

"Why do I have access to this building?"

"You were given access on oh-six-one-two-two-oh-nine-seven by Stephen York."

"What is today's date?" Leah asked. She knew, of course, but wanted to see if the system's time was correct.

"Oh-six-one-two-two-oh-nine-seven."

"Who is Stephen York?"

"I'm sorry, I don't have that information."

"What is this place?" she said.

"I'm sorry, I don't have that information."

Leah stared at the pad and the door as if it might offer more, but of course it didn't. The canvas's voice was a program, not a person. She couldn't ask it if she should be scared, why the man whose journal she'd seen in Crumb's head would have given her access to a restaurant in China-town, and how it had happened today — possibly a few seconds before, as she'd stood out front lightly tugging at her dreadlocks. The whole thing had the feeling of someone watching her then buzzing her in.

"What the fuck is going on?" Leah asked.

The polite voice said, "I'm sorry, I don't have that information."

Not at all sure that she was being wise, Leah stepped inside. The door — an ordinary, old-fashioned shop door from the front — closed behind her on a pneumatic hinge to reveal a solid Plasteel backside. The place had a small entrance foyer, but behind a partial wall was what had once been the interior of the restaurant she'd seen on the train. Today, it wasn't remotely similar. The main room was bright and mostly white, with everything alight from wall to ceiling to floor. The place seemed to be covered in old-model Beam-enabled surfaces, back before they'd developed IntelliResin and started mixing it into paints to create the subtler surfaces most new homes used today. Once upon a time, this room — sparkling clean and dust-free, apparently maintained by bots — had been beyond state of the art. It was now an antique, but thirty years ago it had been the best of the best…of the best.

There were countertops along the walls and a pair of what looked like immersion rigs near the room's center. The rigs (if that's what they were) had the clunky look of old technology, but unlike the Beam surfaces, Leah couldn't shake the feeling that even as old as the rigs seemed, they were well beyond anything she had ever known or tried. The place looked like a white and sterile high-end lab. But amidst all of the lights and geekery, there was one thing that didn't fit. Along one wall was a large king-sized bed with a white comforter that appeared slept in and unmade. The bed's frame was heavy wood.

Leah thought about the security that had kept this place safe, realized it must be formidable, and wondered if she'd be allowed to leave or if she'd be locked in forever to die here. From the outside, the soaped-over windows had seemed to be glass, but now, inside, Leah grew certain they would be transparent steel. The walls would be soundproofed, locked down with electromagnetic bolts as big as her fist. She'd walked into a monster, and it was up to the monster if she would be allowed out.

She crossed the room, watching as the strangely soft surface underfoot glowed to follow her footsteps. Lights chattered in small clusters on the walls. As she approached one of the workbenches, the light over the bench lit to greet her. Instruments Leah didn't recognize turned on and came to life. She touched the wall behind the bench, trying to swipe a window open, but the walls either weren't equipped to create windows or weren't willing to give her access. She could try speaking, but the room's silence seemed almost holy. She had the feeling of being in a temple, and of speech here amounting to sacrilege.

On a shelf, standing on end with a few other volumes, Leah found a book with a leather cover. On the cover was the single word *JOURNAL*. She opened it, already knowing what she'd find: an attribution that read, *Stephen York.*

Leah flipped through the journal, finding entry after entry from decades in the past. The name Noah West appeared throughout — usually as *Noah*, as if Stephen York had known West personally. As she flipped through the handwritten pages, something fluttered out from the journal's back pages. She stooped to pick it up. It was an old 2-D, printed on actual paper. Strange, the idea of putting a 2-D on paper, but it actually made sense coming from a man who'd wanted to record his thoughts *on paper, in a paper book, using an ink pen.* It felt like a ritual to Leah. Leo was like that, too. Sometimes, he did things the old way not because it made sense, but because he simply wanted to experience the ritual of doing it. As a Beam-native, Leah had no attachments to such inefficient methods of communication as some older people seemed to have, but she did understand it. She had just walked all the way from Midtown rather than taking a faster, easier method of transport. It was the same way of thinking: Sometimes, the harder way was the better way, and just because you could do something didn't mean you had to or even should. Sometimes, the act of putting foot to concrete (or, she supposed, pen to paper) was a tiny act of rebellion, showing the world that you refused to be owned.

She looked at the paper in her hands. The 2-D showed a handsome young man with round-framed glasses sitting in a restaurant she recognized with a plate of noodles in front of him. Beside him — beside Noah West, circa 2030s — was another attractive man with a square jaw, long brown hair, and a neatly trimmed beard that had to be Stephen York. The two men had their arms around each other's shoulders, smiling at the camera like great friends.

Leah recognized the second man's eyes, which hadn't changed in all the years that had passed since the 2-D had been taken.

It was Crumb.

Leah looked around the room — around the converted restaurant-turned-elite-lab hidden in Chinatown — and then down at the photo of the crazy vagrant she'd known all her life with his arm around the most famous man who had ever lived.

Aloud, she said, "What were you part of, Crumb?"

The lights on the workbench and in the panels above, below, and directly to Leah's sides faded, becoming an unresponsive gray. Surprised, she stepped backward, out of the dark. As soon as she did, another ring of lights went black. She turned and stepped forward again, and more lights dimmed. She was being herded forward, toward the foyer. One by one, the lights went off in rings around her until she stood in the small area where, a long time ago, customers had sat and waited for a table to sit and eat their noodles.

The front door opened on the pneumatic hinge.

The last of the interior lights clicked off.

Leah, with Stephen York's journal in her hands, stepped into the street.

The door closed behind her, and Leah turned to look at it.

She could try to re-enter, but was sure that if she did, she'd be told that her access had been revoked by Stephen York, oh-six-one-two-two-oh-nine-seven.

| Episode 5 |

Chapter 1

STEPHEN YORK'S JOURNAL, Selected Entries:

Dec 22, 2032

Dad got me a journal. He called it an early Christmas present. He said, "Stephen York, you're going to be someone someday, and any life worth living is worth recording." Totally a Dad thing to say. I asked him if he'd just quoted Tony Robbins again. He does that. He went to see Tony live last year. Tony has to be in his seventies but still jumps around on stage like in Dad's old videos. I don't get it. But whatever.

So Merry Christmas. I got a book. And not even a book I get to read, but one I have to write in myself.

Dad said, "What do you want instead, Stephen? A toy? A video game?" I got his point. That's what most of my friends want, but only the rich kids are still dicking around with that kind of stuff these days. I'm lucky my parents can give me a book, that nobody in our family has been sent to the wars, and that we haven't been drowned in the floodwaters that would have covered the whole island if not for the levees and hovertech to hold them.

Anyway, I got employee of the year today. Pretty fucking boss, considering how hard it was for me to even land the job. They gave me a plaque. Wilson gave a little speech, said it was for "excellent work integrating nanotechnology into fluid gaming environments." I can't believe this is my job. I could be working at Sloppy's to help my family pay the bills, but instead I get to play video games. Javier was pissed, by the way. He was twenty-four when he won last year, and they made such a big deal about his being so young, and I beat that by nine years. He said I got lucky. I called him an old man.

Dec 23, 2032

I got, like, ten calls today from recruiters. Apparently, Javier got them too when he won, but he turned them all down because he said he had a secure, steady career at Zenka Games. He said he used the other offers as leverage to land a big raise, but that going to a new company felt too risky. He said that when you're the new guy, you're the first to go if the company gets into trouble. He said times were too uncertain, and that if the east invaded or if global war broke out or even if people just got afraid, the economy could collapse. He didn't want to end up in the rabble. Jobs are precious, and he'd built up a few years of seniority at Zenka.

I told him that was stupid and that playing it safe was the way to end up accomplishing nothing. He said I was fifteen, so what the fuck did I know? I told him that I'd check back with him when I was twenty-four, and we could compare notes. Either I'd be dirt poor because the world collapsed, or I'd be famous and rich because I had balls and went for what I wanted. I told him that if the world collapsed, it wouldn't fall into recession. It would COLLAPSE. If that happens, seniority won't mean anything anyway so we'll all be fucked. It's not like Zenka will keep making video games after Armageddon. Why not aim big?

Anyway, I don't want to play it safe at Zenka. I like what we've done with nanotechnology, but there's only so much you can do with it in games. The biggest advances are in other fields.

I got a lot of calls and four solid job offers. One was from Google, which is supertempting given what they're doing with omniarchiving and global cyberenvironments, but the one I got really excited about was from Quark. QUARK! If Quark made fan posters, I'd plaster my walls with them. In the end, I think Quark's focus inward, on improving the interface between people and technology networks, is a better direction than Google's external, data-driven approach. The Internet is getting bigger and bigger, but we already have more data than we can assimilate. We need better ways to use and interact with the data we already have.

I mean, WOW. Yes, I'd probably make a ton of money at Quark (I looked it up…their number of employees per dollar in earned profit is by far the highest in the industry, AND they offer profit sharing and a stock program), but really I'm most excited just because they're Quark. They're the biggest company in the world for a reason. They're visionary, and they get where the world is really going. They took the ashes of EverCrunch and made something from that shit heap in like a week BECAUSE they understood that unlimited data means dick until you tie it to data that people actually care about — something EverCrunch missed.

Fingers crossed. I'm meeting with a woman named Carol Wok after the holidays. She's talking press coverage and every-thing, and of course she's giving me that crap people do where they tell you how excited they are. Maybe they're excited and think I'm a prodigy, maybe not. We'll see.

JAN 3, 2033

Second day of interviews at Quark. I can't decide if

they're paranoid or just really thorough. So far, the skills tests are stupidly simple, but there have been a million hours of them. I kept wanting to ask if they were screwing with me, but it's possible they think the tests are hard and that I'd come off as cocky by asking. So I just did them. I hope they're almost over, because I'm getting bored.

Jan 4, 2033

Okay, I take back what I said about the simple tests. Today's were INSANE. What I did the last two days was all simple coding, but now that I think about it, it reminded me of doing times tables in school, where you had to do simple multiplication over and over and over until it got stuck in your head. Wait! I know what it really made me think of. Dad has a rip of this old movie (old enough that he had to rip it from a DVD…and because we don't know anyone with a DVD player, he had to take it to a place and pay for the conversion) called *The Karate Kid*. The tests were like "wax on, wax off." They just wanted me to do simple stuff over and over until I was a ninja.

But today's tests were insane by comparison. Data stream manipulation, combinatorics, numerical analysis. It was almost like codebreaking and advanced encryption. When I said that, one of the guys testing me admitted it used some of the classified EverCrunch algorithms. I actually got lost working on it, and after a while I thought I might be spouting garbage, but they said I did well. Really well. Even though I barely remember doing it — like I was in a trance.

I'm nervous for tomorrow. Carol told me that the next round of tests are psychological, but I can't decide if that means they're going to mess with my head or not. They can't do that, can they?

I also asked about the job. She wouldn't tell me any details but did imply that I'm pretty much hired once I get through these tests. She also said the pay was "ridiculous."

Jan 5, 2033

Holy shit! Today was awesome.

No reason to sweat the psych tests. They were actually sort of fun. It was all what-if stuff, but they shot them at me really, really fast. I guess the idea was that I wasn't supposed to think about the answers — just answer off the top of my head. Some sort of a reaction-versus-logic thing. I asked about it, but they wouldn't elaborate, just said they "need to know how I think." It was superhard and stressful at first because they'd give me something really complex like "What would you do if you encountered an if-then loop in a string of code that hung in a situation that numerically occurred only 0.001 percent of the time but resulted in total data loss when it did" and expect me to answer it in literally one second. I wanted to know the details. Had the code been shipped? What other systems talked to it? What was the error? Was there something particular and predictable that happened that 0.001 percent of the time? But I couldn't ask; I just had to answer. I felt like I'd give the wrong answer, because it was totally ill-informed. They said it didn't matter. After about ten questions, I was getting freaked out, so the guy came in and explained that it was no big deal, that I wouldn't be held to my answers, and that I would be assessed based on the psychological implications of my answers, not their accuracy. After that, I eased up, and it got a lot easier, even fun. They asked those questions for hours, with only one break for fifteen minutes. There may have been ten thousand questions, I don't know. They weren't all about work, either. A lot were either totally random or moral, like "Would you kill one person to save fifty" and "Which color is the most upstanding and honest?"

After the tests, they took me into an empty room with one table and no chairs. I asked if the room was part of the test, like an interrogation. Carol was sitting on the edge of the table. She said they would be hiring me. I asked if I'd done well, and she said that "well" wasn't really relevant to the psych tests, but that I was "hand-picked."

Then she told me that I'll be WORKING DIRECTLY WITH NOAH WEST! She told me that he'd been watching me since I won the NYC science fair three years ago with my desalination project that got the write-up on the *Times* site. I didn't have the guts to ask, but I almost get the impression that I wasn't being pitted against other Quark applicants at all. I think I was the only one tested, like they just wanted ME.

I'm so going to make Javier Cortez eat it.

Aug 20, 2033

After eight months working with Noah West, I've decided that he's barely human, if at all. The man is astonishing. He never stops thinking and never gets tired. I thought I was good (working with the best in the world at sixteen, rah-rah), but Noah makes me look like a punk. He's not really that much older than me, just in his twenties I think, and he runs an empire that's taking over the world…AND doing it while the planet collapses and everyone else whines. Maybe I'm just isolated and coddled, but it's like the world never stopped from where I'm standing. I'm dimly aware that the coasts (save NYC, of course) are flooded, that millions (maybe billions) are homeless or dead, that there are riots and fires and little civil wars and all of that, but it's true what they say about ivory towers. I almost never leave Quark, and the only people I really talk to are my family, who I set up in what's becoming a very fashionable, high-rent area in — of all places — Little Italy. So I don't even see the rest of the world. From where all of us stand, the future's never been brighter. Everyone at Quark feels that way. They say it's like it's 2025 again, with the world still rising in the New Renaissance. Maybe it makes us apathetic, but what the hell, Quark gives a ton of money to restoration and recovery projects in the US, Mexico, and Canada. Nobody wants to say it, but it seems as if the rest of the world may be beyond saving. Quark still funds groups who do what they can to help, but it's like spitting on a fire. People think there's anarchy in America, but I hear Europe is terrible, and they're even talking about cutting off totally, trying to make us self-sufficient.

But still, it's like none of that exists at Quark or in my new circles. Everyone is upbeat and excited. It's hard not to be uplifted by Noah. He's exhausting but totally inspiring. Every idea is brilliant, and he'll explain each if you let him — talking a mile a minute so you can't follow along.

We've been working on this latest project since I was hired, and I can't keep up. I'm exhausted but exhilarated. I barely sleep. I wish I could blab on about the new project (we're "laying the blanket" for it, in Noah's words) but I'm afraid to, even in my own journal. It's THAT secret, and I don't want to be the guy who fucked it up because his apartment was robbed and his journal got stolen.

But it's astonishing. The most amazing thing I've ever seen — maybe the most amazing thing anyone has ever seen.

Noah says it'll be done in maybe five years. I'd figured ten or twenty at the very least. But it's hard not to believe Noah West when he says he can do the impossible.

March 25, 2035

Work with Noah West continues to be beyond nuts. The Crossbrace Project (I think it's funny that the press uncovered the name but not what it is…their guesses are hilarious) is insanely over budget. But it's not just over budget…it's costing Quark a half million dollars per day. Noah says he doesn't care and keeps repeating the same words: "better and faster, better and faster." Carol always seems worried, and the board of directors keeps telling Noah to slow down or speed up — whichever will balance the company's bleeding against actual, finished product the soonest. The board says that Quark, even as rich as it is, can't afford to sustain Crossbrace development. But Noah keeps saying that it can't afford NOT to.

Then, because he's Noah Fucking West, he usually adds that the world can't afford not to have Crossbrace, either. I wish I could say more, but I will say that I tend to agree, especially now that the borders are closed. This continent needs to de-globalize and become self-sufficient.

Now that I think about it, the notion that "the world" needs Crossbrace might be overstating things.

Oct 26, 2040

MAJOR breakthrough today. As always, I wish I could elaborate if for no other reason than that repeating things, even to myself, helps me to clarify, but I can't. Not yet.

But yes, we've had an absolute breakthrough…and about damn time! This project is a monster — a monster I believe in fully, but a monster nonetheless. It seems laughable now that Noah thought this would all be done in 2038 "at the latest, young Stephen!" It's been so frustrating to slave and slave, to get yelled at constantly by the board, but also to know our sunk costs are so deep that there's no way out other than to keep going forward. The only way to save this project is to complete it, and it's stressful and frustrating to know that until that happens, we're only digging in deeper.

But I feel, despite this major step today (one I still can't commit to the page…hopefully I'll remember what it was if I ever read this back), that we're on borrowed time. It troubles me. Not just with the project, but with the world at large. There were a lot of murmurs when the borders were first closed and people started to wonder how the US could ever be self-sufficient. Conversion to hovertech and Stimulin's development of Pocket Fusion helped because at least the oil monkey was off our back, and the discovery of the riches under the ice up north helped a lot more. But...to cut off from the world? It hardly feels stable, especially considering the "hyperconnected" nature of what Quark is trying to do.

A lot of people felt relief when we dropped the US/Mexico and US/Canada borders and formed the NAU because we at least had a few other hands and minds in our camp, but the world still feels like a powder keg, and I can't help but think that everything we're working on will be missing the point if that keg blows while we've still got our hands in our pockets. There's too much desolation and fear in the rest of the world. It's too polarized. I do feel that the NAU's formation was a good thing, but just think about it: the three richest countries in the world following the collapse (and also with the least internal strife, relatively speaking) getting together to form the world's only truly stable government? Hell, we might as well paint a giant target on our backs. How long until we the world stops fighting with itself and comes here to take what's ours? Look at us. That pill, EndLax? It's a fuck-you to the starving people of the world. Or look at the Ryan brothers. I saw Isaac Ryan the other day at a participatory Internet VR event, and I'd never noticed before that his title is the Directorate's Czar of Internal Satisfaction. How can we not think we're in trouble...worrying about our "satisfaction" enough to have appointed a czar for it while the rest of the world burns?

Even the NAU's situation feels like a house of cards. There's a ton of potential in what we're building to bridge the gap between the upper and lower classes (not that I'm a socialist — far from it!), but until it's rolled out? It troubles me.

We have a system where the upper class pops EndLax at endless, gluttonous banquets, living at the top of skyscrapers that keep growing taller and lusher. More fortified, like castles. Meanwhile all that old Park Avenue real estate keeps crumbling to shit, Central Park East and West are going to gangs, with robots using hovertech keeping them in line rather than anyone working to solve the problem…oh, hell. I could go on forever. People say I think too much for someone my age, but that's been the case since before the Fall, when my parents belonged to Stonegate Country Club and wouldn't let me invite Jimmy Swinton to the pool. "He's not our people," they said. And this, today? People around me are full of optimism, saying things have never been better — but I just think they're being willfully blind to the world around them.

Okay, stopping with the downer stuff now.

The new project will help close the gap, and we're finally getting close to rolling it out. I DO think too much. Maybe this new world CAN survive. It's true that the "us versus the world" feeling inside the NAU has reduced internal turmoil. The new Senate? The Directorate? The Enterprise? All good. Give people a choice, and they'll feel satisfied even if both options are equally lousy; the jam study proved that decades ago. The Senate is shaking all the right hands in appointing Noah the Secretary of Practical Advancement. When Crossbrace rolls out, that might actually mean something.

Deep breaths. We're in the home stretch.

<u>Nov 14, 2040</u>

Still going strong. It's hard to maintain enthusiasm (well, not for Noah; he hasn't slept in seven years, I swear), but the scope of Crossbrace is insane, and even as the days drag on, I keep reminding myself that things are moving quickly if you look at the big picture. The board keeps bugging Noah for a schedule, but he says no one can make a schedule for changing the world. They press him, and he grudgingly commits that within two years, the new technology will be rolled out nationwide. That will change everything. It'll touch everywhere in the NAU and be affordable for even the lowest classes (though not at a very sophisticated or immersive level).

The Beatles said they were bigger than Jesus, and that became a problem for them. Crossbrace won't be bigger than Jesus, but that's just about all it won't be bigger than. The printing press? The telephone? Cellular technology? The Internet? Tablet computers? The Internet's evolution into 3-D, VR, and immersion? This new emergent AI shit? Crossbrace will dwarf them all.

Now, Noah West? He'd tell you that HE will be bigger than Jesus.

Feb 24, 2041

I'm twenty-three. Noah is…wow, I don't even know. In his forties? He has to be, but I swear he hasn't aged since I met him. That's crazy.

But whatever, he has to be twenty years older than me, and he's firing on three or four hours of sleep a night. I'm falling asleep at my workbench. I'm making mistakes. Noah is making them too, but don't tell him that. He needs to sleep but won't. And I simply can't understand how he's doing it. It must be the fire in his gut.

We're essentially roommates. We both live at the office and lab. I'm his prisoner, in a way. Noah moved in, first with a blanket and a pillow, and before I realized it he was sleeping there every night. He was there when I showed up early and stayed after I left late. One day, he gave me a guilt trip about leaving, laying the burden of both company and world on my shoulders, so I stayed. It was late, so I slept on the reception couch. The next day, a pillow and blanket arrived, and I realized that I was living there too. Now we leave just once a week, and I can only leave when Noah does. He's cranky. Angry. Getting sloppy. Still a genius, but overeager. He needs to slow down. We both do. I'd like to date, maybe one day start a family. Call me selfish. But right now, having a life takes a backseat to Crossbrace. The project is getting close. Noah says everything is there, and that we only have to "untangle the knot." We try — me, him, the other team members and techs who have lives but still work eighty-hour weeks — but the knot is tight, with too many loose ends. Too many knots. Every time we untie one, another is there, often two. It's taking forever, and I can't help but feel like we're chasing a ghost. Something is running away from us. Whenever we sleep, it gets farther ahead.

Noah snaps all the time. Setbacks make him furious. When we talk, I'm always wrong. He says I'm trying to solve problems with the same thinking that caused them. He acts like I'm in his way. I FEEL like I'm in his way. Where is that desire they had for my "prodigious genius"? They recruited me like no other I've seen since. I literally have more money than I could ever spend. I called Noah on it, asked him why, if I fuck up all the time, he keeps me around. Let me go, I say. Let me have a life, if I'm such a liability. But he only says that mistakes are opportunities to learn. He says that mistakes, frustrating as they are, are gifts. Then, insultingly, he thanks me. He thanks me for all the gifts that I give him.

Sep 18, 2042

I should be elated, but I'm just too fucking tired. Now that we've popped the cork, I'm planning to sleep for weeks — to bunker myself in and refuse to come out. Then I plan to drink heavily. Make up for the college experiences that I hear, via mail but never in person, that my friends have had but that I have not.

Today, Noah told the world about Crossbrace. He outlined what it was and how it would become like a universal sixth sense — how it would give every single person access to all of the world's knowledge. "Imagine a world made just for you," he kept saying, and I know it was something written for him by a genius in marketing. He's describing things that our Internet 5.0 (we left 2.0 and behind in the dust) will do as if they were extensions of sight and hearing. He says it will be like living in an environment that will do whatever you want, without having to be asked. It knows which hand has opened the fridge, and hence which items to rotate to the front. It knows which programs you like to watch, no matter where you call for a screen. Every enabled surface becomes a tablet. Those little gadgets people are starting to wear — the evolution of that stupid Bluetooth earpiece my dad used to wear — will be tied into Crossbrace. Crossbrace will know where you are. Your information will follow you. You can allow yourself to forget, because Crossbrace will remember for you.

It's strange that nobody at Quark is jubilant as the world cheers us. After ten years of work, we've stared at the project long enough to see its every flaw, and worry about all the flaws we don't see. Is it truly secure? Have we put enough redundancies into the parts of Crossbrace that touch security, life support in hospitals, and "life enhancement" in homes? Are we totally sure that homes will not accidentally poison their owners, swapping bleach for soda? Can it be hacked? What about all of this new emphasis on nanotechnology, and the AI that runs it — the AI that talks to resident AI in Crossbrace? Right now, AI is nowhere near as scary as people have thought since the term was first coined, but it's clearly reached singularity. The machines can learn then learn from their learning. We all saw *The Terminator* and the old *Matrix* movies when we were kids, so of course we have safeguards on top of safeguards to prevent the proverbial Skynet disaster. But are the safeguards sufficient? Noah laughs at me when I mention it then explains it to me with calculations and complex math. He explains the idea of an asymptote. I understand, Noah. But there are not only the things you know to worry about. There are not only the things you don't know to worry about. The worst of all are those things you DON'T know that you DON'T know. What if we didn't even think of something that will end in catastrophe? The scope of Crossbrace makes "epic" look small. Crossbrace is thousands upon thousands of times more pervasive (with millions more touchpoints and inputs) than the aging information superhighway. Simple chaos theory clearly states that the potential for disaster is massive.

Carol, on the other hand, is worried about global outcry. We've changed the world, literally. The connectivity of Crossbrace will empower the poorest of the poor and provide fountains of opiates to hush them. For at least a few years, we can say goodbye to most of the class strife inside the NAU borders. But the borders themselves are the problem. Crossbrace only touches the NAU and isn't accessible outside of it. Other countries are already starting to complain, saying this is the NAU's attempt to consolidate their power and rattling their rusty sabers. Quark PR is pacifying them, but Noah intends to keep Crossbrace here in the spirit of triage. He says the rest of the world is beyond saving. I don't know if that's true, but I do know that adding Crossbrace to our pile of riches won't make those other countries love us any more. We've increased the size of our target. I should feel like we've popped the bubble, but to me, the bubble only seems to be growing.

Noah says I worry too much. I can't be sure. I need to sleep.

JUNE 12, 2050

I'm amazed to see a resurgence of Noah's energy. He's talking about a complete overhaul of Crossbrace, again speaking like a revolutionary. Of course Crossbrace just became integrated into daily life inside the NAU, and of course people, as excited and amazed as they were at launch, simply absorbed it. They stopped marveling at how their houses changed the projections of art on the walls based on moods read from those who entered. They began to complain about system latencies and bugs, about the fact that they didn't want peripherals to experience what just became another Internet. Of course the most popular sector was immediately porn. At first, I was indignant, calling the NAU ungrateful, until I realized that people can't help their nature. You can't remain amazed every day. Ultimately, the most astonishing things become commonplace. It makes me wonder why I bother sometimes. You change the world, and people say, "It's always been this way, and it sucks."

Still, I should be grateful. That new lattice dome around the continent handily solved the global crisis I'd worried about. Now the Wild East can yell and shoot at us to their hearts' content, but they cannot hurt us even with the biggest rocks they have to throw. I live well, and I work much less than I did during the heady years. I make more money than most people I know added together. They say that puts me in the top 1 percent of the wealthiest people in the NAU and hence makes me what they're calling "Beau Monde," but I can't help but hear it as an insult. I don't want to be a part of a class pompous enough to give itself a French name. I'm seeing something I made wedge the classes further apart while the lower tiers think it's drawing us all closer.

I'm seeing technological elitism. There are dealers who will only sell the best upgrades to this Beau Monde. I see Crossbrace technology (and modified hovertech) incorporated in those upgrades. People are having actual implants put in their bodies! Nanobots are being injected! And I say that with lots! Of! Exclamation! Points! because it's all so hush-hush. The poor can't buy anything like it; they've no awareness, or access if they did. So what happens? Crossbrace connectivity increases for those with money, and decreases for the rest.

Noah tells me to smoke weed. He says I need to go with the flow. He acts like a merciless businessman one minute and a hippie Organa the next. I try telling him that technology doesn't relax, that it has always made life more harried and more complicated.

Noah is talking about the second version of Crossbrace, which will embrace all of the new biological add-ons and nanotechnology. Forget about your environment knowing where you are. Soon, it will know what you think. What you see. What you feel. What you desire.

I keep telling him that I can't do it all again. We've given the NAU internal supports of a sort — a way of holding us up and interconnecting our isolated society. It's serendipitous that Noah named the network "Crossbrace," seeing how perfectly the metaphor fits today. And so I asked him when we can be finished, when enough will finally be enough. But Noah doesn't listen. He says that he wants something better. Something stronger. So I asked him how much stronger and more robust the mega-network could possibly be. He just laughed, as if I was stupid and naive, and told me that while it's nice that we've propped up a world in trouble with a bit of Cross-bracing, Crossbracing is always triage, always temporary and useful only until something more sturdy and sound can be built on top of it.

Accordingly, he's calling Crossbrace's evolution "The Beam."

Feb 18, 2061

Noah is sick. Of course I'm affected. Over the years, he's been a friend and tyrant, but in the end, he's more the first than the latter. He feels his mortality, although his appearance is still remarkably young. I suspect he had access to nanobot injections before the rest of the world knew they existed — the Beau Monde of the Beau Monde, a group which has always skimmed the cream for itself while keeping its secrets. And of course even today, the "lower 99" (as the elitists call them) know nothing. It makes me wonder what else is out there that even we don't know about, and how high the tiers of ignorance are stacked.

I asked Noah how old he is. He said, "I'm old enough," then smiled to show it was a joke, and I didn't have the heart to insist that I really wanted to know. So I let it go. He's weak. I don't know what's wrong with him, but it must be something nanobots can't cure. I hear there are nanos out there that can, in certain cells and under very restricted experimental conditions, stop apoptosis and telomere shortening. I hear it's a tough nut to crack, but once they do, it'll be one more step toward immortality. It will come too late for Noah. He wants to live long enough to see the launch of The Beam, which he says will "change the world of Crossbrace as much as Crossbrace changed the world of the Internet." He also says he wants to live forever inside The Beam. I told him that he already does — his voice is the voice of Crossbrace; avatars and representations of him show on every tablet, every handheld, every screen, and every canvas. He is the soul of Crossbrace and will be the soul of The Beam. People live with him every day. He is friend to billions — the savior many never had.

But Noah didn't want to hear it. He said Crossbrace is nothing and that I cannot imagine what The Beam will become. I tell him I understand it perfectly because I'm working on it too. But I can't help but believe that Noah has a final ace up his sleeve, and that he won't be content by simply delivering better virtual meeting places, better VR, and more intelligent AI.

. . .

<u>March 3, 2061</u>

I was right. The son of a bitch had an ace up his sleeve all right, and it's one fuck of an ace. The little wrinkle he wants to add to the Beam project will delay us a full year. Sometimes, I want to kill him, even though he's already sick and dying.

I can't write (yet again) about the change, but I'll just say that as part of it, he's moving our R&D into Chinatown. That's right, CHINATOWN. For what has to be nostalgic reasons, he bought that restaurant we used to love to eat noodles at back when we first started working together and has converted it into a lab. The logistics of moving the project, wholesale and in secret, are insane and muddle an already ridiculously complicated project. Noah's turned paranoid, saying our rivals (he uses the word "enemies") have spies in our midst and are watching the Quark labs.

Moving to a totally new secure location (just the two of us plus Jenna and Hal, with Noah sick in bed most of the time) is stupid and paranoid. But the Beam project isn't costing Quark in the way Crossbrace did, seeing as how Crossbrace-related profits have made Quark as rich as the NAU itself, and easily as powerful.

I'm beginning to regret my ironclad nondisclosure agreement. When I signed it originally, I thought it was standard. Each time I re-signed, I thought the same thing. It all seemed logical: to focus scrutiny on the fabulous Noah West and keep me, as his partner, silent and hidden so that I could do my work without worrying about PR. But now with Noah dying, I wonder if this wasn't just another genius move. I wonder if he didn't know EXACTLY what he was doing from the very, very beginning. He's already an icon and as powerful as the Senate. (He'd have to be to nudge through the Tagging Law, marking all new babies with a Crossbrace ID at birth. Nobody but the messiah he thinks he is — and is seen to be — could pull that off without a revolt.) And with me behind the curtain, I'm invisible to the world. Nobody would listen to me. Nobody even knows I exist. And of course, nobody can challenge the will of the great Noah West. Quark will go on when he's gone, but it will just be a company again. Its icon will already be in the aether, having died a martyr's immortal death and living on in the everyday lives of the continent.

Jan 23, 2062

I had an idol, once. By age forty-five, you'd think I'd know better than to idolize anyone, but it seems your heroes can always amaze you, enchant you, and…well, we'll see if this is something I shouldn't be doing. I believe in the power of The Beam. I believe in people, and that they are inherently good. Some would say I'm naive, maybe weak. We'll see.

Noah's been mostly too sick to work on the Beam project. He started out at the lab, but he's been absent for a while, mostly staying in his apartment. I give him updates. Today, he asked, and I told him about our recent successes. I told him we should be running in alpha by the end of the month. He was pleased. Back in the days of Crossbrace, he would have mocked me, yelled at me for being slow and making too many mistakes. But today, he was the man I first met when I was only a kid who looked up to him as a hero. We had dinner in his apartment like we used to, even ordered Chinese noodles — from a different restaurant, seeing as our old one is a lab now. I felt plied, placated. He was Noah West again. I was sixteen-year-old Stevie York, awed to be near him. He told me, very casually as if it were reasonable, that I would have to finish the Beam project alone. Jenna and Hal would no longer be allowed in the new lab; they would be ordered back to Quark HQ and told that work on The Beam was finished, and that techs would handle implementation. Then I was to finish the rest of the work solo. Noah said he would guide me then pulled up a screen and showed me six months of development already outlined for me. It was intensely detailed. I was awed. I still am. These days, the man can barely breathe on his own. He looks like a bag of bones and never leaves his apartment because he can't. And here, he'd done work that I couldn't even imagine. A new module of an entirely new technology that is quite simply beyond belief, incredible in scope, finished just inches from his own death.

Noah told me he would move to the lab and that the two of us would finish The Beam together. It sounds absurd to think about it now, but I don't know that I even protested when he suggested it because I was too spellbound by his last magic trick. He told me he'd require a bed and would need me to give him some light medical assistance (no nurses or doctors, though), but he'd made peace with his impending death. Noah wanted only to end his days working, and to see The Beam live. I didn't feel like I had a choice. I had to help him. Just he and I, working side by side, like in the old days.

It was absurd. I said no. Then, after a while — of course — I changed my answer to yes.

Noah said this went beyond an ironclad NDA, and that I couldn't tell anyone anything, ever.

I told him I wouldn't ever divulge what we were doing, but despite my earlier willingness to do my idol's bidding, I'm now uneasy. So I will compromise and tell this journal, so that at least a sliver of history has a splinter of record.

In violation of Noah's trust and in legal violation of my contract with Quark, I will commit his final wish to paper:

Noah West has found a way to live forever.

June 4, 2062

Succession plans for Noah's death are in place. The Beam has been live for two months and is already being embraced (and obsessed over) to a degree I'd not have thought possible.

With the project's details handled, I've handed over official word that Quark is opening the Beam's source code for developers to do with as they wish. Free enterprise is the best way to ensure that The Beam will continue to evolve forever, and that there are enough proprietary pockets in The Beam to allow us to do what we must.

I remain skeptical about both what Noah wants and my role in it, but at this point, it's tossing dice. There's tremendous potential for good in this, and I cannot turn my head.

What Noah was developing in secret — probably since the start of Crossbrace — was a process for uploading the content of a human mind to The Beam. Over the past five months, we've been ironing kinks, using Noah as the first subject. His reasoning is that if the process kills him or fries his mind (the rich kids who get upgrades these days call frying your brain "getting burned"), it won't matter because he's nearly dead anyway. Besides, his mind is kind of already on The Beam. Once the new generation of VR and holo-immersion went online, every upper-class household gained a Noah West butler. Every canvas, by default unless changed, gained a Noah West voice. Noah's preferences, tendencies, image, and mannerisms made it seem as if there was a face on the AI that ran large sectors of The Beam, but it was only farce. Noah avatars speak like Noah and act as if they are him (some versions more burned than others), but they don't know everything that Noah knows. And more importantly, Noah isn't a part of them at all. He is in our lab, in the other room even as I write this. The Mindbender Project will, if successful, duplicate not just the map of Noah's neurons and their habitual firings, but the emergent properties that go with them: consciousness, emotion, logic, intelligence, presence. It sounds terrifying to me, living as a series of ones and zeroes, but Noah says it will be as amazing as it is beautiful. He'll have a billion eyes and a billion ears, able to be everywhere at once. He makes it sound almost religious, almost as if we're bypassing bodily death and uploading his consciousness directly to Heaven.

Quark will announce the Mindbender Project soon, once we determine that it's viable, but the public version involves great thinkers uploading their intelligences — not their true minds or spirits, if there are such things — to The Beam's data stream. It's hard to argue the elegance of the idea behind it. Imagine if today we could get Einstein to think for us!

But what the public won't know right away — though it's only a matter of time before the Beau Monde is told because they will want to buy it — is that Noah will actually *be* on The Beam. He will not simply duplicate his intelligence, but he will actually move there. And as the rest of The Beam goes open source, his mind will not. It will look like proprietary AI, not attention-drawing because there's plenty of that out there. People will see their Noah avatars and think they are Noah. But his true self will be behind it all.

As I've said repeatedly, I am not without my reservations. But in the end, the brain is a big computer, and I'll admit to my fascination. All visionaries sometimes appear as the devil.

Everything is in place. We will attempt Noah's upload in one week.

JUNE 11, 2062

It is 2:15 a.m. I'm beyond exhausted.

Noah's upload took all day, but the data's integrity seems solid. There's no way to know if what I currently see as a massive data file has any life on its own, though I can access it in parts and verify that the information itself is there. But is it a life form? Does it have consciousness? Will it function and act of its own accord, or is it simply a repository?

For now, Noah is still alive. He looks dead as he lies in his lab bed, and it is as if — perhaps literally — his soul has been sucked from the husk of his body. But I spoke with him briefly afterward and before he collapsed, and he is still Noah West. So if his soul and consciousness is still in his body, can it also be in the data we uploaded? Is it as if we've duplicated Noah West, and now there are two? If it is *him* and not a copy, shouldn't he be able to see through its eyes? Shouldn't he feel it as if it were himself? I'm pulled back to philosophy texts I read as a kid. All of the disciplines fall into this one. Epistemology, ontology, every question together with a single beating heart. Which is the true Ship of Theseus? Is it the body in the bed, or the file on The Beam? Must Noah the man die in order to imbue Noah the data with consciousness?

I'm too tired to contemplate the enormity of what we're trying to do. This is a question for philosophers.

<u>Aug 14, 2062</u>

Noah West is dead. The NAU is in mourning.

I kept my word. I gave Noah a scan cap and a pocket recorder and sent him home. Once The Beam was live, we no longer needed to live in the lab, though I of course still spend an inordinate amount of time there. I didn't disassemble Noah's bed because I promised I would allow no one else into the lab, and without anyone to help me (or anyone to care), I just stopped letting its presence bother me. It has become simply another piece of furniture.

The recorder live-capped Noah's newest thoughts until the end then uploaded them in a batch each night. When his heart and brain waves stopped, Noah's canvas alerted me and only me, as directed. I went to his apartment, verified the uploads from the night before then manually copied the final batch in the recorder. The thing was set to not upload that last grab — the one that happened after his brain went flat — automatically. Who knows what happens at the moment of death? We didn't think it was prudent to risk putting a death online, so I clipped the tail, completed his master file then sent it into the stream. It felt like spreading ashes. I do not know what will happen with that tremendous archive — whether it will be a living thing or a great many recorded memories and nothing more. People have asked me if I'm sad. I'm too exhausted for sorrow. Simply: I am finished.

Noah was already the voice and personality of The Beam. But now I fear I may have created a god.

Chapter 2

"Micah."

Micah wanted to pretend he didn't know who was calling, but of course the caller's Beam ID was embedded in the transmission right there in the bottom right corner of his screen: Jason Whitlock's official Enterprise Capital Protection photo, smiling in a starched, white, collarless shirt with a red band tie, wearing a shit-eating grin. The agent looked so faux-respectable that the photo made Micah want to shove his fist down Whitlock's throat.

He settled for being rude: "What the fuck do you want?"

"What?" Now Whitlock sounded faux-indignant. "I went out to get your girl. Got her all spiffed up. She's behind me now. What did I do wrong?"

They were voice-only because Whitlock was on his screet-bike on his way into the city, so Micah allowed himself the exasperated luxury of closing his eyes. He reminded himself to have something painful or humiliating done to Whitlock later. Whitlock didn't get to be indignant right now because Whitlock was still paying off a debt of trust. Micah hadn't forgotten the way he'd hooked up with some piece of ass during the Natasha Ryan riot and had woken the next day wiped. If not for his mind's firewall, he might have gotten himself data-raped. Whitlock was proving to be the worst sort of incompetent — the kind who doesn't realize just how big of an irresponsible asshole he is.

"Never mind," said Micah.

"Kane had her."

"I know Kane had her. *Why* did he have her?"

"Apparently, she was with Stahl when they caught up with him."

"So they just took her in," Micah said, pacing his office. "Why not slumber her, do a quick wipe, and leave her?"

"Micah, she took out two armed Beamers. Ripped their balls off. This isn't just another pretty face."

Micah closed his eyes again, this time allowing his head a slow shake. Of course she wasn't just another pretty face. She never had been, even back when Micah had first met her. She'd struck him as a scrapper from the first second — a woman who'd fight to the death and never flinch from doing what had to be done. Even before her first nanos and her first defensive add-on, Kai, codenamed Kitty, could sneak up on a man and break his neck between her legs. She'd been resilient and dangerous from the start. She reminded Micah of himself. He thought of her like the deadly daughter he'd never had.

"You fucking idiot," said Micah. He was being somewhat unfair (nobody knew Kai worked with him, for one; that particular trespass had been an accident), but not much. You don't involve bystanders in things like this. You took what you wanted, you slumbered, you wiped, and you ran.

"Hey, *I* didn't do it," said Whitlock.

"Same group of monkeys. None of you are competent."

"You wouldn't have told them to pick up Stahl?"

Noah Fucking West. Why was Whitlock debating him? Who worked for whom, here?

"Stahl, yes. The girl, no. Oh, and by the way…*my brother's fucking speechwriter?* Also no."

"He was in Stahl's apartment, Micah. He might actually be in on this."

And that was true, too. Isaac had always been jealous of the way Micah had gotten the larger slice of their family's empire. He'd been jealous of the arctic windfall and of Micah's involvement with Xenia. Was sabotage and theft through Nicolai really beneath Isaac? But Micah shook the notion away. He'd known Nicolai since the 30s — not as well as Isaac, but enough to have a good feel for the man — and knew that Nicolai wasn't a spy. Nicolai shot straight and aboveboard. He was a regular Boy-Scout with a crossbow, content only to kill the bandits who tried to swipe his picnic basket.

"Keeping him there was a bad call," said Micah. "I should have been informed."

"Kane says that once they realized who he was, they just asked him some questions, never put him on that machine of his, then Gaussed him, and sent him home. He's there now, safe and sound and totally unaware."

Something in Micah snapped. This wasn't supposed to be a discussion, and he sure as hell didn't want his agent telling him about how everything was going to be all right.

"Why am I arguing with you?" he spat.

On the other end of the line, Whitlock made a noncommittal noise.

This whole thing was so irritating, so ready to blow up in everyone's faces. Nicolai might realize he had missing time. Kai might realize that the people who'd rescued her were the same people who'd taken her in and tortured her to within an inch of her life. Micah could lose her loyalty. Isaac, through Nicolai and the disappearance of Nicolai's upgrades dealer, might come to suspect the depths of Micah's dealings.

Micah didn't like losing control, and those assholes at Xenia had given him a tempest.

"Just bring them in," he told Whitlock.

There was a pause. The pickups on the Stark suits had near-perfect noise cancellation, so the line was silent as Whitlock measured his response. Micah imagined him rushing toward the city with Kai behind him, his face working, his delay telling. Even before Whitlock spoke again, Micah's heartbeat had already picked up. He took a cigarette from the box on his desk and lit it, taking a drag.

"Well…you wanted the *girl*, right?"

"The girl and Stahl."

"You told us to get the girl."

"I told you to get them *both*." Micah took another drag on his cigarette. He was controlling his voice, but he could feel a vein in his forehead starting to throb.

"You told us we could get him later, but that she was the important one now. To…you know…*save* her. From death. Which we did. *I* did."

"Noah *Fucking* West, Jason…if you don't tell me what you've fucked up now, I'm going to…"

"Stahl got away. It's no big thing, though." Whitlock was talking fast, trying to squeeze in his entire rationalization before Micah blew. "We ID'd his spoof. He can try to shuffle it, but he doesn't know our tracking technology. It'll be easy. Really. We didn't even bother to track him yet because…"

"You didn't bother to track him?"

"Yet! Judgment call, okay? We knew you wanted her first. The Neuralin stabilized her, but she'll need more. Soon. We've got Stahl's map. Unless he goes in for a full genetic refurb, he'll light up any system we tag the second he passes a sensor, and he's right on the outskirts of…"

"You DIDN'T BOTHER TO FUCKING TRACK HIM?" Micah was losing control of his voice, but he couldn't help it.

The best vengeance might be served cold, but right now Whitlock deserved to have flames licking his idiot skin. Micah had half a mind to call Kane and ask him if he could hot-hack the nanos in Whitlock's Stark suit. He wanted to command the suit to squeeze the agent to paste, like a banana clenched in a fist.

"We've got him already, okay! I know where he is! I could circle back right now if you wanted, but this girl? Kitty? She'll be in danger if I do. When the Neuralin wears off and she goes back into shock..."

"Stahl was the *one* person you assholes were *actually supposed to get* in the first place! Not her! Not Nicolai Costa! *Stahl! Stahl* was the one who infiltrated Xenia! *Stahl* is the only one of the whole group that you stupid motherfuckers were supposed to take into custody, the only one who was ever authorized to go onto the Orion, the only one who was expendable, the only one who was supposed to go into the evaporator! I know you're all idiots, but tell me — tell me for real, Jason. What would *you* have done? How would *you* have handled this? When Stahl got in to see the Beau Monde upgrades, would you have skipped Stahl entirely because he was too obvious? Would you have solved the problem by driving directly to my brother's right-hand-man's apartment and wiping him, finding a random woman and killing her, then shuttling over to give Thomas Stahl a hand job?"

Whitlock barely had a voice when he replied. Very softly — likely too soft even to be heard even by his passenger on the screetbike — he said, "We'll go back for Stahl."

"Not *now*. Noah *Fucking* West. Where are you?"

"Brooklyn." Everything in his voice said, *Yes sir. Whatever you say, sir.*

"Send your partner back to find him and watch him, if he can manage that. You do what you have to do at HQ with Ka...with Kitty. Then..."

Micah paused. Something was coming to him: a way to mitigate the damage, to make this clusterfuck a tiny bit less clustered. He had to wait for it, though, and while he did, Whitlock was blessedly silent. Good thing, too. The way Micah felt right now, keeping his fucking mouth shut might have saved the agent's life.

"Then take her back out," Micah finished.

Whispering, he said, "Take her *back?* You mean *after Stahl?*"

"Yes." He stopped and took a long drag on his cigarette. "Have her kill him."

There was a long pause on the other end of the line.

"I didn't get that, sir," said Whitlock. *Sir* now. Usually, Whitlock called him Micah. About goddamned time they change that, too.

"You heard me fine." He spoke plainly, knowing that even with Kai behind Whitlock, she wouldn't be able to hear Micah speaking through the agent's cochlear implant. "The girl is Stahl's friend. If you'd managed to do your job and bring Stahl in, he could have either been wiped or died 'accidentally.' She might have bought that. But now, thanks to your idiocy, he has to be killed. She's not stupid. He shows up dead after running from us, she'll know who did it and why. I don't want her as an enemy. She works for me, and I need to know if I can use her again. So if he's got to die, she has to do it. Not you, *her.* She either will do it, or she won't. Make her do it, and keep your distance so she can't get to you first. If she refuses…" He sighed, knowing that sometimes, hard decisions had to be made. "If she refuses, then take her out. Permanently, not with a slumber. Do you understand?"

"I understand."

"And Jason, do you also understand that there is no record of this conversation and that you will never be able to prove I said any of this?"

"Of course, sir."

"Good. Then listen carefully: if at the end of today, Kitty and Stahl are both still alive, I will see to it that *you* are strapped to that Orion…and that you'll feel every cell inside your body as it's slowly ripped to atoms."

———

Leo paced his small house, occasionally glancing out the window at the mountain community while waiting for Leah.

According to his handheld, the mag train had pulled into DZ station on time. That was hours ago. Leah would have had plenty of time to hop into a cab, head into the city, hook into The Beam, and do whatever voodoo was needed to find Crumb. At least, that's how he figured it.

Truth was, Leo hadn't been in District Zero in over thirty years. It was foreign territory — maybe even enemy soil — and he had no idea how the city's geography might have changed, how people in the city habitually accessed The Beam, or where Leah might be going. The last time Leo had visited DZ, the best connections had been in underground parlors in the tech ghettos, where hackers clustered in rundown, police-ignored buildings. But even then, Leo had hardly known the city's Beam underbelly. So he had to admit that he couldn't know where Leah had gone, what she was doing, or how long it might take her to do it.

Still, Leo was uneasy. He didn't know what to expect, but he wasn't willing to settle for ignorance. His lack of expectation only made him more curious. What was Leah trying to do? She'd implied that she could track Crumb despite his lack of a Beam ID, and the way she'd said it had reminded Leo of a mother animal's almost psychic ability to track her offspring. Or of one twin feeling the other's pain from a distance. Or — and Leo found this one so much cooler — of the way quantum-entangled but separated particles could synchronize across distances as if they were two sides of the same particle. Leah made her quest sound like that — like she'd sampled part of Crumb in Bontauk, and would now forever feel his mind through The Beam no matter where he tried to hide. As if they were now one.

As Leo paced, two voices fought to be heard in his restless mind.

She said she'd call as soon as she had something to report. She hasn't called, so there's nothing to report.

But what if she's in trouble?

She's not in trouble. She's done nothing wrong.

That you know of.

Somewhere, in a distant part of Leo's mind, he knew he was being unreasonable — and not just about Leah. He'd had that unreasonable feeling that Crumb, who'd been a quirky part of the Organa community for decades, was evolving from crazy rants to (*Go ahead and admit it,* he told himself) *prophetic* rants. That hadn't been unreasonable enough, so he'd sent Leah to Bontauk to take the rather unreasonable and dangerous step of trying to hack Crumb's mind. Unreasonably, they'd then let Crumb vanish, and now Leo had sent Leah into the city on an unreasonable psychic flimflam journey. And all of this unreasonability was happening at the worst possible time, too — while fights were continuing to break out in the village over the moondust shortage and with Dominic, as their dust savior, now MIA. The only news he'd had that remotely involved Dominic was that anonymous mail he'd gotten this morning indicating that Dominic had called in a parcel for Leo. This "parcel" hadn't yet arrived, but the whole thing stank to Leo. It felt like everything was starting to change, as if they were on the lip of a cliff and about to spill over. Things were changing, rotting slowly from the inside.

Maybe the Quark police picked Leah up again. Maybe they decided her stunt last week was more than digital trespassing. Maybe they discovered the way Dominic had covered for her, and maybe that was why Dominic wasn't responding to Leo's mail. What if the Beam clerics had discovered the nanos Leah had fabricated behind her little fingernail factories and loosed in their system?

Leo, out loud, told himself to get a fucking grip.

Across the room, Leo's handheld trilled. He picked it up. The call didn't show a Beam ID, but half of the people Leo knew didn't have an ID. He remembered back when everyone had called everyone using their cellular phones, and the phone numbers themselves would tell you who was calling. These days, when you could call from almost anywhere — from a desktop to a high-end toaster — the device itself gave the recipient little information of its own. Apparently, technology didn't always improve with time.

Leo set the handheld down on his desk, propping it up, and told it to accept the call. Leah's pink-dreadlocked head appeared on the small screen. Leo suppressed a relieved gasp then touched the handheld's corners to activate the magnifier. Leah's image, now projected in front of the phone in a hovering square, grew to life size.

"Leah. Thank goodness."

Leo realized what he'd said, but it was too late to take it back. He felt dumb for being worried, but Leah didn't seem to have heard. She was practically bouncing, and smiling broadly.

"I know who Crumb is," she almost squealed.

"You found him?"

"Well, I haven't exactly found *him* yet, no. But I found something else. Something much more interesting." She held up a leather-bound book.

"A book?"

"One to rival your collection, Leo. This one isn't just paper; it was written in with pen."

Leo paused. "Is that the journal? The one you saw in Crumb's head?"

Leah was nodding, still grinning widely. "Yes. And like I said, I know who he is now, and you're not going to believe it."

"Is he Stephen King?"

"What?" said Leah.

"Sorry. I meant Stephen York. I was reading Stephen King earlier."

"Who is Stephen King?"

Leo waved at the screen, refusing to get into another debate over Leah's refusal to sample classic literature. This wasn't the time.

"Never mind. So that's the journal of Stephen York. And York is Crumb."

"I think so, yes. The journal was inserted into the honeycomb metaphor as a back door, meant to be found by someone and meant to be significant to whoever found it. And I have a 2-D you'll want to see that came out of the book."

"A photo?"

"Yes, but 2-D. On paper."

Leo, who still thought of two-dimensional paper photos as the default and not worthy of specifying as such, nodded.

Leah appeared to be in a private cubicle at a Beam parlor. If she was smart, which she was, she would have already verified the place's Privaseal so she could be sure that no one could see her stream or hear her speaking. She was sitting, staring straight ahead at either a Beam-enabled wall or a dedicated screen. But now, as Leo watched, she pulled a small piece of paper from the journal and set it facedown on the desk. She used her finger to trace a rectangle around it. There was a chirp, and Leah continued to grin up at him like a lunatic.

"Well?"

"You're going to shit, Leo."

"Just show me."

So she did. A small paperclip icon appeared in the lower-right corner of the magnified communication screen. Leo touched it, wondering if the software's developer had ever used or even seen a real-life paperclip. A photo unfolded from the icon. Leo dragged it into the center of the screen then used his fingers to drag it larger. He could still hear Leah behind the photo, chuckling.

"This looks like Noah West," said Leo.

"It is."

"So?"

Leah tittered. "Who's *with* him, Leo?"

To say Noah West was famous would be a vast understatement, so when Leo had looked at the image, his eye had been drawn to West like a moth to a flame. But of course there was another man in the picture with him. A lanky man with sharp features and fiercely intelligent eyes, a man who, now that Leo thought about it, looked an awful lot like...

"Holy shit."

"I know, right?"

"Holy shit. Holy shit, Leah."

"I ran a bunch of searches on Stephen York after finding that Easter egg in Crumb's mind, since we sort of figured at first that he might be Stephen York. But the name is too common, so I couldn't narrow the results to one specific York who was definitely our man. But once I had this image, I was able to pattern-match the face in that photo and repeat the search from the other direction, using a bit of software I picked up and that you are hereby not allowed to bitch at me about. The man in that photo is definitely Stephen York, and unless I'm imagining things, the man in that photo is also definitely Crumb."

"You're not imagining things," said Leo. He looked more

closely at the image, still listening to Leah. He could see her shoulders articulating beneath the picture.

"Stop staring at me, Leo," she said.

"I'm staring at the photo."

"Close it then. You're creeping me out."

Leo pinched the photo closed. If he were anywhere other than in the mountains with only a shamefully hidden hand-held for access, he'd have dragged the photo to one of the walls. Then, with the photo out of the way, he looked into Leah's eyes. That was one way technology had improved: Leo remembered a day when the cameras never quite lined up, and the person you videochatted with always seemed to be looking in the wrong place.

"So who is Stephen York?"

Leah said, "According to The Beam's official version, he's nobody. I found some social profiles, nothing special. Says he worked at Quark a while back as a low-level guy, up through the 60s. Then he died."

"But you feel differently."

Leah again held up the book. "*This* feels differently. You should see what's in here, Leo. Crumb is York, and York worked with West. *Closely.* Unless he was crazy when he wrote this, which he pretty obviously wasn't, he was one of *two* fathers to The Beam. The father who'd had heavy reservations about what The Beam would be able to do and what its implementation might mean for the world. It reads like they must have had some heavy NDA shit in place to keep York's name off of pretty much everything. He let West take all of the credit while he worked just as hard in anonymity."

Leo trusted Leah's research and hacking implicitly, but her claim was immense. West was The Beam's unquestioned genius. And now their crazy old mascot was supposed to share West's spotlight? It was insane. Try as he might, Leo couldn't make himself believe it. He remembered back when a politician named Al Gore had implied that he'd more or less invented the Internet. That became a joke that had lasted as long as the net itself.

"You don't buy it," Leah said, looking at Leo.

"It's hard to," he replied. "*Very* hard."

"Later I'll tell you where I found the journal and how I got in to get it, and you might change your mind. The pieces fit, even though they're hard to believe. York either cocreated The Beam or was a very involved, implicitly trusted assistant of Noah West's. Either way, he was there for the whole thing. I recorded the place where I found the journal for you, but when I came out and tried to unspool the video, it was blank. It wouldn't let me record. So you'll have to trust my judgment and memory."

Stuffing down his doubt, Leo asked Leah to read from the journal. She told him that although her end of the connection was secure, his might not be. Leo said his connection was plenty secure and that he used it regularly to call Dominic *because* it was secure. Leah laughed and again told him to trust her. He'd have to hear the rest in person, or at least via a totally secure connection — the kind not available in the mountains. They'd probably said too much already.

Leo asked if Leah knew where Crumb was now — because as important as it had felt before to find him, it now seemed a hundred times more important — and she told him that she was working on it. She said she thought she'd have an idea in a few hours.

Leo said he could think of a good way to kill those hours then asked where he could meet her.

Leah laughed with surprise. Leo hadn't been into the city in Leah's lifetime, and she was probably already imagining all sorts of hilarious fish-out-of-water scenarios wherein Leo could embarrass himself. But he wanted to go. He *had* to go. This was too coincidental. Captain Dominic Long of the DZPD had brought the Organas *Noah West's partner*. No one had ever known who was guarding their gates and ranting at them through every day of sun. Did Dominic know? Leo doubted it. Dominic claimed to have saved Crumb from Respero when he'd shown up ranting in Times Square, and said he'd done so because something in the vagrant had compelled him. Much like something in the same vagrant had recently compelled Leo to send Leah to Bontauk for an unreasonable hacking.

Dominic was meant to save Crumb.

The Organas were meant to have Crumb.

Which meant that at all costs, they *needed* to find Crumb.

Leah didn't argue, as amused as she seemed by the thought of Leo coming to District Zero. For all Organas, everything was interconnected… but for the hacker elite, the sentiment was almost literal. When you combined Leah's intuitive, borderline spiritual approach to navigating The Beam with The Beam's ubiquity, fate started to look like a mere side effect of hyperconnectivity. Complex networks were like vast, living brains. At a certain point, you could stop talking about the airy will of the universe and start talking about the calculable will of the system itself.

Chapter 4

THE NPS AGENT sharing the room with Dominic was at least a public servant. That made Dominic more comfortable, despite his newly found shit heap of trouble. Quark wasn't running this operation, and the agent was just a regular Directorate Joe like Dominic, earning a (probably decent) dole for doing an honest job. Dominic decided he could live with whatever was coming. He might be going off to a domestic prison or to one of the prison islands outside the lattice, and there was even a fair chance he'd be going to Respero. But as long as Dominic was being judged by public sector humans instead of posturing Quark insiders and clerics, he would try to accept his fate with a smile.

"Come on, Captain Long," said the agent. "Just look at this cap." He gestured to the wall, which displayed a nearly life-sized recording of his earlier encounter with Omar in the abandoned glass warehouse. The agent cranked the volume with a gesture. Dominic listened as he incriminated himself. The cap couldn't have been more perfect for the NPS's case against him. Either Dominic had subconsciously known he was being set up and wanted to get caught trafficking moondust, or Omar was an exemplary theatrical dialogue partner.

Watching the cap was like watching a scene from a movie — the scene where the bad guy confesses using all of the oddly perfect words.

"We've got you up one side and down another," the agent continued. "You're a smart guy. I've reviewed your service record. It's exemplary. You *deserve* to be captain. If I may be so bold, your salary — your direct, real, legit salary — has got to put you in the Presque Beau, notches from the top. You've worked hard for a long time and have earned your success. So let's not do the thing where we posture back and forth. You know we've got you. You know what you did. So let's talk."

It sounded reasonable to Dominic, but the agent had toggled between being a nice guy and a total cock so far, seeming to take on the roles of both the good and bad cop. Although, Dominic decided, even when he was being a dick, Dominic couldn't help but like him. He was kind of a lovable asshole.

"*If* I did anything wrong, discussing it with you would just get me to tell you things you don't already know," said Dominic. "That's how I've landed some of my best leads."

The agent — whose name was Smith but who wanted Dominic to call by his first name, Austin — rolled his eyes so far up into his head that they nearly vanished. He sighed loudly, his level of exasperation exaggerated for Dominic's benefit.

"Cop to cop, Dominic," said Agent Smith (Austin), still angling for a first-name trade, "you don't have much left to expose that we don't already know. Hell, you let it all hang out on this cap, so we don't *need* to know more." He indicated the video, still playing as a two-dimensional rendering on the wall, muted and on a loop. Dominic watched Omar verbally bend Dominic over, his bright-white suit making him look like an angel, a player, or both.

Dominic shrugged. He was sitting. Agent Smith (goddammit if he wasn't starting to think of him as Austin) was standing, occasionally sitting on the edge of the table in front of Dominic. The two couldn't have been more of a cliché. If not for Beam surfaces (which could see into a room as easily as they could display information), Dominic knew there'd be a large two-way mirror at the end of the room to complete the tableau.

Austin stood. "You bought dust from Mr. Jones and sent it to the Organas. If I may be totally frank, we know that unless you are very, very, very good at covering your tracks, you haven't made any money at this. None whatsoever. You have received money from the Organas and have paid the exact same amount to Jones. And I do mean *exact*. To the point-credit."

Dominic watched Austin Smith circle the table, still like a cliché. Apparently, the agent didn't realize how transparent all of this was to a seasoned cop like Dominic. The familiarity, the air of confidence, the use of first names, the small room, the pacing and the causal sitting on the table — all of it obvious…unless, Dominic supposed, Smith's openness was actually genuine.

"Actually, it was the other way around," said Dominic, unable to help himself. "I paid Omar first *then* got money from the Organas."

"Like reimbursement for expenses when you work for a company."

"Exactly like that," said Dominic. And it was. Leo even had a form Dominic filled out. He used a pseudonym, of course. He signed the forms *Dick Huffington*. The forms didn't matter anyway, seeing as the monetary transfers were more obvious than digital paperwork. Besides, Organa record keeping was a joke. They did half of it on paper.

"So essentially, you're a courier. Why would anyone do that, Dominic? You're a police captain, well respected, bringing down a hefty legit dole after so much time and seniority with the force. Your family has a history right here in

DZPD. We know you don't even spend all you make from your dole. So why deal drugs?"

"I'm not *dealing* them," said Dominic. "Like you said: I'm a courier."

"Why?"

Dominic said nothing, watching the agent.

"Let me make a supposition," said the agent. "We're friends, right?"

"Since that's what the 'good guy' script says, sure."

Austin pulled something from inside his jacket. It looked like an old-fashioned bottle cap. He set it on the table then pushed down with one finger. It separated and sprang up into a long, thin stalk with one bottle cap on the tabletop at the silver stalk's other end. Then the stalk spread out into thin limbs that were anchored to the center, turning the device into something like a giant, ten-legged spider. The device sprang from the table and began circling the room's periphery, touching the walls. When it reached the wall that was replaying Dominic's encounter with Omar, the image flicked off, and the wall went back to being just an ordinary wall.

Dominic was watching the thing, aghast. "Those are illegal," he said.

"As illegal as shuttling moondust?"

"They'll notice that they can't see us," said Dominic.

"Not with this one," said Austin. "It's a really good one. Got it from a guy in Little Harajuku. It's more than a privacy jammer. It'll spoof the surveillance feed based on conversations we've already had. Besides, nobody's watching live." He stood and walked to the door, which had a Beam sensor but also a plain old-fashioned thumb lock. He turned the lock and said, "No, sir, we're alone."

Dominic looked at the agent with fresh eyes. A small, knowing smile lit Austin's lips at the corner. The smile asked if the professionals understood each other, cop to cop. Agent Smith had just exposed himself with an illegal privacy bot, and he'd removed both of their civility masks. It was a move that encouraged Dominic to speak openly — not because the agent wanted to build a case against him, but because if they could get past the bullshit, they might be able to shoot straight and help each other.

"I don't think you're a bad cop, Dominic," said Austin. "You're too good to be a bad cop. You're like an *imitation* of a bad cop. The dirty cops we see, they're working angles. They have a vibe. They have a bearing. You? You're a Boy Scout. Three generations on this force, and as far as we can tell, you've *all* been Boy Scouts. Your grandfather refused a Mafia bribe back in the 2010s. The rest of the department took the money, but not your grandpappy. *And* he didn't testify. He just didn't take the money. Your father…"

"I know my history," said Dominic. Something had shifted between them, their footing leveled.

"Nobody's listening. So c'mon. Tell me why you did it. Why send moondust to the Organas?"

Dominic watched him, silent.

Austin sighed. "All right then. Let me tell you a story," he said, again sitting on the table's edge. "A few years ago, we were on the case of a serial child rapist. We caught up with him in this shitty little apartment near the park. It was me and my partner at the time — a nice guy named Clem who retired last year. We were tipped that he was in the building, but the witnesses couldn't agree on which apartment. We think it was because he moved around, seeing as so much of the building was abandoned and empty. They'd sent in bots, but it was during that sun storm, when the bots were all acting glitchy, and we'd gotten tired of fighting with our hover's canvas to try and get them to cover us, seeing as we thought he had a victim with him at the time. So we went in ourselves. Clem took one corridor, and I took another, searching what was open before barging into the locked apartments — basically trying to cover ground and kill time while waiting for the sweepers. I ended up surprising the guy in an unlocked apartment. Surprised myself, too, seeing as I wasn't expecting to find him out in the open. Let's just say I caught him red-handed. So I pointed my slumber at him and told him not to move. The guy raises his hands, and I see a red ring around his right wrist."

"A pass." Dominic had heard about passes. A red ring around the right wrist was supposed to say what license plate medallions had said back in Grandy's day — that any person who a cop encountered wearing one had been tapped by someone important as being untouchable.

Austin nodded. "But I didn't want to let him go. I have kids, see. Two of them. So I kept my gun up, started to get out my cuffs, and opened my mouth to call for Clem. But then I looked again at that red ring, and I realized that even if I did the right thing, this fucker would be let right back onto the streets by someone less righteous than I was. So I lowered my slumber and pulled my grandfather's old service pistol from my shimmer holster, and since there's no record of that weapon, I shot him twice."

Dominic's heart was racing, but he doubted it showed as he stared at Austin as he waited for the man to finish.

"Clem heard the shots, of course, but Clem's a good man, like I said. We backed out, taking the kid he'd had with him back to the hover, all the while waiting for the sweepers to show. But they never did. We got lucky. The kid we recovered played along, told the recorder that another degenerate had shot his abductor and that he'd run out of the building and right into us. Nobody investigated further. Just another nugget of shit dead in the ghetto."

Austin turned to Dominic, looking him in the eye.

"So yes, I get it. Sometimes, you have to break the rules you're supposed to uphold if you want to do what's right. I think that's what *you* do, too, Dominic. Somehow, some way, you're doing what you think is right. I know about your sister, and I think you bought her way out of Respero. I'd have done the same. So what you're doing with the moondust and Omar Jones and the Organas…all I can figure is that there's a reason there. A *moral* reason. Tell me that reason, Dominic."

Dominic chewed on his thoughts, not knowing how to respond. He could explain the situation with the Organas. But was there more to this? Did Austin know about the station's security breach? Did he know which specific record was accessed, and did they know about the second person Dominic had bought out of Respero? The subtle, under-handed way the record was stolen suggested its importance to someone, somewhere.

Austin continued to watch Dominic, waiting.

Dominic believed every word of Austin's story and knew what a risk the agent was taking in telling him. It was hard not to reciprocate. Austin had also sealed the room and made it private using an illegal device, so even if Austin could use what Dominic said against him, it would be stupid to do so without Dominic's permission. Dominic now had something on Agent Smith, just as Agent Smith had something on him.

Austin asked, "Is it the same reason you let Leah go?"

Dominic's resolve broke. He looked at the privacy jammer, which had moved into a corner and was standing still, idling.

"Yes."

"Are you helping them? Trying to stage some sort of a revolt?"

Dominic thought of the riots in the city, and how he hadn't tried particularly hard to beat them down. But those didn't involve Organa at all.

"I'm helping them. I believe in their cause. But I don't believe they're planning a revolt."

Austin looked askance at Dominic, seemingly trying to decide whether to believe him.

"What do you mean, 'you believe in their cause?'"

"It's like you said. My family has always been cops. We're blue-collar, hard-working people. We have blue-collar, hard-working friends. Yeah, I make a good dole from the party. But even if it were small, like my dad's, I'd still be Directorate. It's how we're wired. We do our work as best we can, and then we go home. But more and more, folks like me and folks I know are vanishing into The Beam. They stop worrying about life because they can take their dole and plug in all day. The Organas think The Beam is an opiate, and that in the end it just helps the rich get richer and the poor get poorer. I tend to agree. So I think Organa represents an important movement. A sort of check and balance."

"But you aren't helping them plan a revolt."

Dominic sighed. "They're just a bunch of hippies. They have huts in the mountains and use their 'extensive funding' to buy paper books and smoke moondust."

"But they have hackers among them."

"A few. But…come on. They're addicts. You know how addicts are. And you know what happens when addicts run out. I didn't start them on dust, but I don't want to see them die when they can't get it. That's all."

"So this is a 'save the people' sort of initiative? Like a charity?"

"If I stop, they die. That's all."

"And again, when you say they're 'important'…"

Dominic didn't know how to explain it any other way and didn't feel like trying. He felt broken and tired.

"Take it however you'd like." he said.

Austin stood up. "Okay. Fine."

Dominic stood to match him.

"There's just one last thing," said Austin. "I need to know something about a person who's at the village. Someone who maybe has more going on than you might think."

Dominic wanted to close his eyes and give up. They knew about the vagrant, who the Organas called Crumb. They knew that Dominic was supposed to send him to Respero but had taken him into the mountains instead. This was the reason for the security breach at the station. That was how, somehow, they'd learned about Dominic and Omar. The vagrant. The vagrant, who he'd always somehow worried would be his undoing.

Austin touched the wall behind him, calling up an image that must have been stored inside the room ahead of time, seeing as the jammer was still idling in the corner. But the image on the wall wasn't of Crumb. It was of an old man with two gray pigtails, a beard, and a bright rainbow headband.

"Tell me everything you know about Leo Booker," the agent said.

Chapter 5

Kai gripped the man in the liquid metal suit, her hands feeling the cold alloy as it shifted under her hands. Now that they'd visited whatever passed for the soldiers' station (and, by extension, somehow Micah Ryan's station; she didn't totally understand that) and they'd given her a second, stronger, more evolved dose of whatever drug they'd given her back in the shack, she felt as if she was mostly back to being herself. Her memories of the Orion weren't gone, but their traumatic edge had been dulled. It felt now as if she'd been in a fight instead of having been tortured. When she'd first come off the Orion, her very foundation had been shaken, her very reality thrown to question. She hadn't been able to trust her feet or arms. She'd felt helpless, at the mercy (or cruelty) of something she couldn't see or prevent. At any time, it had seemed, the pain might return. She'd flinched not only literally, but psychologically as well, and with all of her soul at once.

But now that fog had dissipated, and the memory of being ripped apart seemed only to harden her, like a well-earned scar. Kai's high-end nanobots had had time to finish their work; her bruises and cuts were mostly gone. Her muscles felt tuned, not at all sore. She was ready to rumble.

But now, according to the soldier, Kai was supposed to rumble against one of her friends.

They were retracing their steps, once again speeding away from District Zero, blitzing through the air a dozen feet above the roads, then houses, then trees, then rivers and grasslands. Kai didn't have a mask like the one worn by the screetbike's driver, so whipping wind stung her eyes, and she had to keep her head behind his for protection. The sound of the air screaming by them was a constant, high-frequency thumping. Beside them, the other soldier drove his screetbike with no passenger behind him. But one way or another, the loose end of that missing passenger would soon be resolved.

Kai felt an itch on her nose and wanted to scratch it, but both of her wrists were wrapped in liquid metal at the driver's front. The soldier in the suit had waited until Kai had re-mounted the bike and re-wrapped her arms around his waist to tell her about Doc and what she was supposed to do to him. Before he'd said a word of it, his suit had fashioned the built-in cuffs to hold her in place. Kai didn't understand how the suit worked, but it seemed to respond to the man's will or perhaps his brain waves. It (he?) had made a wise choice in restraining her, seeing as how her own brain waves weren't very friendly right now. Still, she couldn't help but feel flattered. The man's suit made him incredibly strong and incredibly fast, and it even seemed to be able to manufacture weapons at will. Only a small portion of the soldier's face — just his mouth and chin — were visible. If he was genuinely worried that the unarmed, unarmored, 115-pound woman might be able to harm him, then Kai was scarier than she thought.

"Do you at least know where he is?" Kai yelled into the soldier's ear. She hoped the answer was no. She was with two heavily armed, heavily augmented men. Even with her own defenses, Kai was essentially naked. She'd never be able to fight, outrun, or outmaneuver them. It was kill or be killed — but she and Doc were the only two people in that equation. A stalemate was the only way out, and the only way they'd get one would be if Doc managed to stay hidden.

"We know *exactly* where he is," the driver yelled back. Beside them, ten feet away, the other bike's driver nodded, having heard Kai's question through his partner's input.

"He's sneaky," she said. "He can elude you forever."

The driver turned his head long enough for Kai to worry that he might run into something. Even over the wind's whipping, she heard his small, condescending laugh. "You don't know shit about what's going on here, lady."

Strangely, the soldier's use of the word "lady" bothered Kai more than anything else he'd said during their hover back to the scene of Doc's escape. It was so belittling. He said "lady" the way you'd yell at a crazy bag woman. At a customer in a store who was being an asshole. At an incompetent ditz who couldn't get her canvas to turn on the lights or make macaroni and cheese.

He turned back. Kai swallowed her irritation. She had to figure a way out. So far, there was none. They claimed they could track Doc as if he had a siren mounted on his head — and based on what Kai had seen of Micah's more covert dealings, she had no reason to doubt that they were telling the truth. There were things Micah had access to — things he seemed to know or be able to do — that defied what Kai thought was possible. Nicolai had told her he'd seen some of the same things from Isaac. But whether the Ryans and their ilk had access to technology that Kai didn't was immaterial; the point was that she knew they'd find Doc faster than she wanted. Their superior tracking would defeat his inferior efforts to hide. Once they found him, their superior speed and agility would defeat his inferior human flight. They'd hold him using their superior restraints. And then they'd sight her with their superior weapons and bring the ultimatum down to brass tacks: Kai would kill Doc, or they'd kill her...and then kill Doc anyway.

The situation made Kai furious. She'd never precisely considered Micah a friend, but he'd always been good to her. He'd picked her up off the streets and given her a start when she'd needed it most. He'd taught her most of her subterfuge and cruelty skill set. He'd saved her ass in a few cases where she couldn't save herself, and just a few hours ago, he'd responded to her beacon and sent two iron men to defeat the Beamers — Beamers who, if she understood right, were more or less on his side. He'd refused all of her advances (the ones she'd intended as returned favors and the ones she'd made because Micah was very handsome and magnetic), insisting that he couldn't think of her as sexual. But if she was in any way like a daughter to Micah (something he'd said many times before), how could he torture her like this?

Kai knew the answer; it just wasn't something she wanted to see. The reason was that Micah always took care of Micah first.

What made it worse was that as twisted as it seemed, Kai could almost sympathize with Micah's thinking on the matter of *The Troubling Issue of Thomas Stahl*. Micah (or those who worked with him) had had a compelling reason to detain Doc — apparently something to do with what he'd seen at Xenia. Doc's escape made him a ticking bomb, and Micah, caught between a rock and a hard place, had to know if Kai was ticking, too. Maybe, as repugnant as she found the idea, she'd have to find a way to do it. There might literally be no other way. She'd done Micah's dirty work plenty of times before, after all — had killed dozens of people on his orders. He'd paid her well, knocked her status right to the top of the Presque Beau. Given what she suspected about the elite tier just above hers, she seemed to be on the cusp of crossing a few final, critical inches. If Micah decided she could be trusted, then she might be able to move up — into this "Beau Monde" she kept hearing in whispers.

If she ended up having to do it, she told herself, it would be nothing personal. A job was a job. Kai was sometimes paid to stop a heartbeat, the same as an engineer might be called to stop an out-of-control machine. It didn't matter that she knew Doc or that she considered him a friend. When the boss (and, honestly, the closest person Kai had to a father) said to handle someone, you handled them.

Except that Kai didn't want to "handle" this job at all — no-win situation notwithstanding.

She *did* like Doc. She *did* consider him a friend, as big of an asshole as he could sometimes be. It *was* personal. And what was more, Kai didn't like the idea of being controlled. She'd always chosen whom she fucked. She wasn't like a taxi with her light on, for hire by any Joe who could manage the fare. And so far, she hadn't precisely *chosen* her hit jobs (because a body was, in the end, just a body), but she also *had* chosen them in a way. She'd been up for each, and opposed to none. She hadn't known any of the victims, either in person or by association. They had all been adults, mostly male, shifty enough in bearing that Kai could, the next day, look her pretty self in the mirror and convince herself that they had earned their demise. Kai had never been sicced on anyone too young, ill, pathetic, or helpless, and if she had, she'd have refused because she wasn't a taxi as an assassin, either. She'd never gone after anyone who couldn't put up a fight. And she'd never gone after a friend.

Possibly the worst thing about the Doc job was that doing it would make her a tool wielded by someone else. *Someone other than Kai would be deciding what Kai was going to do.* The only decision she could make would be to decide whether or not she would allow that to happen — whether or not she would permit someone else to decide for her.

And once she thought about it in those terms, the answer became obvious.

Besides, Doc *was* a friend. He was also a client and a supplier. Kai even admired him — admired how he'd scrapped his way up from the bottom, just as she had. He wasn't proud of everything in his past, just as Kai wasn't proud of everything in hers. It wasn't healthy to be proud of everything you left behind you in life. Everyone who had ever achieved anything had done so by taking chances...and when omelets were made, eggs got broken. Humans were flawed creatures. Untarnished people made Kai nervous. Unflinching honesty was a dishonest way to live, and there were too many bullshitters, layabouts, and whiners in this world to waste a perfectly good Doc Stahl.

But how the hell was she going to get out of it? *Could* she even get out of it?

If the men in the so-called Stark suits had working brains (and with Micah at their heels, they should), they wouldn't give Kai a projectile or immobilizing weapon to use against Doc once they caught up with him. They'd keep their distance and watch her closely. They would stay with her, two against one. She had a few defenses, but nothing that was of any use against a casing of intelligent metal. She saw no holes to exploit. Maybe she'd get lucky — maybe they'd give her a weapon or stand too close — but she doubted it and refused to count on it. And even if she was somehow able to turn the tables, *should* she? If she managed to flee, she'd make an enemy of Micah, and the same went if she somehow attacked or killed the men in the suits. Kai didn't want to do that; Micah was useful. And Micah was a powerful enemy to have at your back.

She could try and talk to Micah. But of course that wouldn't work. Micah wasn't good at empathy when it conflicted with his personal interests.

She could try to escape. But no, she'd already considered

that. She'd be putting her life in danger, surrendering everything she'd achieved. Goodbye to her client base, her apartment, her belongings and money, farewell to her security and her nest egg. Farewell, in fact, to Kai Dreyfus herself. Running from or fighting Micah would mean starting over at best, ending up dead (or back on the Orion) at worst.

She leaned into the soldier, trying to peek around him. She could see a Beam tracker displayed on the small screen between the screetbike's handlebars. Maybe she could try to help Doc somehow — find a way to contact him and give him an advantage, tell him what he was facing and that more severe preventative measures might need to be taken. But the chances of getting to Doc before the soldiers and then facilitating his escape in a non-overt way seemed wafer-thin at best, especially considering the fact that she was literally welded to one of the soldiers at the moment. And what could she suggest that they wouldn't be able to circumvent, anyway? She didn't know enough about the technology at Micah's disposal. Would a complete ID wipe (well beyond what Stanford was going to do for Doc) even hide him? Or had they learned to follow a person's DNA, brain waves, or something else that couldn't be altered or masked?

There was no way to win. None of the options were any good.

Kill Doc.

Run.

Die.

Those were her only three choices, and they were all terrible.

She leaned forward and shouted into the soldier's ear, her limp arms tethering her to him like cargo straps.

"I want to talk to Micah!" she yelled.

The soldier snickered.

"I'm not kidding!"

He said, "Whores don't talk to the boss."

"If he learns later that you didn't let me talk to him about something that bears directly on what we're doing now and the whole thing gets fucked up, do you think he'll be happy?"

The soldier's head twitched. "Just tell me, and I'll tell him."

Kai already knew she had him. A girl learned a few things over the years about when men were being resolute, when they were bending, and when you could break them.

"Fuck you," she said. "I called for help, and he sent you running. I'm more important to him than you are."

The soldier looked like he was about to retort but was probably working out the truth in Kai's words. After a few seconds, he said, "You have an implant?"

"Of course."

"Fine. Coming back at you."

Kai's cochlear implant made tiny chirps as the soldier sent her the call. A moment later, she heard Micah in her ear. Her Beam ID must have shown on his end because without preamble, he said, "Yes. You have to do it."

Kai felt naked. She was usually a creature of subterfuge and secrets and didn't like how transparent she always was to Micah, knowing how he'd see her doubts and this call. It was a sign of weakness — something that never increased a person's stock in the eyes of Micah Ryan.

"That's not what I wanted to talk to you about."

"Yes, it is. Don't lower my opinion of you by giving me a line of bullshit. I expect you to be resistant, but I also expect you to do as you've been told. You understand this, Kitty. I know you do."

Kai considered making up a reason for talking to Micah anyway, but she knew he'd never buy it. If there was one thing Micah respected less than weakness, it was lying. Lying which implied that the liar though he was stupid was the absolute worst. So she caved and answered him directly.

"You *know* I'm on your side. You don't need me to kill anyone to prove it. I've killed for you before."

"Not like this. He has to go. Whitlock can do it, or you can; he'll be just as dead either way. I'd hoped Stahl could be wiped, but he's too much of a wild card. I can't be sure enough that it'll take."

"Doc isn't a threat to you," she said. But that wasn't enough for someone like Micah, who didn't understand mercy, so she added, "He could be a huge asset. The people he knows…"

"Too much of a wild card," Micah repeated.

The thought hung in the air. Kai remembered something else she'd wanted to ask — something that would bear on how she felt about Micah, and what she might or might not be willing to do for him.

"What happened to Nicolai?" she asked.

"Costa? Wiped and released. He doesn't have a cortical firewall. *Not* a wild card." Micah paused. "Did you know him before yesterday?"

"He's a client," Kai said, hiding her relief that Micah's story jibed with Kane's.

"Hmm."

Micah said nothing more, waiting for her to resolve the issue.

"I won't kill Doc for you," she said.

"Then I can't trust you."

"Because I won't kill a friend? It crosses the line. Would you kill your mother?" Kai stopped there because not only was the comparison inapt (Doc wasn't exactly Kai's mother), but she also knew the answer. Micah and Isaac's mother was in her hundreds, fantastically enhanced with add-ons that never quite took because she'd started enhancing too late in life, after her body had already suffered immense natural degenerative damage. The Ryans loved each other, but that wouldn't stop any of them, including Rachel, from drawing blood if it served their interests.

Micah didn't reply for a while. When he did, it was with a simple repetition of his earlier message: "You understand my thinking. I know you do."

Kai sighed.

"It's him or you," Micah said. "Or rather, it's him or *both* of you. I'm sorry, Kitty."

And that was the worst of it. She could tell he *was* sorry. Micah could be a stone-cold son of a bitch, but he could also be warm and kind. He was just more diligent than most about those he doled his warmth and kindness to.

"I know," she said.

"Just get it over with. Then we'll catch up. It's been too long."

"It has," she said. "Goodbye, Champ."

Kai's implant chirped, and she was back to being mentally alone. During the conversation, her head had lolled forward so that it was resting on the cool metal back of the soldier's suit. She left it there.

"He's in a coffee shop on the outskirts," said Whitlock, in front of her. Under Kai's cheek, his back rose and fell as he spoke.

Kai sighed. This was all her fault. This was happening (her part in it, anyway) because Doc had trusted her. He was about to learn a dangerous lesson, although he'd only know it for a few seconds: Trust someone, and it's only a matter of time before they stab you in the back. In this case, literally.

"Ten minutes," said Whitlock.

Chapter 6

Doc didn't wait for Omar to enter the Starbucks before tackling him. Once they'd entered the coffee shop, Starbucks-Corps would intervene in any altercation (there was a good reason the company employed its own highly trained peace force; hypercaffeine was legal and moondust wasn't, but everyone knew which addicts were more obnoxious), and customers might raise the alarm. Doc didn't want attention, seeing as he was trying to hide. But he *did* want to crack Omar's head against the sidewalk, so this seemed like a reasonable compromise.

One moment, the thin black man in the bright-white suit was marching toward the Starbucks rear entrance with two customer service holograms already forming to help/harass him, and the next Doc was spearing him in the stomach with his head. Doc imagined a million nanobots screaming as he mashed his well-maintained blond hair into the lily-white suit, then listened with satisfaction to the more authentic sound of Omar trying and failing to scream.

While Omar gasped for breath, trying to move his diaphragm back into motion, Doc righted himself, tossed his disheveled hair back, and marched forward to grab the dealer by the back of his jacket. He dragged him from the entrance and toward an alleyway as two holograms tried to sell Omar packets of hypercaffeine quad mocha latte mix with included InstaFoam cartridges. The holograms were intuitive enough to realize their target had fallen to the ground but not quite intuitive enough to realize he'd been attacked. So they bent forward, following Omar as Doc dragged him, asking how he'd like to experience the full flavor of a freshly made Starbucks latte at home.

"What the fuck did you get me into, Omar?" Doc yelled. He punched a Plasteel trash can in a tantrum, crushing his fist and wincing. "You want to tell me what you've been up to, who you've been talking to, what you're doing that has…I don't know…fucking *Beamers and torturers* and shit…all up my ass? You mind telling me that, Omar?"

Omar continued to struggle for air on the alley floor.

"You want to smuggle, fine. You want to get your ass in deep and risk NPS on your tail, fine. I know what a slippery shit you are. But the minute you start fucking with…with people who'd do *that*…" Doc was finding he couldn't articulate himself at all. He felt almost as bad as Kai had looked when the Beamers had pulled her from the Orion and hauled her toward the evaporator. She'd gotten it a lot worse than he had, but he could still hardly think at all. He also felt weak and strangely paranoid, but at least he was strong enough to hit a man in the stomach with his head — and to lift a Plasteel trash can and hurl it across an alley, which he then did while yelling, *"MOTHER! FUCKER!"*

Omar was slouched against the wall, his pristine white suit already dirty. His upper back was vertical, and his lower back was horizontal on the ground. He formed a C shape in the corner, his left hand on his gut as if he'd been shot. He held his right hand up, dark fingers splayed.

"Hang on, Doc. Just…" He heaved. "…just hang on. I

don't know what you're talking about. Tell me from the beginning."

But as half-thinking as Doc was, he knew not to volunteer information to Omar Jones. Omar was a fantastic business partner as long as you were his best option, but the minute something better came up, he'd crumple you like a can and toss you aside. Giving Omar information he might later use against you was like rolling unpinned grenades into the other army's foxholes.

"Fuck that!" he yelled, kicking one of Omar's legs.

"Jesus, Doc! Maybe I screwed you over, and maybe I didn't, but unless the reason you called and told me to meet you here was to kill me, I ain't gonna be any help in figuring shit out if you don't tell me what's up. And ideally…that means you'd stop hitting me." His hand was still out. He wiggled himself into an upright sitting position, testing his breath to see if he'd gotten it back. He started to stand, lowering his hand and using both to brush dirt from his suit.

Once Omar had composed himself, he reclaimed his cool. Doc, his brain still uneasy, told himself to watch it. Omar had an intensely strong presence. For a minute there, Doc had unquestionably had the upper hand, but if he let Omar get too confident, he'd easily end up back in charge. It was how Omar worked — maybe even his secret to success.

Omar brushed his jacket a final time then slowly looked up at Doc, his facial expression still guarded, unsure.

"What's up, Doc?" he said.

"Xenia Labs."

"What about them?"

"You trying to get in? Trying to learn what they're doing?"

Omar shrugged. "I'm always trying to learn things, Doc."

"I mean specifically. Are you trying to…infiltrate them? Actively trying to see what they're developing, what they're selling?"

"I guess. But that's why I've got you."

This was exactly the wrong thing to say. Doc knew he was still keyed up with Orion hangover and that his nanos hadn't yet done all they could with his endorphin and epinephrine balance, but that knowledge didn't stop him from grabbing Omar by the sleeves and slamming him hard against the wall, causing his teeth to crash together.

"You've got me? Goddamn right you've got me, only I didn't get a choice about being your bitch, did I? Now you get to tell me about it! Who's after me, Omar? And why?"

"Shit, blondie!" said Omar, rattled but otherwise only mildly perturbed. "How about you get your fucking hands off me and stop acting burned so we can discuss it? Or would you rather keep fucking my shit up and get nowhere?"

But Doc wasn't ready to settle. He felt his eyes bug out, fury coursing through his veins. "What do you mean, you've got me? Am I bugged? Did you somehow bug me, Omar? To do surveillance for you?"

"Motherfucker, I just meant that you know more about Xenia than I do, and you open up shit to me that I can't get. This ain't new information. What the hell is the matter with you?"

Doc let Omar go then took a step back, running his right hand through his hair. He wasn't thinking clearly. He and Omar did talk regularly, despite having only had that one transaction in the park. Doc was planning to sell more to Omar, and Omar was planning to open more doors for Doc. It had only been a few days since Doc had learned that Xenia had more for sale than he'd ever before been permitted to see. Omar hadn't set him up with Killian and taken his usual man out of the picture. The notion that Omar had sent him in to spy on Xenia was ludicrous. Kane's theories had burrowed under Doc's skin.

"It's been a rough few days."

"I *guess*, shit," said Omar, shaking out his suit coat. He put a hand on Doc's arm in what seemed to be a gesture of peace-making. "Let's go inside. Okay? Get a coffee. You drink coffee, don't you?"

Doc did drink coffee, but something else occurred to him as well. He'd heard those men in the metal suits talking about giving Kai a drug called Neuralin. Doc knew about Neuralin because a few of his clients used it recreationally to enhance the effects of some of the deeper neural implants he'd sold them. Doc had even suggested it to Nicolai for use with his creativity wetchip. Neuralin was a stimulant. Hypercaffeine was easily as strong of a stimulant. The two weren't pharmaceutical analogues, but Doc thought they might be close enough. After his time on the Orion, he literally *needed* a jolt.

"Yeah."

"I'll buy," said Omar. "See how great I am? You kick my ass, and I'll still lay out the green for you."

Green, thought Doc. Then he said, "You have dollars?"

Omar gave him a look. "It's an expression, brother. A common one. Someone really fucked you up, didn't they?"

Doc sighed. Of course. Nobody actually carried green. For one, it was no longer legal tender. He closed his eyes, realizing as he did it that he was feeding Omar power like nursing a vampire from an open artery. The closed eyes, the willingness to let Omar pay. But Doc didn't have the strength to resist.

"I need my coffee," he said, forcing his eyes open. With them closed, he'd felt dizzy.

Omar clapped a hand on Doc's back and led him from the alley and toward the door. "Cool. We'll get you one. We'll get you *two*. Then you'll tell me what's up. And you say it has to do with…"

Omar was interrupted when they reached the Starbucks door and a pair of green-shirted holographic people appeared.

"Welcome to Starbucks!" said the one on the door's right, a thin woman with blonde hair.

The Hispanic hologram on the left shoved something in front of Doc's face. It looked like a giant sugar packet. "How would you like to experience the full flavor of a freshly made Starbucks latte at home?"

"Fuck off," said Omar.

They pushed directly through the holograms. Unperturbed, the holograms followed them and continued to pitch the instant latte packets while Doc and Omar descended a moving walkway to the lower level, where the coffee shop spread out, free of the confining streets above.

The lobby was small by Starbucks standards, seemingly only a hundred yards square. Beam posts were spaced throughout the sitting space, which occupied most of the store. The posts were really only for people who wanted or needed to plug in, and most modern Starbucks had removed them and gone fully to Fi connections. Only the oldest handhelds and tablets operated at substandard Fi speeds, and these days, almost nobody brought tablets with them anyway. Doc never carried one outside his apartment. Why would he? As long as your Beam ID was clean, your data was encrypted and stored on The Beam, accessible wherever you wanted it via any public screen. Sure, some people were paranoid and kept their data on slip drives or personal devices, but those were the same people who still used printers.

A green-shirted, obese male hologram walked up and stood in front of Doc and Omar. Doc was annoyed. He just wanted to sit and have some coffee. He was in no mood to deal with these fucking things.

"Welcome to Starbucks!" said the hologram. "What can I...?"

"Fuck off," said Doc, taking a page from Omar's book. He walked straight at the hologram, collided with it, and bounced off.

"Just using The Beam then?" said the hologram — who, judging by his nametag, was actually a clerk named Greg.

"Sorry," said Doc. "I thought you weren't there."

"I just want a trenta coffee. Black," said Omar. He looked at Doc then apologetically toward the clerk. "What you want, Doc?"

"A shitload of hypercaffeine."

"How about a Suicide?" said Greg.

That sounded splendid to Doc, regardless of whether the clerk was offering him a drink or suggesting he kill himself.

Doc nodded. The clerk's fingers moved at his sides.

"Will that be all for you?"

"Yeah, man, thanks," said Omar.

"Which section would you like? Canvas, VR, immersion…"

"Just chairs, man. Just chairs. Tell me you have plain old chairs."

"We have a section of Beam chairs. There are no dedicated canvases — except for projected ones, of course — but they'll remember your position from last time you were here, how soft or firm you like the cushions, what type of music you prefer streamed, assuming you have an implant…"

"Just *chairs*," Omar repeated. Doc wished they'd both hurry. He was feeling weaker and weaker the longer he stood in the cavernous space filled with Beam zombies. He must have been running on adrenaline earlier, and now he was out. He felt like an empty sack, about to collapse.

"Just chairs?"

Doc faltered, and Omar caught him, glaring impatiently at the clerk. "What the hell, man? *Chairs*. Upholstery! Stuffing! Wood frames and shit!"

Greg's asinine smile didn't falter. Doc seemed to remember reading somewhere that Starbucks's training program specifically coached baristas and clerks on how to deal with rude customers and emerge with their positivity intact.

"Section 14, seats 4 and 5," said Greg.

"Are those seats somewhat private?" Omar asked.

"It's just a grouping of two. Should be comfy." The clerk pointed, smiling stupidly. "Back against the wall, past the gamer area with the VR goggles."

Omar thanked the clerk and, holding Doc's arm, led him toward their chairs.

"You didn't pay," said Doc.

"Noah Fucking West, Doc. He scanned me. What the hell did someone do to you?" Doc thought he detected genuine alarm and/or concern in Omar's voice. That was encouraging.

"Stuff," Doc answered.

He squinted and stumbled, following Omar past legions of chairs and reclining lounges equipped with different Beam hookups. There was a section with huge unfolding screens that were attached to the arms of plush chairs. There was a section where people kicked back with holo-projected screens and airboards. Some areas were open and airy, and some chairs were clustered into what looked almost like library carrels. Toward the back was what looked like a cubicle farm for customers who wanted true privacy. They passed the VR section the clerk had indicated, where a handful of patrons lay motionless save for their twitching hands. Coffees sat on small tables beside the immersed customers, though Doc supposed they had likely gone cold.

When they arrived at their chairs in the tiny non-tech session, Doc's cochlear implant tried to wake up and tell him that his order was ready. He shook his head, annoyed, to turn it off. You couldn't be truly disconnected inside a Starbucks, but he wanted to pretend. The announcement was intrusive, seeing as it was only a proximity echo coming from Omar, who'd placed the order. Doc's own order, had he placed it, wouldn't have worked, seeing as the implant was currently broadcasting his spoof.

"Our drinks are ready," said Doc.

"I heard."

Doc slumped into an overstuffed chair, feeling like he weighed a thousand pounds. Once seated, he was hit with a certainty that he'd never be able to lift himself up again. In front of him, a small circle in the table between the chairs slid open, and a pneumatic dumbwaiter raised two coffees from below. Doc grabbed the nearest one, sipped, found it intoxicating, then tried to gulp. But it was too hot.

After a few minutes of quiet sipping, Doc found his head returning. Hypercaffeine was highly addictive (one reason Starbucks was one of the largest companies in the NAU), but Doc didn't care. Right now, it was humping his neural receptors like dipping into a fine woman, and was perfectly welcome.

"Better?" said Omar.

Doc felt his usual devil-may-care smile crawling back onto his lips. "Better," he said, nodding.

"What happened to you?" said Omar.

It may or may not have been wise of Doc, spilling his guts to Omar, but by this point he had ceased giving a shit. It didn't seem likely that Omar was directly responsible for his recently ditched trouble, and any new trouble Omar could get him into would be gentle by comparison. So Doc told Omar about how he'd been shown into a restricted room at Xenia and that he'd seen something he wasn't supposed to see. He told Omar about how Xenia had tried to wipe him, how he'd kept his memories, and how they'd caught up with him anyway. He told him about the ride into the sticks, about Kai and the Beamers, about finding Nicolai in the cell after Nicolai had been snatched from Doc's apartment, and a lot about the Orion. He concluded by telling the only man he felt he could trust (though he could never actually trust him at all) about how Kai had saved the day by bursting in with two soldiers in strange suits, then how she had then tried to get Doc to stay with the soldiers despite having ample opportunity to escape.

Omar considered the story then said, "What did you see in the room at Xenia?"

"I don't blame you for asking," said Doc, "but that's the one thing I won't tell you."

"I need to know what they're chasing you for."

Doc shook his head, causing his hair to wiggle like a model's. His nanos were back at work, restoring his long mane's old luster. "I'm still not sure enough that you're not in on this. No offense. But they thought you sent me in because you needed to know what they had. I'm not in a rush to prove them right."

Omar seemed annoyed. He took a sip of his coffee, looking out across the enormous room. Nobody was paying any attention to them. That was one thing about The Beam — for something designed to connect people, it did an excellent job of making sure they were distracted enough to pay attention to nothing.

"Fine," said Omar. "Then let me tell you what I know. I *do* want to see what Xenia's up to, but not because I want to pirate it. I want to know because whatever they're involved in, it's tied to Micah Ryan."

"The Enterprise guy?"

Omar nodded. "Micah Ryan is in charge of Capital Protection for Enterprise. You heard of Project Mindbender?"

"No."

"Of course not. No one has. I don't know either, just that it has something to do with brains and computers. New levels of connectivity, way past what you've seen with those wetchips. I've heard rumors from the people I know."

"What people?"

Omar shook his head, shaking a long finger. "No need for that. Just *people*. People with connections. People who make shit happen. Nobody knows what Mindbender is, except that it's draped in black. Something Quark tried to roll out that never got legs."

"What does that have to do with Ryan?"

"Capital Protection," Omar repeated. "That's the people charged with 'preserving mankind's mindpower.' You saw that summit a few years back? Well, same deal. The whole 'Noah's Ark of Knowledge' thing. But you stitch the rumors around Mindbender, and the idea of protecting capital — that's *intellectual* capital, you understand — and the fact that the head of Capital Protection is also a majority stockholder at Xenia Labs..."

"He is?"

Omar nodded. "A place that makes add-ons and has a secret division that us lower life forms aren't allowed to see. Only Beau Monde, which is what the too-goods above even us rich huckers call themselves. I hear there are special salespeople for those folks. Now, I know you don't want to tell me what you saw; okay, fine. But just tell me this: Did you see anything that might represent huge leaps forward in brain/machine interfacing? Anything suspiciously mindbenderish, if you catch my drift?"

Doc slowly nodded.

"Doc, I'll shoot straight. I know about this because if I'm in the right place at the right time, I'm going to be very rich. That's also how you know you can trust me. Because this is about credits — enough to pop both of us into that Beau Monde if we skip rope together. I had to turn on someone today. I don't like doing that, but...well, it was necessary to gather forces to my side."

"I don't trust you at all," said Doc.

"I tell you I flipped someone, you'd be fool to. But you do trust me anyhow because I'm honest with you, seeing as you're as slippery as I am. Big changes are coming, Doc. Maybe a sort of war. It's been on simmer for a long while, but if what I think is going down is indeed going down, this world will soon be split into more than Directorate and Enterprise, poor and rich. Think bigger. Think mortals and gods."

Doc laughed.

"Laugh now," said Omar, looking more serious than Doc had ever seen him. "This may take a hundred years to blow, but blow it will. And I don't know about you, but I plan on living as long as I can — and when this blows, I plan to be standing on the winning side."

Doc took another long sip of his Suicide, wondering what was in it. Whatever it was felt very good. Not only was his lethargy and confusion gone; he felt positively high. What Omar was telling him should have made Doc, who'd just survived inhuman torture over his involvement with Omar, run the other way. Instead, the entrepreneur in him was tickled by potential.

"So what you're saying is that I *did* get fucked up because of you."

"Maybe they just got your subversive ass in advance," said Omar. "But it don't matter, Doc. You need friends on all sides. That *includes* the folks who caught you. You just need to demonstrate your worth. Credits talk plenty loud in the end."

"I need a Beam ID reset. I know you know people who can do it."

"Sure, but you can't hide from these folks if they are who I think they are, and if they can do what I think they can. And you know as well as I do, your best allies are those who were once your enemies. That's because they've already seen your cards. So we'll go to Xenia. To Micah Ryan. You and me together."

Doc looked askance at the thin black man in the white suit.

"You're setting me up. To earn favor by taking me in like you did with your other man. The other guy you turned on."

Omar reached to the side, pressed his palm to a wall beside his chair, and lit a panel. He said, "Canvas. Display my contacts. Micah Ryan."

The screen changed to show a photo of Micah Ryan, headed by a Beam ID.

"You have Micah Ryan's ID?"

Omar nodded. "I've never spoken to him, but it's only a matter of time. Point is, I have it because I know the right people. All I had to do, at any point since you showed up, was step aside and send a ping, and they'd be all over you. Why would I bother to set you up, Doc? This way would be so much easier. I ping, they show. Why would I explain everything first?"

Doc stared at Omar then turned to the pic of Ryan. How the hell did a scammer like Omar have the personal contact information for one of Enterprise's heaviest hitters?

Omar removed his hand from the wall. The panel went blank, back to being nothing but wall.

Doc inhaled then exhaled slowly. "Okay. Say I believe you. What's my role?"

"Same as always. You're a man who can get things. You're good at making friends. You're every bit as slippery and self-centered as I am, and not afraid to get your hands dirty."

"And your role?"

"Deep pockets. Connections. Charm."

Doc nodded. He believed what Omar said about running being futile, based on what he'd seen at Xenia, what he'd heard, and all that he'd come to unwittingly know over the past few days. Doc's best bet was to lean into the threat. To call it out, face it down, and make it his friend. Right now, he was a loose end who knew what he shouldn't. If he could convince his pursuers of his value, he'd become a man with connections who knew what he needed to know. What did you call a man like that?

You called him *Partner*.

"Okay," said Doc, nodding subtly. "Let's see what happens. But first, there's one loose end I'd like you to straighten. Something I caused. Something I feel guilty for."

"The woman, right?" said Omar. "Kai Dreyfus, who you were with when you were attacked by Beamers?"

Doc nodded.

"I thought you'd say that."

Omar was smiling, but his smile made Doc want to punch him. This was about an innocent party he'd put in danger, not getting his pole waxed. Doc was a slippery son of a bitch, but he was still one with values.

"Why?" Doc retorted.

"Because my guys say Micah Ryan has a personal hit girl who matches her description. An escort, who's good at making men believe whatever she needs them to believe."

Doc was about to take the final sip of his drink but lowered the cup. "What the hell are you saying, Omar?"

"I'm saying she set you up. Just like you already know she did."

Chapter 7

KAI COULD FEEL the pod on the back of her head, under her hair. She didn't have to reach up and touch it with her fingers to know it was there; she could feel the thing on her scalp like a poker-chip-sized tick. She'd never seen anything like it, but it made sense to believe that it did what Soldier Whitlock said it did, just to be safe.

Whitlock had told Kai that the pod on her head contained what were known as reapers — a murderous species of nanobots that were essentially spinning food processor blades. On Whitlock's command, reapers would spill from the pod, enter her skull, and use nanoscalpels to turn her cerebellum and brain stem to pulp. He told her that they were a new breed, invisible to all known defensive nanos and able to communicate with their handler via a protocol that was unjammable and easily surmounted firewalls and other so-called protections. Lastly, Whitlock told her that if she tried to remove the pod, the nanos would simply begin their work immediately. The experience would not be pleasant. First, she'd lose her senses of coordination and balance, causing her to stumble and appear drunk. Then she'd lose her lower motor control and collapse. At some point thereafter, her breathing and heartbeat would cease. At that point, the nanos would leave her system, and the pod itself would dissolve, leaving lower-99 police investigators to assume that a bomb had simply detonated inside her skull.

Kai stood casually, out of obvious sight in an alley near the Starbucks entrance, waiting for Doc to exit. Whitlock had told her that he had an exact bead on Doc's location inside the immense building, and she believed him. He told her that Doc had entered through the door where Kai now stood, and she had no reason to doubt him about that, either.

Sooner or later, Doc would leave. The person Doc was with (Whitlock didn't say who it was; maybe he knew, and maybe he didn't know everything after all) was still in there with him, and Kai was to wait until this second party was out of the way before engaging Doc. How she proceeded after that was entirely up to her.

Kai still didn't know what she was going to do. She wanted the limbo she was in to last forever so she wouldn't ever have to decide, but sooner or later Doc was going to come out, and she was going to have to face a choice — should she kill a friend and stay alive, or should she let them both die? Math favored the former, but Kai didn't know that she'd be able to live with herself if she did it. She'd been an *escort* for a long time, but she had never really, truly been a *whore*. She'd always had her standards and had always made her own decisions. She loved sex, and a part of her even loved killing. She had always done both by her own choice, no matter who was painting the targets or paying the bills.

She felt the alley's cool stone at her back, her leg kicked up and her posture sexy like a common streetwalker. Then she realized the comparison and dropped her leg, turning her side to the wall. She could see Whitlock across the street, sitting in a chair at an outside cafe. He had pulled a pair of loose pants and a long coat from somewhere and had dragged them on over his shiny suit of liquid metal to hide it.

A few minutes after sitting, he'd seemed to have remembered the visor and then had done something to make it vanish, and now, Kai could see his face as she looked at him from across the street. She couldn't make out his features, though. And as a girl for whom information was the best weapon, she resented it. His partner, Jameson, sat across from him at the same table, his face similarly vague from where she was standing. On the other hand, given the complexity of their suits, Kai thought it likely that they could see every detail of *her* just fine. They might be able to see her neck pulsing with nervousness or see the messy area at the back of her head where her dark-brown hair had been disturbed to plant the pod.

After a few minutes, Doc stepped through the door of the Starbucks with a tall black man in a bright-white suit. Kai frowned. She didn't know the man, but she was curious about the ostentatious stranger Doc had chosen to run to after fleeing those he'd seen as captors. And with that thought, a wave of irritation welled within Kai. If Doc had simply trusted her and not run — if he'd never decided that Whitlock and Jameson were *captors* in the first place — they'd both have been taken to headquarters and dosed with Neuralin. Maybe that would have been the end of it. Micah and his officers might still have messed with Doc afterward — maybe even killed him — but Kai wouldn't have had to be the one to do it.

Feeling her anger rise, Kai tried to hold onto her senses of ire and irritation. She tried to magnify them. She tried to hate Doc for putting her in this position, tried to summon a desire to kill him or at least to hurt him for what he'd done. If she could just get angry enough…If she could just become furious enough with him…

But then the wave of irritation passed, and the heavy feeling of coming regret returned to her stomach. She turned away. Then she turned back, knowing she had to face it, had to do it regardless of how much it bothered her. She felt the pod like an itch on her head. If she didn't kill Doc, the soldiers would kill him just the same…after, of course, killing her.

The man in the white suit said a few final words to Doc and walked away with a wave. Doc looked toward the alley, and Kai dove out of sight just in time. A moment later, she peeked back around the corner and saw him check his wrist, noting the time. His simple gesture tugged at her heart. Kai had never known anyone with an add-on as stupid as Doc's tattoo watch. It said so much about him. It spoke of arrogance, of a respect for yesterday's style, and of a particularly biting kind of fuck-you to people he grew bored with.

"Doc!" she hissed. She didn't know why she did it. But now that he was turning and seeing her, she didn't know what she would do next. Would she just snap his neck the minute he reached her? No, that would be careless. She couldn't do it right out here in public.

Doc approached her, seemingly back in full possession of his usual swagger. He was still wearing the wardrobe Kai had given him days ago — the one she'd kept for him in the way she kept a set of clothes for any of her clients who wanted to leave one. Blue jeans. A white T-shirt. A light-brown suit coat, stylishly tailored. And, on his feet, a pair of Doc-standard cowboy boots. He *was* a cowboy in his chosen profession, too. He was the only person Kai knew who was just as slippery and underhanded as she was but who managed to be fiercely loyal when it mattered.

She waved him into the alley. Seeing the way she was hiding seemed to remind Doc that he was supposed to be keeping a low profile, so he immediately began looking around, ducking as if a three-inch reduction in height might make him invisible. Kai watched him approach, warring internally. She still wasn't sure what came next. She was in charge, and yet she had no idea what she was in charge of, or how she felt. So when she slapped Doc hard across the face, she was every bit as surprised to see herself do it as he was.

"What the hell, sunshine?" he said, raising his hand to the reddening spot on his cheek, his eyes somewhere between shocked and angry.

"You *asshole*," she spat, surprising herself. "Why did you run? Why couldn't you just fucking trust me?"

"Hey, how could I know what you were up to?" he said, shuffling into the alley beside her. "I get my ass tortured and about lose my mind, then a few guys in silver suits storm in and whisk us off somewhere else, God knows where. And you? You're just going right along with them. They were just like those Beamers, in my eyes. You know…showing up out of the blue to get me. After you left my side, I mean."

"Those men *saved* me! I was dying!"

"You look fine to me," said Doc, giving her lean body a long lecherous once-over with his eyes. "Good enough to eat, in fact."

Kai felt disoriented. This wasn't going how this was supposed to be going. "Because I got Neuralin," she said. "Which we were taking *you* to get, too, if you hadn't run."

"Interesting."

Kai pushed him in the chest. "Are you kidding me with this?" she railed. "You came to me in the first place because you trusted me to help you! I *called* those soldiers, you ass!"

"Why are you so worked up, if you called them?"

"It's complicated."

"Oh, it always is. How exactly did you call them? Robot man hotline?"

"I called a connection. He sent them."

"Oh. I see."

"Someone I trust."

"Who did you call, Kai?" Doc asked her, leaning back and kicking his boots up against the stone wall behind him.

Kai shook her head. Something was wrong. Doc was too upright, too confident, too borderline righteous. The last time she'd seen him, he'd been running for the gutter like a frightened rat. Now he looked ready to waltz into a big sale and knock 'em dead. What had happened between then and now?

"Someone who could help me. *Us.*"

"Someone really powerful, I'll bet," he said with a knowing look. The look felt like an X-ray, as if he could see right through her.

"What's the matter with you? You're still in danger. People are still after you. Why are you acting like a cock?"

"*Which* people are after me, kitten?" said Doc. "Not the people I ran from, right? Because that just plain wouldn't make sense, seeing as you're with 'em and all."

Kai tried to reply but found herself short on words.

"You're right," said Doc. "It *was* stupid of me to run from those silver guys on the bikes, seeing as I'm now in danger from them and they're chasing me. So tell me. How do *you* fit in, if they're with you and they're dangerous to me?"

Then, as Kai watched with shocked eyes, Doc pulled a toothpick from his pocket and put it between his teeth. *The motherfucker put a toothpick between his teeth.* Somehow, somewhere, Doc had taken control of the conversation. He wasn't scared at all. He wasn't acting like a man on the run. Something had solved every problem in his mind between when he'd ditched her and when she'd found him.

When Doc looked away with a snicker, Kai glanced toward the two disguised soldiers across the street. Both were watching them. Whitlock stared back, unabashed. There was something in Whitlock's look that rang a bell inside her, but she stuffed the strange feeling down, turning back to her current problem.

She had to do something to break the situation open. Something disturbing.

So she gripped the front of Doc's suit coat and planted her lips on his, pushing him back into the wall. He flinched then let it happen.

And then, finally, she knew what had to come next.

"And I thought you might be up to something funny," said Doc. "But I guess not, because that was logical."

"You need to come with me," she whispered. She hadn't let go of his lapel. She began dragging him toward the alley's far end, away from the Starbucks entrance. Away from Whitlock and Jameson, across the street.

"You ain't gonna lead me to Beamers, are you?" he said. But Doc was Doc, and regardless of whether he was suspicious of something or not, he was still getting hard. She could see that his pants had already started to tent following their kiss.

"Just come," she said.

"You must say that to guys a lot," Doc replied.

She dragged him stumbling for a few more feet then let him go and walked in front for him to follow. She let her ass do the talking, knowing Doc would watch, knowing him better than he knew himself. He would, of course, know full well that the last thing Kai would be looking to do after finding him and warning him about impending danger would be to pull him into a corner and ride his rocket, but at the same time he would be somehow hopeful that it would happen anyway. It wouldn't matter that he seemed a little irritated — or maybe a bit more — with her, either. Since she'd known him, the brain below Doc's belt had always been more influential than the one in his head.

"Where we goin'?" he said, trying to sound cavalier.

Kai turned to look back, but she wasn't looking at Doc; she was eyeing Whitlock and his partner over Doc's shoulder. The soldiers were already scrambling at their tables, trying to extricate themselves without drawing undue attention. She couldn't run because she knew they'd catch her if she did. But she wasn't going to kill a man in the mouth of a public alley, and getting the soldiers to join the party was her next logical move. There had been something in that look Whitlock had given her — that chiming sense of unresolved *déjà vu* — that practically insisted it.

Kai didn't answer Doc. She continue walking, facing forward, moving at a brisk but even pace. He took a few large steps with his longer legs to catch up, and soon they were walking side by side. And with that, Kai realized she was back in control. Whatever angle Doc had been trying to play a few moments ago, Kai had neutralized it. Now she was leading him around by the dick, and the only question was where it would be best to stop.

They reached the next block, where one alley intersected another. They crossed the small street, skirting a trio of homeless people. You didn't see homeless much in the heart of District Zero anymore. Directorate poor never lived on the street, and Enterprise who failed their way into the gutter usually knew to keep out of sight, holing up under bridges and in accessible basements. These three were either crazy or too new to poverty to know better, but if they stayed where they were, it wouldn't be long before Respero agents improved their situation in one way or another.

"Seriously," said Doc. "Are we headed somewhere fun, or are you leading me to your bosses?"

Kai stopped, turned, and slapped Doc across the face again. Hard enough to knock him to the ground.

"Motherfucker!" she yelled.

"Motherfucker yourself, hon!" he replied.

"Do you think I set you up?"

Doc looked up at her for a long moment. "I keep running into mysterious bad guys with you, is all I know."

"You saw me tortured!" she said, red fury in a collar around her neck. "My sense of time was a little fuzzy, but I'd say I took *two or three times* as much as you took before...before I *came in and rescued your sorry ass.*"

"You could have been faking it."

Kai reared back and, using every carbon-nanotube-reinforced, nanobot-tuned muscle in her long, lean right leg, kicked Doc in the ribs. His body yielded too much on impact, and she decided she must have broken one or more of his ribs.

"I'm supposed to kill you, you piece of shit!" she bellowed, unable to help herself. "You put me in this position! I have to kill you, or they'll kill us both! Do you hear me? And it's your own stupid, stubborn, dickheaded fault, because the people who used to be saving us now see you as the giant cocksucking liability you are!"

Doc groaned then looked up. "Who *are* those people? Who's pulling your pretty little strings?"

She kicked him again. "Fuck you!"

The soldiers had seen the melee start and were trotting up behind them, slinking along the alley's side wall. Doc's eyes went to the soldiers then back to Kai.

"Do it again," he croaked up at her. "I like it rough."

The soldiers reached the cross-alley, glanced at the homeless people, then slowed to a fast walk. Kai watched them approach. She glanced down at Doc, who wouldn't be going anywhere anytime soon, and saw a small, grim smile grace his lips as he looked toward the overdressed soldiers. The smile just pissed Kai off even more.

Fucking Doc.

Seething, she remembered that she had to kill him. Now, while she was pissed off, was as good a time as any to do it. But then she wondered: Why exactly was she pissed off at Doc? Was it because he was being an asshole...or was it because he was being correct?

Kai stood over her prey, her legs slightly parted, her head turned back to watch the soldiers approach. Then, as they arrived, her earlier sense of *déjà vu* smacked her hard, and she suddenly knew why Whitlock's look, even from a distance, had struck a strange chord within her.

"Ralph?" she said, too low to be heard.

From the corner of Kai's enhanced eye, she saw Doc's

reaction as he watched the shocked expression cross her face. But most of her attention was focused on Soldier Whitlock — the man she'd bedded last week as the firewalled mystery man, Ralph McGuinness.

Kai watched Whitlock approach, a torrent of information hitting her like a tsunami.

She hadn't been able to figure out who Ralph was in the end, but she knew a few things about him. She knew he'd had tickets for Natasha Ryan's concert yet had seemed totally uninterested in Natasha's actual performance. He'd been much more interested in scanning the crowd and looking toward the exits — almost as if he was waiting for something to happen. And then when something *had* happened — when the first of the big Directorate riots had erupted — Ralph/Whitlock hadn't seemed remotely surprised. It was as if he'd been expecting it. Because of course he *had* been expecting the riot, seeing as he (and no doubt a well-placed group of others) had been sent to the concert to cause it.

The riot hadn't been started by rowdy members of the Directorate after all. The Directorate had been framed. *Enterprise* had staged the riot as a power play, to denigrate their opposition in advance of Shift.

Whitlock was Ralph. Ralph was Whitlock.

And Whitlock, of course, worked for Micah Ryan.

Kai almost shut her eyes to block out the secret she'd tried so hard last week to uncover. It was a very, *very* dangerous piece of information. Micah was an exceedingly private man. You didn't browse Micah's files; you didn't rifle through Micah's apartment or office; you sure as *hell* didn't try to crack your way into Micah's agents while he was using them for something underhanded. But luckily, there was no way Micah could possibly know she'd tried that last one, was there? It wasn't as if Kai had used a sterile lancet to drop six scavenger nanobots into Ralph's cortex or anything…say, six scavengers that wouldn't have expired or been purged yet. Six little fingerprints still floating around inside Whitlock's head — Kai Dreyfus hallmarks that the technology Micah had at his disposal would easily be able to trace.

Kai realized she'd put herself in some deep shit, attempting to hack Soldier Whitlock. She also realized she didn't *want* to know what she'd just learned and wished she had never tried to learn Ralph's secrets.

But perhaps most importantly, she realized how she could kill Doc Stahl.

Whitlock looked at Kai, last week's well-placed bit of mental fog still obscuring his memories of ever having met her.

"What are you doing?" he said.

"What you told me to do," she purred, smiling and blinking her eyes. It was a rather obvious and clichéd gesture, but that didn't matter because she wasn't trying to seduce Whitlock or his partner. She was trying to distract them from her hands as they moved behind her back — as the fingers of her right hand thrummed a rhythm onto her left wrist.

"You're in the middle of an alley," said Whitlock, unimpressed.

"So?"

"What, are you going to beat him to death right here in public?"

"Kicked to death by a jilted woman seems like a pretty legit crime, from the police's perspective," said Kai. She took a few steps toward Whitlock, stepping like a cat. He should be close enough to smell the enhanced musk that was now churning from her pores. She inhaled, puffing her chest as she cocked her long pale neck to the side.

Whitlock's partner watched, apparently interested. But Kai wasn't trying to seduce either of them; she was exploiting the fact that smell was an extremely evocative sense. Right now, Whitlock's brain should be starting to remember Kai deep down, well below the level of consciousness. Connections were forming. He'd be realizing that he genuinely liked this woman for some reason, almost as if they'd shared a bond. In a strange way, he'd trust her. He'd want to please her. And as the motion of Kai's fingers on her arm reactivated the scavengers in his cortex, his defenses would sigh enough to let those scavengers do their work without resistance.

Whitlock's eyes took on a dreamy appearance. The corners of his mouth started to twitch, as if with memory.

"Let's finish this up," he said, looking into Kai's brown eyes.

"I'd like that."

"End it with something quick."

"Can I use your gun?"

"No," said Whitlock.

She'd known that wouldn't work, but it had been worth a shot. Not that having a gun would solve anything, she realized. She couldn't kill the soldiers, and she couldn't run. She had to *kill Doc*. That was the only way. Kai's unfair influence over Whitlock notwithstanding, the only way out was if Micah knew that she'd done what he'd told her to do.

She lowered her voice to a whisper.

"But maybe we should be alone," she said, glancing at the other soldier.

"Jameson," said Whitlock, still staring at Kai but pitching his voice toward his partner. "Report back to HQ."

Jameson looked confused. "Report what?"

Still locking eyes with Kai, Whitlock said, "Just go back."

"Why?"

"Because you're a rookie, and I'm your superior," Whitlock said.

"I think we're supposed to stay together."

Whitlock turned, his tone becoming angry. Judging by the expression on his face, his own anger seemed to surprise him. *"I* think you're supposed to fucking *listen!"*

"You might need help bringing her back," said Jameson.

Whitlock glared. "You idiot. She's doing this to prove herself. You really think I'll need to restrain her *after* she's done the job?"

Knowing it was over the top, Kai whispered to Whitlock, "You *might* have to restrain me."

Jameson looked confused but was already starting to turn. "What do you want me to tell them?"

"Whatever you fucking want!"

Still uncertain, the second man began walking back down the alley. Kai and Whitlock watched him go. The entire way, he kept glancing back. Then, a few minutes later, Kai heard the distant whine of a screetbike. They watched as it flew off over the low buildings.

Behind her back, Kai continued to tap on her forearm. Then, in front of Doc and Kai, Whitlock folded and collapsed.

Doc, still on the street below Kai, looked up. "What did you do to him?"

"Something you should keep in mind that I can do," Kai snapped, still not over her anger at Doc.

Doc sat up, wincing as he gripped his side. He looked for a moment like he was going to make a joke about what Kai had done to him, but instead he looked at the slumped soldier and said nothing.

"Now we run?" he asked.

"No," Kai said. "Now we make some memories."

<u>| Episode 6 |</u>

Chapter 1

AUGUST 13, 2023 — New York

"WOULD you like me to get something for you while you wait?" the receptionist asked Noah West.

The girl — who was pretty and petite — looked even tinier sitting at the too-large reception desk. Behind her, the word *EverCrunch* was spelled out in eighteen-inch letters. The idea of the huge desk had probably been to impart visitors with a sense of awe, but all it really did was to make the receptionist look ridiculously small. Noah found himself thinking of her as Tinkerbell, expecting her to start throwing fairy dust at any moment.

Noah looked to his left, where a conference table with heavy wooden legs was stocked with a giant coffee urn and more food than seemed necessary for anything other than a marathon pit stop. He knew it was a courtesy table, complimentary for visitors, but it seemed so wasteful. How many people came into EverCrunch on a daily basis? How many of those people needed or even *wanted* something to eat? But that wasn't the point, really. The point was that this was EverFuck-ingCrunch, and when you had as much money as EverFuck-ingCrunch, you could burn wads of cash to warm the foyer if you wanted.

"What kind of something do you mean?" Noah asked the Tinkerbell receptionist.

"Something to eat," she said, smiling. "A cup of coffee?"

Noah looked at the food table, at the receptionist, then back at the courtesy table. He'd been waiting for ten minutes, and she'd pointed out the food when he'd first come in. They had even small-talked about its variety and volume.

"Other than *that* food and coffee?" he said, pointing.

"No," she said. "I meant something from there."

Noah put a perplexed look on his face. "From this table that's right next to me?" He held up his hands. "Are you asking if you can walk around your desk, pick up something from that table, and put it into my hand?"

The receptionist giggled.

"People must really be that lazy if you're offering," said Noah, dropping his hands.

"You'd be surprised."

But Noah wouldn't be surprised at all. His father had busted his ass daily from dawn to dusk for his entire life: working land, driving tractors, repairing machinery, digging and breaking things that had to be broken. Noah had grown up under toil's unending shadow, and all it had given him throughout high school (hell, even into college) were odd, almost pitying looks. Kids whose parents shuffled papers acted like Noah should be ashamed of his father and his chosen profession as a farmer, despite the fact that Ian West out-earned all of their parents. Most people were afraid of hard work and didn't understand the need to reach out and *take* what they wanted. They expected the world to hand it over gift-wrapped instead.

"I'm unnerving you by not partaking in this banquet," Noah said. "Let me fix the problem."

For a second, Noah hung on the F in "fix." It was probably thinking of his father and the ridicule in high school that did it. But he wasn't the farmer's kid anymore, and he no longer stuttered. He wasn't ashamed of his past and didn't want to hide it, but he wouldn't be defined by it, either. A man or a woman of substance wrote their own life story, line by line, no matter how the tale was begun.

Noah stood. Then, making a show for the receptionist, he approached the food table. The girl giggled again. Noah inspected the spread, stealing glances behind him.

The table was covered in food. Easily 90 percent of it would be stale or spoiled by sundown. Noah hoped they sent it to a homeless shelter. There were still quite a few homeless shelters in New York, no matter how uniformly wealthy and optimistic people liked to believe the world was these days. Noah saw six kinds of donuts in the spread (including some fat jelly filled ones that smelled delightful), a few varieties of danishes, various spice breads, English muffins and wheat bread for toasting (there was a toaster and some condiments near the coffee urn), blueberry muffins, and various other carbohydrate bombs. Add a reservoir filled with congealed gray sausage gravy, and it would be like the continental breakfast buffet at a Holiday Inn Express.

To one side, almost neglected, sat a bowl of fruit. Noah avoided the junk and grabbed an apple, which he polished on a napkin. Then he drew a cup of black coffee from the urn and sat, took a bite, and raised his eyebrows at the receptionist.

"Better?"

"Much," she said.

The phone rang. The receptionist answered it, taking the call on a conventional phone with a cord. Noah found that worthy of note. EverCrunch had been built on technology — its compression algorithm that squished petabytes of data into a few megs of space without a corresponding decrease in access speed — and that technology had, through hosting fees alone, catapulted the company to the top of the *Fortune* list. Yet despite the astonishing things the company could do with data, the rest of EverCrunch's world seemed abjectly unremarkable, making its facility with data appear almost random.

For one thing, the company had actual physical offices. Few companies bothered to co-locate anymore, because of the expense and the way it limited the talent pool to the immediate geographic area. For another, EverCrunch used phones that ran on the unreliable fiber network. Sure, they were only using voice, but the company had Internet anyway, right? So why not tie Internet and phone together and cut the cord? Was it possible the building's Internet ran on fiber? Of course not; it'd be G10 AirFi. So then why not use cellular phones instead of corded phones — or better, something like Talkie that used the G10 directly? The oddities were all small things, but they struck Noah as almost troubling. If the company couldn't see around something so obvious (who still used corded phones?), did that explain why they couldn't see how EverCrunch compression could tag-team with the Internet and shift the nature of information forever? What other blind spots were in EverCrunch's way? It made Noah wonder if Ben Stone was actually as brilliant as the press said or if he was just a savant — a man with a beautiful mind for numbers but who didn't know when his shoes were untied.

The receptionist hung up, and Noah pitched his voice toward her.

"Question for you."

It would have been more polite to approach the desk, but Noah didn't want the receptionist to think he was hitting on her. She was cute, in her midtwenties, and around his age. She must be hit on constantly. And just as Noah had a sore spot about laziness, he also had a sore spot around the way women were treated — even in the 2020s, while men were working the moon and the world was finally getting out of its own ass and working together. Noah's sister was attractive. She got a lot of dates, but her ideas at her marketing firm were only really "taken seriously" by the men cocky enough to think they had a chance with her. Besides, Noah wouldn't have the guts to hit on her anyway. He'd grown up as a farming gamer with a speech impediment who could barely read primers at age ten, and had the confidence-related scars to prove it.

"Yes?" said Tinkerbell.

"Have there been a lot of candidates coming in recently?"

She nodded. "It's like Willy Wonka announcing he'd let a tour through the chocolate factory. The minute they listed the job, résumés poured in like the faucet had stopped working."

Résumés. Of course EverCrunch would receive *résumés.* Probably on *paper*, stapled in the corner, and detailing five years spent getting official degrees that were obsolete before the ink on them had dried. It was like the corded phone and the failure to see the applications of their own code. What did a *résumé* tell a company, other than that the applicant was proficient at listing bullshit on a template?

"How did they sort through all of them?"

The girl giggled again. Noah thought it was distinctly possible that *she* liked *him*, but having never been a lady killer, he had a hard time believing he wasn't imagining things.

"What?" he said, not understanding her lack of response.

She shrugged. "I don't know if I should say."

"Trade secret?"

"Maybe."

Knowing he was being manipulative but curious to proceed, Noah said, "No offense, but if it were a trade secret, do you think the receptionist would know about it?"

She could have gotten offended at that, but she didn't. Instead, she seemed to agree and then answered the question. "I guess not. Okay, they shredded them."

"Ouch."

"You know how they call Mr. Stone 'Buddha's Brain'?

Well, it's not just because of the shaved head. He's really into Eastern thinking." She looked around as if keenly aware of her lips loosening. She became louder after noting that every door into the offices was closed. Electronic soundproofing would be standard in a building so new, which meant that whatever she said, no one else would hear. "Anyway, he got an idea from…I don't know, a monk test or something. They kept rejecting people, tossing their résumés. Then they would wait to see who came back in spite of being turned away."

"And those people got interviews."

"Well, I think they're scheduled," she said, looking upward as if in realization that no actual interviews had been conducted.

The phone rang again, and the receptionist took the call, but Noah had already decided not to press her further. He drained his coffee and chewed his apple to a core, mentally stringing the pieces together. If the girl knew more about the hiring process, she really *shouldn't* tell him, and he already knew what he needed to anyway. Even the die-hard applicants for the EverCrunch opening, who'd kept coming back after being rebuked, hadn't landed face time with the boss. And yet here Noah was, ready to meet Stone in person. And what was more, he hadn't called them; it was EverCrunch that had made first contact. Why?

But Noah had a guess about that, too.

The job posting had come with an attachment — a form EverCrunch wanted applicants to fill out in consideration for the job. It looked like a personality assessment, which made sense given EverCrunch's secretive and paranoid reputation. (Whispers said employees had to sign a contract — something between the world's strictest nondisclosure agreement and a loyalty oath, and secrecy surrounding EverCrunch's code was CIA strong.) Asking applicants to fill out a screening form wasn't at all surprising. But Noah had been as curious about the form as he'd been about the receptionist's corded phone because it wasn't fillable. Applicants would have to print the form out and fill it in by hand. At first, Noah was almost insulted; how could such a simple detail be overlooked by a tech company? But as he'd begun to pull at the question's frayed edges, he'd discovered a few hundred K of code that comprised a background image on the document. Only on further inspection, that block of extra code proved to be not just an image, but also a puzzle.

Intrigued, Noah had examined and then cracked the puzzle like a Rubik's Cube. When he was finished, those few hundred K of code had bloomed into something larger (Ever-Crunch compression in action), unfolded into a virus, force-executed on his machine, then died. As best as Noah could tell, the virus did nothing other than send a single email. Noah saw that email again when buddhasbrain@evercrunch.com sent a reply to it, asking him when he could come in for a meeting.

Something dinged unseen on the receptionist's computer. She lifted her head and said, "Mr. West?"

Noah looked up.

"Mr. Stone will see you now."

Noah stood, smiled at the receptionist…and then, feeling guilty for having objectified her as Tinkerbell, noted her nameplate.

"Thank you, Denise," he said.

"Do you want me to take that for you?" she said, indicating the empty coffee cup in Noah's hand that contained his spent apple core.

"Are you asking if you can walk around your desk, take this cup from my hand, and drop it in that can that's five feet in front of me?"

She laughed. "You'd be surprised."

He tossed the cup into the garbage, gave her a serious look, and followed a hallway to a door that had just opened at its end. Behind him, Denise the receptionist laughed again. Yes, she seemed to like Noah West just fine.

The man in the open doorway looked like a poorly outfitted assistant — barefoot, dressed in a loose-fitting blue T-shirt and gray yoga pants — but Noah recognized him from photos on multiple covers on many of his favorite magazines. Ben Stone *never* seemed to dress up…or, for that matter, act remotely businesslike enough to justify his spot at the helm of one of the richest, most desired companies in the world. Stone shaved his head to a shine and had a warm, welcoming smile. Noah felt an instant kinship with him. Based on what he'd read about Stone, he knew that the icon had also grown up as a gamer and had fought with his parents to turn a fierce love of gaming into something that looked less dope-smoking-on-the-couch unproductive. Stone was barely thirty, just five years older than Noah. He'd started EverCrunch as a school project and, as the billions rolled in, never seemed to treat it any more seriously than that. His office had a yoga mat on the floor and a few cartoon figurines lined up along the front edge of his unas-suming desk. The figurines were arranged in chronological order like a 3-D timeline: a 1940s-era Mickey Mouse, a Bugs Bunny, an Opus, a Phineas beside a Ferb, a Finn and Jake from *Adventure Time*, a Molly Destructo, and a Bill the Borg from *Dumb Space Opera*.

Stone closed the door behind Noah, crossed the room, and sat on his yoga mat. The move could easily have seemed pretentious, but somehow it worked. Noah knew if he sat on the mat near Stone, it *would* seem pretentious, so he sat on an overturned crate instead. Whether the crate was supposed to be there or whether it was a holdover from a delivery of some sort, Noah had no idea. But he had to sit on it if he wanted to sit at all, given that there appeared to be no chairs in the room.

"You solved Buddha's Box," said Stone without introducing himself or shaking Noah's hand. He'd sat on the mat then stated the truth.

"Sorry?"

"The puzzle. Did you catch the allusion?"

Noah felt like he'd walked into a funhouse. "Sorry?" he repeated.

"I'm a bit of a pop culture nerd," said Stone, gesturing at the figurines on his desk. "My dad was one, and so I became one too. I learned to love his favorites, so I'm not just a pop culture nerd; I'm an *oldies* pop culture nerd. But that's how you get cred as a nerd. You make references that no one understands because they're too obscure. Like being into punk rock, actually." He waved a hand. "Anyway. The box? It came from an old horror movie called *Hellraiser*. That's what the background image was: the puzzle box from that movie."

Noah shook his head.

Stone seemed disappointed. "I figured someone would see the image, recognize it, and get the idea that it might hold a puzzle."

Noah shrugged, wishing he could participate.

"Bah," said Stone. "Just as well. The box in *Hellraiser* opened doors, and creatures came out. Who wants to crack *that* puzzle? So. Without catching the reference, how did you even know there was anything there to solve?"

Noah realized he wasn't sure himself. He answered the best he could, wondering if he was telling the truth: "I just like to take things apart."

"Interesting. Anyway, you were the only one," said Stone. "Well, you and the NSA. But they keep bugging me, and I'm *not* hiring an NSA agent. I haven't trusted them since the WOPR in *WarGames*."

After a silent moment, Stone made an *I-give-up* gesture. If his applicant didn't even know what a WOPR was, there seemed to be no way they could speak on common ground.

Noah felt lost. He'd been so cocksure when he'd seen what

Stone was calling the Buddha's Box puzzle. In the two weeks since, he'd rehearsed his enumeration of EverCrunch's glaring business oversight in the mirror. He'd spent so much time deciding that EverCrunch's CEO had simply gotten lucky and didn't know what he was doing that he now felt totally disarmed. Sure, Stone was outdoing him on obscure trivia, but he was outdoing him nonetheless.

"Fine," said Stone. "I'll stop. But you're really missing out. It's not like I'm that much older than you. If you're going to work here, I'm at least going to need you to see *Star Wars Episodes* 4 through 6 and the *Matrix* movies. There *will* be a quiz. Anyway. This is your time, so let's hear from you, not me. I need new blood. Someone very, very, very smart. The pay for the position I have in mind will make your brain explode, but you'll have to promise me your soul. I'm only kidding. But also not really. And I *will* need you to convince me."

"I solved the puzzle," said Noah.

Stone waved his hand. "Yes, yes. But so did the NSA, and I hate those bastards. You still have to make me believe. Who *is* Noah West? Why do I care? What do you have to give the world? What the hell makes you think the world will care to remember your name when you're gone?"

"Big questions," said Noah, feeling disarmed.

Stone shrugged. "Yeah, well, I'm a Buddhist." He sat, cross-legged with bare feet and waited. Noah stared at him for a minute. The CEO stared back, his expression polite but anticipatory. Stone had finished, and now it was Noah's turn.

"I'm good with computers," said Noah. "With code. I can see a million ways to improve Internet connectivity — not just bringing it to more people, but helping it to evolve, and…"

"Yawn. Move along."

"I have unmatched scores in the fields of…"

"Oh, Jesus. The other shit was better. Don't start giving me your grades. Next thing, you'll be sending me a résumé."

Noah almost laughed at that, but instead he found himself getting irritated. Stone was too cavalier sitting on his mat, letting Noah do all the work, making him jump through hoops while he sat in judgment.

"I think you're missing vast sections of the marketplace for data archiving," Noah said, speaking quickly, almost sniping with his words. "Your compression destroys everyone else, and the only reason everyone isn't using EverCrunch is because they're too lazy to switch or don't realize that staying with another provider is…"

Stone moved as if to stand. "Okay. Thanks for coming in, but I don't think this is going to work out."

Jesus Fucking Christ. The asshole wasn't even listening. How was he supposed to judge Noah's ideas when he wouldn't even hear him out? What did he expect? What the hell else would *anyone* do for his company with its dumbass blind spots, its CEO sitting around doing fucking yoga while missing the entire point of data compression…not to store it, but to move it faster. *That* was how EverCrunch would benefit if they hired him, if this asshole would just listen for a second instead of…

"Why do you use corded phones?" Noah blurted.

Stone was halfway to standing. He paused, one arm propping him up, his right leg on the mat, his left leg in a squat.

"I'm sorry?"

Noah reached over and flicked at the cord hanging from Stone's desk phone. "Cords. Your phones have cords."

Stone sat. "Yes, they do. Why does it matter?"

"Tell me why you have corded phones," said Noah. He was out of line, but it looked like he'd blown the interview already anyway.

"The office just came that way," said Stone.

"But you pay for the phone bill. It's not bundled in."

"Right…"

"Well, you're the world's biggest technology company. And you're not fucking paying attention."

Stone shook his head. "I'm sorry?"

"You're using technology that no one uses anymore 'because it's the way things have always been done.' You want a sign that you're not innovating and just got lucky with one big hit? That's it. You aren't asking *why* or *how.* You got into the lead by luck, and now you're just coasting. You're following."

"I don't see the big deal. It's nickel-and-diming. What would we save? A few hundred bucks?"

"It's not about money," Noah snapped, suddenly angry. "It's about blindness. You discovered you could take data and make it very, very small. Good for you. But that's not enough. Remember Dropbox? You're Dropbox 2.0. That's great until someone else comes up with a 3.0. You're thinking one-dimensionally. Who gives a shit if you can make data small? Storage is already dirt cheap. What are you going to do when people figure out that small doesn't mean much in a world where storage is unlimited?"

"Now wait a minute. We do more than just compress data for storage…"

"Oh, sure. You *sync* it. You make data small, and then you sync it. People everywhere who enjoy things that are small and synchronized, rejoice! Just imagine the sponsorship opportunities in midget water ballet!" He made jazz hands. "But all you've done is nudge our same old way of thinking a bit further down the line. For a while you'll be ahead…until someone smarter catches up. You haven't changed the paradigm. Google changed the game. Amazon changed the game. You've taken the same game and made it better."

Stone looked angry. From where Noah was standing, it felt great to see the Zen flee his eyes.

"How the hell are *you* going to change the game?" he said.

Noah lowered his tone, made it more conversational. "You need to use the network. Don't be Dropbox 2.0. Be the *Internet* 2.0. What would happen if you applied EverCrunch compression to data packets on the net? You can compress and decompress on the fly, so what's to stop you from baking that into the fabric of a new network that could ride on the current one's shoulders? Right now, data people — that's you — want to make information *smaller*. Network people — that's the ISPs and the G10 companies — want to make transfer *faster*. But what I'm shocked that you of all companies can't see is that there are two ways to effectively make things happen faster. One is to move the same amount of data faster. The other is to move at the same speed, but shuttle a lot more data."

Stone's mouth hung open. "Holy shit."

"Think of what could be sent using a data stream that's as compressed as you could make it. Holography. True VR. Maybe, some day, teleportation. And that's just transfer across distance. You've heard this new stuff with nanobots? You know the problem with nanos, right? They're tiny, but the atoms needed to make them up don't get any smaller. Trying to build nanobots is like trying to make a highly detailed six-foot-tall sculpture with Legos the size of my torso. They can't have many moving parts because until mankind manages to shrink atoms, the building blocks are just too damn big. But what if what they lack in brawn could be made up for through intelligent cooperation?"

With that, Noah stopped. He'd already given Stone one trillion-dollar idea, and he'd almost handed him a second. If Stone hired him, the first idea was worth the surrender. Later, when Noah started his own company, he could develop the second. And the other was a *doozy*. Data compression and highly coordinated transmission could make nanotechnology infinitely viable and applicable — much, *much* more than was currently thought possible. Once engineers could stop worrying about freezing a nanobot into one configuration forever and sending it out into the world as a one-function drone, the world's potential would split like an overripe coconut.

Stone stared at Noah. He lowered his head then raised it again.

"When can you start?"

"Are you offering me the job?" Noah asked, trying to bury his growing elation.

"Yes," said Stone. "Absolutely." He appeared shell-shocked.

Noah raised palms to ceiling. "You haven't told me what the job pays."

"All the money in the world," said Ben Stone.

Chapter 2

Leo arrived in the city, out of place and looking mystified. Leah couldn't help but laugh. She knew he used to visit the city semiregularly back before the wars and the bombs, before the second Renaissance people called the Renewal, when it had still been called New York. Leo, in Leah's mind, had the same tendency as most old people — a peculiar way of seeing things as they used to be. Old people never stopped being surprised that Beam walls lit when you touched them, no matter how many years they'd been seeing it. And in the same way, Leo had apparently never stopped seeing District Zero as it had been in the first part of the century.

"You look like the country mouse," Leah said, watching him approach.

Even in a city as diverse as District Zero, Leo seemed out of place. He looked around at everything; he sniffed the air; he seemed amazed by the hoverskippers and hovercabs that jammed the streets like a sprawling Tetris puzzle. If Leo had had an ocular implant, he'd probably have been raising his hands in front of him like a picture frame to indicate images for capture, like a tourist. He'd told Leah that he'd been active in old New York during the 2030s turmoil, and Leah had gotten the impression that he'd even led a group — perhaps a precursor to Organa. But that was a long, long time ago.

"It smells here," said the old man, still standing while Leah remained seated.

She had waited for him in a SoHo cafe. SoHo could be a dangerous neighborhood, but it was a sunny day, and Leah had taken the precaution of sitting outside. She hadn't wanted to stay in Chinatown. For a reason she couldn't explain, doing so felt like a jinx, like staying at the scene of the crime. It had taken a while for her to shake the feeling that Crumb, who seemed to have somehow let her into and out of the secret lab, was right over her shoulder. She hadn't stopped walking until the strange sensation had gone away. That had happened near Houston. She'd stared at the burned-out boutiques and the gang tags, shrugged, and figured that good luck and fate had been on her side so far. So she'd sat.

"You mean that it *doesn't* smell," said Leah. "You haven't been here since they added the air filtration, have you?"

"Air filtration?"

"Read a feed article or two, Leo," she said, laughing.

"I read plenty," he said, apparently uninterested in hilarity at his expense. "I read every word of the distillation sheets that come to the co-op. But there's a lot more to the NAU than District Zero, you know."

Leah held up her hands. "Okay, okay. I hereby retract my mockery about you not reading The Beam and will focus any *new* mockery on you being an insufferable hermit. How long has it been?"

"Since they added air filtration, apparently," said Leo sniffing. He sat in a wrought Plasteel chair opposite her. "Did you find Crumb?"

"I think so, yes. Or at least, I know which direction to go."

"You know 'which direction'?" said Leo, puzzled. Then he nodded slowly. "So you *don't* know where he is."

"It's hard to explain. I think he wants me to find him,

though. I'm confident that if I head in that direction and access along the way, I'll find the trail."

"What, like a map?"

"No, not like a map. And not a series of clues on The Beam either, like a scavenger hunt."

It was hard to explain the sense she had — that a cloud of intuition was floating above her, across the whole city like a low fog, and that all she'd need to do to access it would be to stand up into it. So in order to break Leo in, Leah told him how she'd found the building in Chinatown, how Crumb's mind had seemed to let her in, and how she'd felt him behind her all the way to SoHo. Leo, who couldn't help thinking of The Beam as a super-Internet despite knowing better, didn't seem to get it at all. So Leah sighed and repeated that it was hard to explain and that he'd just have to trust her.

Leo asked to see the diary. Leah showed it to him. Then Leo read it from start to finish, taking his time, while Leah sipped on a soda. Finally, he looked up.

"This is amazing. Do you believe it?"

"Oh yes. I was *in* the lab. If Stephen York isn't who that diary claims he is or if Stephen York didn't write that diary, then whoever did is a very smart, very creative impostor. There's stuff in there about The Beam that I never realized, but that I recognize as true now that I've read it. The fact that there's a subtle wireframe beneath it, for instance. If you just 'use' The Beam, you'll never see its layers, but if you hack, you'll find yourself delving into its guts. And now I can see the way the modern Beam was built on something older that must be Crossbrace. The old Internet is there too, even further down. The Beam infrastructure touches pretty much everything, but did you know there are still sectors where the systems use TCP/IP? Some of the AI clusters use it to talk to others, like a dialect. And it's not just protocols, either. Sometimes, you can find stuff in L33t."

Leo shook his head. This was common when she talked to

him about pretty much anything. At first, she'd thought it was simply a Leo affect, but she later realized he pretty much only did the head-shaking thing to her. Maybe it was because Leah — enhanced and technically gifted — was such an oddity amongst the Organas. She just had a way of talking over his head.

"I have no idea what you're talking about," he said.

"AI has personality, is all I'm saying. At a certain point, you have to stop thinking about The Beam as a computer network and start thinking of it like a community. It's like DZ itself. There are digital neighborhoods inside of The Beam's programming. Different AI appropriates different elements from its environment to create its 'culture.' The oldest structures inside are relics of our earliest attempts at connectivity. The oldest ones harvested CompuServe and AOL to build their neighborhoods. Some seem to have learned from 1980s hacker forums, and do things like speak in L33t."

Leo kept shaking his head.

"You never understood," said Leah. "Just trust me."

"Of course I trust you," said Leo. "When it comes to The Beam, it's all you all the time. I don't say this enough, Leah, but Organa can't survive without you. It's one thing to sit in the mountains and smoke dust, but another to understand the system enough to make our way within it."

Leah smiled, touched.

"I try to understand," he said. "But to me, what's in this journal is simultaneously troubling and unbelievable. Don't get me wrong; I *believe* it just fine. What I mean is…West's mind is *on* The Beam? We know he's out there because he's the default on every canvas. Go into a public building, and a Noah West holo will probably be there to greet you. Hell, on my train ride over, Noah West came into the compartment and insisted I watch a safety demonstration because I don't have a Beam ID, so it couldn't confirm that I'd ever been on a train before to see the demo. But this is different, isn't it?" He tapped the journal's leather cover.

Leah sighed. There was something she could tell Leo that might help him to understand, but she'd never told anyone before and didn't really want to open herself up that much, even to Leo. But then, Leo had his own secrets, didn't he? Everyone did. Leo didn't like to talk about his old days in New York. It was a soft spot for him. But they were embarking on a long, strange trip together, and so Leah figured she might as well be the first to roll over and expose her underbelly.

"Leo," she said, "have you ever heard of anthroposophy?"

He shook his head.

"It used to be a kind of scientific approach to spirituality, but once people started getting so connected to The Beam and everyone on the network got used to its presence 24/7 as if it were part of them, it started being about The Beam's reality instead. I guess the original idea of anthroposophy was to discover the real, objective world of spirituality, and what has happened is that modern anthroposophists believe The Beam has given us access to that world."

Leo looked at the journal then at Leah. "Is this like what happened with the church?"

Leah felt slapped. "Oh God, no. This is closer to...well, like the alternative spiritualists you've told me about from back in the day. Where people would take cocaine to get in touch with themselves?"

Leo laughed. "Cocaine didn't exactly get you in touch with anything other than hyperactivity."

"Well, whatever. *Drugs.* Hallucinogenics. Head trips. Like us with moondust, only real." Leah wrinkled her nose. She was as addicted to dust as the rest of the Organas and loved the glaze it gave her, and there was some truth to the idea that moondust showed you a deeper truth from reality. She needed dust for hacking, but in the end it still felt like a poseur drug. Leah had never liked doing something that everyone else did (mainly because she wanted to be unique, even among a group of people who all insisted on being unique in the exact same way), and a part of her resented that she used dust, given that it was exactly what people expected an Organa girl with pink dreadlocks, piercings, and various bright sarongs to do.

"Not that moondust isn't real," she charged on, not entirely sure if Leo, who kept the village supplied, might take offense. "I just mean…*more* real."

"It's okay," said Leo. "I know what you mean."

"When you sent me into DZ for training and I was away from the community for a while, I started meeting people at the college. Some of them were into this old drug that was supposed to purge you in a way and show you the truth." She looked up at Leo to see his reaction. He nodded. "It was superexpensive, but some of the kids in DZ? Well, they have good money. Anyway, you were supposed to drink this stuff. Like shots. Then you purged."

"Purged?

"Barfed. They even started you with a bucket. The buckets were red." As if that mattered, but the red in Leah's memory was as vivid as the black that came later. "After that, you'd experience something unique to you, and you'd have to overcome it. Flushing your demons, I guess. Purging bullshit the world had laid over you."

"Then what?" Leo asked. He was watching her closely. It dawned on Leah how strange it was to be teaching Leo anything. He was a spiritual yogi. He'd done his share of drugs, plus plenty of other people's shares. Little old Leah finding something he'd not done, didn't know about, and that *she* could guide *him* through was downright surreal.

"For me, I felt this deep sense of connection. I don't know how to describe it any other way. It's like the earth was my body. I could feel everyone at once; I could feel the trees; I could feel the sun and the sky and the clouds. Is this making me sound like a total spaced-out idiot?"

Leo shook his head. "No. But I'm really curious about what the hell it has to do with Crumb and The Beam and West."

"Once I was in that place, Leo — once I'd gotten past some of the worst of the darkness inside me, mostly having to do with my mom and being abandoned, I guess — I started to think about The Beam. I hooked in, through my port, which I'd installed not long before. The idea to do it was just *there*. And once I'd hooked in, I started seeing through the infrastructure, code, and hardware. I don't know how to describe it, but it was like I went *into* The Beam. I didn't feel like I was plugging in and surfing or even Beamwalking. I didn't feel like I left my body, but my body became like only *part* of me, as if it were just my leg or something. The rest of me, I realized, was something more. I could feel The Beam as if I were all of it, and a part of everyone connected to it. And The Beam was its own thing, too, quite separately — complete with its own identity. I saw how we're all connected, and that while The Beam wasn't necessary for that connection, it was like a lubricant. A facilitator. The Beam gave us a new way to feel the connection that was already there.

"I explored for what felt like days, though it was really only hours. I reached out with what felt like new arms and could see the entire whole world at once. There are old, barricaded data pipelines leading out of the NAU on The Beam, and I could see right through their obstructions. I experienced the Wild East. I experienced the sky, where the data goes out to satellites. I took parts of it into me and felt like I left pieces of myself behind, like you would leave something behind if you stirred a pot of hot soup with a spoon made of melting chocolate. And while I was in those many places, I realized that wherever I went, The Beam was a thing within a thing within a thing. And at the very core, like the center in a piece of candy, was something I can only describe as human will. It was like the first networks had been started with an idea, and the creators had left that idea inside. They had wanted to connect people, and the idea had remained as if pieces of those creators were still there. Every layer added to the technology has been a bigger and better attempt to fulfill that original idea, but the thought has always been there at the core, realized to a greater or lesser degree. To me, that core of human will felt like a pond with a bunch of straws poked into its surface. The oldest straws — to the first systems connected to the pre-Internet — were small. The newest straws, leading out to The Beam, were like giant pipes. At the time, since I felt so connected to everything, the solution to fully realizing that core idea seemed so obvious, and it was something that the Internet, Crossbrace, and The Beam have all missed — at least in their original, tangible construction."

"And what they missed was…?"

"That the network had evolved to a point where it's more than the sum of its parts," said Leah. She shifted in her chair, feeling District Zero's clean breeze in her hair. "You know how I talk about The Beam like it has a soul, personality, will, and all of that? Same idea. I did a lot of studying in the months following that drug trip. I wanted to find out if any of what I'd experienced was true or if I'd just been whacked out. And when I studied, I found some interesting parallels. For instance, think about brains. The simplest life forms don't have brains. They have ways to sense their environments, but it's all stimulus and response, like bacteria moving toward food. Higher up, things get more complex. You get ganglia, which are nerve clusters — closer to brains, but not quite. Bugs move toward lights. Worms seek out food. And so on, up the chain. Squid identify patterns and understand what's a fish and how they can capture and eat it. Octopi can use tools. Apes are damn near like us. At a certain point, you'd say there's a 'mind' there. Nobody can agree where that line is (most people agree that dogs 'think' like we do, but it's harder to say that about bugs), but there's no doubt that once a collection of neurons becomes complex enough, they do more than the neurons should be able to do in and of themselves. The Beam is like that. It started as a network, but it became a mind. Now it can tap that original pond — that sense of human will and intention at its center — on its own. Quark, West, and York didn't build a mind, though. They built a system, and the system evolved. Because it saw its own purpose — that first spark of an idea that begat its creation — and sought to fulfill it."

"You talk about The Beam like it's alive," said Leo.

Leah shrugged. "Maybe it is. But really, where is your mind, Leo? Not your brain, but your *mind?* Is it in your head? And if it is, where does intuition come from? Where does creativity come from? When you go into a moondust haze and feel like something is working through you, what is that something, and where is it coming from? I'm telling you, Leo. Today, Crumb has been *with* me, right over my shoulder. I haven't even been plugged in. He guided me to the lab; he let me in. Maybe West really is out there too."

She stopped, taking a long drink from her soda and giving Leo time to react. It was all out there now. She doubted Leo would judge her, seeing as he led a hippie community filled with drug addicts, but he might think her airheaded and ungrounded. The mountain Organas kept their heads in the clouds, but Leah was supposed to be the objectivist. She was supposed to be the anchor. Leo had sent her to QuarkTechnic and a dozen specialized schools to steep her in hard, ones-and-zeros skills. She was Organa, but she was also not Organa at all. Leo might be disappointed that he'd ended up with another spiritualist instead of the realist his community needed.

Leo remained silent, apparently still digesting what she'd told him.

"You think I imagined it all, don't you?" said Leah.

"Maybe. But maybe not. If I didn't think there were bigger truths out there in the world, I wouldn't wear headbands like this." Leo touched his forehead. Today's headband was powder blue and sported a peace sign. "I guess the question is, can you find Crumb? Because if you can, it'd be hard not to believe you."

"Oh yes," she said. "I get the impression that he's looking to be found. But there's another thing, too, and I have no idea what it means."

Leo raised his eyebrows.

"Wherever he is and whoever he's with, it all feels very familiar to me, like déjà vu."

"Like déjà vu?"

"Wherever Crumb is," said Leah, trying to articulate the odd feeling she'd been wrestling with over the past few hours, "feels to me like going home."

<h1 style="text-align:center">Chapter 3</h1>

Nicolai sat in Central Park, near the monument, thinking about how when people said the world was your oyster, they only focused on the pearl. But even before the ocean outside the lattice went toxic with fallout, oysters were edible only by those who didn't mind pollution. Sure, the world could be your oyster, and sure, that might mean that every once in a while, you might get lucky and find a pearl. But nine times out of ten, you just cut the fuck out of your hand with the shucking knife and were rewarded with a stinking booger full of the world's purified shit.

Now that he was free of Isaac (and, honestly, feeling more than a little guilty about it), Nicolai could do whatever he wanted. The world truly was his oyster. But how to find the pearl amidst all the looming shit? He'd almost certainly move to Enterprise when Shift came in twenty-three days, but what then? The implication that the ability to do anything automatically translated to a better life was based on faulty logic. Too many options left few guarantees. Nicolai had been nursing dissatisfaction for months (okay, years), but he'd never given serious consideration to what he might do instead. He had the whole ocean to move about in, yes. But his boat had no rudder.

Nicolai knew what he *wanted* to do. He *wanted* to write; he *wanted* to paint; he *wanted* to learn to play the fantastic piano collecting dust in his apartment. Sure, he had the credits to be pointlessly artistic for a while, but then what? He was well-off today, but he was still Presque Beau, not the mythical Beau Monde. The ultra-rich could achieve critical mass if they invested right; they could use their existing money to stay wealthy forever. But Nicolai's bank account, while large, was finite. *He* didn't have critical mass. Every day he eschewed a job and acted like a future starving artist, his account would lose a handful of credits. After enough time — probably before the next Shift in 2103 — he'd run empty. Then what would he do with his writing and piano playing? He'd be just another creative soul in the gutter, selling the fantastic piano for another year's rent in a middle-of-the-road apartment.

Of course, that was the worst-case scenario, and not at all likely. Nicolai had gone from an insane amount of family wealth to nothing while crossing Europe before he'd returned to crazy (not-quite-insane) wealth in America. During his days of wandering, he'd hunted animals to live, built shelters, killed those who threatened him, and ambushed those who had what he needed. There was no shame when civilization's cheery mask crumbled from its face — no honor among thieves, one might say. Nicolai had no doubt that if he were thrown naked and penniless into the darkest Enterprise ghetto, he'd claw his way out in a matter of weeks. He wasn't the kind of man who fell under another's foot. He wasn't usually arrogant, but truth twas truth: Nicolai was far too fine for the gutter. The best and most cunning always survived, Nicolai knew he was both.

But right now, he *wasn't* poor, and he *wasn't* being thrown into the gutter. He was rich, and if he made the right moves now, he could stay rich forever. He could even remain Directorate, collect a dole, do nothing all day, and let his accumulated wealth sustain him indefinitely. But Nicolai wasn't like that. He couldn't be idle. He couldn't leave his abilities in their holsters. He had to come out blazing and do something remarkable. The question was: What?

Nicolai didn't want to crawl back to Isaac. He didn't really want to go to Micah Ryan's camp either, though that was probably the most logical move. For one, Micah was everything his brother wasn't and didn't need a right hand. Every politician needed strong, persuasive speechwriters, but Nicolai wasn't cut out to be just one man in a stable of others. He wouldn't want to be *a* speechwriter; he'd want to be *the* speechwriter. And really, he didn't want to be *a* speechwriter at all. Wasn't that what he'd been lamenting for years — the feeling that he was whoring out perfectly good talent to manufacture half truths and outright lies? No, he didn't want to be in politics. And he didn't want to work for Micah Ryan.

Nicolai saw Micah in a way that Isaac was blind to. Micah was ruthless. He hadn't led Ryan Enterprises into the empty north when the ice had melted to seize unseized spoils. He'd driven out those who were already there, already staking their claims. He'd aggressively bought them out, made threats, and (Nicolai suspected but couldn't prove) hired roughnecks to sharpen the point on his message. Micah's men had a way of getting into trouble with the law then suddenly no longer being his men. Sometimes, Micah's men vanished. Yet Isaac was blind to his brother's manipulations — his brother's manipulations of *Isaac* prominent among them. Micah could play his brother like a fiddle, and Isaac never quite saw it happening. They even met once a month in private, despite their public rivalry. Ostensibly it was "a brother thing that Nicolai would never understand," but it wasn't just Nicolai who was excluded. Nobody was allowed in those meetings — not Natasha, not Micah and Ryan's mother, Rachel, not anyone — and Isaac always came back from them beaten.

Nicolai had been urging Isaac for years to cut his brother from his life, but Isaac always said that blood was blood, and you didn't turn your back on blood.

It was beyond frustrating. Nicolai's job was to give Isaac advice to help him succeed and keep him safe, but when it came to Micah, Isaac flat-out didn't listen to anyone. The brothers shared the responsibility of taking care of Rachel — mainly shuttling her to her many enhancement appointments; she was nearly 130 years old, so her add-ons never quite took — but Isaac always ended up doing most of the work. Micah sat with Rachel; Isaac ran errands for Rachel. Micah had long discussions with his mother; Isaac hired contractors to do work around her house and walked her dog. Nicolai tried to point out the inequity in the relationship, but Isaac was willfully blind. Rachel still controlled the family fortune and held the majority stake in Ryan Enterprises, which their father had founded. Micah was gaining favor, strengthening his position as her favorite. Isaac, on the other hand, was checking off her list of to-do's.

Well, fuck Isaac. If Isaac was too stupid to see how his brother, his mother, and his wife used him like a puppet to get what they wanted, then he deserved what he got. Nicolai didn't want to — and now, no longer had to — be part of it. Not part of Isaac's faltering machine or Micah's steamroller… and definitely not part of *Natasha's* machine. Hers might be the most dangerous of all. She'd tried to get Nicolai into bed no fewer than a dozen times over the years they'd all known one another, and she'd nearly succeeded several times when Nicolai had been weak or lubricated. The fallout, had he succumbed, would have been disastrous. Nicolai liked Natasha. He kind of wanted Natasha, when he wasn't loathing or afraid of her. So maybe it was best to stay away from her entirely now that he'd cut the cord.

Nicolai's ear rang. He answered without bothering to ask for the caller's ID then nearly fell over when he heard

Natasha's voice. She'd bloomed from his thoughts, grabbing him by the cortex and scrambling over him like a spider, a black widow, a beautiful and deadly thing that…

But it was only Kai Dreyfus.

"Nicolai! You *are* alive!"

It was a bizarre thing for Kai to say. He thought he might have misheard, but Kai had spoken as plain as day.

"*Me?*" he said. "I was trying to reach *you*."

"When?"

"Yester…" He stopped mid-word, remembering his missing day and a half. Yeah, that was another thing he needed to spend some time working out. "The other day," he finished.

"You're not pleasantly surprised that I'm alive?" she asked.

Okay. He could play along. "Sure," he said. "Go, you."

"Are you hurt?"

"Hurt? Why would I be hurt? No, I'm not hurt."

"Did you get Neuralin? Are you hiding, or did they really let you go free?"

Nicolai cocked his head to the side. His implant thought he was trying to add another party to the call so he kicked his head the other way to cancel the accidental request. He'd have to go right at this. The games were driving him nuts. "Kai, what the hell is going on? Just give me the full rundown, okay?"

There was a long pause. Nicolai heard a thumping on Kai's end, as if she'd dropped an armload of laundry. He thought he heard someone grunt. Kai sounded almost out of breath. She wouldn't call him while screwing some guy, would she?

"Oh," said Kai. "Nicolai, when did you talk to me last?"

"Few days, I think. When we went to Vesuvio. I left you a message or two after that."

"I see."

"What?"

"I'll explain in person. Now unfortunately, this is going to seem stranger to you than it should, so just trust me that there's a reason for it. Promise?"

He wasn't about to promise shit regarding this particular conversation. So he just said, "A reason for what?" He felt both bothered and intrigued. Kai was never like this. For one, she was being so mysterious. She was normally dead straight, and not into games. And secondly, though Kai had always been honest with him, Nicolai had never heard her so…so *real*. Kai the escort had a way of speaking, a way of breathing, a way of lilting her voice that she'd trained herself to do and could now no longer help, even when she was with Nicolai. This wasn't Kai the escort. This was Kai the woman. This was her as she'd been born, with no posturing, seducing, or bullshit added. This was her naked voice — ironically, the voice she'd use when there would be no getting naked anytime soon.

"I need you to get me into the Ryans' penthouse," she said.

She might as well have said she needed him to dress like a clown and run the DZ marathon pulling a wagon filled with Twinkies.

"What?"

Now she sounded even more out of breath. She was almost heaving. Nicolai gave Kai a lot of latitude and not a lot she did could bother him, but he didn't think he wanted to hear her have an orgasm. Or fake one. But then, as he listened, there was another thump, and she yelled at someone on her end of the connection. Something about "stop dropping him."

"What the hell are you doing, Kai?"

"I'm sorry. I'm taking a heavy load here."

"Gross."

"No, not…hang on." She yelled at the other person again. This time it was just swearing, nothing specific. When she returned, she was all business and to the point. "Noah Fucking West, Nicolai. Just trust me, okay?"

"Um…"

"Where are you?" she asked.

"In the park."

"Where in the park?"

"By the monument."

Pause. More out-of-breath noises.

"Okay. I'll meet you there. Ten, fifteen minutes. I'm bringing Doc Stahl. You know him, right?"

Doc?

Something desperately wanted to connect in Nicolai's mind. Doc had something for Nicolai. He grasped for what it was then found it. *His chip.* His upgraded creativity wetchip. He'd been so eager to get the chip. He'd been bugging Doc about it for days. Doc had called him and had left a message telling him it was in. Factoring in his missing time, that had to have been days ago. So why hadn't Nicolai picked it up? Reflecting, he seemed to remember being excited, anticipating, going for the chip. Yet he didn't have it; he couldn't sense it inside him. How had his trip to Doc's ended? He had a vague sense that he'd arrived to find Doc gone then went home empty-handed, content to try the next day. The memory was dull but ill-fitting, like a patch-job. When the brain had a hole, it tended to make up something to fill it. So was that the beginning of his missing time? What had happened between going to Doc's on Friday night and waking up this morning?

"Yeah, I know him. Ask him if he has my wetchip," said Nicolai.

Kai laughed. Her voice pitched to that same someone else, who was apparently Doc. She asked him if he had Nicolai's wetchip. Doc laughed, dry in the distance. Some joke was passed between them that Nicolai didn't get. But at least he was beginning to believe they weren't having sex.

"He says he'll give it to you if you get us into the penthouse," Kai said.

"I don't even work for…" Nicolai started, but then the connection broke as Kai ended the call. "I don't even work for him anymore," he finished.

Alone again, Nicolai stood and strolled listlessly around the monument. It showed an enormous stern-faced soldier in an American military uniform holding an old machine gun over his shoulder. Nicolai had never understood the monument. It was supposed to commemorate the shelling of New York, but the preserved bomb crater near Houston commemorated the same thing and was much more impressive. The greenbelt had barely been struck; the (at the time) high-rent apartments and shops and lower Manhattan offices had taken the brunt. As far as Nicolai knew, there hadn't even been any soldiers in DZ at the time. That was why it was such a tragedy. So why was the monument of a soldier?

He walked in circles, pacing. Nicolai always did his best thinking while he was in motion, but even after making many tiny laps, nothing made sense. He could call Kai back, but there was little point. She'd be at his side in a few minutes, and based on all that grunting and heaving, whatever she'd been doing was keeping her hands full in the meantime. Besides, she'd been speaking in a subtly guarded way that Nicolai (as a high-ranking political official) and Kai (as a high-strata escort with a secret second life) were both fluent enough to use when it seemed possible that their conversation might not be private.

It must have to do with his missing time, he thought. The day and a half in which Micah Ryan had made an incendiary speech, Isaac had felt abandoned, Nicolai had given Kai reason to think he might be hurt, and she had given him reason to think she might be dead.

Nicolai suddenly, out of the blue, wondered if he'd been right to leave his post with Isaac. It had nothing to do with Kai and her odd need to break into his penthouse. It had to do with the unknowns. Nicolai had never before, to his knowledge, experienced missing time. Was this what a mind wipe felt like? He'd heard it was possible. He'd read an article or two and viewed a handful of Beam vidstreams made by conspiracy theorists who announced that all of their paranoid fantasies had come true, that the government could now officially control minds. There was also a handful of vidstreams made by nut jobs who wanted to tell the world that their memories were erased, and aliens were real. The latter had kept him busy for an entire night, laughing until he cried. But it all seemed so fringe, so unnecessarily paranoid.

Nicolai had wanted out of his job as a speechwriter so he could finally create, could finally take risks and build his own future, could finally get out from under Isaac's passive-aggressive thumb and Natasha's unrelenting seduction. But he'd made his decision without having all of the information. What might have happened to him during the missing weekend? What might have happened to *Isaac?* Maybe Isaac had really, truly (for real this time!) needed Nicolai. Maybe whatever had happened (and what might happen next) was the pearl-in-the-oyster he had been waiting for. Nicolai was *paid* to turn lemons into lemonade — or had been until a few hours ago. Weren't conspiracy and scandal excellent lemons? Maybe he'd screwed up.

Nicolai spent the next few minutes pacing the monument, pondering the soldier. Maybe it represented the proud military who'd fallen in battle, if not specifically in the shelling. But then why position it as a monument to the shelling rather than to the conflict as a whole? The bronze plaque clearly said it honored those lost during the shelling of District Zero. Nicolai looked up at the soldier, mystified.

A noise behind him turned his attention to Kai as she pulled up behind him on a screetbike, inexplicably wearing a baseball cap and a large wrap around her neck and shoulders. Alone.

"That's an interesting look for you," he said.

"Get on."

"Where's Doc?"

"In an alley," she said, brushing a runaway strand of long brown hair behind her ear. "In a dumpster with another man."

"Is that a gay joke?"

Kai didn't seem to be in the mood for joking, and Nicolai, always observant, saw things in her manner that he didn't like as he climbed onto the bike behind her. She looked around nervously, as if afraid of being followed. Her clothes — blue jeans and a plain white shirt — were clean and unassuming (if far less sexy than her usual wares), but there were spots of dirt and what might be caked blood on the back of her neck, as if she'd changed quickly but not had time to properly shower. She seemed to have spritzed herself with perfume, but under the flowery scent was an earthy smell tinged with sweat and adrenaline.

"What happened, Kai?" he asked.

"It's complicated."

"I was there, wasn't I? Whatever you're running from, I was there."

She looked back at Nicolai, and for a moment, he was afraid she might strike a woman pushing a baby carriage down the sidewalk. She turned forward, jogged the bike around the woman, and said, "Yes."

"I've been wiped?"

"Sounds that way. What's the last thing you remember?"

Nicolai told her about going to get the wetchip from Doc on Friday then knowing nothing after that.

"So you don't remember the simulator. Fighting with Doc. Me being tortured then taken away for evaporation?"

"Jesus. No. Why?"

Natasha and Isaac's apartment, where Kai said she'd left Doc and another man named Whitlock, was across town from the park. So during the long ride through traffic, Kai told Nicolai a story that chilled his bones.

When she was done, she told him about the rock and the hard place she found herself between. Then, she told him exactly how she planned to kill Doc Stahl inside the Ryans' lush uptown penthouse.

Chapter 4

In 2041, Natasha won a Best Artist award from the Music Artists' Alliance. It was a particularly brilliant honor, and the one award among her many that Natasha particularly cherished. The MAA was the recording industry's first truly meritocratic organization. As early as the turn of the twenty-first century, musicians were breaking out without needing help from the big businesses who had grown comfortable raping them, but at the time, truly independent artists were the exception rather than the rule, and it was hard to buck the system and distribute music on your own. Things had progressed nicely by the '20s, and around the time the world was celebrating its AIDS and cancer cures and the unparalleled scientific discoveries being made on the new lunar base, it looked as if musicians might finally get their fair shake on a more global level. But then the weather went bad and the chaos started, and people stopped caring about music for a decade. In 2038, however, the MAA was formed, structured as a virtual co-op that granted artists a 60 percent cut of music they produced on their own. Musicians rejoiced. And in 2041, Natasha won the MAA's most coveted award. The award statue was simple but beautiful. Its base was brown marble formed into the shape of a shallow bowl. A solid ball of brushed metal rested in the bowl's basin. Natasha didn't know what kind of metal it was, but it was heavy, about the size of a shot put and maybe half of a shot put's weight. She loved to pick the ball up out of the bowl, feel its heft in her hands, and read her name. The legend read *Best Artist of 2041* — and below that, *Natasha Ryan*.

When Isaac said the thing about her being fat, the award was sitting on a shelf near Natasha's right hand, so she threw the metal ball at him hard enough to punch a hole in the wall. The hole was perfectly round and looked as if it had been removed with a large cookie cutter. Isaac, who had parried to the side to avoid a direct hit to his face, looked at Natasha with something like disbelief. He looked more afraid than angry. *He would be more afraid than angry*, she thought with spite. *He was so goddamn weak.*

"You could have killed me," he said.

"Fuck you, Isaac!" she yelled.

Natasha was so furious that she was starting to cry. She wasn't sure anymore how the argument had started, but it probably had something to do with Isaac, his fucking work, and his fucking inability to cope with his position. 'Directorate Czar of Internal Satisfaction.' What a joke! He didn't have any satisfaction himself, so how was he supposed to help the members of his party be satisfied? And really, what reason did they even *have* to be satisfied? The Directorate was shit, in Natasha's opinion. She hated it, hated its ethic, hated that she'd allowed Isaac to talk her into shifting to Directorate and being saddled with the baggage that came with it. Any decent self-made person was Enterprise, and any Enterprise person worth anything would see Natasha's Directorate Shift all those years ago for what it was: a political move and a cop-out. She was married to a man who was thought of as "Mr. Directorate" by the press (but only because he was Micah's brother; 'Internal Satisfaction' wasn't important without the Ryans' drama) and had needed to become Directorate to make his party look less shitty. But it *was* shitty. Natasha was in a party of layabouts, most of whom sat inside all day long plugged into The Beam, receiving a government dole for contributing nothing. Enterprise had always been more Natasha's style. The Directorate said that Enterprise was ruthless — that members would slit each other's throats in order to reach the top — but Natasha didn't see it that way. Or, perhaps, she didn't care. What did it matter how many throats were being slit at the bottom if you were good enough to reach the top?

"Okay, I didn't mean that," said Isaac, backpedaling. "You *weren't* fat back then. It just came out. I just meant that there was more to your appeal than…"

Natasha threw the award's marble base. It hit Isaac in the side, causing him to buckle forward.

"Noah Fucking West, Natasha!"

"Your stupid fucking party! You and your stupid fucking job! Who gives a shit? It's all about appearances! All smoke and mirrors! Being raw and real and taking risks *is* what got me where I am. Go ahead and say it again, Isaac! Say that 'real' meant fat too! *Fuck you!*"

But he wouldn't say it again because Isaac was a coward. A coward who represented a party of cowards. She hated the Directorate. Being Directorate these past years had made her weak, like Isaac. She hadn't truly struggled in decades, not since she'd started receiving a fixed Directorate salary based on her track record as a top-billing performer. It would have been different if she'd stayed Enterprise. Even after reaching a high level of fame and fortune, Enterprise still offered an artist a reason to grow and develop. She could always create another best-selling album. She could win more awards, increase her creative cachet. She could connect with more people and change more lives. But what incentive had there been since she'd been Directorate? Every concert became an obligation. There was no reason to perform the concerts, or to perform them especially well. There was no reason to sing her heart out and to give her all. Her accolades and remuneration were always the same no matter how much effort she exerted. For Natasha, it had never really been about the money, but at least credits were something she could count. Credits told her how she was doing. Credits were her cookie at the end of a meal — not that Natasha ate cookies. She had dieted nonstop for years before getting her first nanos, and she'd built up enough ingrained food guilt in that time to last a lifetime. She could eat a buffalo today and not gain an ounce, but she was programmed to eat right. Just like Directorate had programmed her to lie around like a diva, halfass her performances, and believe she had nothing to strive for.

"Jesus, Natasha. Calm down." Isaac held up his hands. Surrendering, like a coward.

"I hate this life, Isaac! I fucking hate it!"

"Oh, but you're happy to use the things we have. To have a driver and a fancy hover. To spend millions and millions on shit..."

Natasha walked toward him, slinking like a serpent, animating her face with drama. "Oh, but I do those things just to fill the emptiness in paradise, love. When there's no real reason to get up in the morning and work for something, there's a giant hole that begs to be filled. And a girl's *got* to have her holes filled, baby." She put her finger to her lips and made an *Oops!* face.

"What the hell does that mean?"

"When life stops getting you off...well, you've got to get off on *something*." Her eyes flicked toward her office.

Isaac's eyes followed hers, looking toward her office. The door was ajar, her immersion rig fully visible.

"What...I mean..."

"Having a hard time forming a sentence without your speechwriter?"

For a moment, Natasha thought he might hit her. But that

was one of the inequities of marital fighting: She was allowed to flail and throw things at him, and he wasn't allowed to do the same. His eyes became like hot glass. Then he pushed by her, stalking toward the center of the apartment. That was a low blow, and it had landed squarely in his chest. Like all low blows, it hurt because it was true. Isaac would be lost without Nicolai, and the panic was eating him alive.

Of course, she could still make it worse, so she did.

"Look on the bright side," she said, walking closer, talking at his back. "Maybe he didn't quit because you're an asshole. Maybe it was your shitty party that drove him away. You can't blame Nicolai. I'll bet he was just tired of being a whore. Smart, creative, attractive man like that? Emphasis on *man*. You remember what he was like, before you ruined him? He never did give us all of the details of what he did in the Wild East, but he showed up at the border with a *crossbow*. I'll bet he really knew how to use it. The things he must have pierced with those hard shafts. Oh, that really turned me on. I remember a few times, when you were away…"

Isaac turned, his eyes flashing, and slapped Natasha hard enough to rock her head on her shoulders.

"Maybe you are a man after all," she said, shocked, a hand to her warming cheek. "Man enough to hit a woman."

"You're barely a woman." He looked Natasha up and down, from her nano-slimmed waist to her nano-sculpted cheekbones to her nano-firmed breasts. "Hell, you're barely human."

"Fuck you."

"You're so original. So creative. You think Directorate is so terrible? Then leave it. Put your money where your mouth is." He watched her, gauging her response to the change in his usually timid demeanor. He was going to call her bluff. She'd always been the blusterer; being a temperamental, bitchy prima donna was what she'd built her career around. When she'd been young, Natasha had written songs about the wrath of a scorned woman. When she got older, her songs became about the wrath of a stalked celebrity. Everything she'd ever done had been centered around hot air.

"I don't need to prove anything to you," she said.

Isaac turned his back and began to move, leaving her behind.

Natasha found herself incensed. Suddenly, *he* was the one walking away. This time, she followed *him*. She wanted to throw something at his back, but she'd already rolled over to expose her soft belly, and now he was going to win the fight. That was unacceptable given that she was, without question, right about all of this. She looked at her office, jonesing hard for Andre's embrace. Andre could make all of this pain and anger go away, and Natasha taking some vengeance cock would show Isaac who had the power. But rushing to her virtual lover would change nothing. An hour from now, Isaac would return to being a weak toady for his millions of layabouts, and she'd go back to being the diva on the divan, living a pointless life filled with everything she'd never want.

But he couldn't resist getting in another barb, so once he was a few feet across the apartment, Isaac turned to face her again.

"You're all smoke and no fire, aren't you?" he said. "You *used* to have fire. Back when you were that little pudgy girl bringing the world to its knees, you had fire."

"I had fire because I had to! What's the point of having fire in the Directorate?"

"So leave," he taunted, now walking toward her again. "Do it. Shift at Shift, and go to Enterprise. Lose that gigantic salary of yours so that you'll be free to sink or swim. I don't have to share my dole with you, you know. That'll give you your fire back. But will anyone listen to you when Directorate isn't paying your way? Or do they already know that you've sold out? How many free seats are at your concerts these days? How many contest winners? How much could you really make if your future was in your hands again? Do you think you have any credibility left? Natasha Ryan, who used to be so raw and real until she decided to enhance the shit out of herself and get comfy, Natasha who started raking in credits for doing nothing but sitting around on her not-fat-at-all-anymore ass." He crossed the last few paces between them, backing her up to the steps up from the sunken living room. A snake's grin crawled across his face. "You don't have the guts. And no matter how much you scream and yell and posture, you know the truth: you *did* sell out."

From deep, deep down, a young girl with heavy thighs and a thick middle spoke up inside Natasha. Knowing she'd almost certainly regret it, she said, "Fine. I'll do it."

Isaac's grin vanished. "What?"

"I'll shift. I'll go Enterprise. I don't need your money. I'll still have your house. I'll eat your food. Thanks for supporting me while I make my comeback...hubby."

"Wait."

"You can't divorce me. It'd look terrible, and I'd get half of what you own. So you're stuck with me. How long is left until Shift? Three weeks?" She put a thoughtful finger to her chin. "Just enough time to tell the sheets all about it. I'll bet I could even sell the story. It'd be okay; I'd just insist that they pay me after Shift, after I'm officially Enterprise. It sure sounds juicy: 'Natasha Ryan, famed songstress and long-suffering wife of prominent Directorate asshole Isaac Ryan, rejuvenates her career with a bold move reminiscent of her early years — turning back to her true people by shifting from her husband's shitass party.'"

"You wouldn't."

"I would. '"It was my husband's idea, says the fabulous singer.' Will that make you look good or bad, Isaac? I figure it's a toss-up. You'll look like a loser and a two-faced hypocrite to your party, but you'll be popular with soccer moms. Well, unless they're Directorate."

"Natasha, wait. Let's talk about this."

Natasha felt the power slide right back to her side of the fence. She turned and walked away from him, and this time, *he* followed. As it should be.

"Natasha!"

"This is such an excellent idea, Isaac!" she shouted over her shoulder as she made her way toward the bedroom. "It solves everything. I never wanted to shift anyway. Now I'll be free. I'll get my credibility back. You can't call me a hypocrite anymore, but I can still call you one. And hey, if I fail, I've still got alimony to fall back on."

"There's no goddamned alimony in Enterprise!" he shouted, now practically running after her.

"There is in Directorate," she said. "I'll bet I could get the courts to see it my way."

"Look. Let's talk about this."

"Nothing to talk about."

"Natasha! Noah Fucking West! You...you can't do this!"

"You *told* me to do this."

Isaac grabbed Natasha by the shoulders and spun her around. His face seemed desperate, which was the way she thought it looked best. She smirked, knowing the expression would made her both wrathful and beautiful.

"Look. I'm sorry. Don't do this, Natasha. I take it all back. Okay? I was upset. This thing with Nicolai. You're right; I need him. I don't know what to do. I need you. I need your support. I can't take this big of a hit. It'll be a serious blow to the party. I'll lose my position. Natasha? Help me. You *have* to help me."

She looked at him, seeing the pleading in his eyes, hearing the appeal in his voice. He looked like a turtle, rolled onto its back. Natasha couldn't help but feel sorry for him, like she would for the turtle.

"Isaac," she said, reaching out and touching his cheek.

"I'm sorry. I'm sorry for saying what I said. I love you."

She sighed, ran her fingers through his dark hair.

"You're so weak," she said. "So pathetic. You are nothing without Nicolai, me, and Micah. I'm sorry too. I'm sorry you're so weak."

She walked into their bedroom, grabbed a light bag, and tossed a change of clothes and her concert travel bag into it. She grabbed her dog purse, cornered Kiki, and shoved him into it. As long as she had her purse, she could buy anything else she needed. It was important to walk out now, before he regrouped. She'd be back. For now, she had to go, and leave him to break.

"Where are you going?" she asked.

"Micah's."

"Micah's?"

"Don't worry, dear. I'm not going to fuck your brother. But he and I need to talk." Then, to show she wasn't just bluffing, Natasha zipped her bag and brushed past Isaac, back into the living room. She buttonhooked toward the door, knowing seconds counted. Maybe she was bluffing and maybe she wasn't, but she had to be out the door fast so that if she needed to backpedal, she could make it look like Isaac had begged her to. She had to go to Micah's. This crap, with Isaac belittling and ignoring her and fitting her into his farce of a life, had gone on too long. Whether she shifted or not, Natasha was for goddamn sure reclaiming her life. Isaac could go with her to Micah's if he wanted, but she was going.

"You can't go. James has the car," he blubbered, grasping at straws.

She shrugged, loving the way he was falling to pieces. "I'll take a cab." And then she made for the front door and walked through it.

Isaac chased her down the hallway, followed her like a dog, tucked into the elevator behind her, and continued to grovel for the entire stomach-dropping ride.

"You're not really going to Micah," Isaac pleaded. "Don't.

Don't tell him. For the love of West, Natasha. He'll use it to crush me."

"Maybe."

"You can't do this. Please. I'm begging you."

She looked at him, almost laughed, and wanted very badly to reply by saying, *You absolutely are, Isaac.* But instead, she let it go. She had won. No need to twist the knife.

When they arrived at street level, Natasha strutted, and Isaac tumbled out the front door and right into Nicolai Costa. He looked as shocked as Natasha felt to see him. Natasha gave herself two full seconds to fall into Nicolai's beautiful brown eyes then another two to ensure that Isaac saw her do it. Then, without a word to either of them, she stepped into a driverless cab that had seen her coming and was waiting at the curb with its door open.

Isaac grabbed the door as she started to close it. He leaned inside, his shoulders rising as his torso sank, his posture above her like a mantis.

"Don't do this," he said. "Don't go to Micah." He glanced back at Nicolai, who was watching and listening with an uncomfortable expression on his face.

She looked at Nicolai then started to pull on the door again. Then, with an air of spontaneous decision, Isaac fell in beside her and closed the door. Apparently, he was going too. Which meant her chance to bluff, if she'd been considering it (she still wasn't sure) was gone. Ironically, Isaac had sealed his own fate. Now they were going to Micah's for sure.

Natasha looked through the window at Nicolai. Feeling bold, she waved then turned from Isaac and delivered Micah's address to the cab while her husband continued to plead his futile case beside her.

Chapter 5

Jason Whitlock stared at the small pretty woman in front of him, her dark hair lifting in a light breeze. To Jason's side was a brick wall. His boots stood on hard gray concrete. As he watched, the woman turned to look at him, a tortured look painted on her face. She held a heavy pipe in one hand — a weapon that Jason had allowed her to pick up after he'd stepped back, wary despite the centurion suit he was wearing. Micah had warned him about the girl, whom Micah had called Kitty. She was deadly, Micah had said. Jason should keep his distance, ideally aiming a weapon, until she'd done what she had to do.

Kitty said, "Don't make me do this."

"Just get it over with," he told her.

"*You* could do it. He'd be just as dead. I won't stop you. You could make it quick. You have a gun. A *real* gun." Her eyes — deep brown and pleading, not at all deadly looking — locked on his. "Please."

"Boss's orders."

Below her, kneeling with his lower legs crossed behind him as ordered, Thomas Stahl was begging for his life. He didn't seem to know whom to beg. He pleaded with Jason and Kitty both. Since this tense little stand-off had started, he'd vacillated between shouting and whimpering. Jason had tried to remain unaffected, but it was hard. He knew the two were friends, and he wasn't so cold that he could get his head totally past it. What he was watching was heartbreaking, but Micah had ordered that she kill Stahl, and Jason had already failed Micah twice. You didn't get three strikes with Micah Ryan. As it stood, he wasn't entirely sure he'd get away with two.

"I can't do it," she said.

The torment was killing Jason. He pulled his slamgun from its concealment and cocked it. The hammer on the gun did absolutely nothing. CP weapons were at least six or seven generations past the last guns that had required hammers to fire, but the designers continued to add them for effect. Nothing put an exclamation point on a sentence quite like the tiny noise of a cocking hammer, even in an age when it was nothing but bluster.

"I'm telling you, I can't do it," she repeated. Now she was crying. *Noah Fucking West.*

Jason raised his gun. One way or another, this had to end. He wasn't good with crying women or pleading subjects, and right now he had both. He wasn't even good with killing people. Always hated it. He didn't want this to happen either, but he wanted even less to end up in a box himself.

"Do it," he said.

The woman seemed to focus then put her other hand on the pipe. She raised it over her head.

Below her, Stahl raised his hands. "Jesus. Sweetheart. No. Don't do it. Don't. Please."

She looked at Jason, the pipe now shaking. He twitched his gun, giving her just the one last chance. He knew she was an assassin. Making her kill Stahl was cold-blooded as fuck, but she could handle it. She'd done this kind of thing plenty before today. She had made her bed, and she'd have plenty of other men to lie in it with her.

Kitty inhaled and swung. Her eyes closed on the downward curve as she threw all of her enhanced strength behind it. Her speed made up for her small frame. The first blow glanced off of Doc's right hand, snapping a finger the wrong way before striking him in the side of the face. He started to scream. Above him, chest heaving, Kitty raised the pipe and swung again, apparently eager to finish. The second blow split his scalp, still not knocking him out. Blood flew up and flecked the woman's chest and face. This time, she screamed. It was nothing compared to Stahl's wails. Jason wanted to turn away but couldn't. He watched as she raised the pipe again. And again. And again. The pipe was heavy, and Kitty was strong, so Jason was shocked at how many strikes it took to close Stahl's eyes. *Seven.* It took seven hits before he went down and stayed down. After that, she was just bashing a lifeless form, gasping and heaving and crying all at once, blood and gore on her cheeks, on her shirt, in her long dark-brown hair.

She turned toward Jason, her arms away from her sides and the bloody, hair-specked pipe in her right hand. Her face was a mask of blood. She looked at him with the fury of Hell, and Jason felt himself quail under her gaze, thankful he'd put some distance between them.

"There!" she shouted, spittle flying from her lips. It didn't clear her face but drooled down her chin instead, mingling with blood. When the liquid reached her chin, it hung like a bright-pink balloon. "I'm fucking done! I hope you're *mother-fucking happy!*" She reared back and hurled the heavy pipe at him as hard as she could. It came at him spinning end over end, and he dove to miss it.

Jason felt a spike of anger then reminded himself of what he'd just made her do. He stuffed it down, raising his gun again and training it on her chest. She looked ready to murder again, but he didn't plan to give her a chance. He tossed her a pair of handcuffs and ordered her to cuff herself. He said he wanted to hear them click. When they clicked, he made her hold her hands up and show him that there was no gap between the edges of the cuffs and her small wrists. Then he told her to step back and kneel as Stahl had, with her lower legs crossed behind her.

Only then, with the woman neutralized, did Jason approach what looked like a sack of pulverized meat. He toed the limp pile, keeping Kitty in the corner of his sight. He looked for Stahl's face but couldn't find it. He poked the corpse further, looking first out of curiosity and then, eventually, out of confusion. The man *had* had a face, right? But then he realized that he'd been looking at Stahl's former face the entire time and almost vomited. He made out a triangle of flesh that was probably once a nose. A deeper, pulpier cut was likely a mouth. He couldn't see the corpse's eyes, and didn't really want to.

The woman, still boring holes in him with her eyes and panting, said, "Did I do it well enough for you?"

"Almost," said Jason.

He took a step back to mind the splatter then fired a shot through what used to be Doc Stahl's head. His precautions against splatter were inadequate, and his lower half was specked with blood as if a bomb had exploded. It didn't matter. He was due to remove the clothes he'd draped over his Stark suit anyway, now that his time of lying low was over.

"Okay," he said, looking toward Kitty. "Now here's what I need you to do if you're coming with me."

After he finished the sentence, there was a beat of nothingness. It felt like his great grandfather's record needle skipping in a groove. But the skip was uninteresting, and he paid it no mind. It happened again and again. But it was all so uninteresting.

Somehow, Jason later imagined, he must have finished his directions to Kitty. But in real time, a gray cloud rose from below, and it all just kind of stopped mattering. His mind had seen the cloud twice before — first on the night of the concert riot and then again shortly before Kitty had killed Stahl. The cloud didn't feel like a hole, or like missing time. It didn't feel like anything. It was just a slip in which he'd forgotten unimportant details, as happened countless times every day, like when he found himself unable to remember what he'd had for breakfast the day before or where he'd placed his hover keys.

That was the thing about the human brain. When you gave it something it didn't understand, it drew its own conclusions. It was how people blocked incidents of abuse, how brain trauma patients could function after losing years of their lives and pick up where they'd left off as if no time had passed. It could cause a person to question the nature of reality. Was reality something truly objective, or did everyone have their own?

Chapter 6

____

When Kai sat up in Natasha Ryan's immersion rig, all she could hear were bloodcurdling screams. Whitlock was still in the rig beside her, plugged in and silent enough to be sleeping. The office door was cracked. The screams were coming from outside.

She made it through the office door just in time to hear the screams cease and to get a face full of Doc Stahl. He was on top of her in the Ryans' living room before she knew what was happening, his arms pinning hers to the floor and his not-unsubstantial weight on her chest and pelvis. Behind him, Kai could see Doc's rig and the unoccupied one beside it, Doc's inputs sticking up at the head of the thing like the legs of a dead spider.

"Fucking bitch!" Doc screamed. Spit flew from his lips and struck her in the face.

Nicolai rushed forward and grabbed Doc by the shoulders. He was trying to pull Doc off Kai, but Doc was too strong. Nicolai, however, turned out to be the better grappler. He easily off-balanced Doc and rolled him to the Ryans' polished wood floor, Nicolai now becoming the man on top.

"Goddammit, lie still!" Nicolai shouted. "Let it pass!"

Doc drew three slow, shambling breaths then threw Nicolai away from him in a burst of ill temper. Kai watched, thinking that Nicolai had let Doc toss him to vent steam. But he would be okay now; Doc was past the precipice and coming down fast.

Doc glared at Kai as if she'd just beaten the shit out of him with a pipe. Which, of course, she had.

"Do you have *any* fucking idea how much that hurt?" He met Kai's eyes then turned to stare into the office at the rig he'd been on a moment earlier. "What kind of sick shit is that?"

"I'm sorry," said Kai, standing and brushing herself off. "But let's try to remember that I just saved your life."

"Fuck you!"

Doc hawked and spat. The blob of spit struck the wood floor and huddled up into a dome on the floor's thick coat of synthetic wax. It didn't matter; Kai was planning to have the Ryans' bots do some housekeeping after they left anyway. Given the way she'd been able to roll back the canvas's clock back to yesterday — a time when Nicolai's ID gave him valid clearance to enter the apartment — she could easily hack the cleaning system and make it forgetful.

"That was harder for me than you think," she said, getting to her feet. And it had been, too. Dark fantasies aside, twenty-four hours since her spin on the Orion had been enough time to convince herself that high-end immersion couldn't possibly have been as real as she remembered it. But what she'd just experienced *had* been real — as real as right now — and killing Doc in a virtual world hadn't been any easier than killing him in the actual one would have been. She'd felt the weight of the pipe in her hands. She'd felt the way each strike telegraphed through her bones. She'd heard the crunch of his skull, then how his body yielded too much on the following swing. She'd felt the draft in the alley as it ran through her hair. She'd been in the real version of that alley an hour earlier, and where she'd been a moment ago had been exactly the same. *Exactly.* For a moment, coming out of the rig, she'd had a moment of vertigo, not knowing one world from the other. And on the heels of that thought, a frightening thing occurred to her: If you were immersed and someone programmed the simulation to seem to end when it actually hadn't ended, you'd never know. A person could live the rest of her life inside without realizing she wasn't in the real world.

"Oh, I'll *bet* it was hard, sunshine. Just as hard as it was for me. You could have at least warned me."

"You heard me tell Nicolai to put us on the city map in the alley down from the Starbucks. I told you I was going to ask the simulation for a pipe and that you had to let me beat you to death with it. Where was I unclear?"

"You should have asked it for a fake Doc Stahl when you asked for the pipe."

"I don't think it has you in the database," said Kai.

Doc cracked his neck one way then the other. He shook out his arms. "Hell. I didn't know it was going to be like *that.* Shouldn't there be failsafes on shit like this? Pain preventers or something?"

"Maybe Natasha and Isaac are into S&M," said Nicolai. "Maybe they turned the pain up."

Doc looked into the office as if it had tried to bite him. Which, really, it kind of had.

"Shit. Well, anyway. How's your boy?" He jerked his chin toward the other office, where Whitlock was still motionless in the rig. "You think he bought it?"

Kai nodded. "I think so. He was there with us, and his brain will plug the holes on either side of the memory. He saw it happen. He even shot you at the end, just to be sure."

"Oh, I know," said Doc. "I felt it. The rig didn't stop feeding me shit after I died. And let me tell you: Getting your head blown off?" He made a thumb and forefinger circle. *"Fan-fucking-tastic."*

After making sure that Doc and Kai weren't going to tear each other's heads off, Nicolai walked into Isaac's office then Natasha's. He came back out, motioning at the others to make haste.

"I've reset everything on all of the rigs. I unplugged Whitlock and erased the cache file on the machine. I think I did, anyway. It's not like I've ever seen anything like those rigs before."

Doc looked into the offices, apparently recovered. "Yeah, me either." Then, when he looked back toward Kai, she recognized a look in his eyes. Doc was an opportunist first and a person second. She realized he was seeing dollar signs. The man had just been beaten to death with a pipe, and all he was thinking about right now was that he wished someone would let him sell what he'd just used. The irony was, if Micah had hired Doc instead of trying to have him killed, it would have solved the problem for everyone.

"We need to go," said Nicolai, looking around the apartment for evidence of their intrusion. "While it's nice that I didn't have to lure them away for you, the fact that they're off on their own makes their return less predictable. She said something about going to Micah's, but that doesn't mean she won't change her mind and come right back. Natasha is kind of…well…" He stopped, apparently unsure how to finish the sentence.

"Go do your shit with funboy then," Doc said to Kai. "Sex him up."

Kai did. She got Whitlock ambulatory and led him to the street, where they climbed onto his screetbike. She cuffed his hands around her waist then fought his impossible, sluggish weight as they flew back to the alley they'd come from, where Kai told her nanos to let his fog dissipate. It wouldn't matter that there was no corpse on the ground when his coherence returned. His brain would fill in the gaps. He would assume he'd called the police and reported a corpse, and that the police hadn't asked questions once they'd learned who was called it in. Then he'd report the deed as done and, presumably, take Kai home once Micah agreed that she could be trusted. Based on Kai's experience, it would take less than a day before he committed the patchwork lie to memory as if it were true.

The next morning, Micah Ryan called Kai. His earlier menace was as gone as the threat of Doc Stahl.

He told her about his big plan, and that he had excellent news for her.

Chapter 7

They walked for hours.

Leah didn't have a Beam ID, but the system seemed to know who she was anyway. Every few blocks, she'd press her hand to a wall or a glass window, and it would light up and register her as anonymous. Then she'd tap around on the Beam window for a while (verbal never worked quite right in public and made you look like a tourist), and the system would soon act like it knew who she was anyway. It always took a minute or two, as if there was something in the area — possibly at her last access point — that needed time to sniff her out. But then the window would begin to shift in barely perceptible ways. She'd do a search and find that it autocompleted from a list of recent searches made from her earlier access points. The few times she visited retail pages then revisited later, items she'd recently looked at would appear, as if cookied. She'd find the keypad set to her most natural, preferred position. Search results would end up strangely tailored to someone her age, gender, and level of enhancement.

Block by block, entirely on foot, they spent the day wandering from SoHo's burned-out studios and shops all the way into one of Manhattan's most upscale neighborhoods. As the sun set, they found themselves in a trendy section of Harlem. They both felt underdressed. Harlem wasn't exactly snobby, but it was affluent and not modest in the least. Most of the men wore suits and expensive band ties, and the women wore long, flowing dresses. There weren't many jeans, headbands, gray braids, pink dreadlocks, or rainbow sarongs at all.

As uncomfortable as Leo had been when he'd met Leah in the cafe, Harlem seemed to press the boot heel harder against his back. Leah found the old man's discomfort cute, despite feeling slightly out of skin herself. Leo talked all the time about the need to follow your internal compass and not care what others thought, but he clearly had a bit of self-consciousness and peer-think in him after all.

Finally, to Leo's sighing relief, Leah slapped the wall of a large gray building. It looked as out of place as Leah and Leo, but for different reasons. While the rest of the buildings were glass-and-concrete spires or high-end apartments, the building Leah indicated had a large wooden arch across its front that was surrounded by abstract stained glass accents. The area beneath the wooden arch was chrome broken by two enormous windows. Or at least, they *looked* like windows, but they weren't. They showed clouds in a blue sky instead of the building's interior, which meant they were Beam displays, and as soon as Leo and Leah walked under the arch, they saw that the clouds protruded from the building's front as 3-D holos. The holos were barely visible from the street, but once under the arch they seemed almost real. Leah felt like she was hiking through the sky, with concrete steps underfoot.

Leo glanced up at the floating clouds. "This looks like a church," he said. Then he walked over to a small plaque, read it, and returned to Leah.

"Is it a church?" Leah asked.

"It's a school. A school for gifted children. Why is Crumb

at a school?" He paused. "No, wait. Why did a school *steal* Crumb from his hospital room and then erase all trace that he'd ever been there?"

"I don't know."

Leo looked at the building, the clouds, and Leah. Finally, he looked out into Harlem, seemingly at the long and winding route they'd taken to get here.

"You're sure about this?" he asked.

"No," said Leah.

Leo chuckled. "Good enough."

The school's lobby was as odd as its outside. The cloud motif was repeated, and Leah found herself waist-deep in a small cumulus as she approached a reception desk. At least, that's what she assumed it was. The desk was the most intricately carved thing Leah had ever seen. It was all waves and whorls, its surface rippled like whipped cream. It was roughly desk-shaped — but only roughly, and its surface breathed with a Beam projection of rippling water. The wave projection tumbling across the curved surface made Leah dizzy, and she had to look away as she approached it.

The attendant was as odd as the desk. He was a boy of maybe eight, with thick, messy brown hair. He had large ears and a charming smile and seemed unable to sit still. He stayed behind the desk, but the area behind it was wide and long enough for him to pace. He did so the entire time he was talking, making gestures with his hands.

Leah realized she didn't know what to say. Why *would* a school have taken in a strange, sick vagrant? Would the kid know about any of it? And if he did, would he know Crumb as "Crumb," or "Stephen York?" Or neither? And if the place *did* have Crumb, would his presence here be a secret? Would Leah and Leo need to connive their way in? The notion, as she considered it, seemed absurd. Something in the school (or perhaps the school itself) had been drawing Leah toward it all the way from lower Manhattan like a dog on a leash. Whatever that something was, it wanted her here. It almost felt like it *needed* her here. To Leah, the force felt almost magnetic. As odd as it was and as impossible as it would have been to describe, she almost felt like she was on both sides of that magnetism, simultaneously being drawn toward the school and doing the summoning herself. She hadn't even really felt the mechanics of their journey. Aside from stopping occasionally to access The Beam, the walk here had felt almost like sleepwalking.

"She's been waiting for you," said the kid, pacing, barely looking up. His fingers traced the interior edge of the liquid desk, following its contours.

"Who?" said Leo.

The kid gave Leo a brief look. It wasn't impolite or unwelcoming, but it wasn't like the look he'd already given Leah. *She* was supposed to be here. Leo, on the other hand, was tagging along.

"The headmistress," said the kid, speaking to Leah.

"What is this place?" Leah asked.

"It's a school."

"What do you do here?"

The kid shrugged. "Learn about the world."

"The world?"

The kid nodded.

"Like what about the world?"

"The way the world is. Where to go. How to use it."

"How to use the world?"

"How to travel the world. How to make the world," said the kid. Then, without slowing his pacing, the lobby's floating clouds winked out of existence. The strange, fluid reception desk seemed to vanish as it blended into the walls and floors. The entirety of the lobby's surfaces became moving images of a beach. Waves seemed to crash from one side as a hologram plugged the doorway through which Leo and Leah had entered. Leah felt a breeze touch her bare shoulders and looked out at the surf, her senses already buying that it was real surf rather than projection. Out in the surf, enormous rocks jutted up from the breakers like fingers jabbed at the sky. Leah looked down and saw sand. She was wearing sandals and standing still, but the reality was so complete that Leah felt certain that if she slipped off her sandals, she'd find herself standing in actual sand. So she did. She slipped off a sandal, stepped down, and felt sand.

"We're in a simulator?" Leah asked the kid.

"No," said the kid. "We're in the world."

"But we're in a simulator in the world," Leah clarified.

The kid stopped pacing and looked at Leah, earnest and confused at the same time. "We're *at a beach* in the world," he said.

Leah watched Leo trying to get his bearings, amused by his wonder. Leo knew simulators existed, of course, but he'd probably never experienced one this good, or this fully.

"No," Leo said to the kid. "She means this room. This school lobby. We're still in the lobby. The lobby is a simulator, and it's simulating a beach."

"We're at a beach," said the kid.

"A beach that was made by a simulator."

The kid scrunched up his face. Leah saw his innocence and felt vulnerable in its glare. "What's a simulator?"

Rather than stretching the argument, Leah let it go. She sighed, closed her eyes, and accepted the breeze on her skin. She listened to the breakers. She smelled the air. It was an astonishing simulation, and an astonishing simulator.

"Whatever it is, it's beautiful," she said. "I almost feel like I could throw a rock into those waves."

So the kid, because he was a kid, picked up a rock and threw it. The rock whistled and skipped, plunking into the surf twenty or thirty yards away. Leah felt like she'd been punched. Something in the world had just gone very wrong, but it took her mind a few seconds to realize what it was. Then it came to her: the rock hadn't hit the real walls of the school's lobby as it should have.

"What is this place?" she whispered.

"It's the world," said the kid. Then the beach faded, and the lobby reappeared around them, the kid back behind the liquid-looking reception desk. That was another thing; he'd never come out from behind the desk. Yet a moment ago, she'd been standing beside him and had seen his whole body.

Leah didn't know what to say. So after an odd moment, the kid finally came out from behind the desk then took Leah's hand as if she were the child and began to lead her down a long hallway.

"Where are we going?" she asked.

The kid said, "Somewhere else."

At the end of the corridor was a door, and behind the door was another corridor. They walked it for a long time, passing rooms that were bright and sun-filled despite the fact that they were clearly at the building's interior. The suites were filled with children and looked like sparsely furnished class-rooms. The hallway itself was spotless and reminded Leah of the secret Quark lab in Chinatown, but she wasn't sure if the surfaces were Beam surfaces or not. Nothing seemed to be responding, but everything was familiar. Yet Leah knew her past well enough to know she'd never been there.

"You're intuitives," said Leah.

"We're kids," said the boy, still holding her hand.

"You're anthroposophists. You walk The Beam."

"We learn about the world," said the kid.

"By using The Beam."

"Well," said the kid, "what do *you* use?"

"I don't know. Eyes. Ears. Hands."

"The native five," said the kid.

"Excuse me?"

"You just use your first five senses. It's cool. Most people do. The others are better."

Leah felt lost. "What do you mean, 'others'?"

"The other senses," the kid replied, seemingly unable to accept Leah's naiveté.

"The Beam isn't a sense," she said. "You're learning technology, not reality." But then she thought about the rock falling into the surf thirty yards away.

"What's the difference?" he said.

They'd reached a wide set of double doors. The kid let go of her hand.

"Just wait in here," he said, smiling. "The headmistress will be here soon."

He pushed the doors open then nodded at Leah and Leo to enter. Leo looked at Leah. Leah looked at Leo. She wanted Leo to see trust in her eyes, but she couldn't summon the feeling herself. They settled on mutual uncertainty. Leah looked at the kid. He looked back at her, placid.

Both Leo and Leah turned to look into the room. There, in a large chrome-framed bed with bright-white sheets and a heavy comforter, was Crumb.

They entered as the double doors slowly closed behind them. The room was large and stark, with windows every few feet. Outside the windows was a bucolic meadow with a red barn in the distance. The red barn had white trim and an arm mounted above the loft door, swaying slightly in a breeze that made the grass puff and dance. The room's interior was simple; other than Crumb sleeping in the large bed, there were only a few chairs and a small end table with four glasses on top. Beside the glasses was a clear glass pitcher, empty.

Behind them, the kid had vanished. Neither had heard him go. The room itself was quiet. The corridor hadn't been loud, but kids' laughter had rumbled through the air like a machine's constant hum. But inside the room — which almost looked like a lush hospital suite, minus the machines — the silence was absolute. Leah could hear her sandals squeak as her body shifted and balanced.

Leo turned to Leah.

"I'm tripping, right? We did a lot of moondust."

Leah knew Leo was kidding. Moondust didn't work like that. It enhanced sight on The Beam and made you mellow but didn't make you see things.

"A hell of a lot," said Leah, smiling.

"I guess I believe you," said Leo. "About that crazy shit with Crumb and The Beam. Because here we are. And there he is."

They walked forward. Crumb seemed to be asleep, his breathing low and regular. Leah wasn't sure how she knew, but she was sure it was sleep that had him, not coma. Whatever damage she'd done to his brain back in Bontauk was healed. Leo looked at him closely then at Leah. Crumb shifted in his sleep, rolling onto his side.

They backed up, speaking in half whispers.

Leo said, "He's better."

"I know."

"They cleaned him up. I think his hair and beard have been trimmed," Leo added.

"I don't see shit in his beard. No crumbs for Crumb." Leah laughed, but the sound was hollow in the big white room and made her want to look around self-consciously.

"I don't want to be here," said Leo.

"We *need* to be here."

Leo swallowed. "I still don't want to be."

"You think we're in danger? That *he's* in danger?"

Leo looked at the end table. "I want a drink of water."

Leah didn't know what to say, so she told him to go ahead. But of course, the pitcher was empty.

"We passed a bathroom on the way down," said Leo. "At least I think it was a bathroom. I intuited that it was a bathroom using my native five senses. But it's cool. Most people do that."

"Maybe it's a beach," said Leah.

Leo told Leah that he was going to fill the pitcher. He said it with a swallow, as if announcing he was about to cross a minefield. Leah told him to go ahead. It sounded odd, her giving him permission, but he seemed to be asking. So Leah gave her blessing. And after Leo had taken the pitcher and ducked out (strangely, the sound of kids from the hallway didn't enter the silent room even while the door was open), Leah approached Crumb. She resisted the urge to pet his hair. It seemed like a cliché, and no matter what she'd learned about Stephen York, he was still mostly Crumb to her, and touching Crumb was gross.

Leah had put him here. But of course, she also hadn't. He wasn't Crumb and never had been. This was Stephen York, one of The Beam's fathers. All of those deep thoughts in the leather journal stashed in Leah's backpack had come from this man's mind. It was impossible to believe. Crumb spoke about squirrels, and conspiracies, and squirrel conspiracies. How could he have thought all of the things in the journal? He'd accomplished unparalleled feats. He'd changed the world and then fretted about the implications of changing the world, asking the question so few people asked: *Sure, we CAN do this. But SHOULD we?* Some would say that what this man had done had resulted in a kind of utopia. Others would say he'd just forged another set of chains, given the masses another pill to pop.

"Where is Noah West now, Crumb?" Leah whispered.

"I wish we knew," said a voice behind her.

Leah jumped. Then she turned, finding a girl of maybe eighteen or nineteen standing just three feet to her rear. The room was tomb quiet, like outer space, and still the girl had managed to sneak up on her.

"Hi," said Leah.

"Hello, Leah," said the woman. She was wearing a long blue dress and had pale skin sprayed with freckles. Her hair was red and silky smooth, a trim under shoulder length, flowing around her narrow face like the sun's corona. She was young, but somehow she projected a much older aura. Her manner was upright and confident, infused with authority.

"How do you know who I am?" Leah asked.

"We called you," the girl replied.

Leah wanted to protest that the girl hadn't called her at all but knew it was wasted breath. She knew what the girl meant, even if she didn't understand it…or who "they" were.

"Who are you?" she asked instead.

"My name is SerenityBlue." The girl extended a pale hand for Leah to take briefly but not shake. "One word. Two capitals. I know, I know. But it's the name I was created with."

"Created?"

"We were all created," said SerenityBlue. She walked to Crumb and fluffed his pillow. Leah followed the girl with her eyes. She was rail-thin and looked almost insubstantial. When she stood between Leah and one of the false windows, her arms nearly vanished as the bright sun tried to wrap around and swallow them. "You came for Crumb."

"You know his name?"

"It's the name you registered him with at the hospital. It's the name he calls himself."

"But he has another name," said Leah. She thought about holding back, but going too far was no longer possible. "It's Stephen York."

Serenity closed her eyes briefly then opened them and said, "Yes. It is. Thank you."

Leah felt like she was dreaming. There was nothing unreal about the girl or the room, but the elements within it were like a dream. Everything seemed to crawl. The girl's voice was hypnotic, her movements ethereal and other-worldly. The room was too clean and too sparse. It looked like a vision of a bedroom created by a person who'd never had one. The bed wasn't against one wall; it was in the middle, like a showpiece. It wasn't the way anyone would design a real bedroom, a real sick room, a real classroom…whatever this was.

"You took him from the hospital," said Leah.

"Yes. We needed him more than they did."

"For what?"

"I'm not sure. None of us are."

"But that didn't stop you. That didn't stop you from breaking into a hospital, unhooking a man from support he may have needed, and leaving no trace for people who might have been looking for him. It didn't stop you from erasing records or wiping memories."

Serenity didn't seem remotely troubled by Leah's tone or the undercurrent of her words. She circled Crumb's bed, adjusting his covers. Beneath her hands, he stirred. Leah thought he might be waking.

"No, it didn't stop us," said the girl. "We saw him, and we went to him. I have followers everywhere, and we've been looking for minds like his. When his surfaced, we went to it. I went with the others, in my body. We asked his mind to go, and it agreed. So we moved the rest of him. We did not seek to disturb others, and the children wished for them to stay unbothered. We left no trace, each going our own way. Now we're here."

Leah didn't know what to make of any of it. She thought of the kid they'd met earlier, how he had turned the lobby into a beach, and his casual disregard for any line between a person's native senses and the extra ones provided by The Beam. She'd decided he must have been an intuitive. If they all were intuitives, then at least Serenity's logic would make sense to her. Whether it agreed with the normal rules of reality was something else entirely.

"What is this place?" Leah asked.

"It's a school. For children who find themselves out of place, born into a world they can't control."

Leah thought of the NAU, the Wild East, the impervious

lattice covering the continent, the rich in their spires and the Enterprise poor in their gutters, and the billions in the middle, poor but pacified.

"None of us can control the world."

Serenity said, "But my children can control their worlds in other ways."

"The Beam."

Serenity shrugged, as if Leah were splitting hairs.

"Becoming proficient on The Beam isn't reality," said Leah.

Serenity looked at her and smiled — a kind smile that was somehow apologetic.

On the bed, Crumb's eyes began to blink and open. He looked around, seeming to be momentarily confused by either his location or the presence of the two women — his old friend and his new guardian — here together. He stirred and propped himself up on his elbows, looking at Leah. The crazy was gone from his eyes. He looked like a man who'd seen a lot and had lived long without ever blunting his edge.

"Leah," he said.

It was only one word, but the way he said it chilled her to the bone. His eyes were steady and steely, his voice calm and sedate and in control. This was not the same man who had wandered the Organa community her entire life, guarding the gates and chasing squirrels and talking about conspiracies with a beard full of garbage. Whatever Leah had started back in the burned-out house in Bontauk, it had clearly peaked, crested, and rolled on to completion. The wall she'd seen in his mind must have collapsed and fallen, leaving Crumb as the man he was supposed to be.

"Crumb?"

"I suppose," he said. "Though Serenity helped me somehow reach out to you, I dreamed that you found a journal. I think it belonged to me. Did you?"

Leah, finding herself unable to speak, held up the journal.

Crumb looked at Serenity. Her replying look said, *I told you.*

"Then you know my real name," he said.

"Stephen York," said Leah.

Crumb looked around the room, looked down at his open hands. His eyes rolled back. Then he said, "Yes, that sounds right."

"Do you remember?"

"I remember remembering."

"Do you remember Noah West? Quark?" Leah had to rein herself in. She was blabbing too far out of line, revealing too much. She still didn't know who this strange girl was or what she wanted. She clamped her lips shut and waited.

"No," said Crumb.

Leah looked at Serenity. For the first time, she wondered where Leo was. Was he really just filling a pitcher of water? He'd looked freaked out enough to run, to head all the way back to the mountains and dismiss his ill-advised return to the city as one long, bad trip. Leah found herself able to sympathize.

"Why are you interested in him?" she asked Serenity.

"I don't know. His mind feels different on The Beam. It's stronger, wiser. Maybe you know." She looked at Leah. Wasn't Leah supposed to be the guest? She was hardly the guide.

"He worked on The Beam," said Leah. "He helped create it."

Serenity nodded. "Thank you. Then what I've felt makes sense. The Beam was birthed from the same wellspring we all draw from, when we are inspired and create art. Every artist leaves a splinter of himself in everything he does. Every painting is a self-portrait. Every character in every story is the creator in disguise. Every song is the sound of the singer's soul." She turned to Crumb. "If you worked on The Beam, you left a part of yourself in it. We've sensed your echo. What's in this bed is the corporeal piece of yourself, but there may be many others. Those parts may seem separate, but they are all connected beneath the surface. You are like a chain of islands in the ocean. We see many distinct drops of land, but they only appear separate because we can only see their tops. Beneath, they're all part of the same thing."

Leah's skin prickled. Serenity's message reminded her of what she'd felt during that strange trip in college, after taking the drug and purging into the red bucket. She'd felt that same sense of under-the-surface connectivity, as if she and the trees and the planet and all the other people around her were strands of the same energy, apparently separate but actually connected. She remembered an abiding feeling that it would all be okay, because it always was and could never be otherwise. She remembered feeling as if she'd left part of herself behind in The Beam in the way Serenity had described Crumb doing the same — that strange sense of herself as a spoon made of chocolate, melting pieces of her soul into a pot of hot soup as she stirred.

Serenity, without further word, turned and paced to the far end of the room and began staring through one of the false windows. Leah looked past her, to the glasses on the end table. She was thirsty. If Serenity was as intuitive as she seemed to be, she'd pour Leah a glass of water from the full pitcher and bring it over.

Leah turned to Crumb. There was probably no reason to keep her voice low, but she did anyway, wanting to exchange a few words with the new Crumb while SerenityBlue was out of earshot.

"Are you okay?" she asked him. Leah tapped her own head. "In here, I mean? You're so coherent. But do you remember the shack in Bontauk?"

"I remember that, yes. I also remember being erratic, but my mind never went away. I was just trapped."

"I thought I might have killed you. Or burned you. Whatever wall you had inside…it started to buckle. It had an intentional failure point. It was as if your mind had decided it would rather self-destruct than let anyone in."

"I've felt the wall. But I think I'm fine now."

"Who did that to you? The wall, I mean? Why? When? Do you know? Do you remember?"

"I don't know. I don't remember."

"So now you're just going to lie here like a convalescent and let a pretty young girl take care of you, huh?" she said, ticking her head toward SerenityBlue. She smiled. "I see how you are."

Crumb shrugged. It was so odd. Leah had looked at this man hundreds or thousands of times, but she'd never really *seen* him. The man in front of her was totally new. The face was the same, but the spark in his eyes was different. Leah realized she should start to think of him as Stephen York, but her mind refused to think of him as anything but Crumb.

"She seems so familiar," said Leah. "I can't shake the feeling that I've been here or that I've met her before. Is it just this place? Do you feel it?"

"I feel something," said Crumb.

"She reminds me of my friend Alison, from years ago," Leah whispered. "The sense of familiarity is so intense."

Crumb said, "She reminds me of my mother."

Leah looked at Crumb. His hair was mostly gray, peppered with the rare strand of stubborn brown. She remembered the 2-D from the journal, showing Noah West beside a young Crumb with long brown hair. She looked at Serenity, puzzled.

"Your mom was a redhead?" said Leah.

"No," said Crumb, furrowing his eyebrows.

Leah looked at Serenity again. Her hair color wasn't ambiguous. It wasn't strawberry blonde or reddish-brown. It was red, as in red-red. Like Alison's.

"She looks like your mom other than the hair, you mean," said Leah.

"No," said Crumb. "My mother had long dark-brown hair with light streaks in it." He pointed. "Just like hers."

Leah looked from Serenity to Crumb, from Crumb to Serenity. At the end table, the girl turned. She'd picked up the pitcher and was pouring a glass of water, turned slightly so that Leah could see that she really *did* look like Alison — Alison, whom Leah had last seen the night she'd swallowed drugs and purged in a bucket, whose hand she'd held as she'd realized they were all connected. She thought of how she'd felt later, when she'd dove into The Beam. The way everything had, for a while, made sense. Leah melting inside it. The feeling that she was touching everything, that everything was touching her. The feeling of unsettling a balance, of stirring, of leaving a part of herself behind.

Serenity finished pouring the glass of water and returned the pitcher to the end table.

"Wait," said Leah, watching her. "Didn't Leo…?"

But Leo could answer for himself because he'd appeared in the doorway, holding a pitcher of water. He looked at Leah, then at Serenity, who hadn't been there when he'd left. His mouth hung open as the pitcher — the same one he had taken from the end table to fill — slipped from his fingers and crashed to the floor.

"Noah Fucking West," he said, still flitting his eyes back and forth between Leah and SerenityBlue. "You two could be twins."

Across the room, Serenity blinked then smiled. A flash of understanding crossed her face, as if something had finally snapped into place.

"So that's why you seem so familiar," she said to Leah.

Chapter 8

"You want to know about *Leo?*" said Dominic.

He blinked in the room's dim light. NPS Agent Austin Smith had thrown him for a loop. He'd thought the agent was going to ask him about the vagrant he'd picked up in Times Square back in the 2060s and shuttled up to the Organa community instead of sending him to Respero as ordered. But no, Smith was throwing him this curve ball about Leo.

"Leo Booker," Austin repeated. "And let me be honest with you, Captain Long. We've been after you for a while. We took you instead of your buddy Omar (who flipped the minute we were able to make him a good enough deal; so eager for his own advancement, that Omar) because we were after you more than him…but the good news for you is that we're after *Booker* more than you. It's like I said: Yes, you've done things that aren't by the book. We all have. But your intention has, as far as I can tell, always been honorable. So if you'll help us get Leo, you can go. Remember — " he gestured at the privacy jammer still idling in the corner, " — this is all off the record. This arrest won't even show on the books. It didn't happen."

That was appealing, but it wouldn't solve Dominic's problems. The Organas still needed their moondust (the bunkered supply Omar had stashed and enabled Dominic to ship with his phone call wouldn't last forever), so he wouldn't be able to retire as a trafficker unless he wanted blood on his hands. Besides, he was still all but incriminated in other ways. The Beam would have records leading up to the pickup itself, just lying around for someone else to find and use to pull Dominic's puppet strings.

"What do you want with Leo, anyway?" Dominic asked. "He's not hurting anyone."

"Not yet, maybe. But what happens when his group decides to stage a revolt? We have reason to believe they're planning a Beam outage — maybe a long and rather disruptive one."

"So what if they are?" Dominic didn't think Leo was staging any outage, but he didn't see the big deal if he was. So people would have to open their own doors and beat off to stored pictures instead of holo shows. Big fucking deal.

Austin stood and began circling the table. "Dominic," he said, "do you realize just how essential The Beam has become to most people…to the NAU in general? Not only does its AI run practically every system we have; it's also plugged into just about every citizen. Not literally, of course, but think about all of the people out there who lean on The Beam for the simplest of daily tasks. How many people in the city do you think know how to use a stove? A radiant cooker? How many people know how to open a can? What about the cold climates and the hot climates? Most people don't know where their heating and cooling controls are, or what settings are appropriate…and that's assuming their systems would work without The Beam, which they usually wouldn't. Did you know that in an unmodified hot climate, you should drink a lot more water to keep your body from shutting down? I didn't. I grew up poor in the north, so I do know about cold, though. Most people don't. People with internal heaters would walk out after the heaters stopped working and freeze to death in their shorts and tees. Literally *to death*, because they wouldn't know what cold feels like and wouldn't recognize the source of their discomfort. Most people don't know how to drive or navigate. If they get in trouble, they wouldn't know how to call for help. And what about the veggies who sit in one place all day, plugged in and walking The Beam, watching holos and filling their heads with obscure trivia that doesn't matter to anyone? Do you think those people know how to read a plain old paper book to keep themselves from going nuts? Assuming they could even stand without their assisters, do you think they know how to go out and socialize, use a non-Beam communication device, play non-Beam games, or just sit and think? Those people aren't used to being alone with their thoughts. They don't know how to handle the inputs of unplugged daily life. They haven't built any internal defenses or filters. They'd go mad. The chaos that would come from a widespread, sustained Beam outage would be catastrophic."

Dominic shrugged. "Are you trying to convince me?" he said. He knew how dependent the NAU was on The Beam. It was just one more reason to be disgusted by people, and Dominic had been bitching about it to bored friends for years. Grandy had had a cabin in the woods with no electricity or plumbing. He could head up there with a bow and an axe and live for weeks, hunting and cleaning and eating his own game. Grandy could survive Armageddon, and in the '30s, he almost literally had. Most folks today could barely survive through the interruption of a pop-up ad. Dominic wouldn't feel bad for the people who would have to learn in a trial by fire just what humanity was all about.

Austin shrugged. "Just making my case about what would happen if Organa got their way. If you'll help us get Leo Booker, then…"

"Are you kidding me?" Dominic interrupted Austin with a laugh. "Leo isn't planning a revolt. Leo just wants to sit up in the mountains and do moondust and think about the good old days. He's a hippie."

"Is that why he sent his girl Leah to some of the best schools to learn about networks and systems and how to bend them to her will? Is it why he sent her into Quark?"

"Leo distrusts The Beam. He wants to be prepared, to know his enemy. He talks like the world might be better without The Beam. But as far as actively doing anything about it? Forget it."

Austin shook his head. "You're being naive. What he has up there is a cult."

This time, Dominic laughed harder. "A *cult?* I've *been* up there. It's a group of people who want to be unique, so they all got together in order to be different in the same way at once. There have always been fringe groups. Organa is harmless. They don't have a stockpile of guns, and I've never once heard or smelled a hint of revolution. Quark has its panties twisted over Organa too. It's cute. You're all so worried about a bunch of junkies with beards and colorful clothes."

Austin pulled the chair from under the table and sat on it backward, his upper arms crossed over the chair's back.

"When did you meet Leo, Dominic?"

Not knowing what else to do, Dominic shrugged and played along. He told Austin about how Leo had been his high school biology teacher and how he'd taught young Dominic, who had wanted to be a cop, how to track biology-based evidence. He taught Dominic how the scientific method applied to everything, not just to problems in his courses. He showed the boy how to form hypotheses, how to test them, how to see pieces of the puzzle that others couldn't. Dominic had aced biology and wrangled a two-year virtual university scholarship thanks to Leo Booker. He'd then risen through the ranks of DZPD quickly once his superiors had taken note of his "natural" skills. There was more, of course, but Dominic didn't want to volunteer it. It was too personal — like how when Dominic's life had started to fray, when his parents got divorced and his father was killed in the line of duty, it had been kindly Mr. Booker who'd helped him pick up the pieces.

"So," said Austin, eyeing Dominic and weighing his story, "that was…what? Mid-50s?"

"Fifty-five, I think," said Dominic. He'd graduated in '57 at age seventeen, and he'd been in Leo's class as a sophomore.

"How old would you say Mr. Booker was at the time?"

Dominic thought. "Maybe forty? Late thirties?"

A sly smile crawled across Agent Austin's lips. "In 2055, Leo Booker would have been seventy-nine."

Dominic tried to hide his shock. His first thought was that Austin was lying, but to what end? It was a hell of a thing to toss an age out there and be so specific. Dominic knew all the tricks, but this didn't feel like one.

"It's the truth, Dominic. He was born on March 23, 1976. He's 121 today. Still think you know this man, given what he's been hiding from his good friend Captain Long?"

"Bullshit."

Austin reached behind him, toward a counter at the back of the room. He removed a folder filled with papers then opened it and rifled through the contents. After a few minutes, he pinched a piece of paper and extended it toward Dominic.

"This is a very old file," he explained. "They should scan it all and put it on The Beam, but a lot was still being done on paper when this file was started. We've got the same problems DZPD has. Nobody wants to pay for it."

Dominic took the sheet of paper. It was a copy of a birth certificate. Someone had stapled a duplicate of an early Beam ID card to the birth certificate. Both were Leo's.

"This could be anyone's birth certificate."

"Well, it was 121 years ago. They hadn't started genetic marking yet, so the ID is supposed to act as a bridge, to help you believe the cert is Leo's. I'll admit it's shoddy evidence. You can choose not to believe me, but there's plenty more in this file, one bit after another. Taken together, you may find them hard to deny." He held the folder in front of his chest. It was in a sort of yellowish, thick paper sleeve that Dominic remembered Grandy having had in his office.

Dominic set the paper on the table. Austin left it where it was.

"Let me tell you about your pal Leo," said the agent. "The first part, which you've already figured out if you even halfway believe that certificate, is that he's not organic as he pretends to be. He has nanos in his blood, just like a lot of the people he rolls his eyes at. He also has a handful of add-ons. They're old ones, circa 2030s and '40s, when add-ons were new. Leo was getting enhancements well before most people. Before it was fashionable, say." Austin leafed through the folder then pulled out another piece of paper. "Here. 'Polycarbonate radius and ulna, surgical steel core, right arm. Surgical steel plating with nanotube mesh resin coating, metacarpopha-langeal joint, right hand. Commensurate splint reinforcement of metacarpals, right hand.' Next time you're with Leo, ask him to punch through a wall for you. I imagine it's impressive. They called that a 'warrior's fist' back in the day — popular with splinter groups during the riots. You'd split your skin when you punched something, but there was a numbing salve they used to carry in a pouch at their sides like climber's chalk. And hey, that's just his arm and hand. There's also…"

"You're telling me Leo has an iron fist?"

"Well, surgical steel. There was a movie back around when Leo was a kid, called *The Terminator.* The idea for the warrior's fist came from that movie, from the arm of a kind of human robot in it. They apparently tried to make the full arms, which looked like the innards of an angry toaster, but in the '30s, the medical technology just wasn't there. The things looked good, but they couldn't generate any power and were too slow. So they did this hybrid thing, stapling new materials to what was already there. It was all the rage in certain quarters. Really just the next step for a lot of folks. In the early 2000s and up through the catastrophic years, there was this huge upsurge in body modification. People started piercing more of their dangling parts then started hacking huge holes in their earlobes. Then when things got good and it looked like we might finally have world peace, some people couldn't take all the joy and started doing things like implanting spikes under their shaved scalps so they'd look more fucked up. There was a wave of people who tattooed their whole bodies. Then there was digit replacement, when people started having their middle fingers amputated and replaced with the Terminator's middle finger, so they could tell the shiny happy world to go fuck itself with a chrome salute. But hey, that was just the warm-up. After the world went to shit, the wackos thought nothing of giving themselves metal fists. Luckily, Leo opted for an approach that was useful rather than just flashy. He also had structural enhancements added to both legs. He also has an early covert communicator that works on RadioFi, which means it's just a hunk of crap in his head today. Rudimentary vision enhancers. None of it Beam-enabled, of course. At the time, those mods were state of the art. But who knows how much of it works today, if any."

Dominic felt like the air had left his lungs.

"You're lying," he said. He had never studied the old mods, but Dominic knew Leo. Leo had always been kind and gentle. He'd given Dominic countless lectures about peace, moderation in (not elimination of) technology, being fair, and trying to live and let live. Agent Smith wasn't describing Leo. He was describing someone else — someone horrible. Leo had been forty back when Dominic had met him, and now that he was in his eighties, he was growing old gracefully and naturally, without age enhancement or nanobots.

But suddenly, it was Dominic's version of the story that was starting to smell like bullshit. According to Austin and apparently a whole file's worth of paper, his old friend was practically a cyborg.

"Oh, I'm afraid not," said Austin. "Don't go out drinking with Leo and get to the point where you have to carry him home, because I'd guess he weighs nearly three hundred pounds with all that old hardware in him. But don't blame Leo for being vain, Dominic. Back then, he needed those doodads. I don't suppose you know Organa's roots?"

Dominic shook his head.

"No, of course not. Nobody does, except for a few old-timers on the fringe who nobody listens to. If you don't believe me, look it up sometime. Organa's history goes back until around 2048 and then just stops like it was cut off with a knife. But in '48, you'll see mentions of large groups with complex hierarchies, stuff you'd see in a mature organization. And at first, you might say, 'Wow, this group got its shit together right away, as soon as it was formed.' But if you're not a stupid cop, which I know you're not, that tune will whistle sour. If you're smart, which I know you *are*, it'll look like an organization that's been around for years but has no recorded history. And that's exactly what it was. Because in 2048 — and this is the part we'll deny if you ever mention it publicly — the NAU cut a deal with them to erase their history from The Beam."

"You cut a deal with Organa? Why?"

"They started calling themselves 'Organa' in '48 or so, when Mr. Booker had a public change of heart about his group's mission and decided it was important to be natural, blah blah blah. Before that, they were known as Gaia's Hammer. Have you heard of Gaia's Hammer?"

Dominic had vague recollections of dinner table discussions in his youth, remembered hearing that name used between his father and Grandy. But even then, those discussions had the feel of ancient history — two old soldiers swapping old tales. But he couldn't put his finger on it for sure. He shook his head.

"Paramilitary organization, founded and led by your buddy Leo. Very fringe. Their premise was that the ecological disaster in the '20s and '30s that fucked the world right up the butt was humans' doing, which of course it was. They said that people had refused to listen for decades while signs kept mounting about how we were damaging the planet. They said that the old hippies were well intentioned but soft, and that peace was all well and good except for the fact that nobody paid it any fucking attention. So after the chaos, as the country started to get back on its feet and build the same old machines back up, Gaia's Hammer took it upon themselves to stop it all from happening again. They said they wanted an organic world, without polluting factories and big, self-interested businesses. Same as the old hippies, except that Gaia's Hammer didn't just sing Kumbaya and smoke bongs. I suppose the way they enhanced the crap out of themselves was intended as some kind of poetic irony — harnessing technology to fuck technology. The group grew fast because apparently people were plenty pissed off after the Fall and wanted someone to blame. They stayed mostly hidden and staged massive, well-coordinated, well-targeted attacks on recovering infrastructures. Quark's Crossbrace project, which was the first version of The Beam, was constantly set back by Hammer attacks. Hammer had people everywhere. In 2034, fifteen politicians were assassinated at once, in the same day, all throughout different locations in the satellite government offices outside of DZ. All were reconstructionists who wanted to pause previously established ecological programs so they'd be able to fast-track the rebuilding of industry. Gaia's Hammer burned factories, bombed network centers, and murdered whoever was in their way. It was all for the greater good, they said, to avoid another catastrophe. They said they were on the Earth's side, and would keep hitting hard even after she herself stopped delivering punches."

Dominic blinked then stared up at Austin. "I've never heard any of this."

"Like I said, it was mostly hidden. They weren't showy. They must have had insiders because they always hit in the right places and did plenty of damage without drawing any more attention to themselves than was inevitable. Then they made that deal in '48, and it went like this: The NAU government said, 'Let us rebuild and leave us alone, and we'll do it within agreed-upon, ecologically sound boundaries.' You see, there was dissent in their ranks, and a lot of people wanted to leave Hammer, but Leo ran it like a Mafia don. When lieutenants tried to get out, they ended up dead. But in the end, Leo was tired, too. The deal gave both sides a way to stop the war and start fresh without losing face. Both sides were able to claim victory. All records pertaining to the Hammer were expunged, leaving only memories. Those memories faded fast, and today you'd have to find someone directly involved to hear the story I've just told you. But it's the truth, Dominic, and you're a good enough cop to find evidence to verify it now that you know what you're looking for."

Dominic considered. He didn't want to believe anything Austin was saying, but he was right about the last bit — Dominic could easily investigate and find out for himself. Austin had given him a bunch of clear steps to verify pieces of the puzzle: somehow check Leo's weight, ask the right people about Gaia's Hammer. He could be bullshitting, but there would be no point if Dominic could confirm or deny so easily.

"So what happened to Gaia's Hammer?"

"They settled down, apparently. Reinvented themselves as Organa — which became, very soon after, an ineffectual hippie group like the ones Leo used to laugh at. He started talking about peace and connecting with the planet and eschewing technology. He stopped actively fighting to stop progress, and in the intervening fifty years, he seems to have mellowed. He even looks the part. We think he got pulse treatment to kill off his nanos and is now aging naturally, which seems about right based on his appearance. For a while, after a few years of mistrust, the NAU thought he might have actually chilled out completely. Like he finally got tired of his old ideals. He's been actively hiding the group's past and his old ways, and apparently he's been showing himself to people since the '50s — " Austin opened his palm toward Dominic, " — as a kindly, granola-munching, tree-hugging hippie. And maybe he is. But he didn't used to be, and we have good reason to suspect, now, that he hasn't entirely given up his old revolutionary ways."

"They're harmless today," said Dominic, wanting to believe it himself. "Even if what you're saying is true, which I'm not saying it is, they're not a threat anymore. At all." He thought of the teacher he'd met, the friend he'd had, the village he'd visited, the peaceful man he'd known for forty years. They'd had their arguments, and Dominic had never detected one iota of threat from Leo — or even significant anger. How could he square his entire life's impression with Austin's portrait of Leo as a ruthless revolutionary and killer?

"We don't think that's true," said Austin.

"I do."

"Because you know him, right? Because you know Leo Booker — the man he is today, even if it's not who he used to be."

"Right," said Dominic.

"You're *sure* you know him?" Austin almost smiled. "Totally, completely, absolutely sure?"

Dominic hesitated.

"Because, Captain Long," said Austin, "what I've told you so far is just the beginning."

Chapter 9

NICOLAI PACED HIS APARTMENT, feeling more conflicted than he ever had in his life.

In the past few days, it seemed as if everything in Nicolai's world had flipped end-for-end. He used to rank high in the Directorate; now he was planning a shift to Enterprise. He used to have a good, high-paying job; he'd just quit then broken into his ex-employer's home. He'd spent sixty years at Isaac Ryan's beck and call, but now, after Shift, he'd find himself under the eye of Isaac's brother.

The thought of ending up in Micah's camp — not by intention, but because the younger Ryan would no doubt seize on Nicolai's defection as a PR bomb in his favor — felt to Nicolai like diving into oil. There had been a day when he'd spent time with all of the Ryans, sure, but Micah had always bothered Nicolai. Micah had a way of being obliviously self-ish, as if he were so single-mindedly focused on his own aims that it never occurred to him what damage he might do to others in his pursuits. He reminded Nicolai of the proverbial bull in a china shop. The bull didn't necessarily even realize that it was too wide and too strong or that its horns were too sharp. It only knew it wanted that pewter salt and pepper shaker set at the back of the store, and it would pay no mind to the little old ladies who were underfoot between here and there.

Nicolai had hoped to avoid Micah, but he'd been kidding himself. There would be no avoiding Micah. He'd avoided Micah for years — had, in fact, wasted a lot of breath advising Isaac to do the same — but a shift to Enterprise would mean inviting Micah back inside. Nicolai was a valuable piece on the Ryans' chessboard (a rook, at least), and Micah wouldn't allow him to silently switch affiliations. Micah would be on him the minute he heard Nicolai's traitorous news — which, because Isaac was Isaac, he'd probably hear soon no matter what Nicolai did. Because Isaac himself would tell him, and then Shift would be all over for the Directorate.

But, arguments aside, Nicolai had been with Isaac for six decades. It didn't feel right to abandon him so completely. Isaac was infuriating, but he was also helpless. Nicolai couldn't help but pity him.

Nicolai paced his apartment, running his fingers down the slanted top of the gorgeous grand piano that he would now, finally, have a chance to learn and play. He'd suss out his other wetchip — from another dealer if not from Doc — and he'd spend a lot more time writing the things he wanted to write. He'd put a blank canvas on his easel and paint. But before he could do any of those things with a clear conscience, he had one last bit of political business. He owed it to Isaac.

"Canvas, get me Micah Ryan. Audio only, track and follow."

While the connection sniffed out Micah, Nicolai set a hand on the flat part of the piano, his back to the beautiful instrument, his eyes looking out across District Zero. The light had mostly bled from the day. He could see an almost-full moon in the sky, its luminance dimmed only slightly by the NAU lattice that kept Nicolai safe from his old home in Europe…trapped in paradise. He told himself to keep his call to Micah direct and brief. He'd propose a deal: Nicolai would make an exclusive announcement for Micah later if Micah would keep his mouth shut about his brother's speechwriter's defection until Shift was over. Once Micah agreed (or disagreed; he could only try his best), he'd get off the line. He'd keep the conversation businesslike, and he wouldn't go to video for Micah to read his facial expressions. If he could do those things, Micah might never suspect that Nicolai had learned what had happened during his missing days, who Kai had said was behind those erased happenings, or the other things she'd told him about Micah's dealings — about just how heavy the bull was willing to tromp as it smashed and gored its way toward the objects of its desire.

"Well, isn't this a delightful surprise," Micah's voice said as they connected. "I thought you might call, Nicolai."

Stupid, Isaac. If Micah "thought Nicolai might call" after years of radio silence, that could only mean that Isaac had already blabbed news to his brother, probably in a vain hope for sympathy. The idiot worked so fast to disembowel himself.

"Then you know," said Nicolai, not bothering with pleasantries. He'd never been truly acrimonious with Micah despite his wariness, but Micah respected precision. Being direct served both of Nicolai's goals: getting business over with quickly and refraining from being pleasant to the man who'd tried to kill one of his friends. Or maybe two.

"Yes," said Micah. "Isaac and Natasha came over last night. She was in one of her huffs. You know how she gets. Isaac was a mess. He said you'd quit and that you were probably heading over to join me on the dark side."

"Not *join you*, really…"

"You know what I mean. But what would be amusing if it weren't so tragic is that Natasha is planning to shift, too."

"Natasha is going to shift?" That was a shock. But also, it wasn't a shock at all. She'd started as Enterprise and had only switched for Isaac. She could also be a spiteful bitch.

"Looks that way. Not a good week for Team Isaac." Micah chuckled.

"Look, I wanted to offer you a deal," said Nicolai. "My Shift would be big news for you, right?"

"That had, in some small way, occurred to me," said Micah, still chuckling.

"Well, I'll talk all about it for you. Do a press conference and everything. I'll even stand right up there beside you if you want, and I'll say…"

Nicolai could imagine Micah waving his hands in an impatient gesture as he cut Nicolai off. "…if I'll just wait until after Shift to make my brother look like a fool. Right?"

Nicolai tapped two fingers on the piano, annoyed at Micah's foresight. Eventually, he said, "Right."

"Of course. That's no problem at all. *You yourself* are the prize, Nicolai. Not the timing, or a political advantage. I got what I wanted. Even got my sister-in-law as a bonus, though I don't know if Natasha counts as a 'bonus.'" And for the third time, he gave that infuriating little chuckle. The chuckle said he'd known exactly what was going to happen and was amused to see the inevitable play on its stage, watching pawns in his game feigning choice.

"I'm out of politics, Micah. No offense, but I don't want to work for you." He thought of Kai, Doc, and the blood on Micah's hands. "I don't want to work *for* Enterprise at all. I just want to shift *to* Enterprise."

"I understand," said Micah. "I figured as much. But again, it doesn't matter. Do you remember how hard I lobbied to get you to join us all those years ago? I know how much it tempted you, too. But you were too loyal. You were like a mouse who feels he owes something to the trap because it gave him cheese."

"I remember you lobbying," said Nicolai, sidestepping Micah's conception of his loyalty to Isaac as a trap.

"You were *meant* to be Enterprise, Nicolai. It was a crime

seeing you in Directorate. I've seldom known anyone more naturally Enterprise than you. Except for me, of course. And your father…had he lived to see the birth of Enterprise."

Nicolai felt his hand slip on the piano. He slid backward, ramming his hip into its side. Something inside the great instrument tinkled on impact.

"I'm sorry?"

"Your father. Salvatore. It broke my heart to watch you slowly die in Directorate, Nicolai. I know you don't want to work for me, and that's okay. It's enough that you'll be where you should have been all along. Maybe the things you'll be able to do in Enterprise will change the world, like your father's inventions."

Nicolai, feeling dizzy, slid along the piano's length and slumped onto its bench. He felt levels of vertigo stack high above him. He hadn't breathed a word of his father since seeing him dead on the ground. He hadn't told the Ryans (or anyone else in the NAU) about his father's business, his immense wealth, or even his name. And *nobody* knew about his inventions. Nicolai himself hadn't even known about them for more than half his time in Italy and had only found them by accident because sometimes an inventor's teenage son manages to gain access that even the AISE (or the American CIA, for that matter) can't get. He'd been told his father was a professor, and even after he'd learned that his father worked for Allegro Andante (but not what he did for them), Nicolai had been told to keep telling the professor lie to his friends. Only decades later did Nicolai manage to piece the puzzle together, finally understanding the gadgets in his father's usually locked study and in the so-called arsenal room his father had explained he'd only be able to access in an emergency. As best he could tell, Allegro had had an ironclad NDA with his father. Salvatore invented, and Allegro Andante would publish (once the technology was ready) without giving him credit. The untold millions of euros in the family's bank account must have been Allegro's way of making up for stealing Salvatore's rightful fame.

But then the chaos had begun, and his father's inventions had never been released. Salvatore had died in his living room, and Nicolai himself had burned the mansion and all it contained. When he later saw hovering objects in the NAU, he assumed Allegro Andante (which had burned to cinders too; he'd trekked to Rome and seen the shell) had leaked some gadgets before expiring. But regardless of how those gadgets had made it overseas, Salvatore Costa's name wouldn't have been on any.

"What do you know about my father's inventions?" said Nicolai. He felt weak. It had been seventy years since he'd found his family slaughtered in their mansion on the hill, but now it was as if he could see their bodies laid out in front of him. He closed his eyes. Behind his lids, blood flowed. A house burned.

"I know they don't get the credit they deserve," said Micah.

"You mean *he* didn't get the credit *he* deserved," said Nicolai.

"That too, yes. But also the inventions themselves. They were more than just hovering bots, you know. Your father suspected the potential of hovertech. I never knew him, of course, but my grandfather did. My family had ties to some powerful people in Italy at the time, and I've heard the stories. Making things float!" He laughed. "Yes, it's a neat little novelty. Think of all of the kitchen floors saved from the ravages of scraping chair legs! Think of the advances in sweeping under ottomans! And finally: flying cars. How long have we been promised flying cars, Nicolai? Every science fiction film I've found from the twentieth century promised us flying cars, and finally we got them. The world rejoiced. Am I right?"

Nicolai felt blind-sided and punch-drunk by the line of

discussion. He'd seen the flying cars, the hovering ottomans, and all sorts of other things that floated. He'd been secretly proud of each, but only in his own little way. Those things hadn't exactly changed the world.

Micah, not waiting for a response, went on.

"But what not a lot of people know — but which I know because my grandfather's company was among the first to work with hovertech in the States — was that hovertech nanobots were the first to use an intuitive distributed network. See, your father didn't just want things to float. He wanted his nanobots to be able to respond to commands, to move around, to float various different objects as needed. Simple to solve, right? Just add processors. But the problem is that nanobots are just too damn small, and when people tried to give them more than the most rudimentary processors — and I do mean *rudimentary*, on par with using a rock as a can opener — they became way too large to do their jobs. So your father asked a question: What if he modeled the human brain? The brain isn't just one big chunk; it's a collection of discreet neurons that all work together to create thought. So to make his bots compute, Salvatore found a way to spread the processing functions out over *many* bots instead of giving a complete processor to *each* bot. Just like neurons in a brain. A single neuron isn't very useful, but if you get a ton of them together and they work in harmony with each doing a little bit of the work…well, then they can become damn intelligent. Intelligent enough, in hovertech's case, to come up with their own intuitive goals. Intelligent enough to farm raw materials from their environments and build other kinds of nanobots to help them as those goals demanded."

Nicolai fought to keep his bearing. Micah might be bull-shitting, but in general, Micah Ryan didn't bullshit. He *lied*, but he didn't bullshit. There was a difference.

"Without your father's work," said Micah, "we'd have been sunk. Literally, in some cases. Hoverbots kept the levees in place so that District Zero could be saved when the oceans rose. Bots ran the desalinators, giving us clean water. But I don't need to tell you about all the things that intelligent nanobots do today, Nicolai. You've got plenty in your own system. You should be proud, my friend. Salvatore Costa's work saved the NAU and made our way of life possible. Hell, even The Beam's evolution was facilitated by the pollination effect."

Nicolai remained silent. Micah had won. Nicolai wasn't even sure what game they were playing…but whatever it was, Micah had the medal. He felt all of his moments collapse into one disorderly pile. And to think: he'd believed he was in control of his life all along.

"You still there, Nicolai?" said Micah.

"Of course."

"You're so quiet."

"I'm just…my father's work was very secret. His name wasn't supposed to be on anything. The work itself wasn't even supposed to be released because they never quite finished before the riots and wars broke out. I've looked it all up. The company was run by a bunch of isolationists. They had this vision of turning Italy into the next Japan, wanting Italy to command hovertech the way Japan commanded the electronics market at the time. I don't even understand why they released it. Did they release it to your grandfather?"

Micah laughed a bitter sort of laugh. "Oh, no. They were very protective of it. It was like you said: nothing for the *Americani* until it was finished and they had gotten their big head start. Believe me, my grandfather's people tried to convince them. They tried *hard*. I'll even tell you a little secret, now that it's no longer fresh news: They were ready to *steal* it from them. But then, like you said…the wars. And then Allegro Andante was no more."

"Then my father…"

"He wouldn't budge either," said Micah, "and they tried hard to persuade *him*, too."

"Then how did it get here?" he said.

Micah gave another chuckle. For the briefest of moments, Nicolai closed his eyes. In the darkness, he saw the mansion burn in a fire of white phosphorous. He saw his family's bodies laid out on the living room floor like macabre trophies. He saw himself alone, at seventeen, surviving the massacre — finally able to access the arsenal and its microscopic wonders once the others were dead. In his mind's eye, he watched the last Costa walk away with only a few scant belongings and a crossbow like a voyager heading off into an unknown wilderness. Like a pilgrim heading off on a pilgrimage. Like a heroic warrior heading off on a quest.

"You brought it to us," Micah told him.

Or like Typhoid Mary, off to seed a plague.

Enter the Truantverse

When it comes to stories and the worlds they live in, books are only the beginning.

Visit JohnnyBTruant.com/join to get my best books sooner and cheaper than the other stores.

My list doesn't suck like so many author email lists. Seriously. It has unicorns.

The Magic Bunch

Unicorn Genesis

∾

FAT VAMPIRE:

Fat Vampire

Fat Vampire 2: Tastes Like Chicken

Fat Vampire 3: All You Can Eat

Fat Vampire 4: Harder Better Fatter Stronger

Fat Vampire 5: Fatpocalypse

Fat Vampire 6: Survival of the Fattest

The Vampire Maurice

Anarchy and Blood

Vampires in the White City

Fangs and Fame

Game of Fangs

∾

INVASION:

Invasion

Contact

Colonization

Annihilation

Judgment

Extinction

Resurrection

Save the City

Save the Girl

Save the World

Longshot

THE INEVITABLE:

Robot Proletariat

The Infinite Loop

The Hard Reset

Cascade Failure

Reboot

En3my

DEAD CITY:

Dead City

Dead Nation

Dead Planet

Dead Zero

Empty Nest

THE DREAM ENGINE:

The Dream Engine

The Nightmare Factory

The Ruby Room

The Pandora Core

The Engine Convergence

The Tinkerer's Mainspring

Fiends

Decoy Wallet

~

NONFICTION:

The Fiction Formula

Fiction Unboxed

Iterate & Optimize

The Story Solution

Write. Publish. Repeat.

The One With All the Writing Advice

9 781964 578187